THE CIRCUS OF MACHINATIONS

TALES OF CROW #4

CHRIS WARD

ALSO BY CHRIS WARD

Head of Words
The Man Who Built the World
Saving the Day
Ugly Thirteen

The Fire Planets Saga
Fire Fight
Fire Storm
Fire Rage
Fire Flare
Fire Hunt

The Endinfinium series
Benjamin Forrest and the School at the End of the World
Benjamin Forrest and the Bay of Paper Dragons
Benjamin Forrest and the Lost City of the Ghouls
Benjamin Forrest and the Curse of the Miscreants
Benjamin Forrest and the Rise of the Pure Blood

The Tube Riders series
Underground
Exile
Revenge
In the Shadow of London
Genesis: The Rise of the Governor

The Tales of Crow series
The Eyes in the Dark
The Castle of Nightmares
The Puppeteer King
The Circus of Machinations
The Dark Master of Dogs

ABOUT THE AUTHOR

A proud and noble Cornishman (and to a lesser extent British), Chris Ward ran off to live and work in Japan back in 2004. There he got married, got a decent job, and got a cat. He remains pure to his Cornish/British roots while enjoying the inspiration of living in a foreign country.

He is the author of the *The Tube Riders* series, the *Tales of Crow* series, and the *Endinfinium* YA fantasy series, as well as numerous other well-received stand alone novels.

Chris would love to hear from you:
chrisward@amillionmilesfromanywhere.net

PROLOGUE

THE ROBOT AND THE INVENTOR

A COLD WIND was whipping in from the south, bringing with it flurries of hard ice ripped off the top of seasons-long snow drifts standing like dirt-streaked grey sentinels by the side of the road. Victor Mishin stopped one more time to tie up his hood, but the string was frozen stiff. He scowled, cursing under his breath. Dipping his face away from the wind instead, he turned back to make sure the cart was still following.

From both sides of the road, the dead eyes of Brevik's abandoned houses watched him with their broken door grins. From inside flickered torchlight, accompanied by the faint peal of nervous laughter. Many became temporary crack houses and brothels after dark, living crypts filled with the skeletal remnants of men and women put out of work by the closing mines and factories.

The first rock to clang off the outside of the cart's casing made Victor jump. The echo of laughter from a shadowy alley that followed made him shiver.

'We see you, old man.'

It was the voice of a kid, throat dry from too many cigarettes and cheap local homebrew. Brevik started its youngsters early, and only a kid would ever call him old. Victor wasn't yet thirty.

'Come on,' he told the cart. 'We have to hurry.'

The machine's head snapped up, a vaguely humanoid oval. Twin lights at the front gave a wild flicker. 'Rolling, rolling.'

Another stone landed in the snow at Victor's feet. He grimaced. Even the prepubescent kids were built out of wire passed down through generations of miners with playful fists, and Victor was no fighter.

'Level up,' he said to the cart. 'We have to move. Now.'

'Roger that, partner.'

The cart, a silver rectangle, rocked back on its caterpillar treads and lurched into an upright position. Smaller central treads unfolded from the ends of its main propulsion system. It was activating its sprint mode, but in the snow and ice its motors would only last a couple of hundred metres. It would have to be enough.

'Move it,' Victor said, as another stone clanged off the cart's casing.

Shadows shifted behind him as he started into a run, morphing into the shapes of four, five, six kids as they bolted from the alleyway. Victor squeezed his eyes shut as the cart's accelerator runners spun in the snow, then clunked as they caught on something buried under the surface.

He didn't want to turn around to see his most treasured invention pitch forward onto its robotic face as the group of laughing urchins descended on it, thrown stones rattling off the metal like machine gun fire, but he had no choice. The cart was dear to him; he owed it a single icy tear frozen against his face by the chilling wind.

He glared for one long moment at the feral children as they engulfed the cart in a flurry of thumping hands and kicking feet, then turned and hurried for home, feeling at least some scant relief that its sacrifice had allowed him to get away.

It was not yet four p.m. but full dark had descended upon Brevik like a galloping black horse, bringing with it a cold so dense it was like an iced blanket draped over the streets. The man in the shawl shivered. The cold made his bones ache to the very brink of what he could stand, but that chill gave comfort to the many scars on his savaged body.

Across the street, one of the brothels had fallen near silent, the last sounds the tired grunting of one last couple as they concluded their transaction. The man in the shawl headed out into the street, stepping through footprints left by others where he could, wary that the wind could be fickle and might choose to leave his tracks unburied.

The house's door hung on one hinge. The man in the shawl pushed inside, pausing a moment to listen to the rutting underway in a room to his left. A ratty carpet hid his footfalls as he peered in through a doorway to see a naked ass rising and falling between two skinny, pockmarked legs in the flickering light of a trashcan fire, accompanied by a series of halfhearted grunts and moans. The man in the shawl moved on, deeper into the house.

In a room near the back he found what he was looking for, an unconscious man plump enough to be new to this game. Two crusty circles of blood lined the man's nose, and purple bags hung from his eyes as if he hadn't slept in weeks. His body leaned against the window, and only ragged breathing indicated he still lived.

The man in the shawl reached into his jacket and pulled out a metal bar about two feet long, curved at one end for pulling up floorboards. He pulled back a strip of threadbare carpet and worked up a couple of boards. Then he dragged the man over and laid him on the ground with his forehead pressing against the side of the hole, his neck over it.

With expert precision the man in the shawl pierced the unconscious man's main carotid artery, then held his head steady while the man bled out onto the freezing gravel two feet below. It took several minutes before the man in the shawl was satisfied that any mess he made would be easy to clean up, then he set about sawing off pieces of the man's body and dropping them into a sacking bag lined with plastic. It was a crude operation, but the intense cold made it easier. Any blood that was spilt quickly froze into tiny droplets that could be brushed into the under-floor space.

He sometimes wondered why he went to such lengths to cover his tracks. He had observed long enough to know that no one cared about these people. Had there been anyone to miss them, they were long faded away into the smoke of the belching factories, ground down so far by their own misery that the death of a loved one might go so far as to incite jealousy. People in these towns toiled in the snow and ice, and if their factories failed they died if they couldn't find another before the fingers of temptation took hold. And once they took those first steps along the path to the crack houses in the downtrodden Lenin District, there was no coming back.

With the choice cuts secured in his bag, he pushed the rest of the body into the under-floor space and lowered the floorboards back down, covering them over with the carpet. The next gang of fiends to use this building might notice the creaking of the loose boards, or the way the carpet seemed to slip more on one side than the other, but the man in the shawl felt confident that the underlying dread that shrouded these communities would keep them from letting their inquisitiveness take control. They would turn away from their suspicions and embrace the blind acceptance of their own crumbling paths.

He stood up and hauled the heavy sack up over his shoulder. The house was silent now, the sounds of rutting gone, the light dying down as the cold stepped back in. The man in the shawl shivered, feeling the creep of the chill on his skin, but it wasn't an unpleasant feeling. The cold, tormentor of most, was his greatest comfort.

As he reached the door he heard the sound of breathing, and turned to see the whore still lying there, her legs wide as if waiting for the flickering of the dying trashcan fire to become her next customer. Now that he could see her clearly, the man in the shawl marvelled at how haggard she was, almost skeletal. Had he been desperate there would have been no meat worth taking, and he wondered how it was possible to find pleasure between legs that were little more than skin stretched over bone.

Her eyes studied the shadows where his face was hidden. Unable to resist, he put the bag down by his feet and squatted down.

'A penny for your thoughts, sweet princess?' he asked her in a good impersonation of the Russian dialect spoken in these parts.

'Are you him?' she asked, and he wondered whether she meant Death, or perhaps someone more welcome. 'Are you … him?'

The man in the shawl smiled. 'I'm him and them and everyone,' he said.

'Do you want me?'

Again, her meaning was ambiguous. The idea of screwing her was almost as repulsive as she would find his face—were he to reveal it—but perhaps she was searching for a different kind of answer. There was little brightness in her eyes, only a flicker that pulsed in and out of view, a candlelight struggling to stay alive.

He reached out a scarred, bony hand and ran one hooked, claw-like finger up the inside of her thigh from her knee to her pelvis. Her eyes continued to flick across the shadows under his hood, but she made no other reaction.

Even after everything, he couldn't resist setting in motion a little game. Would it work out for her, or wouldn't it? She would cast the die. And she would either live, or her candle would be extinguished forever.

'Not yet,' he said. 'But I am following at your shoulder. Whenever you look, I will be there. Outrun me if you can.'

'I'm so tired.'

'Sleep now, but when you wake you will remember me only as a dream, one to fear, one to speak of to no one.'

He slid a finger into the shadows between her legs, feeling damp warmth. Still she made no reaction.

'Are you him?' she said again.

'I am the worst creature in the world. I am the end of all things.'

With his finger still inside her, she smiled. It was so unexpected that he tensed for a moment, wondering if perhaps he'd been sucked into some kind of trick.

'No,' she said. 'No, you're not. I know where he is.'

The man in the shawl pulled back, alarmed. He glanced behind him, but the room was empty, the punter gone. When he looked back at the girl her eyelids had fallen half closed, and she gazed at him with a drugged nonchalance.

Who did she mean by *he*? The man in the shawl stood up and took a few steps backwards. There had been an intensity to that one word that set his nerves on edge. The days when he could hide out in the open were gone; now he was penniless and alone, cut off from the resources that had so long sustained him. And he was hunted. He knew it as surely as night followed day.

He left the girl alone to her own devices. Either she would stand and leave and live or she would sleep and die, as the trashcan fire burned down and the killer cold returned. The temperature was often minus ten even during daytime, and at night minus twenty or more was not uncommon. It could take the unprepared quicker than a knife to the throat.

Outside, he slung the bag over his shoulder as he moved quickly up the street. It hadn't snowed in several days but the air was filled with flurries of ice shards ripped off the top of the last drifts.

The building he had chosen to make his lair was a gutted Soviet-era apartment block. While the upper levels were populated with a similar assortment of nobodies and has-beens to those he preyed on, the old basements were his alone. It was easy to keep people away. The scraping of his nails on the metal door frames, a shriek from his fire-damaged throat, the shadow of his ghastly shape on the walls, were more than enough to deter the curious. For the most part he was left in peace.

Something was lying in the road up ahead. Knocked over on to its side, it had the size and shape of a shopping cart. The man in the shawl glanced left and right as he approached it, fearing a trap, but it was late now and only the foolhardy or the desperate were out on the streets.

It was covered with a dusting of the ice-snow. It looked like a motorised transportation cart, but when he leaned down and ran a finger along its metal casing he heard a ticking sound coming from somewhere inside. A spherical object, bent and dented, tried to twist around to face him, but its mounting had been cracked and it could only turn halfway.

'Ever ready, always ready to help.'

The man in the shawl started. It was some kind of robot. Battered and damaged, left to rot out here in the snow.

An old awakening stirred in him, and a purring sound rose in his chest. It had been so long. Years of stumbling further north where the temperatures were easier on his skin, moving from place to place and living like a beggar in the streets, or a wraith in the bowels of some forgotten building, his old pleasures had become a sideshow rather than the driving force that had once been his obsession.

The thing tried to lift its head again, but the mounting cracked and it bumped against the side of its body.

'Can you move?' the man in the shawl asked.

'Ready and willing to take orders,' it said, although it didn't move.

The man in the shawl inspected its outer casing. In one end a handle had been fitted, perhaps for the very event that its propulsion motors might fail. Slinging his bag of human flesh into an empty carry compartment built into the machine's top, he unclipped the handle and began to pull the cart along behind him. He was far stronger than the scrawny body gave away, but every few steps he had to stop to clear away an accumulation of scraped ice from around the machine's caterpillar treads.

As his building appeared like a grey shadow out of the gloom of the winter night, his excitement grew. His raging hunger was long gone, replaced by an impatient desire to begin tinkering with the machine, to open up its body, to investigate its components.

Sometimes, in his darkest days, he felt like none of his life had ever happened, that he wasn't an aging monster so disfigured as to be more scar than skin, but that innocent child sitting around on the floor of his mother's hovel, taking apart junked video players and food processors and pieces of circuit board and fashioning them into something wondrous.

Back when he had just been a boy who made robots.

PART I

THE COLD LITTLE TOWN IN THE MIDDLE OF SIBERIA

1

THE MAN WHO CONSUMES OTHER MEN

HE HAD FORGOTTEN many things over the years, but one thing he had always remembered was his name.

It was pronounced *ku-row* and written in Romanised letters as *Kurou*. It was the British businessman Rutherford Forbes who had first named him for the bird that his name so resembled, in part for his inability to pronounce an unusual Chinese name and partly for what the boy's face reminded him of on those few occasions when he had no choice but to look at Kurou eye to eye. The bony outcrop where the nose should have been, the thin, pinched lips reminiscent of a bird's tongue, the tiny black eyes, and the tufts of calcified hair that looked like the feathers of some starving, emaciated bird. Kurou's body, too, was misshapen, twisted and scrawny, the wiry strength greater than two bigger men combined no consolation for a need to hide himself from every reflective surface.

In some ways it was ironic that Forbes had bought him to attempt the very thing that he wished he could bestow on his deformed young charge; remove a mind from one place and insert it into another.

It would be easy to exclaim that his childhood was harsh, but after being taken from his mother he was never mistreated. He was merely institutionalized, a lab rat, grown up in a sterile environment and given all the tools necessary to develop into the scientific genius Forbes had predicted from the moment his clumsy foot unwittingly crushed Kurou's most prized robot into the muddy floor of a dirty Chinese hovel.

That genius came easily, in a rush that built momentum as the years passed, a flood of scientific knowledge that washed away any possibility of normal human emotions. The seedlings of such primitive feelings as compassion or love or empathy were ripped from the ground and swept away, while darker sensations such as anger and resentment took years to flourish as he became more of a machine than those he was charged with building.

Inside his own world of manic, relentless creation, he was content. He needed nothing, wanted nothing that wasn't provided on whim, and in exchange for maintaining his day to day comforts, all he had to do was what he had wanted to do all along: experiment and build. His master would occasionally make requests, and while as Kurou's teenage years gave way to young adulthood he began to realise that he was controlled far more than he had realised, it was an easy favour to return. Improve the crop yield of X seed, increase the muscle percentage of X cow to X percentage, build a missile that can hit X target at X range. It was all too easy. His mind was a box filled with assorted jigsaw pieces. All he had to do was tease each pretty picture out.

THE ROBOT FASCINATED HIM. It was no more than the work of a keen amateur, but there were modes and components in its electronic makeup that brought back fond memories. It was designed as a work companion, an automated transportation machine, capable of bearing heavy loads over uneven terrain. It was old though, and while Kurou found signs of love in the attempts to repair and maintain it, the replaced components were poorly fitting and showed signs of wear, most likely picked out of the remains of junked electrical appliances.

Some of the handiwork made him smile. His own hands had fashioned such imperfections many times over the years. There was never an end to the learning curve. No matter how accomplished you became—and he was the best he had ever known—there would always be a million things to learn. You could never learn everything, because then you would be God, and there was no such thing.

With the stink of cooked human flesh as his accompaniment, he worked long into the night, tinkering, adjusting and repairing, using what crude tools he had accumulated over his years of seclusion to restore the robot as best he could to working order. Were an outsider to peek through a crack in the door Kurou could imagine what he might look like; a deformed, scarred outcast striving to restore life to a semblance of a friend.

His motives, however, went far beyond.

Repairing the robot was just the start. He wanted to find the owner.

HE AWOKE to a chill breeze gusting in from the chimney, the shaft of which emerged at street level. He disentangled himself from the mess of stinking blankets he called a bed, and looked at the repaired robot by the opposite wall. A wire fed out of an electrical outlet into a little power generator. Kurou wasn't sure if the batteries would charge, but there was only one way to find out.

'Do you still sleep?'

The robot lifted its head. 'Coming in loud and clear, master … oh. No. You're not.'

'Where is he?'

'Who wants to know?'

Kurou scraped a handful of tile shards off the floor and flung them at the robot. They cascaded off its metal casing like hailstones off a tin roof.

'Bending you to my will is easier than driving a car, robot. Giving you a life of chewing rocks is easier than climbing a rope. Tell me where he lives and I'll make sure he gets you back.'

The robot, outwardly unperturbed by Kurou's thinly veiled threats, rattled off a complex-sounding Russian address. Kurou knew every street in Brevik by heart, having made it a point of his residency to do so. The inventor's location was a mere ten-minute walk away.

'Thank you for your compliance, robot. You just earned yourself a ticket to freedom.'

The robot stared at him. Its strange head bobbed up and down as if some pendulum mechanism inside was propelling it. The lights positioned where a human's eyes might have been—a quaint but often useless touch that many amateurs used in their pursuit of an anthropomorphic creation—flickered as if the robot was blinking. Kurou stood up, giving it a wide berth as he made his way towards the room he used as a kitchen, mildly concerned about the possibility of hidden weapons.

As he returned with a slab of dried flesh and a handful of nuts he had pilfered before the winter set in, he heard a clicking sound coming from the robot's chest.

'You're recording me, aren't you?'

'Sound and visuals.'

'Why?'

'I'm not at liberty to say.'

'Erase all visuals. That's an order. Remember what I said before?'

The robot's head continued to bob up and down. 'Visuals erased.'

Kurou smiled. 'Wow, compliance. What a wonderful thing. Tell me, robot, are you alone?'

'Alone?'

'Are there more of you? Did your master make you alone, or are there others?'

'Others.'

Kurou nodded slowly. 'How many?'

'I don't know.'

'He has equipment?'

'I don't know.'

'Are you transmitting information about me back to him?'

'No capability. Just recording for review later.'

Kurou rubbed his chin. He wanted to meet this young inventor, but it was unlikely the inventor would appreciate meeting him in return. He would have to engineer the situation, gain the inventor's trust first.

THE KNOCK on his door was barely audible over the roaring of the fire. At first Victor thought it was the splitting of a log, but then it came again, short and sharp, three quick raps.

Was that the police? What could he have done to attract their attention? Or what if it was one of the gangs? He had heard about people being dragged out of their houses and beaten to death in the streets for no reason other than to alleviate the boredom of the out of work factory workers turning to crime and drugs to numb themselves against the pain of a broken future. He had been working on something downstairs in his basement that could protect him, but it was unfinished, held up by a couple of design flaws he couldn't get his head around.

As the minutes ticked by, no more knocks came. At first Victor felt relieved, but his relief soon gave way to curiosity. It was only five o'clock, but the sun had been gone for hours already, hidden first behind the grey skies and later the snow-covered hills to the west.

In the corridor outside his small living room the cold had taken hold, and he shivered as he wrapped a blanket around his shoulders. The over-large Soviet-era front door loomed huge, hiding the world and its secrets. The handle was ice cold. Victor felt his thudding pulse in his wrist and winced at the chill.

Opening the door a crack was not an option. The moisture in the air made the wood swell enough to make it drag on the stone step, meaning only with a heave could he open it. Once there had been a spy hole, but it had long since gummed up. Composing himself, Victor twisted and jerked the door handle, flinging the door open on to the storm of a Siberian winter like some Dickensian villain.

The few street lights that still worked illuminated circles of swirling ice flurries and the closed doors of his neighbours, people he rarely saw and avoided when he did. Further up the street he heard the rumble of a car and for a moment twin cones of light swung across the front of his house and then were gone.

Something was sitting in the snow on the pavement in front of him. At first he had mistaken it for a pillar or post because the ice had done its work, covering it in a film of blue, but his nerves had imagined a structure there where there had always been none.

He stepped forward and swiped away the ice, gasping in surprise.

It was the cart.

Someone had returned it to him.

'Cart?'

The head swung up out of the front of the cart's casing, and its eyes flicked on. 'Ready and waiting for orders, sire.'

It wasn't until a couple of days later when Victor had taken the cart down into the basement and opened up the casing that he found the note.

It had been written on the back of a scrap of cardboard in a coppery coloured ink that for some reason made Victor shiver. The extravagant curls and flourishes that looked out of place with the Cyrillic script identified the writer as a foreigner, albeit a learned one. It came as some relief to Victor, who held on to a suspicion of every part of the world he knew best like a generations-old family feud. Whatever stranger this was who had found the cart, he was trying to help, although Victor guessed that suspicions ran both ways, otherwise the stranger would have waited around to talk to him.

I have repaired your machine for you. I have made some small changes to improve its performance. If you have other machines that require amendment, leave them in the location I advise.

At the end of the note was an address for an abandoned café on the outskirts of town. It was the kind of remote place where not even homeless people would bother to hole up, and Victor was certain his mysterious correspondent lived nowhere that could be linked to either the café or Victor's place. From the handiwork on the cart's systems it was obvious that the man was thorough.

Victor spent the rest of the day running tests on the cart, figuring out what the other man had done. There were a couple of modifications to the cart's front casing that remained a mystery, but he felt sure that with enough investigation he would work it out. More of a mystery was the identity of his mysterious benefactor, and even more so his motivation. Finding someone in this dead end town with a will to create rather than destroy was akin to winning a prize on the state-run lottery.

Night had fallen, bringing with it the deeper chill that the weak sun spent all day trying to shake off. Victor was beginning to think about retiring for the evening, when a sudden muffled boom shook the glass in his windows and made a vase on the table top fall over.

At first he thought of earthquakes, but this part of the world was far from a plate boundary. Something had happened to one of the factories. A gas leak, perhaps. It happened from time to time. No matter how much the pipes were insulated, the cold had a way of stripping away the layers until whatever was underneath just popped.

It was no particular concern of his. By day Victor was a general electronics dogsbody, everything from wiring to computer programming, a perennial fixer of problems for people wealthy enough to have them. In a society where few new products were available and people had to make do with old and dated technology, his skills were in great demand. Had he chosen to move to a larger city he could have made real money, but he had been reluctant to leave his old town for reasons he could still barely understand.

The sound of shouting came from outside. His curiosity finally piqued, Victor went over to the window and pulled back a corner of curtain to look out on to the ice-shrouded street outside.

A handful of people were walking northwards up the street in the direction of the industrial district. So, his guess had been right then, he thought, but something in the way the people were gesturing and conferring made him nervous. There was a greater urgency than there should have been for a simple gas explosion. Dangerous as they could be, they were too regular to be a surprise anymore, yet here people were milling about in greater and greater numbers as if some disaster were about to engulf the whole town.

He pulled a thick jacket off a hook behind his door, pulled a fur hat down over his ears and went out on to the street. 'What's going on?' he shouted at the nearest person, a bearded man in his fifties with the bloodshot eyes of someone never far from the filthy homebrewed vodka that soaked these parts.

'We just got hit, Comrade,' he said, using an old greeting that Victor hadn't heard in years. 'They're coming.'

'Who?'

The man gave victor a grimace that revealed the blackened stumps of what had once been teeth. 'All of them. Time to put us to rest at last. That's the munitions factory they just took out.'

'What … I don't—'

'We're under *attack*, Comrade,' the bearded man said. 'Time for the last curtain to fall.'

With those last ominous words, the man hurried off, leaving Victor standing in his wake, dusty swirls of week-old ice kicked up by the wind around him.

2
———

THE WOMAN WITH THE WILD HAIR

DRONES.

That was what people were saying. The munitions factory had been taken out by drones. There was some optimism that with the sole valuable asset of the town now a smouldering ruin, there would be no further attacks, but the general consensus was that a land attack would soon be forthcoming. Brevik was not so far to the east to be of no strategic value, but for the townsfolk there was literally nowhere else to go.

A couple of days later, Victor attended a hastily arranged public meeting in an old auditorium where only one in three overhead lights worked. On the stage the mayor, Pavel Andrev, and his chief aide Lena Patrova, alongside other members of the town council and several prominent local businessmen, outlined vague plans for protecting the city or moving the people out.

Victor knew about the war in the west, of course, but Russia was so huge that her western frontier might as well have been a world away. Few people cared as long as the war stayed there. The harshness of life here in central Siberia would switch the skin off the back of anyone who let their guard down, so what was happening thousands of miles to the west was of little concern. Victor guessed that the products the great smoking factories made went to aid the war effort, but once the trucks and trains left the city limits they belonged elsewhere.

The meeting descended into a debacle of name calling and arguments, culminating in a section of the crowd throwing their chairs towards the stage. Victor slipped out of a side entrance along with other disgruntled members of the crowd, unsure quite what the final decision had been.

Unless ordered, he had no intention of leaving. Brevik was all he had ever known, and he couldn't leave his life's work behind. Without it, he might just as well string himself up from the nearest petrified tree.

HE DIDN'T HEAD HOME. Instead, he turned north and hurried through the freezing streets towards where Isabella lived. She hadn't spoken to him in almost a month, but if ever there was a time to end their estrangement, it was with the threat of war hanging over their heads like a great big thundercloud.

Isabella's father, Robert Mortin, was a foreman in one of the copper mines in the hills north of town. His wife had died some years before and now Isabella tended a cold, charmless house while looking after two younger siblings so wild as to be almost feral. Unlike most of the town's young women, she had neither been pushed into an unhappy marriage nor fled for one of the cities further to the south, preferring her father's protective influence, rough though it might be. There were rumours, of course, that in her mother's place Isabella warmed not only Mortin's house but also his bed, but Victor tended not to listen to the hearsay spouted by the drunks who littered the bars around Brevik's only train station.

The Mortin house came up on the left, a three-storey townhouse separated from the two houses on either side by a polite space wide enough only to remove the term terrace from its description, and to leave it flanked by two vicious wind tunnels that whistled so loud in the dead of winter that you could believe the house was about to be torn off its moorings and whisked away into the snowy hills to the north.

A single light was on in a downstairs window, a tiny glimmer scratching at the thick air-raid curtains that had been hung across the glass.

So, it appeared Isabella had heard the rumours too.

Whether by some sixth sense or a CCTV system that was invisible to Victor's searching eyes, Isabella must have known he was coming, because she flung the door open and stepped out before he had even turned through the rusty gate at the bottom of her path. She stood there with one hand on the door and the other buried in hair ruffled by the wind like a creature born of storm and snow.

'What are you still doing here?' she shouted as soon as he was close enough to hear. 'Are you crazy? Get out of here before the whole town gets destroyed!'

She reached down, grabbed a handful of ice, and flung it at him. He flinched and stepped aside, holding up a hand to shield his face, and continued making his way towards her. Her gesture might have been for aesthetic purposes, but she tried one more time before giving up and stepping back inside to let him into the house.

As she pulled the door shut behind him, he shook the ice off his jacket and turned around. Before his eyes had even focused, a hard, cold hand cracked him across the side of the face.

'Who do you think you are, coming here, Victor Mishin?' She glared at him, her nostrils flaring, little flakes of ice caught in her unruly mop of hair.

To call Isabella wild was akin to calling a mad dog rabid. It was a wholly appropriate description, but only told half the story. She was a product both of her upbringing and her environment, a young woman who in better times and places might achieve greatness in some field or other, or at least become a battalion at the centre of a large and fruitful family. Stuck here in Brevik with her unflinching father and rampant younger siblings, she rebelled in the only way she could, by lambasting any and all who treated her with a modicum of respect.

'I wanted to see you,' he said. 'Just in case, you know.'

'In case of nuclear war? In case of a second Holocaust? How thoughtful! Why not just write me a letter?'

Victor sighed. 'We'll be fine,' he said. 'No one wants this place. *We* don't even want it.'

'Speak for yourself! The enemy is coming and you know it. In less than a week I'll be lying on my back getting systematically raped by a squadron of European Confederation solders. Where will you be then, Victor? Playing with your stupid robots?'

He shrugged. He tried to think of something witty to say, but such comments rarely worked to stem the tide of Isabella's fury. Instead, he just said, 'Probably.'

'Well, it's all right for some!'

'I guess it's all right for you,' she said, and he sensed her temper starting to level out. 'You have actual skills. You'll be assimilated, assigned to build weapons so they can kill even more of us. You'll probably even get paid.' Her eyes gave one more flash of ire. 'Spend it on something good, Victor! Make sure you have a good time in some sleazy bar while I'm getting gang-raped!'

He opened his mouth and waited for a reply to form, but she had already pushed past him and headed for the living room further down the hall. Victor glanced up at the stairs across the entranceway that led up to the second floor, but there was no sign of her brother and sister. Her brother ran with the gangs who terrorised the Lenin District in the southwest part of town just beyond the area where Victor lived, while her sister, not yet fifteen, was rumoured to be making a merry penny in the alleys around the train station. It was clear that despite Isabella's best efforts, her siblings were following the path assigned to most of the town's youth, but the merest suggestion that Isabella's surrogate parenting was proving counterproductive would find him cast out into the snow and ice, the door slammed in his face.

'I'm so glad you finally came to your senses,' she was saying as he entered the living room. A fire blazed with welcome heat from a hearth in the far wall, while a heavy pine table in the centre was neatly adorned with cups and saucers and a steaming kettle. Unless she was pre-preparing for possible guests or even refugees, she had to have guessed he was coming. Victor felt a mite of satisfaction knowing that much of her anger had probably diffused itself in the hallway while she waited for him to arrive. Isabella was like a lit fuse; she could briefly flare bright, but her anger never lasted long.

'I have to say, I wondered if I would ever see you again,' she said, handing him a cup of steaming tea. Just the aroma of it was enough to make his senses melt. 'I've heard trains are leaving for the east and not coming back. Going anywhere they can. The Baikal Oasis, or even on to Vladivostok. That horrible city must be so full of refugees by now that it's a surprise our whole country doesn't tip up and send us all pouring into the Japan Sea.'

'I'm not going anywhere.'

'I should hope not. I couldn't live without you.'

Victor didn't want to point out that she did a fine job of it during their extended periods of estrangement. 'I'm pretty sure we'll be safe here,' he said. 'That hit on the munitions factory was just strategic. They have nothing to gain by occupying us.'

Isabella dashed around the table and ran up to him, taking his hands and holding them against his chest. Up close it was easier to see the humanity behind the feral exterior; her eyes shone with both hope and fear.

'How can you be sure?'

The truth was that he couldn't. All he could do was spout wild speculation in the hope of reassuring her. 'I was at a council meeting before I came here. There's nothing to suggest that the airstrike was any more than a one-off.'

'I hope you're right, Victor. I'm so terrified. Can you stay with me tonight?'

There was nowhere Isabella was wilder than in the bedroom, where her internal fury made for sessions of lovemaking that left Victor breathless for days afterwards, but today he shook his head. 'Nothing would make me happier, but I have work to do,' he said.

She pushed away from him. 'You'd turn down time with me to go and wire some rich bastard's fuse box? You swine, Victor. Get out!'

He'd expected such a reaction and was already moving towards the door. As her open palms swiped at him, he backed away until he could turn and jerk open the front door without opening himself up to attack. As he stood there on the threshold with the wild winter billowing at his back, he lifted a hand and blew her a kiss. 'I'll be back soon with more news.'

'Get out!'

The slamming door missed his fingers by inches, and as he stumbled backwards Victor was lucky not to slip and fall, twisting himself into a staggering pirouette and regaining his footing before the rocks hidden under the ice greeted his face. Behind him, he heard Isabella shouting something on the other side of the door, but whether it was directed at him or some other unseen person, he couldn't tell.

Their meeting had gone better than expected. A request for protection and an offer of sex certainly outdid the threats of death and the waving kitchen knife he had expected.

Despite the threat of impending war, the day was looking up.

3

SECRETS AND MESSAGES

THE SECOND ROBOT was some kind of surveillance machine, built to burrow through deep snow to stealthily approach its target, then capture visuals and sound using a periscope-like instrument that could rise up through the top of the snow, then transmit the data back to a source computer.

It was crude and awkward, the kind of thing a university scientist nerd might build to spy on his cheating girlfriend. It looked stupid, had a fragile, ungainly shape, and didn't even work.

Kurou thought it was a masterpiece.

As he picked it apart one circuit board at a time, He tried not to think about the multi-billion-dollar fortune that was just out of his reach. He had once travelled the world surrounded by state-of-the-art machinery to which even governments had no access, with an endless source of funds available from anywhere at any time. People said money couldn't buy everything, but the fallacy of that assumption depended on your circumstances. When you were in control you could buy yourself a plateau that stood higher than the law. When you lost control all that excessive wealth did was tie a beacon around your neck that brought your enemies running.

He was hunted by someone even more dangerous than him. If he tried to access his money, he would be found.

The only thing that was more important than money was power, and right now Kurou had none.

All he had was a room full of junkyard electronics, and the awe of a young man who thought he was a god. It would have to be enough.

The security robot's A.I. component was too complex for his crude computer systems to access, but he was able to figure out its role. It was primitive, something that technological development had far surpassed in the last couple of decades, but gave the robot the ability to made its own decisions based on its target's actions, be them to continue to observe or to make a subtle retreat. It had no weapons systems, but there was a data wiping function that would activate when the machine was captured or tampered with. The inventor was obviously an amateur, because Kurou's interference would have triggered it had he not been careful to check for such a device first.

Now he had full access to the data collected by the robot so far, but it was pretty boring stuff. It had been sent to spy on the inventor's neighbours, returning pointless statistical information about meal times, pre-sleep rituals, the duration of usage of lighting and heating systems, and other inane information of no use to anyone. Everything stank of experimentation, that the inventor had built this machine on a whim with no idea what he really wanted to do with it.

Kurou had found it in the place he had requested along with a couple of pages of notes written in formal Russian that had pushed his understanding of the language to its limits. The inventor's tone was one of overzealousness, a burgeoning enthusiasm for his work, but at the same time lacked direction. Kurou quickly realised that rather than some incumbent member of the science community, he had discovered a hobbyist who had no idea how progressive his creations were. Of course, compared to what Kurou called innovative they were simple and crude, but for someone growing up in this throwback nowhere town at the end of the world they were startlingly impressive.

Kurou needed to know more, so he modified the surveillance robot as best he could and set it to work.

Spying on its creator.

Victor waited three days and then he went out to the abandoned café on the edge of town to see if his broken robot had been returned.

As he ducked through the partly collapsed entrance, he was disappointed to see that the single remaining table was bare. He glanced behind him, afraid he had been suckered into a trap, but there was no one there. He headed back towards the entrance and then noticed a piece of paper held down by a rock in the lee of the wall, out of the way of the icy snow gusting in through the entrance. Victor snatched it up and read it over with a wild grin on his face.

· · ·

I NEED a little more time to make my modifications. I also need more equipment. I would greatly appreciate it if you could provide me with the following items:

WHAT FOLLOWED WAS a modest list of items ranging from computer equipment to power tools. Several model numbers were specified, all of which were long out of date, as if the stranger had been living off the grid for quite some time. The wish list had a very childlike air about it, reminding Victor of his first forays into scientific experimentation as an adolescent with a chemistry set borrowed from school, where every puff of smoke or spark of light was a revelation. The note could have come from his own younger self.

Victor wasn't sure he could provide everything without going up to the secret place. He hadn't planned on going up there again until spring, because at this time of year the road would be waist-deep in snow and the entrance so well hidden that it would be a trial to find it at all, let alone get inside.

The few visitors that passed through the town—usually in transit to somewhere else—often felt like the winter was never-ending, but from April through to September there was a significant thaw. Permafrost was common higher up in the hills, even around some of the mines, but the town itself became a veritable oasis of moderate warmth. Some evenings Victor didn't even need to build a fire. Once the snow came though, anywhere not regularly plowed quickly became inaccessible.

Victor didn't know if the city council knew about the secret place. It was possible that they did, but he had never seen anyone up there. If he made a request for a team to clear the trail of snow, however, the secret place would no longer be secret, and whatever dreams he had had for its contents would be lost.

His mysterious benefactor would have to make do with what Victor could find in his own basement. Hopefully it would be enough, but even as he got home and began to rummage through drawers and cupboards, Victor began to worry that the stranger might be angered by his inability to cope with the requests. What if he gave up on Victor altogether and decided to leave or find someone else? Perhaps the road up into the hills that led past the trail to the secret place was worth the risk. The mining companies often ploughed the roads privately, not waiting for the council to get to it. If he left early tomorrow he could make it up and back before dark if it wasn't snowed in. But, spending the night there didn't bear thinking about, and if he got caught halfway when night fell....

HE LEFT the goods he could find in the old café on the way to his afternoon work assignment. A factory that built car bodyworks had been experiencing trouble with its alarm systems, and Victor was commissioned to fix them. The alarms had been heard going off in the middle of the night, even when the security teams found no sign of any intruders. After inspecting the computer programs set up to control the system, Victor found some kind of downloaded virus that was disrupting the timing, making the alarms fire at random times. The virus had caused a number of fuses to blow, which was making the problem worse.

He gave the management an estimate of three days to fix it, and quoted them a price. After a little negotiation, a deal was struck and Victor headed home to collect the tools he needed. It crossed his mind that an assistant might prove useful, and wondered if a work assignment might draw out his mysterious benefactor. He took a detour out to the café, thinking to leave a note.

The café stood a hundred metres from the entrance ramp to the main highway that passed Brevik on its southern side. At this time of year traffic was always sparse, but as Victor reached the café he saw the lights of a number of vehicles in convoy making the turn off towards the town.

They were Russian military, old Soviet vehicles that wouldn't have looked out of place in a museum. One was riddled with gunshots and another had a broken windscreen partly covered with a clear tarpaulin.

Overhead, the grey skies seemed to carry more dread than usual as the line of vehicles limped along through the snow, heading for the town centre. Victor ducked inside the café door as they passed, afraid to be seen. Through the side windows he caught glimpses of grim-faced military officers, their expressions carrying the weight of a far distant war that was slowly, inexorably drawing closer. As he watched the vehicles disappearing into the gloom, their tracks already being filled by fresh snow, he couldn't shake a feeling that today marked a threshold, that from here onwards things would be different.

Inside the café, he found another note, this one with a request that surprised him.

4

KNIVES, BLOOD, AND WOLVES

LEOV ROLLED the knife across his palms as he waited for the drug to take effect. Amazing it was, he thought, that in a place where it was so hard to find basic necessities like food or work, narcotics were as abundant as fruit on the autumn trees in the Baikal Oasis Zone.

He had never liked his job until the day after it ended, when he realised there would be no more money coming. Forty-three years old, he had lived his entire adult life in a series of dormitories owned by his employer, Navakov Deep Shaft Operations. The explosion that had killed thirty of his colleagues and rendered the mine unsafe for further excavations had also ended a neatly rounded twenty-five years' employment.

He had been added to a waiting list for vacancies at other companies, but with his days open to a boredom he hadn't known existed, he had followed the river down into the same addictions that had swallowed many of his former colleagues. Only yesterday he had shared a crack pipe with his former foreman, and then woken freezing next to the man's stiff body, the crust of blood around his nose frozen into a pluming ice flower that had lifted off his face as it contracted like a hand waving goodbye.

The knife, a coating of rust parting around the blade edge where he had sharpened it on the edge of a broken porcelain bowl, had come from the bins at the back of one of the bars near the train station, discarded because the wooden handle had split down the middle. Leov had wrapped a piece of cloth around it to make it easier to grip when he decided the time was right to use it. As he felt his senses beginning to dull, he knew he was close.

There was a dead man in the adjacent room. How much longer it would be before the council or one of the companies took notice,

Leov couldn't tell. The bodies of disillusioned, out-of-work miners and factory workers were stacking up like flies. Leov had found one swinging this morning in one of the bare rooms upstairs. A man whose face he recognised from another shift, come down to play one afternoon with a child's skipping rope in his bag, and here he was swaying in the chill morning breeze. Did he have kids? A wife? A home? Did it matter? No wife would stay with a man without prospects if there was a city councillor with an empty bed, not if she still had the looks to pull it off. Otherwise they might come down here hand in hand and swing that skipping rope together.

A shadow fell across the entrance. Leov tried to lift his head, but the stuff was taking over now and with his chin only a couple of inches off his chest he gazed up past his own brows at the cloaked figure standing in the doorway.

Stooped like an old man, the hood hanging low, claw-like hands holding a cloth bag containing something that made angles through the material. Leov gasped, or thought he did, as the Reaper's head swung towards him. The hood slipped back and a gnarled, ancient bird's beak poked out, surrounded by scar tissue that encircled two shadowed eye sockets.

Something was stirring in Leov's gut, a strange hurricane of force that had once held his arms steady behind the cutting machines in the dark places below ground, kept a stoic grimace on his face as the air filled with dust and the deafening roar of machinery. With a gasp that was nearly, but not quite, a war cry, his fingers clenched over the knife and he guided it through the air towards a placement in the Reaper's body.

The air filled with a banshee wail as the knife fed between folds of cloth and found a home in the meaty area above the creature's left hip. Leov twisted the blade as he felt it strike something hard, plunging it deeper through fat, muscle and sinew until the cloth handle came to rest against bone.

His fingers opened to release the knife, but those claw-like hands had closed over his wrist, holding him tight. Leov stared at the back of the Reaper's hand, at little tufts of what resembled feathers, at the hard scales in between, and the scar tissue that ran rivers through both. It was the strangest hand he had ever seen, certainly belonging to no human. There even seemed to be pieces of metal moving about beneath the skin.

Blood was pooling around the Reaper's left foot, which was shoed, Leov saw now, by several twists of a filthy cloth bandage which had turned copper brown and glistened in the shards of light sliding through the boards over the window. The Reaper still held Leov's arm by the wrist, as if the creature was planning to return through the doorway to its own world, dragging him behind.

Leov wasn't ready to go yet. He twisted his arm and slipped out of the Reaper's grip, turning to crawl away. The floor suddenly seemed impossibly close as his hands fell out from under him and his chin struck hard stone.

He felt something crack near the left corner of his mouth. He hoped it was just teeth breaking, but when he tried to grimace a sharp pain raced around the inside of his skull.

Something was holding on to his leg, twisting him over. It was hard, as strong as the metal pincers he had once used to break up lumps of rock in search of their valuable contents. He grunted as he was flipped over on to his back, the breath knocked out of him. The Reaper stood there in front of him, hood fallen away to reveal a monstrous face, like some ugly bird thrown into a fire to burn. One single eye glared at him and a crack opened beneath the lumpy beak to give him a smile.

'Goodnight, sire,' the Reaper said, a dry, crusty cackle that lacked any of the humour suggested by the smile. 'I'll enjoy you.'

Leov saw his own knife in the Reaper's hand, and as the creature squatted down between his legs he almost laughed. In his hysteria it looked like the Reaper was sitting down at a banquet table to eat.

Then a sharp pain carved up the inside of his thigh, jolting his hips and making him arch his back to scream. The Reaper's knife had opened up a major artery, and Leov's own blood warmed his freezing legs. The world began to go blurry and faint. The last thing Leov saw was the knife slicing into the flesh of his leg in neatly spaced incisions like a butcher slicing up a joint of meat.

KUROU STAGGERED BACK through the snow, his bag dragging along behind him, his left leg slick with his own blood.

He had berated himself a thousand times already, but it made no difference. He had got sloppy. After all these years, the prankster in him still lifted its ugly head at the most inopportune of times, and now it might cost him his life.

It had been a lucky thrust, but it could have been avoided with a little caution. Now there was a knife wound in his side and he had lost a lot of blood. With each step his vision grew fainter, and he worried that he might not reach the safety of his basement lodgings before he collapsed in the snow.

Something howled behind the whistling wind. It was far off, but coming closer. He cocked his head, letting his keen ears work for him, identifying the sound.

Wolves.

They got bolder in winter, he thought. Here, too close to the town limits, they had picked up the scent of blood on the wind. What power, he marvelled. Even now, perhaps soon to become a meal for a hungry pack, he couldn't help but feel impressed at their skills. God had taken his face and in return given him the eyes and ears of a hawk, but his sense of smell was no different to any other man.

He dropped the bag of human meat on the ground. It was his only chance. He'd taken little anyway, his knife hand too unsteady and his need to leave escalating with every stalling moment. The man's corpse lay where it had fallen, in the abandoned building back in the Lenin District, to be discovered cannibalised sometime tomorrow, he expected, after which a manhunt might ensue. After so many years of meticulous caution his very survival now lay in the balance.

Leaving the bag of human remains behind him, he staggered ahead into the snow as the howling of wolves rose above the crying of the coming storm.

$$5$$

STOLEN DRUGS AND BAD BROTHERS

I'M HUNGRY. Bring me food. And I'm sick. I need basic medicines. Especially antibiotics. Tonight if you can.

THERE WAS a hint of desperation in the note. The Cyrillic script, previously so neat and tidy, was skewed as if written in a hurry. And there was no mention of the missing items.

Victor took a pencil from his bag and scribbled a quick reply.

I'll come back as soon as I can. I hope it's not serious. I'm excited to meet you someday soon.

As he headed back towards the town, he wondered if he had time to return to the café again tonight. With the weather on the turn again, the temperature after dark would drop into the killing zone, minus thirty Celsius or lower. In the snow he would easily become disorientated, and even the shelter of the café wouldn't save him.

He hadn't been back through the Lenin District since the gang of kids had damaged the cart, but now he found himself heading towards it as it offered a short cut home. For half an hour he had been following the tyre treads of the military vehicles, but now he left them behind and found himself trudging through several centimetres of fresh snow. The blizzard was getting worse, and soon he was surrounded by curtains of cascading snowflakes, the houses to either side of the street barely visible, their hazy lights his only comfort. From time to time other people appeared out of the snow, walking quickly with their heads down.

As the houses and old company buildings became more dilapidated, so the streets lost their people, until Victor was walking alone through a shadowy dystopia of broken windows and smashed doors, collapsed fire escapes and roofs fallen onto the road. As a child he and his friends had dared each other to go inside these buildings, a rite of passage that had ended abruptly when a boy named Eric Devolov, a year younger than Victor and pretty in a cherubic way, had not come back out. The police found his body the following morning in the alley at the back of the building, thrown from one of the upper floors. He had been beaten and raped, his neck broken before he fell.

No one was ever arrested, but the suspects had all assumed the faces of the two greatest enemies of Brevik's townsfolk: unemployment and poverty.

He turned a corner and blinked. A flashing light called to him out of the snow. As he stumbled closer he saw a police car parked at the side of the street, outside one of the houses. The tracks of its tyres were the only ones he had seen since those of the military vehicles.

A police officer stood outside the door. From inside the house came the sound of a woman screaming and someone else shouting for calm. Whatever had happened, too much interest might make him a suspect. Victor gave the house a wide berth, unsure whether to worry more about what had been found or the gangs that might have been displaced by the police presence. He could only hope that the snow would keep them inside.

He reached his home a few minutes later. He filled a bag with food and as many medical supplies as he could find, mostly basic items like gauze and bandages. He had some ointments, but no antibiotics. They were hard to procure without cause. No doctor would prescribe them without ample evidence they were needed, so his only option other than robbing a pharmaceutical store was to ask Isabella. He wasn't sure which was easier.

With his bag slung over his shoulder, he headed back out into the snow, warier than ever as darkness fell. When he reached Isabella's house he was pleased to see that her father wasn't yet home. The man was far more terrifying than his daughter, and there would be no way past him. Isabella might be talked into helping him, but Mortin would likely throw him back out into the snow.

When she opened the door though, instead of berating him she rushed out and pulled him into a tight embrace. 'I'm so glad you came,' she gasped. 'It's so thoughtful of you to think of me at this time.'

Aware that asking what she meant would give him up, he said instead, 'I had to see you, to make sure you were all right.'

'What are we going to do?' she sobbed. 'They're abandoning us to die.'

Victor was desperate to ask who, but Isabella needed him to be strong. He held her tight, stroking her back as she cried against him. 'Don't worry, we'll be all right.'

'How do you know?'

'I just do. It'll all be okay.'

'We'll be cut down like wild dogs when those bastards come through here,' Isabella said. 'They'll string us up and flay the skin off our backs. They might even rape us. Do you know how it feels to be raped by a robot?'

As often with Isabella, Victor felt that the best answer was silence. He tried to um and ah in the right places, all the while hoping she would let him into the house before he froze to death on the front step.

Finally she pulled him inside and shut the door with a theatrical slam. She excused herself to go and freshen up, so Victor wandered into the living room where a radio was broadcasting news reports. Isabella's brother, Esel, was sitting with his feet up over the end of a sofa, smoking a cigarette. The boy, tall and broad for a fourteen-year-old, gave Victor a quick contemptible glance, then turned back to a magazine he was reading.

'What's going on?' Victor asked.

'About what?'

'The war.'

'Oh, don't you know, robo-boy? Lying to get into my sister's pants again?'

Victor would happily see Esel fall off a cliff or be torn apart by wolves. He would hold a camera and then upload the video to the internet with a huge grin on his face. 'I've been busy,' he said. 'I work. You should try it.'

'Go and eat yourself a dick.'

Victor knew from experience that getting sucked into an insult-throwing contest with a teenage asshole was a waste of time. Taking a slow, deep breath, he asked, 'I saw some military vehicles come into town.'

Esel flapped a hand towards the radio without looking up. 'They just made an announcement on the radio. Moscow has fallen.'

Victor gripped the edge of the nearest chair to stop himself stumbling. 'Are you serious?'

The boy looked up. 'Of course I'm serious, what do you think? Who cares? It's been on the cards for weeks. And it's not like they were of any help to us, were they?'

Before Victor could reply, Isabella came bustling into the room like a sudden squall out on Lake Baikal, her hands flapping in the air.

'They'll nuke us,' she shouted. 'The army has refused to surrender. We're all going to die.'

'Shut up, you dumb whore,' Esel shouted, throwing his magazine across the room. He jumped to his feet and looked about to slap his sister. Victor hung on to the edge of the chair between them in a position that could be either confrontational or neutral, depending on how he angled his body. Esel was several inches taller than Victor and had inherited his father's broad shoulders. In a fight to defend Isabella's honour, Victor was destined for a distant second place.

It was lucky that Isabella was more fearsome than her brother. 'Sit down, you little brat!' she screamed at him. 'You know nothing! You think we're safe here? We have no choice but to leave.'

'And go where? I like it here.'

'Vladivostok, and then to Japan.'

Esel laughed. 'So we can live in some tent village eating uncooked fish? No thanks. I'd rather stay here.' He turned to Victor. 'You're not going to leave, are you, robo-boy? Why don't you build us some weapons to fight with?'

Victor glanced from one to the other, unsure what to say. He felt like an ice cube in the middle of two fires, and tried to remember he'd only come here to ask if Isabella had any antibiotics she could spare.

'Well?'

It was Isabella who was looking at him. He shrugged. 'I'm not sure if I can.'

'See?' she cried, throwing her hands up in the air. 'We're all going to die.'

Esel pushed past her to the door. 'Well, in that case, I might as well go and get drunk with my friends. Could be the last time, couldn't it?'

As the front door slammed, an uneasy calm fell over the house, punctuated only by Isabella's sobbing. Victor, feeling like a man who'd just survived a vicious storm, sat down on the edge of the sofa. A moment later Isabella joined him. She took his hands in hers and looked up at him out of eyes bloodshot from crying.

'I don't want to die,' Isabella said.

'You won't. I won't let them touch you.'

'The radio reports said we've been abandoned, that an army is on its way here to take over the region. It's all lies. They're just going to nuke us, I know it.'

Victor shook his head. 'They can't. They destroyed all the nukes and even if they did still have some it's too dangerous with cyber-warfare.'

'What do you mean?'

'Hackers. Wars are fought online these days. You can't launch anything without a hacker coming in and taking over its systems and redirecting it back at you. That why the second Moscow siege happened. They have to use soldiers because men can't be hacked.'

It was a layman answer, but it seemed to satisfy her. The truth was that Victor didn't really know how powerful hackers were in war, other than being a pain in the ass. As far as he knew, localized systems worked fine, it was just long range technology that was at risk, anything with a signal that could be intercepted by satellite.

'We should still leave. Vladivostok isn't so far.'

'It's five thousand kilometres. If there are no more trains, it's a long walk.'

'Now's not the time to joke, Victor.'

'I'm not. Have you seen a car anywhere in town that could survive a journey half that long? Most of them are too unreliable to get from one end of town to the other.'

'So what do you suggest we do?'

'Well, the first thing would be to not panic. Don't believe everything you hear. Moscow might not have fallen at all. It could all be hackers planting fake reports.'

'Do you really think so?'

'It's as likely as not. We can't prove anything unless we see it with our own eyes.' He wanted to add, 'There might not be any war,' but thought better of it. The drone strike and the military vehicles were evidence of some upheaval at least.

Isabella slowly began to calm down. After Victor promised to stay the night, she went to make them a simple dinner. Her father, she said, was working the night shift at the mine and wouldn't be back until some time tomorrow. As for her brother and sister, they would come back when they chose, if at all. She seemed to have it in her head that a platoon of distant soldiers would come bursting through the door at any moment. If there was one thing that Victor wanted to make her understand, it was that wars never moved as quickly in real time as they did in history textbooks and television documentaries. Most wars, like most jobs he thought, consisted of more hours of waiting than of anything else.

It was already late by the time they had dinner, and afterwards they retired to Isabella's bedroom for some unfulfilling sex. The girl clearly had her mind elsewhere, while Victor was thinking about his promise to the stranger. As soon as Isabella had fallen asleep, he got up and crept downstairs. He felt bad about stealing from her, but he had no choice.

In a kitchen drawer he found a jar of what looked like a basic antibiotic, prescribed to Isabella's father. The date printed on the label was from six months ago, so Robert had probably stopped taking them after his ailment had healed. He wouldn't miss them.

Victor was just closing the drawer when he heard the kitchen door open.

'What the fuck are you doing?'

He turned to find Esel leaning in the doorway, eyes bleary and bloodshot, hair ruffled. He was still wearing his jacket.

'I said, what the fuck are you doing?'

'I had a headache.'

'So?'

'So I was looking for something to take.'

Esel advanced across the kitchen towards him. Even from several feet away Victor could smell the vodka on the boy's breath.

'I saw you put something in your pocket. Give it to me, you stealing cunt.'

Victor's heart was pounding. Esel had violence in his eyes, and from the look of a couple of scuff marks on his jaw he'd already had some tonight.

'I told you, I just took something for a headache. I was just going back upstairs.'

Esel shoved Victor hard in the shoulder, making him spin towards the door. 'I don't know what my whore of a sister sees in you, you worthless prick.'

'Don't call your sister a whore.'

'Stop me.'

Victor wasn't stupid enough to start a fight. Instead he backed off, trying to slide around Esel towards the door.

'Come on, robo-boy. Stop me. She's a whore. How much do you pay? How much?'

The kitchen door was at Victor's back. He took one step backwards, reaching out for it, then swung it hard forward just as Esel threw a punch at him. The heavy hardwood, designed to keep out the draft in the long Siberian winters, cracked against the boy's knuckles like a gun going off.

As Esel cried out in pain, Victor pelted for the front door. Of three deadbolts, the drunken teenager had only pulled the top one across, so Victor grabbed it and slid it back, reaching behind him to slip his jacket off a hook on the wall beside the door. The risk was worth it—the cold was far more dangerous than Esel's fists.

He heard feet in the hallway as he stepped outside and pulled the door shut. He took the steps down to the street three at a time, slipping once to land on his back before getting up and hurrying on. The door swung open and a barrage of insults followed him, but the boy didn't. Victor was just reaching the other side of the street when he heard the door slam closed again.

Next time he tried to visit Isabella he would likely face a beating, but he would worry about that when the time came.

The temperature had dropped below minus twenty Celsius. Without his jacket with its thick, fur-lined hood, he would be a lump of ice before he made it back to his house. Even with it the cold was like a net sifting through his body to steal away with each molecule of warmth. He ducked his head and buried his hands in his pockets, heading for home.

6

DECISIONS AND DISCOVERIES

BREVIK'S MAYOR, Pavel Andrev, shook his hands like two old cloths, a gesture that indicated the very fullest extent of his rage. The soldiers had gone, but their words still hung heavy in the air like laden thunderclouds.

How dare those bastards walk in here and then just leave, telling us to fend for ourselves? What happened to the might of the Russian army?

So, it had come to pass. Moscow was defeated, and the Russian army was in full retreat, heading—well, who knew where? The enemy—whatever it was; Andrev, like most people living out here on the fringes of society, wasn't quite sure—was coming, rolling on like a giant, crushing wheel, obliterating everything in its path. And the townsfolk had a choice, to pack their bags and head east, following the cringing tail of their retreating army, or stay behind and hope for the best.

He hadn't planned for things to turn out like this. His own stint in the military had been uneventful, years of sentry duty and occasional skirmishes with insurgents from the states to the south, followed by early retirement and a quaint and prosperous quasi-military post as mayor of this nothing little industrial town hidden among the endless forested hills of Siberia. A single man most of his life, he'd been able to take his pick of widowed miners' wives, eventually settling on a pretty young blonde called Petra, whom he had so far seeded with four boisterous little babies. Life was easy, life was good.

The men barrelling into his office had been nothing more than messengers. Skin chapped and bloody, uniforms scuffed and torn, their appearance had told more stories than their mouths. Moving in teams, they said, their responsibility was simply to pass on the message to each town they passed, now that radio and email could no longer be trusted.

'Will we die if we stay?' he had asked.

It was not a question they had been able to answer. *You might. You might not. The risk is yours.*

Andrev picked up the phone on his desk and asked his secretary to call for his most senior aide, Lena Patrova. A few minutes later the door opened and Lena walked in. As always when the tall, elegant woman entered, Andrev had to look away to avoid undressing her with his eyes. Petra was cute and her legs opened on request, but she had been a distant second choice. Lena was the apple to every eye that beheld her, a glittering river cutting through the icy streets of this hellhole town.

'What do we do?' he said after she had sat down across from him, one perfectly formed leg crossed over another. 'We can't put up a defence. That drone took out the one munitions factory in town. Even if we had enough people to arm we've got nothing to arm them with.'

Lena opened her mouth, pausing a few seconds before she spoke. 'We do nothing,' she said. 'Panicking the people more than they already are would only make the situation worse. What do we really know? There could be no war out there at all.'

'Those hacking bastards,' Andrev spat. 'I can't turn on the television news anymore without doubting every single thing I see.'

'It goes both ways,' Lena said. 'They don't know anything about us, either.'

'But they have guns, we don't.'

'They don't know that.' She raised a perfectly manicured eyebrow at him. 'And we don't know that either. If they've won, will they really need to harm us? We're not fighting the Nazis, you know.'

'Those men had pictures and videos of slaughter,' Andrev said slowly. 'Whole villages of people lined up and hacked apart like dead trees. Fields of chopped limbs floating in a lake of discarded blood.'

Lena rolled her eyes. 'And you trusted their authenticity?'

With a sweep of his hand Andrev knocked a pile of papers to the floor. They spread out around his feet in a fan of grey and white. 'I trust them enough to know that it would be our folly to ignore the threat.'

'Of course it would. But before we do anything perhaps we need to see for ourselves what's going on. Who do you trust most in your offices? Who is the one person you rely on?'

Rumour had it that Lena was ex-secret police. Of course, no one mentioned it out loud.

He gave a slow nod. 'How will you do it?'

'Give me an all-terrain vehicle and two aides. I'll also need supplies and a secure radio linked only to one you hold yourself. I'll go west, only as far as I need to go to see what the stories are in towns closer to the conflict.'

Andrev sighed. He had no way to tell whether she would just break and run with the best resources he had available. Then again, she could have boarded the last train heading east. He had no real choice but to trust her.

'Done,' he said.

KUROU WOKE to a chill that was almost paralysing. He pulled back the heap of filthy blankets and massaged his one remaining eye until the lid felt supple enough to open. A square of cold sunlight illuminated the ashes of a fire in the grate. For any sunlight at all to get down through the shaft, the wind must have been harsher than usual last night, the ice that usually piled up on the chimney top stripped away.

He rolled over and tried to get up, but a wave of nausea overcame him and he slumped back to the floor, his hands clawing through a patch of freezing stone stained brown with his blood after he had tried to sew up the knife wound. He felt it now, the only part of his body that was warm, burning with a feverish heat.

His fingers closed over a radio receiver. He depressed a button and waited until a hiss of static had cleared.

'Has he come back yet?'

The robot he had repaired, in hiding not far from the abandoned café, replied in a series of binary numbers which Kurou took a few seconds to decipher into words: *Negative. Still waiting. Systems cold. Request a reduction of primary power battery.*

Kurou sighed. The machine was primitive, but he would die in the snow if he attempted to reach the café himself. 'Request granted. Maintain visual and audio link at all times.'

The machine replied with another series that roughly translated as: *Thanks, master, nice one.* Even with the agonising pain in his side, Kurou felt a brief flash of the old humour. In different days and different circumstances, he might have got on with the machine's inventor pretty well.

Now though, he depended on him for survival.

Where are you?

He dragged himself across to the old fireplace and managed to spark up the embers. He still had some food, and he pulled a blanket around himself and lay down, chewing on the dried human meat while letting the small fire project its meagre warmth on to him.

He estimated that he had a couple of days at most before the infection became too strong for his ailing body and he slipped into a delirium which would likely be followed by hypothermia. A slow, degrading death caused by one moment of cockiness that his failings really should have ironed out of him by now.

I am the ender of worlds, he thought, as he began to doze off into feverish dreams. *I am the creator of great monsters and the bringer of revolutions. And here I lie, broken and dying, alone and penniless, forgotten by the world that should have fallen at my feet.*

VICTOR LEFT AS EARLY as he could. The snowstorm broke midmorning, leaving the town blanketed in twenty centimetres of fresh snow. As he made his way through the streets, he found himself alone except for a few lethargic snow-clearing machines pushing the stuff into piles on street corners already overloaded with huge mounds of dirty snow and ice. The town carried an eerie stillness reflected by the absence of broadcasts on his radio this morning and the accompanying television blackout. Such things happened from time to time, but in light of yesterday's rumours a glacial feeling of foreboding was beginning to bear down on him.

Change was afoot, and someone high up didn't want the commoners to know about it.

He thought of the secret place, wondering whether he should risk a hike up to the viewing point this afternoon to check that it was undisturbed. The extra snow would make the journey even more difficult, but his afternoon's employer had cancelled, leaving him free. He wouldn't have time during daylight hours again until the weekend, so it might be his best chance.

Over his shoulder he carried a waterproof canvas bag containing the stolen antibiotics, as much food as he could spare, and a few extra bits and pieces that he thought the stranger might need. It wasn't much, but the mention of medicines scared him. This stranger had already done more for him than he could believe, yet what if he was sick? What if he was dying?

The road out to the abandoned café was an untouched blanket of snow. Out here in the open, away from the hills that sheltered the town, the snow had fallen heavier, and it looked like the southern highway was blocked. In this region, each town or city was responsible for its own snow clearing, but outside the city limits there was an unhealthy reliance on the occasional government snow plough that rumbled through. If the highway was blocked, it meant the ploughs hadn't come, and if the ploughs hadn't come, it meant...

War?

Victor pressed on, trying not to dwell on it. When he reached the café, snow had drifted up against the door, and he had to put down his bag for a while to clear a way inside.

There were no more notes. The table was empty. As he reached it, something crunched underfoot, and he looked down to see lumps of ice below the table with strange patterns impressed in them. Something had been inside since his last visit, leaving its tracks behind.

Victor lifted a piece of the ice in his hands.

The impressions weren't from shoes or boots. They looked like tiny tyre treads, or the symmetrical lines of a miniature caterpillar track.

A robot.

His robot.

With a lump in his throat, Victor stepped backwards. The man was too hurt to come here. He was using Victor's robot to deliver the letters.

Victor went to the door and peered out at the snowy road. If the robot had come here recently, there should be tracks, but the overnight snow had covered them.

He decided to hide out for a while, but after an hour there was still no sign, and the temperatures had already begun to drop again as clouds came in to cover the sun. It looked like more snow was coming, and with no way to stay warm he would end up freezing to death. As he left the bag and headed back out into the snow he resolved to come better prepared next time, in case there was a chance he could follow the robot back to where the stranger was hiding.

He still had a little time though, so instead of going straight home, he skirted the edge of the town to the east, taking a forest track that was easy to follow from the line of the trees, until he came to one of the access roads for the mines to the north. Here, he found the roads had been ploughed, so he pushed on, heading up into the hills as the afternoon drew on. A strange feeling of determination had taken over him, and he walked hard despite the chill starting to seep into his boots and the cold sweat that stuck his shirt to his back.

At last he reached the craggy tree with the V-shaped trunk that looked like a giant gnarled arrowhead protruding from the side of the road. Other than its shape, there was nothing to mark it as special from the other pines that stood in rows along the edge of the mining access road.

Looking back, he could see Brevik laid out in functional grid lines in the valley below. Some lights had come on and it almost looked pretty. Further ahead, the road wound on up and over the hill, dropping down into another valley where the copper mines were located.

Brevik had grown up around the miners' dormitories when the rich seams of ore had first been discovered more than a hundred years ago. The town had begun with the workers' essentials—brothels, bars, and gambling dens—before eventually expanding out into shops, banks and even a squat, ugly church. From a distance, surrounded on all sides by undulating hills covered with pine forests, all draped with a blanket of snow, it looked pure and innocent, one giant Christmas tree away from a Coca Cola commercial. Only up close did the degeneration begin to reveal itself.

Highways flanked it to the north and south, while a railway snaked its way through the hills between the two. The southern highway was in disrepair, but the northern was the main trunk route for most of the mining traffic, and was therefore better maintained. The railway served to bring supplies into the town, and take the people out.

Victor turned back towards the tree. Split many years ago, perhaps by lightning, or left by some subtle planter as a sign of something hidden beyond, it served the purpose well. Aware he was leaving tracks in the snow that would take wind or fresh fall to cover, Victor continued up the road some way before climbing up the snowbank into the trees and doubling back to reach the v-shaped tree from behind.

Once he located it, he headed into the forest, walking with the tree to his back, checking over his shoulder every few steps to make sure he wasn't veering off course. Beneath the snow-laden trees the standing air temperature was cooler, but he was sheltered from the snapping wind.

He estimated he had two hours at most. The snow had held off, so as long as he made it back to the ploughed mining road and in sight of the town lights before dark he would get back all right.

A few metres further on, he came to an opening of sorts, where a thinner line of trees stood straight and sentry-like between two taller rows of pines. It was this strange natural phenomenon that had first allowed him to find the secret place. Enough trees had fallen or been felled to turn away the eye of the unobservant, but when you lined yourself up against any one of the trunks, closed one eye and peered out just far enough for the next tree in the line to become visible, a regular arc of trees would appear, slanting off uphill and to the left.

During the previous summer, a bit of digging in the earth around the trees had revealed the remains of laid aggregate, and

Victor knew he was looking at an old access road that had been dug up and obscured by a line of trees planted up its centre.

And of course, as a hobby inventor, the need to discover where it went had briefly overtaken all other needs.

He began to hike up through the snow, following the line of the smaller trees. They wound up into the hills, cutting back around a protruding cliff, through a cutting in the hill, and then dropped sharply into a valley.

This was the point where Victor had initially lost the trail. Sure by now that he was following an old road, it had taken him some days to realise that he had reached an old lookout point, and that it was necessary to backtrack a few hundred metres and then follow another branch that swept down and around the base of the hill, before straightening out at the bottom of the valley.

At first he had been sure he was following the route to an old mine, but the diligence with which the trees had been planted made it obvious someone was hiding something.

Now, as he stood looking down on the concealed valley and the stand of trees that hid the entrance to the secret place, he breathed a sigh of relief. After the warnings from the day before and the visit by the bedraggled military vehicles, Victor had half expected to see activity down there, vehicles moving about in the trees, the lights of torches and spotlights, but it was as he had hoped, undisturbed.

Again, he had left it too late to get down there today and get back to the town safely, but it was relief enough to know it was—

He blinked, unsure if his eyes were just tired or if he had really seen it.

'No…'

There it came again.

A single light, blinking on and off.

7

RELUCTANCE, RELIEF, AND ANTICIPATION

PAVEL ANDREV TAPPED the switch that had failed to turn his office light on, but it made no difference. The room remained dark. With a sigh, he fumbled his way across the room and pulled a chord to ignite an old standing gas lamp in one corner. The dim, flickering glow made his drab office with its desk piled high with papers look almost sultry.

Lena had been gone for nine hours. There had been no word from her, but she had assured him she would only be in touch if she had news. Andrev didn't know if the likelihood of their signal being intercepted was a genuine threat or simple paranoia, but she had felt the risk was enough. Andrev felt like a monkey tricked into a cage by a fox which had then run off with the key.

'Bulb's gone,' he shouted out to his secretary, but when no answer came, he sighed again then went to a utility closet in the corner and found a replacement. However, changing the bulb made no difference.

He was just about to throw the thing across the room when he noticed his secretary standing in the doorway. 'Should I call an electrician?' she asked.

'That would be a good idea. Everything's starting to fall apart.'

His secretary gave him a smile that was supposed to be reassuring, and went out to make some phone calls.

At the window, Andrev looked down at the snowy street. A handful of cars had gathered there, some with their lights still blazing. He could hear the commotion already, some of the richer townsfolk barging into the council offices, demanding to know what had happened to their televisions. It was actually a relief that most of the town was so poverty stricken that the sudden severance of broadcasts had gone largely unnoticed.

'Like a sinking ship with just the rats left,' he muttered. 'Why am I wasting my time trying to save it?'

'Sir?' came his secretary's voice. 'An electrician will come the day after tomorrow. That's the earliest I could find one available, I'm afraid. Um, there are quite a few people downstairs now. They're demanding you talk to them.'

'What about Security?'

'Chief Voltaire said they can't hold them off much longer without shooting people. Perhaps you should speak to them, sir.'

'Fine.'

He headed for the stairs as she went back to her desk. What could he tell them? He knew nothing, and apart from sending Lena off to collect more information, he'd done nothing. The best place for these people right now was their homes.

'Andrev! What's going on?'

The man at the front of the group of a dozen or so was Karl Ostinov, foreman at GTA Mining Industries, and at his shoulder was Jan Markovich, the head of the town's only bank. Behind them was a motley assortment of business owners and local investors. Andrev groaned inwardly. He could have predicted the capitalist bloodsuckers would be the first to get upset. After all, they had the most to lose.

'There's nothing I can tell you that you don't already know,' Andrev said. 'You've seen the same news reports as I have.'

'Except now they've all stopped.' Markovich said. 'Was that your doing, you swine? You never got my vote, you swindling bastard.'

'Your insults won't help anything,' Andrev said. 'All I can tell you is that I no longer have access to television broadcasts either. The whole region is undergoing some sort of blackout.'

'Which means what?'

'Forty men died in that drone attack,' someone near the back shouted. 'What are you going to do about it?'

'Look, there's nothing I can do. I'm waiting for further information.'

'Waiting till the whole town gets bombed off the earth?'

A scuffle broke out in the middle of the group as someone tried to push his way to the front. Andrev took a step back as his two security guards stepped forward. To his left, Security Chief Voltaire had unclipped his gun holster.

'It's getting late. I suggest you return to your homes,' Andrev said. 'I'll do a public address at lunchtime tomorrow to share what information I have. Until then it would be advisable to maintain public order.'

'You useless piece of—'

A fist came flying out of nowhere. Andrev ducked sideways, unsure exactly who had thrown it. Chief Voltaire, a monster of a man at six-seven and a hundred and twenty kilograms, batted the would-be attacker away with ease, pushing him back into the crowd.

Rickard Ustinov, head of the town's largest insurance company.

Voltaire reached for his gun.

'No!' Andrev shouted, putting two hands on his security chief's arm. 'This is over,' he shouted at the crowd. 'Go back to your homes. I'm placing an official curfew in place, as of right now.'

The threat of the gun had subdued them, and with a few mutters and half-hearted insults they withdrew. Voltaire and his colleague secured the front entrance as the cars pulled away, some skidding in the snow in a last display of disobedience.

Andrev stared after the disappearing lights. This was just the start, he knew. They would be back, and they would want answers. What would he tell them tomorrow? How long could he keep putting off a decision?

It was getting late. The thought of Petra's warm body appealed to him. He needed to forget about all this, but there was only so long he could close his eyes. Sooner or later he would have to stand up and be the town's mayor, or get his family on a train heading east and become a nobody.

It wasn't much of a choice.

THE ROBOT WAS BACK. Kurou tried to open his eyes as it bumped down the steps using a series of extendable levers and wheels the inventor had installed. As it reached the bottom its engine fizzed and died, the robot slumping forward, even its auxiliaries exhausted. After sending him a message that the inventor had showed up at last, it had taken a couple of hours to get back through the heavy snow. Kurou would worry about whether it was repairable tomorrow. He would see if he made it through the night first.

He reached for the bag the robot had dragged with it and brushed ice off the outside, holding the zipper close to the fire until the ice had thawed enough for it to open. As soon as he could pull it back, he dumped the contents out on the ground and rifled through them, gasping with relief as he came upon a little bottle of tablets.

The fever that had come on strong in the afternoon left him too weak to read the label properly, so he would have to trust the inventor. Without a second thought, he popped the cap and swallowed three tablets.

A few food items also lay among the bag's contents. There were some tins and dried foodstuffs, as well as a few vegetables and even a tub of vitamin tablets. It had been so long since Kurou had eaten anything with Vitamin C that his teeth felt loose in his mouth. He chewed down a couple, then began to worry that the sudden influx of health food would make him sick.

As the minutes ticked by and nothing happened, he stared into the flames, a drowsiness coming over him. Would he wake up again or was this it?

The young inventor, whoever he was, had saved him. If he was still alive tomorrow, Kurou promised himself that he would at least consider doing something nice in return.

LENA DOZED in the back seat as the aide drove hard along the northern highway in the direction of Moscow. The road was built for the larger tyres of trucks, with the potholes concealed by the snow treacherous for smaller vehicles, but their car was military-grade, one of the few well-maintained vehicles that the council owned. In the back, among their supplies, were a couple of hundred litres of spare bio-fuel. In the event that they found no fuelling stations still operational, they had enough for about three thousand kilometres, fifteen hundred out and the same back. It wasn't far in Siberia, but it would be enough for them to find out what was really going on.

They had seen nothing so far to give them concern. They had passed through a couple of sleepy mining towns where they had found enough shops open to get food and drink. No one had looked at them strangely, or offered any news.

Lena wasn't sure whether to be happy about that or not. Tucked inside her shirt was her secret service-issued pistol, with a couple of magazines of extra rounds. The thought of using it again made her lick her lips. The popping sound as a bullet penetrated through enemy clothing into flesh was as addictive and delicious as anything she'd ever known. She had been too long out of service, working a nothing position as a lower ranked councillor in a nothing little town. The thought of getting back into action made her skin tingle with excitement, even if it might end up costing her life.

With each turn of the highway, each rise and fall of the hills, each time a small town came into view, Lena found herself praying for something—anything—that suggested they might be getting close to a combat situation.

Oh, for the chance to shoot down a couple of enemies again ... Lena could barely contain her excitement.

8

A WAR OF INFORMATION

VICTOR WAS desperate to get over to the old café to see if there had been any response from the stranger, but the snow had closed in again overnight and he had no time before his scheduled work for the day. Even as he made his way across town to the car parts factory he rubbed the bleariness out of his eyes, having stayed up late working in his basement. His thoughts were all asunder after seeing the light up by the entrance to the secret place, and the only way to combat the swirling thoughts going through his head was to busy himself with his ongoing projects.

What if a war really did come to the town? He'd have to give up everything. The thought of abandoning his life's work made him feel sick. For years he had been working on his dream, pushing everything else aside to put in the hours down in his basement that he hoped would one day bring colour and excitement back to the drab, grey wastes of Siberia.

Over the course of the morning and into the afternoon, as he worked away at fixing the factory's computer system problems, he caught snippets of conversation from the workers passing him by. The threat of more drone strikes was the main topic, with other concerns about the apparent television and radio blackout that had swept the town. No one seemed to be talking much about the internet, but it had been banned outside of government offices for years, and the threat of locators had kept the casual user from trying to break the rules. Victor had a computer powerful enough to access it, but he used it sparingly for the same reason, and only ever through a firewall that blocked his location. There was always someone monitoring you.

He stayed late at the factory, hoping to get into a position where he could finish up by the end of the following day, after which he had to visit City Hall to fix up some electrics for the mayor. He hadn't wanted to take the job, but you couldn't refuse City Hall. Even in a town with such a meagre police force, there was always a cell waiting for those who outwardly refused anything for the government.

His work went well, and he finished for the day at five o'clock, heading straight for the abandoned café. He had brought extra clothing with him to protect against the evening cold, but luckily the snow had stopped again, and city ploughs had been clearing the streets all afternoon. He made quick progress, but even so it was near full dark by the time the squat structure rose out of the gloom, a vague silhouette against the dark grey sky.

He pulled a torch from his pocket and went inside, not wanting to use the light until he was out of sight of the road. To his disappointment there was no new note. Victor tried not to panic as he looked down at the empty table top. Had the medicines been strong enough? What if the stranger had died overnight?

Disappointed, he was just about to leave when he heard a whirring sound coming from outside. He dropped down behind a stack of chairs and peered through a space offering a view of the doorway as something pushed its way inside.

His eyes widened as his own little surveillance robot appeared, rolling through the entrance on its caterpillar tracks. It went up to the table, and a little box opened on its side for a robotic arm to extend out, dropping a piece of paper down on the table top.

Victor's heart leapt. He wanted to jump up and hail the robot, but at the same time he had designed it for surveillance; it would be recording everything that it saw and heard, and storing the information in its memory banks. If he alerted it to his presence the stranger would find out Victor was hiding here. If he wanted to discover the stranger's hiding place he only had to follow the robot, but he would have to be careful.

It stopped for a few seconds and then turned and went back outside. As soon as it was gone, Victor climbed out of his hiding place and went over to the table. Aware that he could easily follow the robot's tracks, he stopped for a few seconds to check the note in his torchlight:

Thank you, sire. I owe you my life. Next, I need a needle, and thread. Thank you, kindly.

A wide smile spread across Victor's face, especially the way the stranger had addressed him again using an old-fashioned word usually reserved for a Tsar. It was quaint. Perhaps they would become great friends once they finally met face to face.

Remembering the robot, he hurried back out into the snow. The road had been ploughed but its tracks were still easy to follow, a line of caterpillar tread marks heading back towards the town.

Then, fifty yards further on, they suddenly veered left, into the snow piled up along the side of the road. Victor frowned, then nodded. Of course. The robot was designed for surveillance, and the stranger had programmed it to observe the café from a distance, hidden out of sight.

Would it recognise him? If the stranger knew he was hoping to follow the robot, would he change his plans?

Victor carried on walking. The robot wouldn't return to its new master's den until it needed to bring something. He could bring a needle and thread later tonight if the snow stayed away, although it would be brutally cold, and he didn't like the idea of hiding out. Perhaps he should wait until tomorrow. Finish up at the factory as quick as he could, then hide out in the café until the robot came back.

Yes, that would do it.

Victor smiled again as he headed off back towards the town. He was so excited about meeting the stranger that he was practically tingling with anticipation.

THE FEVER HAD BROKEN OVERNIGHT, and when Kurou pulled back the blankets he saw the wound had lost some of its violence, the sharp reds of the infected area dulled and stabilized. His haphazard attempt at closing it up had failed, the crude stitches broken open, but he had plenty of the antibiotics left so if he didn't aggravate it he still had time.

Much to his pleasure, the robot's batteries had charged up again overnight. He opened the front casing and made a few quick adjustments to its circuitry, implanting some bypasses of unnecessary processes so that its battery life could be extended, then he sent it out into the snow with another note, a simple request this time.

With the robot gone, he took another dose of the pills and then opened a can of processed fruit the inventor had left him. After living off human meat and whatever he could pick from the town's trash for as long as he could remember, the taste of pineapple and mango, however much it had been processed, was like taking a drug. He plucked out each small piece with a tiny fork, examined it for a few seconds, then popped it into his mouth and rolled it across his tongue a few times before chewing and swallowing it down.

He had once controlled a fortune worth billions of dollars. He had travelled the world and been master of a scientific portfolio greater than any in the world. He had built robots and biotechnologically enhanced animals and humans that no one else could even begin to comprehend. He had mastered his field, as close to a God on earth as there had ever been.

Yet here he was, entranced by the taste of pineapple.

Feeling better, he pulled across the bag that the inventor had left for him and picked through its contents. The most interesting item was a little digital radio. During the years of his self-imposed exile, Kurou had cut himself adrift from events in the outside world. He switched it on, flicking through the channels in search of a signal, but at first he found nothing but static, or obvious silences where broadcasts should have been.

Someone or something was blocking the airwaves, but it was an easy wall to get around if one had the skills. He opened the casing with a screwdriver and spent half an hour readjusting the settings on the internal computer display. The tiny, internal monitor screen had enough power to access the internet, but Kurou purposely stayed away, afraid of who might be listening. Instead, he used a few universal commands to access the central coding of the device, an intricate program perhaps written by the inventor. It showed a high level of skill, but there was skill, and then there was *skill*. Kurou had never had an apprentice, but if he ever chose to take one, the inventor showed potential. It would be best, he thought, to tread carefully around the young man.

After an hour of recoding the settings and updating the access permits to allow the transmitter to permeate the external firewall that was blocking out the region, Kurou closed up the casing again and began to search again for signals.

The first was in a language he hadn't heard for many years, but that brought back pangs of nostalgia for those few memories of his childhood not soured: Chinese:

Refugee levels becoming unsustainable.

It was on a loop, a recorded message. He listened to it for a few seconds, then abandoned it, searching for more information.

This time he found a live broadcast. The language was Baltic, not one he knew well. From the few crossover words of Russian that he could pick out, he managed to understand a few short phrases:

...moving east ... air control compromised ... last known position ... talks ... ceasefire abandonment ... options ... battalions under attack ... surrender...

Interesting. Kurou rubbed his chin, picking at a scab, and changed the frequency again.

This time, another language he knew well. English:

Reports are coming in that a hacker hive has been discovered and eliminated in southwestern Belgium, near Bruges. Until further notice the Web remains offline in most of northern Europe while other hives are flushed out and destroyed. Radio contact has been reestablished with the supposed lost battalion near the Ukraine-Romania border, although initial reports are that—the report died in a hail of fuzz and static—*we will now return to scheduled programming. Have you heard that you should be putting away your perennials for the coming winter season? Prune back to one third of the plant's original size, remove from the pot and hang upside down in a cool, dry place. Then, come spring, the plants will be ready to be re-fucking fucking fuck you and die ignore everything you hear the hackers are in control*—

Kurou switched off the radio and leaned back, nodding thoughtfully. How interesting. A new form of warfare was being ushered in, it seemed. A war of information. If you couldn't trust what you heard, how could you wage a war? It had become foot soldiers and trenches all over again. When you couldn't trust a simple radio, how could you believe anything you read on the internet? How could you believe a phone call was from your superior when voice manipulation software was so powerful?

In peace times, of course, it didn't matter. But in times of war, the armies of hackers were more important than the men with guns.

For the first time in years, Kurou felt a stirring of his old desires, as if he had woken up from a long hibernation. Perhaps it was just the euphoria of the antibiotics fighting off the infection in his knife wound, but he felt the urge to find a way back online and create some chaos. He could hack with the best of them, and had once found great joy in manipulating the cyber world from his own computer screen.

Perhaps it was safe now. Perhaps that man who had hunted him was dead, or had found a more exciting target to hunt.

It paid to be cautious. There were programs that could track user activity and hunt out old habits and familiar patterns with more accuracy than people might once have thought possible. Everything from the kind of sites he used, to the frequency, to the times of day and length of time he spent online. Everything he did would be lined up against an immense database of statistics, and he would leave a footprint, however faint, however distorted. It was a risk, but one he felt ready to take.

He contacted the surveillance robot.

'Has he come back yet?'

9
____

PLANS TO ESCAPE

VICTOR WAS ABOUT to leave for work the next morning when he was snapped out of a grogginess caused by a lack of sleep by his old dial phone ringing from the hallway.

As he picked it up, he eyed the clock on the wall warily. More than five minutes and he risked being late.

'Victor? Oh, thank God!'

'Isabella? What's the matter?'

He wasted nearly a minute of his leeway listening to her sob into the phone. He was starting to wonder whether he should hang up and have her call him back when she suddenly blurted: 'I'm worried about Father! He's gone off with some of his friends to start a protest against the council!'

Having met Isabella's bullish, bullying father, it was the city council Victor was most worried about. The man was as dangerous and unstoppable as one of the huge dump trucks that loaded and shifted the mined rock between the towers and the pits to the north of Brevik, his forehead wide and jutting like a bulldozer blade. It was easy to see where Esel got his aggression; Victor could only assume Isabella got her emotion and her sister her coquettishness from their absent mother.

'You have to come to me now, Victor,' she said. 'I'm not sure I can go through this alone.'

'I have to work.'

'No!' A heavy knocking sound came from the other end of the line, like a phone being hit against wood. 'This is one of those times where you have to put everything else aside to be with those you love! Please, Victor! I'm terrified!'

Victor frowned. He wondered if he could get away with going in late. The factory's management was unlikely to fire him because there was no one else in the town who could work with computers and electronics like he could.

'Where are you?'

'I'm at home, you idiot.'

'No, I meant where will you be while these protests are going on? Is it safe to stay in your house?'

'Father said not to go outside, but I don't know. Do you think I should? I mean, where is safe, Victor?'

It was becoming obvious to Victor that Isabella was on the verge of losing her mind. The girl made little sense at the best of times, and her words were now descending into incoherence. It was possible she had been at some of the other pills he had seen in her father's medicine drawer, antidepressants and painkillers that only wealth could procure. He had considered taking a few for the stranger but he couldn't be sure whether they were safe or not. It wasn't uncommon in days gone by for richer landowners to maintain a stash of quick-acting poison in the event that the secret police came knocking. Death by one's own hand had long been preferable to death at a plethora of others.

'Look, just stay where you are,' he said at last. 'I'll be over there as quickly as I can. Don't do anything, just lock yourself in your room until you hear me arrive.'

'Okay. I love you, Victor.'

Knowing she would instinctively notice a hesitation, Victor blurted, 'I love you too,' and then allowed himself a few moments of delayed reflection after he had put down the phone. He was never quite sure if he did love her or whether her bullheadedness had pushed him into thinking that he did, but if there really was a war heading their way, it wouldn't matter much.

He called the factory and told them he had been struck down with a sudden malady that required a visit to the doctor. The foreman he spoke to wasn't best pleased, but there was nothing he could do. Victor promised to be there by lunchtime unless he was officially confirmed as on his deathbed.

Before fulfilling his promise to Isabella, he headed out to the old café and delivered the needle and thread the stranger had asked for. He wanted to wait for the robot to come and take it, but a creeping guilt that he was breaking his promise to his girlfriend turned him away, so he headed off back into town while throwing occasional reluctant glances over his shoulder.

Outside City Hall, a mob had appeared, many perhaps spurred on by the day's temperature; at a degree or two below zero it was as warm as it had been since the first snow fell.

There were a couple of television crews set up outside the doors, while a handful of policemen were making half-hearted attempts to keep order. Perhaps sensing an impending slaughter, a couple of crows had appeared out of nowhere and were perched on the ornate balconies of the building's second floor windows.

Victor hung back, not willing to be associated with such unrest, even though it was obvious that there would be little comeback on it. He sensed that everything he took for granted about law and order was about to be turned on its head.

The main doors opened and the mayor stepped out, flanked by two huge bodyguards on either side. He started to talk, but the mob —which probably numbered fifty or so—started to shout and argue before he'd finished his first sentence. His words were immediately lost in the din, and as he got increasingly more frustrated he managed only to inadvertently create some excellent photograph poses for magazines and newspapers that might or might not still be publishing in a few days' time.

Then someone threw an egg.

That it struck the mayor square between the eyes was only slightly more of a surprise than that someone had intentionally wasted a rare commodity. Indeed, the sudden flurry of commotion from the middle of the mob suggested several of the assembled people felt the same thing.

It was enough for the mayor. He brushed the already-freezing gunge off his face and marched back inside, the doors slamming behind him as a flurry of rocks and lumps of ice   beat out a harsh rhythm on the heavy wood.

As the police backed away against the doors, radios held to their ears as if to threaten calling reinforcements, Victor headed back into the quieter streets surrounding the town square, skirting back up to the north towards where Isabella lived.

The door was flung open before he had even turned on to her path, and the insults that greeted him were softened only by the volume of her sobbing.

'Father says we are to leave,' she cried into his chest, pulling him inside and closing the door with one arm flapping gracelessly around behind his back. 'On the train. Come with us, Victor.'

Again, he felt that hesitation would betray his true feelings, but it was too late. The request was so unexpected that he was momentarily rendered speechless.

'Isabella, I … I don't know if—'

'Do you love me or not?'

'Of course, I love you!'

'Then come!'

'Isabella, this is a knee jerk reaction to a lot of hearsay. There's no evidence—'

'A destroyed munitions factory, a group of soldiers warning us of coming danger, the trains filling up with refugees ... what more evidence do you want?'

An enemy, was what he wanted to say, but he decided to give a noncommittal shrug instead.

'You're not taking this seriously, are you, Victor?'

'I've just been busy.'

'Not too busy for your silly machines, I doubt.'

Victor was just opening his mouth to answer when a car pulled up outside and Isabella's father came stomping up the path. Wrapped up in a huge fur coat he looked like a yeti come stalking out of the forest.

When he pulled back his hood Victor saw a vicious, bloody bruise on the side of his right eye.

Isabella screamed. 'What happened, Father?'

Robert Mortin ignored his daughter and looked straight at Victor. 'We got in a fight with the guards.' He turned back to Isabella. 'Why is he here?'

'He's looking after me.'

As if a switch had been tripped to turn off the conversation, Mortin stalked through into the kitchen, throwing his massive jacket over the back of a chair that rocked with the weight, and turned around to face them.

'The northern highway has been road-blocked.'

'What?' Isabella shrieked, as if hearing her entire extended family had just been slaughtered.

'Trucks returned last night. About eighty miles east there's been no ploughing. The snow was over a metre deep.'

'Can't they drive through it?'

'They tried. We lost four trucks.'

'But we're going west, right? That's the safe way.'

'Forty miles west they found it blocked with old military vehicles. Cowards trying to slow the flow of something they don't want to catch them.'

Isabella began to cry. Victor reached out to pat her shoulder but at a glare from Mortin he dropped his hand back to his side.

'There'll be one more train out. A snow-clearer kept in sidings here in the town. There are some carriages we'll get fixed up to it, but it'll be the last one.'

'When?'

'Three days from now. That's the earliest we can get it prepared.'

Isabella gasped again. Mortin stared at his daughter, his eyes as motionless as if he was staring at a seam of rock.

'What's out there, Father?'

Mortin sighed and shrugged. 'I have no idea. But whatever it is, it's coming our way.'

Victor had been slowly plucking up the courage to speak. He lifted a tentative hand like a shy child offering to answer a question and said, 'There's no reason to believe they would attack us. The munitions factory was the only thing of value to the military in the town.'

Mortin swung his huge head around. His eyes were like lasers, making Victor flinch. 'Where do you think all our ore has been going for the last few months, boy? No one's building roads in the west, they're repairing the ones that have been destroyed.' He turned back to Isabella. 'Don't keep idiots for friends, daughter.'

'Victor isn't an idiot!'

'Why is he even still here? We have preparations to make. Where are your brother and sister?'

'They went to school.'

Mortin scoffed as if the idea was more ridiculous than the thought of evacuating the town under the threat of an unknown enemy.

'If you say so. Start getting your things together.' He turned towards the door and stalked out of the room, pausing in the doorway to look back at Victor. 'You can leave now. Haven't you got somewhere to be?'

Victor did indeed have to get to the factory, so he bid farewell to a complaining Isabella and headed for the door. He was just pulling it open when her fingers closed over his arm, squeezing tight through his coat.

'You will come with me, won't you?' she whispered. 'You'll come on the train with us?'

He had other places to go and he needed to hurry. There was one answer that would pacify her, and in any case he had three days to think about it.

'Yes,' he said. 'Of course I will.'

'Oh, Victor! I love you!' she screamed, pulling him close. Victor gave her a peck on the cheek just as her father's voice boomed from the other room.

'I've got to go,' he said.

THE QUICKEST WAY to the factory was through the Lenin District. Victor pulled his jacket close and hurried through the freezing streets. He thought about Isabella's request and Robert Mortin's assertions.

What to believe, that was the question. He had no doubt that

Mortin was true to his word about the roadblocks and the last train, but Isabella was mistaken. There would be no place for the likes of Victor, or any of the other lowly underclasses. Those with wealth and contacts would leave, the rest would get gunned down by sentries if they tried to board. It was the way of wartime, the world over.

The streets in the Lenin District were busier than usual. Roused from their slumber by the whispers of impending invasion, groups of hollow-cheeked wraiths stood around on street corners, eyeing everyone else with suspicion and more than a little contempt. Victor gave as many groups as he could a wide berth, but as he reached a junction with a larger street, four men moved out of the shadows of a doorway to intercept him.

All four were taller than him, with the ghost of broad shoulders that had once worked mining machinery now slumped and emaciated. Their faces wore the chapping of too little heat, and the acne of too much narcotic.

'Where you off to?' one called to him. 'You got a job or something?'

Victor looked up before he could stop himself. He caught the eyes of the man, two sunken hollows containing a lifetime of failures. Victor looked quickly away again and ducked his head, but it was too late, the man was breaking out of the group to intercept him, moving across to cut Victor off in a way that he could only avoid by breaking into an open run. Even faced by the danger posed by the desperate, he found himself unable to break out of his social conditioning, to show unnecessary panic in public. Instead, he just quickened his pace, knowing that a confrontation was inevitable.

'Hey!' the man called. 'Hey, you! I'm talking to you!'

'I'm in a hurry,' Victor muttered, but the man would not be denied. He reached the pavement in front of Victor and stopped there, leaving just a couple of metres between his shoulder and the snowdrift that was now the edge of the road. Victor didn't fancy his chances of making a dart for it, and if he headed right out into the road he would meet the man's friends, still idling in their loose group halfway across the street.

He had no other choice. He stopped.

'What do you want? I'm busy.'

'What's there to be busy about? Can't you spare a little time to talk?'

'Not right now,' Victor said. Then, before he could stop himself, he blurted: 'There's an invasion coming. We have to get ready.'

Victor wasn't sure what reaction he had expected, but it wasn't the sudden expulsion of laughter like a train breaking out of a tunnel in a puff of smoke. The man slapped his thigh with a hand that was skeletal, the skin chapped and blue. Victor had the urge to ask why he wasn't wearing gloves.

'An invasion, you say? You know nothing. The invasion started long ago. The enemy has been here for quite some time already.'

There was little jollity in the man's tone, and that set the prickles on the back of Victor's neck rising. Delusional drug talk was to be expected, but something in the man's tone told Victor he was deadly serious.

'What do you mean, quite some time?'

The man started to laugh again, cold and sinister. 'You fools in your ivory towers. You're expecting an enemy of flesh and bone you can cut up with your guns. You damn clowns. This is an enemy unlike any you have ever known. It walks among us at night, whispering to us in our sleep, feeding us its lies until on waking we remember them as truth. It stalks us, taking us out one by one, yet it is invisible and everywhere, unseen.'

'I'm sure you're mistaken—'

The man reached out and gripped Victor's wrist with a hand that was both icy hard and freezing cold. Victor tried to pull back but the old miner's strength still remained.

'I saw him,' the man hissed into Victor's ear, the stench of rotting teeth clawing its way around Victor's face, making him cough. 'I opened my eyes and he was there, I closed my eyes and he was gone. All he left behind was blood and death.'

'Where?'

'Where do you think?'

Victor shrugged. The man was clearly crazy. 'In your dreams?'

The man's cold, bony palm came up to slap Victor across the face. 'Fool, you think I'm an idiot? What harm could he do there? I saw him in St Peter's Place. At night. And I saw his marks in the body I found beneath the floorboards.'

'What body?'

The man shrugged. 'I was hungry, I was desperate. I smelled something I thought might be food. It wasn't … not for me, at any rate. I'd rather die.'

Victor gave a slow nod and started to inch backwards. Perhaps if he could create enough of a gap between them he could make an attempt to escape. He was younger and healthier after all. All he'd need was a few metres head start.

'Got no choice, boy,' the other man spat. 'You stay here, you'll die like the rest of us. You leave … he'll find you. Embrace the darkness. It's the only way.'

The man sighed and looked away for a moment. Victor saw his chance. He dug into the snow and kicked off hard, making an angle across the street towards the others, then turning on his heels and heading back the other way. Shouts came from behind him, but there were no signs of running feet. He had sprung the trap, and they were too weary to give chase.

The last thing that he heard before he turned a corner sent a trickle of horror down his back:

'Embrace the darkness before it embraces you! Its arms are everywhere, in every shadow, and he's starting to come back into the light!'

10

SECRET WEAPONS

'HE'S BACK.'

The voice popped up out of the radio, making Kurou jump. He'd been resting, lying atop a pile of dirty blankets with the fire burning a few feet away. His back felt hot and feverish, while his front was chilled and tight from facing the rest of the freezing room. Not for the first time he considered just rolling over into the flames and letting it end him. After all, having dived into a lake of fire once before, there was no amount of pain that he feared. The only thing that kept him up at night was the thought that while there was life left in him there was creativity, the darkest of all kinds, and the chance to dance to its sinister tune one last time would forever turn him away from thoughts of suicide.

He had wired up the radio to replay the surveillance robot's reports in a language he could understand. The robot's batteries were running low, but it seemed the section of road where the old café stood didn't receive much traffic, and its sensors were set to activate with motion.

Kurou sat up. The knife wound in his side still ached, but the infection was fading away. All he had to do was keep it clean and it would heal, adding another scar to the great patchwork of his body.

'Give me details. Are you sure it's him?'

The receiver translated his words into binary and relayed them to the robot. A few seconds later a confirmation came back as affirmative.

'Wait until he's gone and then go inside.'

Kurou propped up some blankets and sat up to wait. He had been hoping the inventor would come up with the last items on his list, but the young man was taking his time about it. With them he could finally build himself something of note, but he wondered if the inventor knew that. Perhaps he was holding them back as bargaining tools for some unknown deal he was yet to serve.

Years ago, Kurou wouldn't have considered such a scenario. He would have had the man gutted, either by his own hand or by that of one of his creations. Now, though, he was in less of a position of power. It might be prudent to let the young inventor think he was ready to strike a deal.

'Follow him this time. Make sure he knows you're there.'

The robot gave him an affirmative. Kurou closed the line and stood up. His body was aching from a thousand wounds, most old, some new. He stretched as best he could, wishing he could do to himself what he had done to so many others: create a new from an old. The years had not been kind, and time had added its own weight too. He was no longer a young man, even inside the leathery ruin of a coat of skin that covered him. He suffered from the same aches and pains that everyone did, a thousand times over, a constant drum beating in the back of his skull, reminding him over and over again that it might have been better to die in that lake of fire he had himself created and been done with it.

Thanks to the young inventor he had enough food for a few more days, but he needed some fresh air. He went out of his rooms and began the long arduous climb up a service staircase at the building's rear. Signs warning of collapse and unstable masonry kept most of the few tenants to the front stairways and the single elevator that worked intermittently, so he found himself the sole passenger up through the freezing levels towards the roof.

By the time he had climbed the nine flights of stairs and stepped out through the rusted door on to the open roof that gave a bleak, foggy view of a winter-shrouded town and the lumpy hills that broke the haze all around, he was sweating, and the chill air was a relief on his burning skin.

He hobbled to the very edge and sat with his legs dangling off, looking out over the barely hospitable little hovel he had called home for the last five years. Like a boil on hell's asshole, Brevik sat discontented and angry, a cesspit of hate and failure. If and when whatever army that was coming rolled through here, it would be a beautiful thing to watch the town's total and utter annihilation, its erasure from existence.

IT WAS dark when he went back down. His legs ached from the cold, and for someone with more human skin it might have been fatal to sit in the biting wind for so long, but Kurou's deformities had their uses. He felt no better, but the pain in his side had reduced to a dull ache, almost enough to blend in with the rest of the clattering background music of agony that accompanied his every step.

When he got back to his rooms a light on the radio was flashing, indicating a recorded message.

'He left you a note,' the robot's recorded voice said.

Kurou tried to activate the command for the machine to restart, but the robot's battery was dead. Controlling his anger until he found something whose value wouldn't be missed, he flung a screwdriver hard against the wall.

He had lost his way to communicate with the young inventor. He would have to go out to the café himself, but it was a couple of miles through snow and freezing temperatures, and he was still too weak.

Still, he had enough food for a couple more days. If he lay low for a while, he might build up enough strength to make the trip.

And if he didn't? Well, he would worry about that then.

VICTOR STARED. His own surveillance robot stood motionless in the road behind him. It had been following him for some time judging by the tracks in the snow leading back down the street, but he would never have noticed it was there if the alarm warning of low battery hadn't blared.

He went up to it, feeling a little uncertain about touching it. Even though he had built it with his own hands, it now seemed tainted, alien.

Part of him wanted to leave it behind. Just the way it looked now made him feel uncomfortable, especially coming so soon after his brief conversation with the drug addict in the Lenin District. Another part knew it might be his only way to find out where the stranger lived. The robot had memory chips that would have stored location data. If Victor could access them, it would display where the robot had been during the last few days.

Whatever he did, he couldn't leave it out in the middle of the street. Within hours wolves—the human kind—would have found it and it would be gone.

It was too heavy to lift. He would need to bring the cart to transport it.

He dragged it to the side of the street, surprised at how heavy it now felt, as if someone had filled up the cavities behind its casing with sand. He pushed it behind a pair of trashcans and partially covered it over with snow. It wasn't perfect, but if he was quick it might work.

He ran most of the way back to his house, slipping several times in the snow in his eagerness to get home. Returning with the cart took a while longer, the tracks of the machine only able to maintain a steady walking pace in the snow. When he arrived at where he had left the robot, he had a shock because the trashcans had gone, emptied or moved back inside, but the robot was still standing back against a wall, looking like a heap of scrap metal poking out of a pile of snow.

He opened out the cart's back section, folding it down into a ramp. Then he pulled the surveillance robot up on to the carry platform and secured it with ropes.

It was nearly dark. He was like a sitting duck, a warship waiting for an airstrike, a blind rabbit waiting for a fox. There was no way back to his house apart from the most open way, straight through the streets.

And by now the wolves would be out.

The whirring of the cart's little motor seemed to fill the stillness of the night. Victor kept as best he could to the side of the street where there were no concealing alleyways, but it was only a matter of time before the cart attracted someone's attention. He thought about finding somewhere to hide it as he had the surveillance robot, but he had got lucky once and didn't expect his luck to hold twice.

He was able to skirt around the edge of the Lenin District, and as fog draped itself over the snowy landscape—what Victor often called zombie weather—he found himself thinking he might make it.

He was only a couple of streets from home when a voice shouted out of the shadows, startling him.

'Hey, you! Where do you think you're off to with that?'

Victor scowled. He turned to the cart and urged it to move quicker, but the machine was already struggling beneath the load of the powerless surveillance robot. With every shift of its caterpillar treads, more shards of ice got jammed into the mechanisms, making their passage slow and tiresome.

A shadow fell across the snow in front of him.

'Look who it is.'

Victor gulped. It was Isabella's brother, Esel, dressed up in a thick Russian coat, only his cherubic little face boiling like a roasted cherry at the centre of a fur-lined hood.

Two others stepped out of the shadows behind him. Both were taller, but seemed more diminished in the glow of authority emanating like radiation from the fourteen-year-old boy.

'What do you want?'

'What have you got there? Don't you know there's a law about hoarding stuff like this?'

Esel began to stroll in a lazy arc around the cart. Victor waited, keeping one eye on the boy's henchmen at the same time. This was not a situation he could win. In a simple fist fight he would struggle to beat Esel alone; he had no chance against three. With the threat of war hanging over Brevik there was murder in the air, Victor could practically inhale it. It had turned the discontented into thugs, and thugs into killers.

Esel suddenly took a step in towards Victor, pushing him back against the cart.

'You fucking thief,' he said, voice low, menacing. 'I haven't forgotten what you did. Where'd you get this stuff? Steal it as well?'

Victor clenched his teeth together until he was as confident as he could be that they wouldn't chatter. 'These things are mine,' he said. 'All of them.'

'Liar,' Esel said, spitting into Victor's face. 'You're a thief and a loser and it's bringing shame to my family that my dumb whore of a sister is hanging around with you.'

Victor felt it was better to say nothing than aim a retort that would bring a fist into his face. Esel stood facing him, even at fourteen a few inches taller, and thick enough at the shoulders to not need his henchmen to cause damage. Victor tried to look around him for a possible escape route.

'Gonna run away, are you?' Esel said, when Victor's eyes strayed too far. 'Like a coward with his tail between his legs? You wet fucking blanket. You're so pathetic I can barely find the words to describe you.'

'Then don't try,' Victor muttered under his breath. 'Just let me go on my way.'

'What did you say?' Esel said, stepping forward, right into Victor's face, the lips of their hoods touching. 'What did you fucking say?'

Victor tried to duck away, but Esel pushed his shoulder, spinning him around. Victor's foot caught on a corner of ice and he fell, his hands landing on the ground, sending stabs of pain up through his shoulders. He looked up as Esel swung a kick into the side of the cart, a sadistic grin on his face.

A fizzing boom sounded and a light flashed. Esel cried out and fell—no, *flew*—backwards, slamming hard against the wall of the nearest building, a puff of smoke exploding out of his chest. He hit the ground and rolled, coming up quickly, but another blast of light burst out of the cart's casing and this time struck him square in the face, sending him cartwheeling backwards to land face down in the snow, his legs bent up to his neck, his back broken.

Out of the corner of his eye, Victor spotted the two henchmen dashing off down the street. The cart fired one last shot which caused a bank of shovelled ice to explode in a cascade of red and yellow flame, then it went silent and still.

Victor climbed slowly to his feet, brushing the snow off his jacket. The street was silent now, the cart sitting motionless, still laden with the surveillance robot.

Victor looked around him. Except for himself and the cart, the street was empty. There were lights in some windows further up the wide, snowy boulevard, but no cars moved, no people walked beneath the few working streetlights.

He hadn't recognised either of Esel's two companions, but if they took their testimonies back to anyone with a running mouth then it wouldn't take long for his own identity to come out. He could hear them now: foreman's son murdered in cold blood by crackpot local inventor.

The truth, as always, was largely irrelevant. Esel was dead. Nothing else was of any great concern.

The cart hadn't moved. Victor looked down at its casing, wondering where the blast of light had come from. He hadn't installed any kind of defence weaponry, so it had been done by the stranger. It had all happened so fast Victor had barely seen what it was. Some kind of incendiary device, something that exploded on impact.

'We have to get away,' Victor said, concerned by the tremble in his voice. The last thing he needed to do now was panic. He had to keep a level head above all else. His life might hinge on it.

He crouched by Esel's body, pulled off a glove and held out a shaking hand to what was left of Esel's mouth, feeling for breath, but there was nothing. Strangely, the thought rotating on a loop was that Isabella would be angry that he had killed her brother. That it would spell the end of their relationship seemed more important than that it would find him rotting in a jail cell in the frozen basements beneath City Hall.

Esel was a dead weight of muscle, bone and furs. Victor dragged the body into the shadows of the nearest alleyway and piled some snow over it. It would be easy enough to find, but having it out of immediate sight eased his conscience, as though he had temporarily erased his association to the crime. While it might be discovered tomorrow, in a best case scenario it would go unnoticed until the spring thaws.

With the deadly cart trundling at his heels, he headed for home, shoulders weighed down by the fear of what might soon happen.

11

GOING UNDERGROUND

Robert Mortin put one large hand on the wooden banister pommel and squeezed, feeling the whole trellis frame shake under his grip. He thought about tearing it off and breaking it into firewood at his feet, but it would just waste valuable energy, and it wouldn't hurry these fucking kids up.

Isabella appeared at the top of the stairs, a bag held in one hand and a dress of some lace description in the other.

'Are you sure I can't take more than one bag, Father?'

'One,' he growled, barely loud enough for her to hear, but the look on his face must have been enough, because she threw her eyes back over her shoulder, huffed, and fled from sight.

Patricia slinked in from the kitchen. Compared to Isabella she was diminutive, barely five feet tall. She had an oval face that was all her mother's, but the cold, unforgiving eyes were Robert's alone. He refused to let her know, but Mortin was proud of his younger daughter to a point that it almost hurt. She was everything her older sister was not: intelligent, calculated, ambitious. He knew what she did around the station at night, but he also knew why; she was a taker, like her father. Not a single finger was lifted without her willing it so, and she would make a great woman one day, fearsome and unflinching. Before the war, he had planned to ship her off to Moscow to a state university, where she could go into management and perhaps even politics.

She watched him like a fox and he met her gaze, refusing to be the first to look away. Esel should have been the one made in his father's image, but while the boy shared his father's callousness, his cruelty wasn't controlled like his twin's. He was erratic, destructive, a bomb rather than a trigger.

'Where is he, Father? He should be back by now.'

'You tell me.'

Patricia shrugged. 'I haven't seen him since this morning. Perhaps he went to school?' The corner of her lips turned up as if it was an inside joke.

'He knows to be ready. He'll be here. I'll leave him if necessary.'

'I know you will.'

Isabella, stumbling and clattering to the top of the stairs, gave them both an excuse to look away. She held up two bottles of perfume. 'I know I can only take one, but I can't decide.'

'You'll take neither,' Robert said. 'This is not a joke, Isabella. Our lives are in danger.'

'But we have to leave so much behind!'

Patricia scoffed. 'Why don't you stay then? It'll make your precious boyfriend happy.'

Isabella opened her mouth to reply, but the wit required didn't come quickly enough. She gave a trembling shake of her head, then stormed back into her room, slamming the door.

'Don't tease her,' Mortin told Patricia. 'You know how she is.'

'She's an idiot.'

'Don't speak ill of your sister.'

'I don't hear you defending her, Papa.'

'Your time would be better spent looking for your brother than talking back to me, girl,' Robert said, taking a step forward and lifting his hand from the banister in warning. He'd struck her before and would do so again, as his own father had done to him. Discipline and love were branches of the same tree, swaying to the same tune, and if you offered too much of one and too little of another, the tree would fall.

She held his gaze another moment, then turned away, stalking back into the kitchen.

Where was that boy? Of course he wasn't at school. He rarely went, and when he did he couldn't stay for long. He had the curse of the spoiled but the elusiveness of the brave, avoiding a beating whenever Robert was in the mood. The truth was that the boy was fast outgrowing his father's discipline; the day would come when he would fight back a little too hard and the balance would shift. Once that control over his son was lost, it would never be regained.

Up on the balcony, Isabella appeared again, her eyes filled with tears.

'You're cruel, Father. Maybe I'll just stay behind with Victor.'

At the mention of the idiot's name, Robert felt his anger rising. His daughter might be an airhead filled with the same misguided optimism her mother had possessed before five years of brutal marriage resulted in the bitter and cynical twins, but even she deserved better than that crackpot she hung around with. Victor Mishin might keep himself employed around the town because he possessed skills that few people in the area possessed, but the daughter of a mining operation foreman could do better than someone who was an odd job man in all but name.

Plus, there was something strange about him. He looked through you when you talked, fidgeted as he answered, every word that came from his mouth sounding uncertain, as if speech itself was an experiment still in the testing phase. His mind was always somewhere else, and it wouldn't have surprised Robert to discover that Victor was the possessor of secrets very dark indeed.

He turned and stared at the front door, willing it to open and reveal his son, red-faced and huffing, having returned from some errand of mischief, but it stayed closed, silent, hopeless.

BACK IN HIS apartment Victor began to pack his things while he charged the battery on the surveillance robot. He piled everything important on to the back of the cart, aware just how small a space he had available to hold thirty years of valuables. After adding and discarding a dozen items—with each moment of indecision grew an awareness that a knock could come on his door at any time—he took only what money he could find, and a handful of computer chips containing his most important work. His robots—his life's successes—would have to remain behind. Perhaps if he was not found, his work would be untouched. It was a fragile hope, but a hope nonetheless.

The bleeping alarm to signal that the surveillance robot had regained enough power to be operated shocked him so much he fell off his chair. Recovering himself, he extracted its memory chips and loaded up the data on to a computer, picking out the coordinates of the robot's recent movements.

His heart sank. An abandoned tower block just off St Peter's Place in the Lenin District. It might be a decoy, but even if it wasn't, the building was notorious, a haunt of criminals and drug-addled wraiths, hiding away among crumbling rooms and corridors that should have been detonated two decades ago. It was the last place he would have expected to find the stranger, and the last place he wanted to go.

There was no choice. He could sit and wait for the police to arrive, or he could try to find the stranger and see if they could help each other. Perhaps the stranger could shelter him until everyone of any authority fled on the last train out of town. After all, with a war looming, the city authorities had bigger problems to worry about.

He had just reached the front door when he heard the sound of a siren blaring.

Clicking like a misfiring clock hand, his heart burst one way and then the other. It wasn't the sound of a police siren like it should be. It meant something different.

Air raid.

'FATHER!' Isabella screamed, leaping the last few steps into Robert's arms. 'What do we do now? We're going to die!'

Mortin put her down, turning in one movement towards the kitchen. 'Patricia! Hurry! There's no time!'

The source of the siren was just half a block south, and the sound cut through the walls of their house like a divine wind. Mortin wondered if the sirens had been designed this way since time immemorial, that long, slow drone that put the fear of all God into you.

Isabella was screaming. Patricia, a small hold-all slung over her shoulder, acting no more fussed than if she were heading out to school, appeared in the kitchen doorway.

'This is a waste of time,' she said. 'They aren't going to waste their bombs on our house. They're after the factories.'

'Better not to take the chance. Come on.'

Half dragging Isabella behind him, Mortin led his two daughters out of the house and down the street to an ancient shelter dating right back to the Cold War, on the edges of living memory. Following other citizens down a flight of cold, damp steps into a dark concrete box with a ceiling so low he had to stoop, Robert wondered which of his daughters would prove correct. There were bombs these days that made concrete no more effective as a defence than sponge, but warfare wasn't like it used to be. Civilians had little value, either as collateral or bargaining tools. It was likely any invading army would sweep right through them, purging the town of anything of use and then leaving its residents cold and hungry in its wake.

Someone charged with directing the human traffic ushered them towards a line of plastic seats that had probably once graced a bus shelter or doctor's waiting room. Robert sat down with a daughter on either side, one leaning in to sob on his shoulder, the other sitting up gun-barrel straight, ready to leap up into action at a moment's notice. He wanted to snap at Isabella to shut up, but the shelter was crowded with people, and down here in the dark there was no social hierarchy like there was up on the surface; they were all ducks lined up on an enemy's wall waiting to be shot. It didn't matter that he was one of the wealthiest men in town, down here in the dark he was just an irate father snapping unfairly at his upset daughter.

Beneath a layer of dirt and concrete, the siren was just a muffled squeal, but as the doors closed behind the last entrants and voices began to die down, the thumping on the walls like a bass drum beat announced the dropping of distant bombs. Robert put a hand down on the bricks behind him and felt it intimately, like a baby's heartbeat. He estimated that the bombs were too far away to damage his own house, but somewhere far off that polite little thumping was wreaking untold destruction.

'We're going to die,' Isabella whispered against his chest, over and over. 'We're going to die and I won't get to say goodbye to Victor.'

Mortin stared ahead of him into the dark. It wouldn't be such a bad thing if bombs were raining down on the poor district where his daughter's worthless boyfriend lived. Sometimes, purges were necessary.

'WE HAVE TO HURRY!'

The cart had no comprehension of human emotion but at the sound of the word *hurry* it boosted its speed to near maximum, keeping in time with Victor as he stumbled across the snowy street. Far to the north, flashes of colour lit up the dark sky like a firework display just out of sight. The rumble and crack of exploding bombs reached him as a series of pops and thuds, loud but not deafening, close but not too close. He was no military technician; he had no idea whether they were coming closer or going further away, nor exactly what the targets were. They sounded too far away to be hitting the town, so it made sense that they were bombing the mining operations that lay over that way.

The streets were surprisingly busy, people heading for air raid shelters or just standing in doorways or peering out of windows, watching the distant bombardment. That so few people seemed afraid struck Victor as a symptom of apathy, that these people had lived their lives so long without any excitement that even the idea of impending death was of interest.

Where possible he kept to the smaller streets, judging that the cold would keep would-be muggers and other criminals inside. At times he had to clear a way for the cart to pass, and sometimes he considered abandoning it altogether, but finally he stepped out on to the plaza known as St Peter's Place and saw the grey rectangle of the abandoned tower block standing opposite him across a field of snow and ice.

Against a sky punctuated with distant muzzle flashes, it was a haunted house of fable and yore, fifty lightless—mostly glassless—windows staring vacantly down at the street, bidding only the brave and the desperate to enter. Victor considered himself one but not the other, and it was the desperation that was leading him. He called the cart to him and started out across the plaza.

Something flashed across the sky, too fast and small to be a plane. There was a sliver of time laden with foreboding and then a building a couple of blocks north plumed with fire and smoke as a deafening explosion rattled Victor's teeth and billowed his face with the first gust of warmth he had felt since the end of summer.

Even as he began to run across the plaza, Victor couldn't decide if he was running towards or away from danger. The gaping, doorless entrance to the tower block loomed ahead of him, twin drifts of snow filling the entrance, leaving between them a thin rift that had been packed down hard by dozens of pairs of passing shoes. Something else fast and small flashed overhead, and he ducked inside before the sound of another explosion rattled the walls around him.

He turned to see the cart squeezing through the gap left in the snow by the tower block's illicit occupants. For a moment a bright light lit up the street behind it, then another boom brought icicles tinkling down around him. Victor slipped down against the back wall of the old entrance lobby and pulled his knees up to his chest, watching the sinister firework display outside.

In his haste, he hadn't thought to write down the details of the surveillance robot's stored data, and while he had loaded a couple of his computer tablets on to the cart, he didn't want to unload everything now. What he remembered though, that the tracking signal had gone faint when the surveillance robot had been inside this building, told him all he needed to know.

The signal had gone faint because it had been weakened.

Because it had gone underground.

The stranger was downstairs, in the basement.

Victor pushed himself to his feet. He glanced back at the floor below him, wishing he had more time to spare. Despite the freezing temperatures, inside this entrance he felt safe, and after the events of the last few hours he just wanted to crawl up into a corner for a while, but he had to push himself on.

To his right a broken door revealed a staircase. Snow had been tracked inside and left dirty marks on the stairs going up, but the stairs heading down were remarkably clean. With the cart using its reversible wheels to follow him, he started down.

12

THE ENTRANCE INTO HELL

THERE HAD BEEN no word yet from Lena. Pavel had tried the secure radio link several times a day, but she never answered. Barely an hour passed without him considering her a traitor, a coward, an infidel who had earned his trust and then used it to escape, except that he knew Lena better than that.

The girl wanted a fight, and she had gone looking for one.

When the bombs started to rain down, Pavel headed straight for the subterranean chambers below City Hall, a relic from the Communists which contained a complete communications control centre capable of running Brevik without ever going up to the surface. Over the years he had ensured it was maintained and updated, so the absence of windows notwithstanding, it was almost possible to believe he was still up in his own office. He had even hung a couple of murals on the walls, and a plastic pot plant stood in one corner collecting dust.

He felt absurd and a little guilty to admit it, but in some ways the bombs provided the evidence he needed that indeed there was an enemy on the way which should be feared. With the armies of hackers employed by every government almost as dangerous as the soldiers themselves, physical evidence was more necessary than ever to cajole a community into action. Now, as they risked total and utter obliteration, people were finally prepared to listen.

The radio on his desk buzzed, making him jump.

'This is security officer Markus Vorstock. Sir, I have some reports concerning the damage received.'

'Code?'

Without hesitation, Markus reeled off a nine-digit number. Pavel cared little about the number, only the length of the pause before it came. There was none.

'Proceed.'

'We've witnessed damage to nine mining operations. The strikes were carried out by drones. Four pits have been sealed by direct hits, while three others suffered peripheral damage. Two others were missed entirely, while seven other strikes hit abandoned mining dormitory buildings, suggesting that our enemy's data is inaccurate and out of date.'

Pavel nodded. It was to be expected. 'Casualties?'

'We're estimating ninety. Mostly nightshift workers. Many more may be trapped underground, but we're working to secure their escape through emergency access shafts.'

'Good. And of the other strikes?'

Pavel could almost hear the shrug from the other end of the line. Markus didn't know. 'Our estimation is that they were warning strikes, no more.'

'Warning us of what?'

Markus's sign mirrored Pavel's own thoughts. 'That they exist. Whoever they are.'

'Thank you. Return to your post.'

There was a slight pause. 'Sir, if I may be so bold as to suggest something....'

'Go ahead.'

Pavel waited, but no reply came. The static seemed to intensify for a few seconds, then the connection died. Pavel switched off his receiver and sat staring at the little radio, wondering if Markus Vorstock was still alive.

THE BOY HAD BEEN WATCHING Patricia for about half an hour, his frightened eyes flickering back and forth from the floor to her face. Her father and sister were sleeping restlessly on the bench beside her, but Patricia was still wide awake. Somewhere out there on the streets was her brother, and she couldn't relax until she knew he was safe. There had been no sound of any strikes for at least an hour, but down in the gloom of the air raid shelter the passage of time was difficult to measure. At some point she guessed they would be given an all-clear to return to their homes, but whether that was tonight or dawn or five days from now, she didn't know. As the seconds dragged past, the idea that they would be stuck down here forever grew and grew.

The assembled crowd probably numbered about a hundred, spread across a space about the size of a couple of school classrooms. At first people had sat in uniform rows, talking to their immediate neighbours in hushed, fearful tones, but over time they had split off into microcosms of society. A few groups of kids sat playing cards or tapping on little handheld computers. Some older people were spread out on the floor in rows, trying to sleep as best they could, while groups of business-types sat in tight circles and discussed company matters or the coming war. The boy sitting opposite her stood out simply because he was alone and detached from everyone else around him.

He was probably older than her, fifteen or sixteen, but he had the vacant, innocent eyes of a perennial follower. His skin was chapped and flaking and the hands he held over his knees looked callused from manual labour. She was sure she had seen him hanging around with Esel, but her brother's friends tended to drift in and out of focus, changing with the seasons and his violent whims. Because they had nothing to offer her, she rarely wasted her eyes on them for long.

But he was staring at her. That meant one of two things: he wanted to fuck her like most men did, or he had something to say. She hadn't yet seen him smile. While he might still want to fuck her, it probably wasn't today.

She got up and walked over, sitting down beside him. In the gloom, her shadow almost seemed to linger behind her, as if reluctant to let her go.

'I don't like people staring at me,' she whispered into his ear. 'What do you want?'

His lip trembled when he spoke. 'You're Esel's sister, aren't you? I've seen you around. He used to talk about you a lot.'

'Charmed,' she said. 'Where is he?'

'Some … something … something attacked him.'

Patricia gripped his arm and squeezed through his jacket hard enough to make him flinch. 'What? What attacked him? Where is he?'

'It was a man, but he had this thing with him. A robot. Esel wanted to push him around, beat up on him a bit. We were just being … lads.'

Patricia wanted to slap the words out of him. She knew about Esel being a "lad". His ever-shifting gang terrorised whole neighbourhoods. Their father, of course, knew nothing, but Patricia, sharing the intimacy of being a twin, often had to listen to his boasts of who they had bashed about, which houses they had broken into, and what they had stolen. None of his former friends would tell and none of his victims would report it through fear of retaliation, so Esel's reign of terror continued unchallenged.

'Where is he now?'

'It … it … shot him.'

Patricia felt the strength drain out of her hands. She clamped them to her knees to stop them from shaking. 'Where?'

'In the Lenin District. Just off Nickolsky Street.'

'Is he … dead?'

The boy shook his head, then nodded, then shook it again. 'I don't know. We … ran.'

Anger replaced her fear. She dug a finger into his thigh, into a weak spot between his muscles she had often used to hurt men who had tried to take advantage of her. 'You fucking coward. If I find out you left him to die, I'll gut you and every member of your family.'

A tear trickled down his face, the surface glossing over as the chill air in the bunker tried to claim it for ice. 'I'm sorry.'

Patricia jumped up from the seat. Her father and sister were still sleeping. While her father could get men together, her sister was useless and would create a scene. The best thing to do was go alone.

She pulled up her hood and looked down at the whimpering boy. She wondered how many fists he had thrown on her brother's instruction, how many old people he had pushed over or kicked in the face, yet here he was, a blubbering coward.

'Remember what I said,' she hissed, then hurried for the stairs.

VICTOR WAS about four levels underground when the bomb hit the building above him. The sound was only a muffled thud followed by a sharp crack, like a cloth being snapped tight. He hung on to the wall until the vibrations passed, noticing a sudden stuffiness to the air where it had been chilly and fresh before. Something somewhere had been blocked, and he hoped it wasn't the only way out.

Once below ground, his only light was from a torch he had packed into the cart, and he held it out in front of him, scanning the shadows below as he moved step by step down into the bowels of the building.

Several times he had come to doors, the entrances to old underground apartments, but those not rusted shut had opened on to dusty corridors of darkness. He began to wonder if he had been mistaken, if the coordinates he had translated were wrong, if perhaps he had unwittingly climbed down into his own tomb, when he came to the final door and saw a flickering light coming from beneath the door.

His eyes widened as he swung the torch over the inscriptions smeared on to the door in untidy paint scrawled over the top of years of others that had faded or chipped away.

YOU ARE ALREADY DEAD IF YOU HAVE REACHED THIS DOOR. ENTER AND MEET YOUR END. THE DEVIL WAITS INSIDE FOR YOU.

Reading about such a thing in a book, Victor might have laughed it off, but standing here in front of the door with the flickering light coming from underneath, surrounded by freezing walls of concrete and earth, he could imagine the door led down into the fires of hell itself. His legs trembled and his hands shook, the torchlight flickering across the words, highlighting and erasing them in turn.

It took him several tries to make his shaking fingers grip the handle and open the door. When it swung wide with a creaking groan that could have been a wraith moaning in timeless agony, at first all he saw was a fire built into the far wall, beating flames up and around a blackened chimney, spitting pieces of broken furniture out on to the concrete floor and the heap of rags and old clothes that were piled in front of it.

And then something shifted on the pile of old clothes, and a spindly, scarred monster rose up, its charred frame a silhouette against the fire behind, its jutting, pointed face twisting towards him in a sneer, one black eye opening and closing in long, slow blinks.

Victor heard a sinister laugh and the rustle of feathers.

Then the room went black and he slumped to the ground, his legs collapsing beneath him.

13

THE END OF EVERYTHING

Lena reached what she considered the frontline on the seventh day
out from the city. After days of driving through nothingness, she
suddenly found herself negotiating her way through lines of
refugees flanked by ragged soldiers and the occasional tank burnt
out by the roadside. In the city of Omsk, on the eastern bank of the
now frozen Irtysh River, she used her old contacts to get them
through roadblocks and into the heart of a military operation that
seemed disorganized and on the verge of collapse.

A convoy took her to the headquarters of the city's defence, in
the basement of an old banking head office, and she was led down
through twisting, poorly lit corridors, past doors guarded by soldiers.

The man waiting behind the desk needed a stick to stand. Lines
scored his ancient face, all of eighty years, if not more. The kindness
she remembered from her formative years in the Secret Service
before its restricting and her ejection were still there, as was the
haunted look that the commander had carried with him from his
own youth, from events he had never shared.

She couldn't keep the smile off her face. Dearer to her than her
old grandfather, seeing him again was like seeing someone brought
back from the grave.

'Alek,' she said, momentarily losing the composure that had
made her one of the service's most feared agents. 'I thought you
were dead.'

The old man smiled. 'I should have died a hundred times, but
I'm still here. How are you, Lena?'

'I guess if I wanted to pick one thing of everything, I'd say I'm
confused. 'What's going on, Alek? What is this war? She threw her
hands up in the air, the weeks of frustration finally getting on top of

her. 'No one can believe anything because of the hackers. Yet calling it the Hacker War seems so trivial, so ridiculous. Wars are fought by guns and blood, not men in darkened rooms with computers.'

'War is fought in many ways, Lena. This is a new one, one we hoped would never come to pass.'

'Why?'

Alek sighed. 'Because this time we're fighting ourselves.'

'A revolution? Is that what this is? All the talk is of Europe and America, pushing us back into the eastern sea.'

Alek smiled, shaking his head. 'If anything they're on our side. It's true that Europe's at war, but not with us. With itself. With its own army.'

'A military coup? Make sense, won't you?'

'I can't make sense because none of this makes sense. Let me show you something.'

Alek pressed a buzzer on his desk. 'This is Commander Politov. I need an escort to take us to the research station on Zenkova Street.'

As he switched the buzzer off, he leaned back, nodding slowly. 'They say that the only way to believe is to see with your own eyes,' he said. 'Over the last two years I have found that to be true. Hold your judgments and your assumptions until I show you what I need to. Then, I think you will understand.'

Patricia ran through the dark, slipping and falling on the ice. The snow had begun to fall again, and after one last explosion to the south the sound of bombs had gone quiet. The streetlights, covered by wooden boxes to hide them from the skies, cast barely perceptible circles of light on the ground, and she ran from one to the next, fearful of hurting herself in the dark.

She was tired and freezing by the time she reached Nickolsky Street, where the boy had told her Esel's gang had been attacked. At first she could see nothing, then as she approached one of the few streetlights in this area she saw the scuffs in the snow of running feet leading from an alleyway, accompanied by a line of lumpy squares of ice made by small caterpillar treads. On another day she might attribute them to a snow clearing machine, but now she followed them back towards the alley, getting on her hands and knees to feel them when the dark got too deep, until she found herself surrounded by the tall walls of two adjacent apartment blocks.

Far to the east, the sky had caught the hazy hue of dawn, but it would be hours before it was light enough for her to see clearly. She made her way by feeling along until she reached a heap of snow piled against one wall.

She dug her hands into it, feeling the telltale crunch of lumps of ice only recently begun to freeze together. And there, a few inches down, she touched something that was softer and more flexible than ice.

The hood of a thick fur jacket.

She knew it was Esel even before she had cleared away the snow and felt the frozen blood caking her twin brother's face.

Staggering back out of the alleyway, she tried to climb to her feet but failed. Pounding her gloves against the icy ground she screamed up at the sky, anger and sadness coursing through her.

'I'll find you,' she cried over and over again. 'Wherever you are, I'll find you.'

ALEK POLITOV INSISTED ON WALKING, even though his pace held up the party as they made their way into a huge warehouse on an industrial estate not far from the river port. Lena walked beside him, while the guards fanned out to either side, protecting them against some potent but unseen threat.

'In here,' Politov said, gesturing to a set of doors and having the men pull them wide. 'Here is where you'll begin to understand how this all went wrong.'

The guards switched on overhead lights that filled the room with a cold, wintry glow. Inside was a lab, banks of computer equipment and tall steel cases filled with instruments, books and sample jars. Beyond a set of tables were several other doors, each numbered in sequence. Only one had a light on, and Politov led Lena across to it, leaving the guards by the door.

'What you are about to see will turn on your head what you know about the nature of warfare,' he said. 'There may be stranger things in the world—' here, his eyes seemed to glaze, as if recalling some long ago memory, '—but every so often a change happens that turns the disc a little faster than is safe. The space program, the invention of dynamite, fire ... sometimes we humans make more mistakes than are necessary, and the world suffers for it.'

He slipped a key into the lock and Lena helped him push open the heavy door. Lying in the middle of the room was what looked like a corpse, a damaged and smashed up human body, only at least twice the size of an average human. Then she noticed wires protruding from where an arm would have been and turned to look at Politov with a frown on her face.

'It's a robot?'

'It's a War Horse, Prototype Level Six.'

'A what?'

'It's a machine. A robotic body suit. It requires a rider, a human who is linked to the machine's systems. We captured this one in battle and brought it here for analysis. Unfortunately, the rider died during transit. The systems of one affect the systems of the other. They share a symbiotic relationship.'

Lena stared at the machine for a long while. Her eyes traced the outline of armour plating she had at first thought were the torn remains of a uniform but now realised were layers of camouflage that could be alternated depending on the terrain.

'It's a newer model,' Politov said. 'It has semi-autonomous control but the rider, once linked with the machine, is only in control of direct and immediate functions, not wider battle tactics.'

'So it's not like driving a tank?'

'It depends on its orders. Due to its complexity, each War Horse typically requires a command team of two to three people.'

'Like with a drone aircraft?'

'Exactly. They have been mass produced, but it's impractical to deploy more than a small battalion at any one time. The manpower required to deploy an entire army would require a command centre and an online presence that would be easily found by our spies and eliminated by our own planes.'

Lena tapped a finger on the metal gurney holding the robot. 'I'm in no way authorised to ask you these questions, sir, but I was sent to find out what the threat is to my city. How many of these things are out there?'

Politov looked at her for a long time and the hopelessness in his eyes was haunting. 'Thousands,' he said. 'Slowly marching across Siberia towards us. They've been separated into multiple groups of a few hundred each so they can cover more ground and cause more destruction, but at the moment all our own armies are doing is slowing the tide. Unless we can find out how to stop them we have no hope.'

'Who built them?'

Lena didn't want to hear Politov's answer, but when it came it was little more than a whisper, as if the air itself didn't want to lend him the strength to say it.

'We did.'

'Then—'

'Who's controlling them? When controlling such a number is for all intents and purposes impossible?'

'Yes.'

Politov shrugged. 'We don't know. They were effectively stolen, several factories at once taken over in a massive concerted terrorist attack. Before we knew what was happening they were eating us from the inside out. Our military was in dismay, and by the time we regrouped we were unable to form a united, fortified front. Our forces are broken, suffering terrible losses whenever we engage the enemy in close combat. Our planes are ineffectual because the targets are so small, giving off no heat unless already damaged, meaning we might as well fire a missile at every parked car. We cannot use nukes on our own country, and surrender is of no use because they do not understand the rules of warfare. Every one of our battalions that has surrendered has been executed immediately. Every town captured has suffered the same. Systematic destruction.'

'My god. Can't you find who's controlling them? If there are thousands of them out there, there will be a command centre somewhere. There has to be.'

Politov shook his head. 'No, there doesn't. Our experiments on those we have captured have retained no stored data suggesting they've been following a series of updated orders. The signs are that a single, elaborate program is controlling them all.'

'A computer? What computer could possibly be that powerful?'

Politov gave a short, choking laugh, like a grieving widow holding off tears. He lifted an old, arthritic finger and poked it against the side of his head. 'What computer is more powerful than the human mind?'

'What are you suggesting?'

'Nothing I can prove, Lena. Nothing that anyone would believe.'

She walked over to the robot, looking down at its humanoid frame. Heavy armour-plating covered its chest region, and she could see the marks of dozens of bullets on the casing.

'How bad is this, sir?'

Politov turned and walked to a chair near the wall. He slumped down on it, putting his head in his hands, shaking it slowly back and forth. Lena suddenly felt sorry for him, that here was a very old man who should have been able to spend his last few years in peace, perhaps sitting on a porch somewhere, looking out at fields, watching life as it ticked by, taking with it all his regrets and failings, leaving his mind at ease.

'It's very bad. Imagine an army of soldiers that do not need to rest. They take dozens of hits to bring down and they suffer from none of the usual issues that make human soldiers easy to fight. The machine protects the rider from the cold and shields the rider so that body heat is undetectable. They're small enough that they can hide, and they can jump higher, run faster, climb better, than any human ever could. They're relentless, moving forward until they've been shot apart, piece by piece. This is what we face.' He lifted his head to look at her. 'If we don't stop them they will eat their way across our country until there is no one left. Then perhaps they will move on somewhere else. They are capable of wiping out the entire human race.'

Lena stared at him. 'If I may ask, sir, what is their fuel source?'

Politov couldn't meet her gaze. It took him a long time to answer, and when he did, it was barely a whisper.

'Believe me, you do not want to know.'

PART II

THE SECRETS OF THE SECRET PLACE

14

INTERVIEW WITH THE DEVIL

'Wake up, won't you, sire?'

Victor leapt up as freezing water doused him, spinning in an awkward circle before scrambling back against the wall. Wiping sleep out of his eyes, he glanced towards the door, but it had been closed now, and was likely locked. The monster sat opposite him, naked as far as he could tell, squatting in front of the fire as if it had been born out of the flames. Its skin was a latticework of scar tissue, like a skeleton dipped in marbling water, punctuated with little tufts of feathers. As Victor watched, it picked up a piece of something from the ground, tore off a strip of what he thought was meat, and pushed it into a small mouth below a huge bird's beak.

'I imagine you're a little cold now.'

Victor could do nothing other than shiver, not even open his mouth. The terror he felt was absolute, but even so, the fire behind the monster looked so inviting.

'I won't hurt you … unless I have to. In some ways I've been looking forward to meeting you.'

Victor said nothing. This couldn't be the stranger, could it? Not this … abomination? The robot must have been stolen, the stranger tricked out of it by this hideous creature….

'Here.' It pointed to its side. 'The knife went in here. You saved me.' The monster tossed the piece of dried meat into the fire, causing a little plume of sparks. 'And I no longer have to eat this, thanks to the food you brought me.'

Victor just stared at the monster, his mouth dry.

'A penny for your thoughts? Wondering what I am, I guess you are? Wouldn't that be close to the truth?'

The creature stood up. It walked a few steps towards Victor, looming large in front of the fire, its scarred body dark with shadow. Victor found it hard to look up at its face, the gnarled crust of a beak where its nose should have been, the bald, scarred head tufted with feathers, the black eye that watched him like a hawk.

'Aren't you going to thank me for fixing up your robot? A little give and take would be nice, wouldn't it?'

Victor coughed. He felt so cold his body must be shutting down. He stared at the creature's gnarled feet, wishing that hypothermia could kill quicker, put him out of his misery.

'Sorry about that little shower,' the monster said. 'But you were snoring, and I hate a man who snores. So rude, don't you know?' He lifted one hooked hand and rubbed his chin. 'But I forgive you, sire. Good neighbour that I am.'

At last Victor found his voice. 'Cold....'

The creature stepped forward and reached down quicker than Victor would have thought possible. A hard, pincer-like grip dragged him up by the shoulder and shoved him back across the room. He stumbled to his knees in front of the fire, and, unable to help himself, shuffled as close to the warmth as he could.

'I won't ask how you found me,' the monster said from Victor's shoulder, the warmth of its breath so close that Victor gasped and squeezed his eyes shut, hoping that if he concentrated, he might wake up from a very bad dream in his own bed. 'But it was careless of me to leave that robot's memory alone. I guess I didn't expect you to have equipment capable of extracting my location. I have come to expect nothing from this disgusting little town.'

'Who...?'

'Who am I?'

The claws took hold of Victor's shoulder again, twisting him around. He gasped, terrified, squeezing his legs shut to stop his bladder emptying. Hard points pushed into one of his eyes and his lids were forced open.

'Look at me, damn you. I don't have to do it, thank the mighty heavens, but you do.'

The monster's face was mere inches from Victor's own, and his eyes filled with tears of fear as he took in the bumps and curves and scars of the worst thing he had ever seen. Had he seen such a thing come out of a woman's womb, even someone as passive as he might have been glad to see it drowned in the nearest river.

The tiny grey lips pulled back in a smile. 'Oh, I disgust you, don't I? What a delightful turn of events. I'm sure you'll sleep well tonight, sire. Like a baby, wouldn't I suggest? Do you have children, sire? Do they look anything like me?'

'No ... children,' Victor wheezed.

The monster pushed him away and stalked back across the

room. Victor, remembering his wet clothes, rolled closer to the fire, keeping the creature in sight as it stalked out through a doorway into an adjacent room. For a few seconds Victor thought about trying to flee, but he was still soaking, and even if he could get out of the door before the monster came back, he would freeze to death out on the streets.

A shadow fell over the stone floor and then the creature returned, something clutched in its spindly fingers. Victor flinched as it squatted down beside him and held out a tiny photograph of an unsmiling Asian woman, her head wrapped in a shawl, sitting on a stone wall outside a shack made of corrugated iron.

'My mother, sire.' A bony finger gave the woman's face a disdainful prod. 'The bitch. I've been hunted across the world yet this fucking photograph follows me like a fly wanting to feast on my remains.'

The monster sat down on the floor beside Victor, holding the photograph up in two hands. 'I really was that child with a face only a mother could love. Yet she didn't. She sold me like a piece of furniture she didn't want anymore. It wasn't even to the highest bidder, because there was only one.'

He sprung up suddenly and flung the picture towards the fire, only to reach out one spindly finger to pluck it out of the air just inches above the flames. 'Oh, mother dear, lost angel of my life, creator of so much yet so little. One day I will say goodbye to you forever, but not today.'

As the heat of the fire gradually sucked the cold and damp out of his clothes, Victor's fear began to reside, allowing for a flicker of curiosity to take its place. The monster was still holding the photograph between two fingers like a delicate flower, and was speaking to it in a language that Victor didn't recognise, like a remarkably ugly character actor preparing for a final performance.

'You … you … you—'

The monster's head swung around. 'What?'

'You … have a name?'

'I thought you would never ask, sire. I am Professor Kurou.'

'Crow?'

'Ku-*rou*. Be the first person I've ever met to get it correct, won't you? Hated and hunted and in hiding longer than I remember. The very same.'

'You're a man.'

'Of course I'm a fucking man, fool!' Kurou turned and aimed a kick at Victor which missed by a good fifty centimetres. Kurou fell backwards like a drunk trying to take a penalty kick and slumped down on the pile of filthy blankets, where he lay with his arms out wide, laughing as though he had just heard the funniest joke in the world.

Then, like a tap being switched off, the laughter was gone, Kurou was sitting up, one arm propping up his head, one eye watching Victor intently, the other—that Victor now saw was false, a ball of some black polished stone—staring off into space.

'Say what you need to say, sire. It will make no different to whether I kill you or not. In fact, I'm quite enjoying your company. I like to speak to the dead—or at least those soon to be—but to be in conversation with someone living is a rare place indeed.'

'You've been scarred.'

'Oh, and the rest! I crawled kicking and screaming out of my mother's cunt like an ugly beetle no one was quick enough to stamp out. Perhaps she did love me once upon a time, who can guess? Before I first showed my face I was probably a treasure, and from there things swiftly went the wrong way of right. There surely must have been people around wanting to toss me under the nearest passing truck, let me pop like a ripe melon and all's done and dusted. What a way to go out, yes?'

Victor cleared his throat. It was as Kurou said—he would either be killed or he would not. The man was insane, but Victor doubted there was anything he could do to make things better.

'I saw what you did to the cart. It killed someone who attacked me. I'm not too happy about it, but I'm pleased all the same. But what you did … you're a genius.'

Kurou gave an extravagant bow. 'All in a day's work, sire.'

'I mean, how did you do that? What was it?'

'A master never tells his secrets, only sells them to the highest bidder. And you don't look like you'd get too far in a bidding war. Would I be right, sire?'

'I do okay. I've always had plenty of work. What about you? What do you do?'

The question seemed absurd the instant it left his lips. As if a man like this could have ever held a real job. He was a creature of dark places, a wraith shunned by society.

Kurou turned to him and smiled. Patches of scar tissue pulsed red, while others were pale white. He looked like the devil's own checkers board.

'I, sire? What might I do?' He leaned forward theatrically. 'I change the world.'

'How?'

'*How?* What kind of question is that?'

'How do you change it? For better or worse?' Victor clamped his mouth shut, but it was too late. Accusing the man of being a criminal might not be the best course of action.

Kurou's eyes narrowed for a moment, then he stood up straight again. 'Well, I guess that depends on your perspective, doesn't it, sire? I am a painter, and the entire world is my canvas.'

Without warning, Kurou disappeared into the other room again. Victor looked around him for a weapon, but aside from the bucket that had doused him with water, there was nothing. The cart, he noticed, had disappeared.

The door was fifteen feet behind him, and now he had got over his initial shock, the strength was returning to his legs. He could make it if he moved right now, if he didn't hesitate—

'Hungry, sire?'

Something landed on the floor to Victor's right. It looked like a strip of dried meat. 'What is it?'

Kurou sniggered. 'Jerky.'

Victor, who couldn't remember when he had last eaten, picked it up and gave it a sniff. It smelt oily and dry, like old clothes. 'Beef?'

'Have you seen a cow in these parts, lately?' Kurou roared, throwing his hands up towards the ceiling like an emperor bidding a crowd to rise. 'I mean, have you?'

'Well, what is it then?'

'It's the fruit of failure, of fallen dreams, the thigh of drug-addled miner.'

Victor cried out and tossed the strip of meat away. It hit the edge of the fire and began to fizzle, little pockets of oil crackling and spitting.

'Don't waste it, fool! Upon strips of flesh like that stone pedestals are raised, empires are built, and wars are fought.'

'Did you kill him?'

'Who?'

Victor pointed at the bubbling strip of meat. 'Whoever that came from.'

Kurou shrugged and turned away. 'He was already dead. Or as good as.' He suddenly spun and leapt across the room, knocking Victor backwards and pinning him to the ground. Victor stared up into Kurou's one seeing eye as it loomed inches above his own.

'Who are you to judge me, sire?' Kurou hissed, his putrid breath making Victor gag. 'I'm hardly the first, hardly the worst. What man wouldn't descend to the depths of all depravity should he have the chance? It's a long way down, I can tell you.'

'You're crazy,' Victor whispered.

Kurou leaned closer, his breath tickling Victor's ear. 'Crazy doesn't begin to describe me,' he breathed, so quietly Victor could barely hear. 'Mankind has yet to invent the adjective that would do me justice.'

Before Victor could reply, Kurou had leapt up again and dashed off into the other room. 'I imagine something more … trivial might be to your taste,' he called back, then a metal can came bouncing across the floor to land at Victor's feet.

Tinned pineapples. A few weeks out of date, but that the paper label was yet to fade made them fresh enough in this town. Victor had left them for the stranger a couple of days ago.

Kurou's voice drifted out of what Victor was now sure was a makeshift kitchen.

'Quite the host, aren't I?'

15

NINE FLOORS UNDER

THE ALL CLEAR for people to return to their homes was given some time in the early dawn. Robert walked back towards his house with Isabella leaning on his shoulder, a light snow falling around him. His heart felt heavy and his hands were itching to get hold of something meaningful he could break.

Patricia had disappeared.

While Robert and Isabella were sleeping in the shelter, she had got up and left. No one could remember her leaving, or had been too afraid to say so. In his anger he had started a fist fight with a group of younger men who had taken umbrage to his insistent questioning, and now his knuckles were red and sore from distributing his frustration across several bearded faces. In return he had a tooth loose in the left side of his mouth and his right eye was swollen half shut.

Where could she have gone?

Esel had never shown up, so she must have gone to find him. How could she know where he was? Or was she blindly wandering the streets in search of him? He guessed she had left hours before the all clear, so she had put herself unnecessarily at risk for her fool of a brother.

If he had to choose ... if he had to choose... It would be Patricia leaning on his arm while the other two rotted in the ground, but such thoughts would achieve nothing.

Their house was undamaged. A crater a hundred metres up the street indicated that a stray bomb had come close, but otherwise it seemed that the drones had kept to the industrial targets to the north of town.

Robert deposited Isabella in her bedroom and set her to packing, the only way to keep her occupied, then headed back out on to the street. His telephone wasn't working, but a couple of doors down he borrowed one that was, and called up several of his closest associates from the stand they had made against the council.

Half an hour later, he had ten men gathered around him on the street.

'My twins, are missing,' he said, remembering to include Esel, even though the fool boy was probably off looting some damaged building. 'I'm asking only that you put your feelers out, see if anyone's seen them.'

The men around him nodded. One, a banker named Michael, raised his hand. 'A friend of mine saw a girl in the Lenin District early this morning, in St Peter's Place. She was looking at the fallen dormitory building. I didn't think anything of it at the time, but—'

'What did you say? Fallen?'

'A drone strike caused the building to partially collapse. It was the only major damage received inside the town limits.' Michael smiled. 'And it's abandoned. Of all the places to hit—'

'What was she doing?'

Robert turned without waiting for an answer, but such was his authority that the men fell into step behind him. At his shoulder, Michael said, 'My friend said nothing at all. Just watching it, like she was fascinated by something.'

'Where did she go?'

'He didn't say.'

As they headed through town towards the Lenin District, Robert sent several men off to put the word out about Patricia. When the rest of them arrived, they found St Peter's Place to be busier than normal, with people standing in small groups as they watched the smouldering dormitory building, which appeared to have fallen in upon itself like a trampled spider.

'She was standing right in the middle of the plaza,' Michael said. 'Still like a statue, my friend told me. He thought perhaps she'd lost someone inside.'

'No one in there but addicts and pit crawlers,' Robert spat. 'No loss to anyone.'

He felt his anger talking, but even though many of the down-and-outs in the town were former mine workers made redundant by pit closures and cutbacks—several dozen by his own firm—no one dared to disagree with him.

A couple of the town's bedraggled fire crews had pulled up, but no one was making any effort to enter the collapsed building. Robert headed across the plaza to where a small crowd had gathered, most of them arguing with each other about whether the drone strike was intentional or not. Most of the streets around St Peter's Place were the haunts of the damned; drug addicts and prostitutes, rapists and muggers, a sea of human detritus committing crimes against each other. There were few streets that would be missed, but a little way to the north the residential area was altogether more respectable, and a direct hit would have caused a considerable loss of well-thought-of life.

'Has anyone seen a young girl?' Robert shouted, barging into the midst of the crowd. 'I'm looking for my daughter. She's fourteen. She was seen in the plaza just before dawn.'

A few people—clearly not aware of his status—shouted angry insults back at him, or pushed him aside. Robert toyed with the idea of starting a fight, then he saw an old man near the front beckoning towards him.

'She about so high?' the old man wheezed through smokers' lungs. 'Wearing a black jacket? Kind of pretty, if that were a thing in these parts?'

It was the clearest description he could hope for. 'Yes,' he said.

'She's gone, I'm afraid. I'm sorry for your loss.'

Robert grabbed the old man by the lapels of his jacket and swung him around. 'What the fuck are you talking about? Where's she gone?'

As someone else waded in, pushing them apart, Robert heard the words he had been dreading.

'She went in there. After it got hit, before it came down. Ain't no coming back out now. I'm sorry for your loss, sir.'

Robert shoved away the hands that were restraining him, but his own strength had gone. He sank to his knees in the snow, his hands on the ground in front of him, and he looked up at the building that had become his daughter's tomb.

'Why? Goddamn it, why, Patricia?'

Nearby, a group of firemen were debating whether to risk entering the collapsed building or not. Something about the disdain rising from their voices set Robert off. He pushed himself to his feet, a ball of rage growing inside him. Pushing everyone in front of him aside, he waded into them, shouting and hollering, fists swinging.

It took three men to subdue him, but it made no difference. As Robert lay pinned to the ground by two burly firemen, the chief commander called the order for a safety zone to be established around the outside of the dormitory building. Entering it was too great a risk. It was supposed to be abandoned after all.

Robert managed to free one arm enough to pound the snowy plaza in disgust. If Patricia was inside, no one was coming to get her.

Pavel made his way up to the roof level and stood looking out towards the Lenin District further to the south. A haze rose there now, like smoke, and he knew from the reports that it was dust from the collapsed dormitory building on the north side of St Peter's Place.

He had ignored all incoming calls, but his gallant secretary—remaining at her post even during the raid—had taken messages.

One was from Robert Mortin, the garrulous mining foreman who might have found his wagging tongue cut out in more imperial times. His daughter was supposedly trapped inside the collapsed building, but with the only evidence being that of a dim-witted old man, Pavel had refused to allow the town's firemen to risk themselves.

A second had come from the head of the local rail district, informing him that the line was undamaged and that a train could still leave as scheduled tomorrow, providing there were no further attacks.

The last was from Lena.

Pavel lifted the secure line radio to his ear and activated the frequency.

'Lena, it's me, Pavel. What have you found?'

16

TRAPPED UNDERGROUND

'WELL, THAT'S US SCREWED.'

Before Victor could reply, Kurou had jumped up and run to the door, flinging it wide. A plume of dust gusted into the room in the moments before he slammed it shut. Then, leaning up against it like some slapstick prankster, he raised a crooked eyebrow and cocked his head.

'Looks like you'll be staying a while, doesn't it, sire?'

'What was that noise?' Victor asked, fearing the answer. The sudden boom that had shook the whole room didn't need an introduction.

The building had been hit by a bomb.

'It was the sound of several floors of concrete deciding to take a little lie down, sire. Probably the best course of action for us, too.'

'Are we going to die? Are we going to get crushed by the building falling down?'

Kurou kicked a dirty blanket against the door to block the draft beneath it that was coughing handfuls of dust into the room.

'Soviet architecture,' he said. Good and lumpy, falls apart like crumbly cake. Makes a mess, but never goes straight down. Up there's a big heap of rocks, but we're safe down here in our tomb.'

'Our tomb?' Victor jumped up. 'Are you serious? There must be a way out!'

Kurou picked up the serrated lid of the tinned pineapples. 'A quick swipe across the neck is your quickest way out, sire,' Kurou said. 'Ask nicely, any time.'

The longer he spent with Kurou, the more Victor's fear of him continued to wane. The man was dangerous, certainly, and insane without a doubt. But he was also a joker, and beneath the hideous exterior, almost childlike in many of his mannerisms. It was impossible not to be afraid, but the paralysing terror he had first encountered had given way to a nervous wariness.

'I meant out of the building. Are the stairs blocked?'

'It's a guessing game, sire. What's your guess?'

'Shouldn't we check?'

Kurou gave a theatrical bow in the direction of the door. 'Be my guest, sire. Your lungs are a lot younger than mine.'

'Are there any other ways out?'

Kurou gave a creepy double wink. 'We could dig a tunnel, couldn't we? Alone in the dark together … cosy, yes?'

Victor glanced up at the dim electric bulb hanging from the ceiling. There were two in the apartment, this one and another in Kurou's filthy little kitchen. The only other light was from the fire—

Victor sprang to his feet. 'The chimney! It goes above ground, does it not? Otherwise we'd have choked to death by now.'

'Ded Moroz in reverse,' Kurou cackled. 'I'm not sure I have anything in red.'

Victor leaned close to the fire and tried to look up, but all he could see was a black-grey hole. It was impossible to tell how wide it was, or how far up it went. It was possible the floors above hadn't blocked it, otherwise the room would be filling with smoke, but it might be a pipe no more than a few inches wide. Kurou might be able to squeeze his spindly frame up something not fit for a snake, but Victor was a little thicker around the waist.

'Perhaps we should try the stairs first, see if there's a way out. If the lower floors are intact, maybe there's a rear access or something we can try….'

'The optimism of youth,' Kurou said, his voice taking on a musical air. 'So delightful.'

'We should try before the lights go out. I'm amazed the electricity has stayed on, but I'm sure the power will go off soon. There might be fires upstairs and everything.'

'Fool.' Kurou gave an exaggerated sigh. 'These are *my* lights. They go off when I say.' He offered no more explanation.

'Shall I look then?' Victor started to get up, but hard fingers closed over his arm and pulled him back down. He could feel bruises forming on his skin as Kurou's face loomed close. Where the strength in Kurou's frail arms came from, Victor didn't know, but as he looked into Kurou's eyes he felt all his horror come flooding back.

'So keen to leave, aren't we?' Kurou hissed, his voice low. 'And we've only just met. I would hate to wave goodbye so soon, sire.'

Victor let out a slow breath as Kurou relaxed his grip, keeping his fingers hooked around Victor's arm as if in warning.

'I'm not trying to escape,' he said, hoping his trembling voice was louder than his pounding heart. 'I'm the one that came to find you, remember?'

Kurou watched him for a few seconds, his beady eye unreadable. Then in an instant he danced over to the door, kicked back the blanket and squatted down to wipe his fingers in the dust.

'Settling,' he said. 'Fortune follows the brave, and since you were brave enough to come here—' he stood up and pulled the door wide, '—I'll let you go first.'

Victor got up and peered hesitantly up into the dusty gloom of the stairwell. The entire bottom floor looked undamaged, but he could only see about halfway up the stairs in the glow cast by Kurou's apartment light.

'I need my torch.'

'My pleasure.' Kurou ran away into the kitchen to retrieve Victor's torch. As he returned, Victor saw a barely perceptible flinch, one of Kurou's hands almost dropping to the wound on his side, a rare sign that Kurou felt pain like normal people. A while earlier, as the fire died down, Kurou had donned a pair of ragged trousers, but he was still stripped to the waist, a skeleton wrapped in scar tissue. The knife wound was a deeper red gash against the blotchy red of old burns, but at some point during Kurou's excitement it had started to bleed again. Victor couldn't remember how many tablets he had left for Kurou. It might prove that the wound would need more. Victor decided to file the information away as a possible bargaining tool in the event that they ever managed to escape.

Kurou tossed Victor's torch in his general direction, cackling when Victor failed to catch it, the torch landing on the blankets at Victor's feet. He picked it up and scowled at Kurou before he could stop himself.

Kurou hung back in the doorway as Victor crept up the stairs, worried that any noise might bring the building down on his head. He had reached the second landing before his torch could make out any signs of damage from above, but when he spotted the huge stone girders that had blocked the stairwell, his heart sank.

He swung the torch through the curtains of dust, looking for a way through, but he might as well have been walled in. What few lumps of broken masonry looked small enough for him to shift could bring others tumbling down.

There was no way through.

He was about to head back down to tell Kurou the bad news when he heard a little cough come from beneath the rubble nearby.

'SHE'S IN THERE,' he said, pointing. 'I don't know how far. I can't get her to answer me, but if I point the torch through this gap I can see part of a foot poking out.'

At Victor's shoulder, Kurou gave a huge looping nod that utilised his whole upper body. He reminded Victor of the flamingoes he had once seen in Moscow Zoo.

'A girl, you think? Tasty, yes?'

'No!' Victor actually felt the temptation to swipe Kurou around the head, but thought better of it.

'Then what did you drag me up here for?'

'We have to get her out.'

'Why?'

'Because … we have to.'

Kurou stared at Victor a moment, then gave a shrug and headed back down the stairs, doing a bizarre hop-skip-jump as he disappeared out of sight. A bang came from below as the door swung shut, and the tiny glow of light that had stretched its fingers to the edge of the stairs below was gone.

Victor was alone with his torch and the hoarse breathing of the trapped girl.

She was about ten feet away, lying in a crux below a V-shaped metal girder holding up a heap of broken masonry. Victor could only see part of her foot, and only guessed it was a girl from the timbre of her occasional coughs. He had called out a few questions but received no answer.

He moved a few feet to his right, to the very edge of the stairwell, looking for some way to reach her. As he squatted down and pointed his torch between piles of bricks and rubble, fallen lintels and hunks of chewed up stone with protruding metal teeth, he tried not to think about the danger he was in. He didn't want to think about Isabella, or the impending war, or the thousands of tons of broken rock and metal just waiting to plunge down and pop his head like a squashed lemon.

He tried only to think about the trapped girl, and that it was his duty to try to save her, even though a large part of him wanted to be downstairs next to the warm fire. It was a simple matter of conscience.

Part of the wall above had broken away and fallen across the stairs. Huge lumps of concrete as large as Victor's chest were held together by metal support rods strung through them like braces correcting a giant's teeth. They had fallen at an awkward angle, and closest to the wall there was a thirty-centimetre gap between the lowest chunk of broken masonry and the floor.

Victor trained the torch on it and gulped. He could just about wriggle through if he got down on his belly, but he would have to go all the way in, somehow get a hold of the girl and pull her out with no way to lever himself other than by jerking his knees back and forth like a desperate swimmer in a dried out pool.

It was as close to a suicide mission as he ever hoped to take on. If the girl was stuck she was as good as dead. Trying to pull her free might kill them both, but even if she was free beneath the rubble he might not be able to drag her back out. He would have barely a couple of centimetres each side to lever himself, and would need at least one hand free to try to push himself backwards.

His heart was pounding harder that it had done on his first meeting with Kurou. He was no hero; this was ridiculous. He was a small town inventor without a brave bone in his body.

'Are you all right?' he called again, but once more received no answer except a creaking groan from somewhere high above. A flutter of dust rained down on him, and Victor stared down at his feet, too afraid to look up.

Before he had a chance to talk himself out of it, he pulled off his coat and top layers, tossing them to the ground beside him. Then he stripped off his undershirt and wrapped it around his left forearm. Naked to the waist, the chill was punishing, but he gritted his teeth and tried to ignore it. Holding the torch in his right hand, he dropped to his knees and then his belly, sliding forward until the huge chunks of masonry were right above him. His breath came in little gasps, the terror greater than anything he had ever felt. Death, if it came now, could be brutal or merciful; he could be crushed in a moment or left to die slowly for days.

A few feet ahead of him, he heard another little cough.

'I'm coming,' he whispered, inching himself forward, digging his soles against the rough concrete of the stairs to push himself forward. He didn't dare lean on any of the rubble around him for leverage out of the fear it would come crashing down.

It had looked to be about ten feet from outside, but now he was pushing himself forward it seemed so much further. Little shards of rock cut into his naked belly as he moved forward, but the little stabs of pain they caused were almost a relief compared to the endless press of the concrete, which was as cold as a block of ice.

'Come on,' he muttered, counting the pressure of his feet as he shifted his weight from one leg to the other. One step, two, three, four—

And then his fingers touched something that wasn't freezing cold or hard like stone or steel.

The sole of a boot.

He tried to give it a little shake, but it was difficult to move his hands enough with his arms fully outstretched. Instead, he inched himself further forward until his hand could reach up as far as the girl's knee.

He could see her better now, a pair of woollen trousers under a heavy jacket, her face hidden by a hood that was still pulled up. She was lying on her front, her face turned to the left, away from him.

It appeared she had been remarkably lucky. From Victor's angle it looked like she wasn't trapped, which meant if he could just get a good grip on her he might be able to pull her free. If she was injured he couldn't tell; her thick jacket would have soaked up the blood from any flesh wound, but none of her limbs looked bent out of shape. It was possible she was just concussed.

Moving one inch at a time, Victor pushed the sleeve of his shirt under her leg and pulled it back over the top. Trying to find the pressure to tie it tight enough took a few minutes, and he couldn't reach her other leg as he had hoped. He didn't know how well he could move her by pulling on just one limb, but it would have to be enough.

With the knot tied as tightly as he could manage, he started to inch his way backwards, pushing with his hands and elbows.

His rescue mission was going well until his shirt went taut. He gave it another tug and the girl's leg moved a few inches towards him, but the rest of her body stayed put. He tried to back away again, but to achieve the pressure he needed to drag her body he would have to use parts of the fallen masonry for leverage.

He was so scared he could barely even breathe. The torch had begun to flicker, the batteries running low. He had perhaps a couple of minutes before he was plunged into darkness, and then he might not even get out, let alone the girl. He had to move, and he had to move now.

He gave the fallen lintel nearest to his leg a tentative kick. It felt stable enough, but if he leaned his knee into it would it stay where it had fallen, or would it shift just enough to cause something heavy above him to come crashing down?

The torch gave another flicker and for a second everything when black. Victor tapped it against the ground and it came back on, but the warning was enough. Ignoring the danger, he dug his knee into the fallen rock and pulled backwards.

The girl shifted a few inches. She gave another little cough, this time accompanied by a groan.

'Don't worry, you're safe,' he hissed at her, digging his knee in again and hauling her back another couple of inches. A gentle breeze ghosted over his ankle, and he realised his feet had found the exit. A little more and he'd be able to sit up and pull her out. They were so close—

Something rumbled far above him, and a sudden pattering of

falling debris fell like rain around them. Victor froze as little chunks of rock bounced down around him, some striking him on the bare skin as they ricocheted off fallen masonry into his cubby hole. One struck the casing of the torch with a hard crack.

Victor gritted his teeth and began to worm his way backwards as fast as he could. The deadweight of the girl's body barely seemed to move as he wriggled back and forth, his body aching from both the chaff and the cold of the floor.

'Where am I...?' came a weak voice.

'Hang on!' Victor called out. 'Don't struggle!'

'Where? What's going on?'

Victor had almost freed his legs when the girl came to her senses and began to struggle. One foot kicked out and struck a large fallen rock that bounced down just inches from Victor's face.

'Stop it!' he shouted. 'Stop struggling or it'll collapse.'

'Who's there?' the girl called, and he thought he recognised her voice from somewhere but couldn't quite place it.

'Victor. My name's Victor Mishin.'

Isabella had been the first of several on-off girlfriends who hadn't found Victor's mild manner to be a sedative in itself, but at the sound of his name his old magic worked its charm and the girl calmed down, lying still while he continued to back out.

The rumble came from above once again just as Victor's shoulders came free and the torch gave a final flicker and died, plunging them into darkness.

'Hold on,' Victor called, terror slipping into his voice. 'Just a little further and we'll be safe—'

The girl's boot slammed into his face. Victor groaned, his neck absorbing most of the impact. He tried to hold on to her but she kicked him again.

'What are you doing?' he gasped.

'Fucking bastard.'

The voice was definitely familiar, but so was the rising thunder from high above. Some other great death-harnessing lump of power was setting itself to fall; Victor could feel the ache in the debris around him.

Then something closed over his feet, dragging him backwards with the strength of some terrible subterranean beast. He was still holding on to the sling around the girl's foot he had made with his shirt, and she slid out after him.

'Let me go!' she screamed as something heavy slammed down just a few feet to Victor's left, invisible in the dark except for the vibrations it sent running through the concrete.

Victor could see nothing. He heard the rumbling of collapsing masonry from high above him, and wondered how many seconds he had left before his life was snuffed out. He still had one hand holding on to his shirt with the other end tied around the struggling girl's foot. Her voice seemed so familiar.

What had grabbed hold of him?

'Looks like you found a live one, sire,' Kurou's voice came in his ear. 'Time for a little grave-robbing. Yours.'

Kurou's fingers slipped over Victor's feet and dragged him across the floor until he felt the first bump of the stairs under his shoulders. With each step he cried out, but Kurou didn't slow his pace, pulling him down the stairs like a child dragging a teddy bear.

Behind him, the girl, still pulled along behind, cried out in her own pain.

A massive crash came from above as the pile of debris shifted and settled. Despite the bruising pain in his back from the concrete steps, he knew Kurou had saved them both.

And then he saw something wondrous: the light through Kurou's open doorway.

The girl had struck her head and been knocked out again. Victor climbed gingerly to his feet and took hold of her ankles, helping Kurou to carry her inside, where they unceremoniously dumped her on top of the pile of filthy blankets. Kurou slammed the door shut.

'Well, a fine catch, sire. Albeit one I'm not certain was worth such a frightful risk.'

'Thank you,' Victor gasped, pulling his shirt back on and picking a dirty jacket from under a pile of Kurou's blankets, the cold helping him to ignore the smell. 'You might not be gentle about it, but you saved my life back there. Why did you come back?'

Kurou gave a lopsided grin. 'I was hungry, sire.'

'We're not eating her!'

Kurou shrugged. 'Let's see how you feel in a few days if we're unable to find a way out. You know her, sire?'

The girl groaned. Her eyelids fluttered. She was wearing a heavy jacket that made him instantly jealous, having left his somewhere up the stairwell. She was young, no more than fourteen or fifteen, with blonde hair and cold blue eyes set into a delicate but beautiful face. He had seen her somewhere before, he was sure of it——

She opened her eyes. 'You bastard,' she spat. 'You murdered my brother.'

Victor, despite being slightly overwhelmed by the intensity of her vitriol, remembered her now. She was a younger, nastier version of her sister, Isabella.

He glanced at Kurou. 'Patricia Mortin,' he said.

17

———

THE CLIMB IN THE DARKNESS

JUDGING by the girl's impressive display of aggression in the face of life-threatening adversity, Victor felt it best that they restrain Patricia before she properly came around. Kurou tied her hands behind her back and bound her ankles, and was going to gag her with one of his putrid blankets before Victor suggested that a piece of duct tape from a roll he had loaded on to the cart might be a less potentially lethal alternative.

Kurou, though, once the girl was safely secured, had retreated into the background to let Victor deal with her vitriol, a smirk on his twisted face.

Patricia wasn't like an old car that needed warming up. From the moment she opened her eyes she was struggling to get at Victor, her anger expressed by a series of muffled shrieks and snarls that no doubt encompassed the worst curses ever coined by humanity. Kurou had also had the foresight to tie her wrists to the leg of a heavy old chair, otherwise, she might well have attempted to bludgeon Victor to death using only her shoulders, elbows and knees. As she struggled now in front of him, Victor couldn't help feeling a little regretful that he had saved her. It had been enough trouble dealing with Kurou. Now he would have to sleep with both eyes open.

'Look, I know what you're thinking,' he said as she struggled and kicked. 'I didn't kill your brother. It was an accident.'

Patricia's eyes bulged. Her arms, battered and bloody from her fall, strained at the bonds.

'I know you hate me and you don't want to hear any excuses, but I'm sorry. I really wish it hadn't happened, but he did attack me—twice, I might add.'

Behind her, Kurou was lying on his back, squealing with laughter. Victor began to feel like he was in the middle of some absurdist freak show. He had to remind himself that he was in a room with a deformed killer who had not only booby-trapped the cart to shoot deadly projectiles at its enemies, but who also feasted on harvested human flesh.

Patricia, perhaps realising the futility of her continued resistance, had calmed down. She watched him through eyes as damning as hot coals as he muttered excuse after excuse. He tried to promise her freedom and a return to her family, but with Kurou in complete control it was possible neither of them might go home alive. If Victor could get Patricia to side with him then they might be able to help each other escape from the professor, but it was unlikely. She seemed certain he was responsible for her twin brother's death.

Finally, Kurou stood up and ambled over. He squatted down behind Patricia's chair and laid two bony hands over her shoulders.

She immediately froze. She looked up at the face leaning on her left shoulder and her breath shortened. The prankster that brought a sun of sorts through the clouds of Kurou's visage was nowhere to be seen; the demon that Victor had first encountered was in full attendance. Patricia, for all her attitude, had never encountered a creature such as this, and was barely controlling the urge to cry.

'Hush, hush, my princess,' Kurou whispered, his voice a gravelly sound like sand paper dragging over stones. 'Calm your sweet mind. Your brother chose his own death by his actions. I'm afraid it is a common trait among your species.' He lifted a finger and ran it down the side of her cheek. 'It would be a shame for you to choose your own death so soon.'

Tears filled Patricia's eyes. The angry, violent young woman had become a child beneath Kurou's touch.

'Who saw you enter?' Kurou asked. 'Will they try to dig you out?'

'No—no one,' she stammered. 'It was dark.'

'How tragic,' Kurou whistled. 'A travesty that could grace great literature.'

The fire was dying down. Kurou's lights flickered, and the cold that had been licking at the edges of everything began to sneak ever closer. Victor was grateful for his shirt and jacket, and even Kurou had pulled a thin tunic on over his body.

'What do we do now?' Victor said. 'We can't just sit here.'

Kurou shrugged. 'We can, sire. I have enough food for several weeks now that you and the princess are here.'

Patricia screamed. 'You can't eat us!'

'Why not?'

'Because—because you can't. We're human beings!'

'The taste of which I can at least tolerate,' Kurou said. 'If no suitable alternative is present.'

'It's not safe to stay here,' Victor said. 'What if the rest of the building collapses?'

Kurou's neck creaked as he turned towards Victor. He looked like a badly decomposed corpse suddenly reanimated. 'So what do you suggest?'

'The chimney. It's the only way.'

'Be my guest.'

Kurou stood up and waved Victor towards the fireplace with a flourish of his hand. Victor turned towards it, then looked back at Kurou.

'Perhaps we should formulate a plan.'

Kurou rolled his eyes. 'I'll leave it for your consideration, sire,' he said. 'I'm tiring of this conversation.' He started towards the kitchen, but as he passed Patricia he paused for a moment, resting one finger on her chin and lifting it up towards him.

'I had a daughter once,' he sighed, then before she could answer, he had gone.

'Don't worry,' I don't think he's going to eat us,' Victor said, keeping his voice low. 'I think he actually likes the company, but we'd probably be best to do what he says, just in case.'

'What is that thing?'

'His name is Kurou. I'm not exactly sure what he is, but he's a genius with machines. It was his modifications to my robot that … killed your brother.'

Patricia stared at him for a long time. Victor felt too magnetized by her gaze to either look away or respond. Instead, he found his cheeks turning red with a mixture of discomfort, guilt and shame.

'Never ever mention my brother again,' she said.

'I'm sorry,' he muttered, his voice coming out like a croak. Patricia scowled and looked away.

The awkward silence was penetrated by Kurou marching back into the room with a coil of rope hung over one shoulder. He dropped it on the floor and then squatted down beside Victor with one end held in his hands.

'What are you doing?'

'If we're going to climb out of that chimney we should practice climbing safety,' Kurou said. 'Hold still.'

Victor was too afraid to move as Kurou tied the rope around his ankle in an elaborate knot, then picked a piece of burning wood from the edge of the flames and melted part of the rope to seal it in place.

'It would be most ungrateful of you to try to escape,' he said. 'After everything I've done for you.'

'I—I wouldn't.'

Kurou patted him on the knee. 'Of course, you wouldn't. I trust you, sire. Just airing my concerns.'

Victor stared at the dying embers of the fire. Pretty soon the chimney would be the only place in the whole apartment with any residue of warmth. It would be worth the climb for that alone, but the thought of hauling his way up that tunnel of black soot filled him with dread.

'Does the chimney go all the way to the top of the building?' he asked.

Kurou shook his head. 'Oh, no, sire. Can you imagine the cleaning that would take? It surfaces at ground level.'

'How high is the climb?'

'Oh, sixty or seventy metres.' We're buried deeper than the Cretaceous.'

Victor gulped. 'Wouldn't it be better to try to get out through the stairwell's rubble?'

Kurou shook his head. 'While you were freeing the young lady, I took the liberty of having a look around. It seems we're trapped. Of course, you're welcome to try, wasting valuable time while our resources dwindle and the cold sets in. Not an unwelcome sensation on a body such as mine, I might add.'

'Do you have anything we can use to climb with?'

Kurou cocked his head and gave Victor a crooked smile. With the uneven tufts of hair protruding from his scalp he looked like a remarkably ugly hatchling. 'Only what you brought with you, sire. I'm a man of few means, so I am.'

Behind the visage of helplessness, Victor knew Kurou was hiding something from him. Probably many things. All of this was a test, he felt, to see if he was worth keeping alive. Kurou might be enjoying their company, but he was a man of many guises. He could switch faces in a moment and find both Victor and Patricia surplus to requirements without any hint of regret. If Victor wanted to keep himself and the girl alive until they had a chance to escape, he had to prove his value.

'It's made of bricks, isn't it?' he said, mostly to himself. He went over to the dying fireplace and peered up, the rope going taut around his foot as Kurou stayed where he was. It was wider than those in private apartments might have been, used perhaps more frequently down in this basement room, but still no more than around forty centimetres square. Victor was the most heavyset of the three of them, but still fairly slight compared to most Russian men. Even with his coat he could just fit, and while the squeeze would be claustrophobic and suffocating, it would count in his favour if the bricks were uneven enough to allow him a grip.

In a show of confidence, he began to kick out the remaining embers of the fire. 'Ready when you are,' he said, feeling anything but.

Kurou spent a few minutes making a brace for Patricia, then tying and sealing the far end of the rope around the girl's waist. He cut her legs free so she could steady herself against the chimney walls, but refused to free her arms even though the obvious logic suggested the threat of her attacking them from the bottom of the chimney shaft was worth the risk of giving her the means to climb. Kurou, though, seemed to consider everything a big adventure.

'Let's go,' he said.

Victor didn't even bother trying to hold a torch. This was one climb where he didn't want to know how far he had gone, or how much further was left. Kurou helped him climb up into the shaft, where he braced his back against one wall of the filthy chimney and jammed his feet against the other. He had brought a couple of screwdrivers with him to possibly jam into gaps in the stone, but it was uneven enough that he could get a grip with his gloves, lift himself a few inches, then move his feet up.

Climbing upwards was a painful, uncomfortable process. He could see nothing, not even the walls of the shaft around him. He knew that if he slipped his momentum would take Kurou and Patricia down with him, yet every few steps the rope would go taut as Kurou struggled to keep up, and Victor would have a few seconds to sit quietly in the dark, listening to the breathing of the others, punctuated by bursts of Kurou's cackling laughter, while trying to ignore the clogging stench of decades of accumulated soot.

He had been climbing for about half an hour, inch by resilient inch, when he saw the first glimmer of light above him. He had suspected that day had come while he had been struggling to free Patricia, but the exact passage of time was measured only by the growing aches and pains in his body.

At some point about halfway up, Patricia had started crying. Her sobbing floated up through the shaft like bubbles, her misery encasing him. Kurou had fallen silent as if listening to it like sweet music, and Victor wondered how much of it was worry at their predicament, and how much was a mixture of delayed shock and grief at the loss of her brother.

The glimmer of light above him grew brighter. It looked so small and distant, a pinprick of hope. He steeled himself, gritted his teeth, and began to move upwards with greater urgency.

He came upon it in a rush, but his excitement was quashed when he saw the chimney shaft ended in a circular concrete tube, barely wide enough for him to reach an arm through. Set into bricks, it was clogged with soot, but effectively sealed them into the shaft.

They were stuck. There was no way out.

Below him, Kurou was coming up, the sound of his movements scraping and sharp like a hermit crab digging its way out of an undersized shell.

'We're stuck,' Victor said, his first words aloud since they had begun climbing. 'There's no way through.'

'There's always a way, sire,' Kurou said, his breathing ragged. 'Aren't you an inventor? Invent us a way out.'

Victor braced himself and then reached up a hand into the tube. The sudden gust of cold air on his hand was so comforting he almost wept.

'You said this opened out on the back of the building. Which side is inside, which is out?'

Kurou chuckled. 'Sire, use your head. Can't you tell from the breeze?'

Victor scowled. It was clear Kurou was going to be of no help at all. Again he got the impression this was some sort of test.

He pulled off his glove and tucked it into his jacket. Then he reached up again, holding his fingers out in the freezing air. The breeze seemed to be coming from his back, but what did that mean? Would the air wrap around the building or be deflected by it?

He tried to remember the layout of the building, of the orientation of Kurou's apartment, but he had lost count of the turns of the stairwell, and his fear had stripped him of his sense of direction.

He opened his mouth to speak, then came up with another idea. He pulled his hand back down, but instead of putting his glove back on, he put his hand against the stone of the shaft walls, feeling through the accumulated soot to try to get at the rock itself.

On both sides the bricks were cold, but they were a little colder at his back than in front of him.

'It's here,' he said. 'Behind my back.'

'Very good, sire. How do we get out?'

Victor pulled a screwdriver out of his jacket pocket and handed it down to Kurou, keeping the second for himself. 'We dig,' he said.

The mortar was old, weakened by heat and cold and most recently the bombing. It took Victor just a couple of minutes to locate a brick that was already lose and begin chipping away at it. He warned Patricia to keep the hood over her head in case of any falling pieces of rock, but the mortar was crumbly and came away in grains.

Ten minutes later, Victor pushed against the brick and it slid outwards, revealing the inside of a drift of snow. A few minutes of hacking at the packed ice and they had light enough to see, and a space for more dislodged bricks.

'A little chilly for you, is it?' Kurou whispered.

'Just keep digging or we'll freeze to death long before we get out of here.'

'As you command, sire,' Kurou answered with a cackle.

Below them, Patricia was silent. Victor could sense her presence, but jammed into the tiny space there was only enough room for Kurou to reach up and help Victor chip away at the loose mortar, leaving Patricia down in the dark. He felt a mixture of guilt for the girl's predicament and unease at her next move. She might understand that her brother's death wasn't Victor's fault, but that didn't mean she forgave him for his involvement. He would do well to avoid turning his back to her.

Victor broke away another brick, making the space wide enough for his head to fit through. A couple more and they would be able to get out.

And then Kurou screamed as Patricia jerked on the rope, sending him tumbling back down the shaft. Victor grabbed hold of a crag of protruding brick, wrapping his arms around it and bracing his legs a moment before the rope yanked his ankle so hard he thought it must have broken right through. Below him he heard the sounds of a scuffle, but unable to help, all he could do was hang on, and hope that their combined weight wouldn't send all three of them plummeting down the shaft to their deaths.

18

THE MACHINATIONS OF WAR

RICHARD KARHOV PULLED up the morning's orders on the monitor and quickly read over them. Satisfied that he knew what he needed to know in order to carry them out, he got up from his desk and wandered over to the coffee machine in the corner. All around him the click and clack of relentless typing filled the air like the buzzing of hundreds of mechanical bees. It was interesting sometimes how old-school some of his colleagues were. Allowed to choose the component parts of their individual workstations from the immense deposits of junked hardware that rose in near mountains of forgotten technology in the warehouses around the base, many had chosen geriatric monitors or keyboards with big, heavy keys, and great walls of fan-assisted hard drive units that rose up around them nearly as high as the walls of the cubicles themselves. Far fewer had chosen the newer touch-screen tablets, the embedded table top monitors and the laptops small enough to fit in your pocket; if your workstation was a reflection of your personality, then it was clear that nostalgia for the old days permeated the base like a heavy but welcome perfume.

'What did you get today?' he asked the girl standing nearest the coffee machine, a plastic cup held up in two hands to her mouth as she blew gently on to its surface.

Miranda gave him a little smile from beneath a mop of brown hair that ballooned around her head as if gravity were rejecting it.

'You know we're not supposed to talk about it,' she said. 'Is that some poor cover at asking me out on a date?'

Richard smiled. 'You know I'd never do that. Just wondering, that's all.'

Miranda shrugged. 'The usual. False weather reports here,

edited news footage there. Oh, and a radio broadcast I have to doctor. Should be fun.'

'Oh, I know you don't mean that.'

'You know what I heard?' Miranda said, deflecting the conversation away from small talk. 'I heard that we're being inspected later today. You hear that?'

Richard frowned. 'No. Where'd you hear that?'

'On the secure line.'

'I don't bother with that. I trust it no more than the unsecure ones. There are the instructions that come in every morning and nothing else.'

Miranda's face hardened as if she found his display of devotion to duty upsetting. 'I'm happy for you, Richard, I really am. I'm sure you'll pass the inspection with flying colours.'

'I hope so.'

Their conversation seemed to be over by mutual consent. Richard gave Miranda a polite nod and then headed back to his cubicle. Thoughts of the impending inspection filled his mind. Things happened every time they had one, usually someone getting pulled up and removed for a display of failure that couldn't be measured in real terms.

The last time, a little over a month ago, a man named Larkin had been removed and replaced without warning. Larkin had scored higher in the commission charts than Richard had, and outwardly had been a model employee. No one knew what had happened to him, but there were rumours, of course. Rumours and reports and video footage, none of which could be verified beyond something that might or might not be true.

He got back to work, planting seeds as he liked to call it. Seeds of doubt, seeds of misinformation. He knew what they were called on the outside, but Richard thought of his job as one of far more importance than simply hacking into websites and altering their content. Yes, it was outright sabotage, but his team and many others were simply undoing the mess than the rest of humanity had created over the past few decades, stripping it back, reducing its use and its credibility, making it unreliable in order to free people from its terrible hold.

For years, scientists, religious leaders, and other crackpots had predicted the eventual enslavement of humanity, they had just expected it to come from without.

Instead, it had come from within.

THE ELEVATOR TOOK Alek Politov and his guards to the top floor of the old Gorbachev Hotel, forty floors of bland but functional business suites, several floors of which were now used by his men for their operations. With the tide—as he liked to call it—set to overwhelm them in the coming days, his crews were currently clearing out, packing their things and preparing for the next step in the gradual eastward retreat.

He wouldn't be going with them. Neither his guards nor those in his command knew it yet, but Politov had reached the end of his own personal crusade. He was far older now than he deserved to be, and the cold would kill him if he tried another overland trek. The war would be lost by summer, but by the time the snow thawed and spring announced itself, it would be too late.

Am I being a coward? He wondered. *Is it not that I don't want to witness the death of my great nation first-hand, that I'd rather remember the good days than witness the coming of the bad?*

The penthouse suite had floor-to-ceiling windows in the west-facing wall. Politov allowed the guards to help him to a chair, then they retired to their posts in the corridor outside. The hum of electric heaters comforted him, warming his old bones, as he looked out at the greying, snow-shrouded city towards the hills far to the east.

They would come from there, he knew. Any day now.

He closed his eyes, leaning back in the chair, letting his thoughts drift.

I know you're out there. I can feel you, always, waiting at the edges of my thoughts, keeping watch on me, not wanting to intrude.

He didn't know if he expected an answer or not. He was so old that often the thoughts drifting through his mind were unrecognizable. Once, though, things had been different. He had been part of something incredible, and while so many had died, he had managed to come through, one of the few last remnants of something that had changed the world.

Out there in the hills, his soldiers, his ragtag army of leftovers and untrained recruits, were bedded in, hidden in their tunnels, their trenches, behind their gun emplacements, waiting for an enemy more terrible than any they could imagine to stride right in amongst them. More than Politov could count had deserted, joining the refugee trains heading east, trudging to their eventual deaths long before they ever made it as far as Mongolia or the Korean Peninsula.

Those that had stayed could not be regarded as brave, merely resigned to a death that would come one way or the other, and they chose to die in the fight rather than on their knees. Politov respected their decision; it was the one he would have chosen were he young enough to make a difference, but the truth was that this shouldn't be his fight. He was holding on to a life that didn't belong to him. For many years he had hoped that things would change, that he could put right the wrongs of the past, but his last chances were gone. Everything he had feared had been set into motion.

He opened his eyes, lifted a pair of binoculars and peered out at the distant hills. At this distance the trees blurred into one another, just an endless expanse of forest dipping and rising like snow-covered waves until it faded into the distance. Would more men make a difference, he wondered? More tanks, more aerial bombardment? They had tried everything, thrown the full might of the Russian army against the enemy, and it had been broken like an old ship on a vicious shore.

Despite everything, Politov found his ancient face breaking into a grim smile. Where armies had fallen and the greatest technology at their disposal had been as effective as blowing bubbles at body armour, reality had taken a backwards step and left in its place room for the incredible, the miraculous, the storybook heroism. There was someone out there, he knew, someone who could find a way to turn the tide.

His smile gave way to a choking sob, and he wiped tears out of his old eyes. The sun was not yet set on Russia, the war was not yet lost. There would be a standard bearer who would step out of the ranks to win the day, there had to be.

Alek Politov just wished he would live long enough to see it.

19

VICTOR'S CIRCUS

IT WAS impossible in the tiny confined space to pull back her hands to strike properly, but Patricia did her best as she found the shaft above her filled with Kurou's bone-thin, leathery body. She slammed a fist into his belly, heard him groan as she struck some old war wound, then bony fingers were crushing her windpipe, pinching her tight in a knowing, practiced way. She tried to gasp and pull back, but there was literally nowhere to go but straight down. For a few seconds she thought about relaxing her feet and plummeting to her death, but Esel's eyes flashed into her mind, bringing with them a message: *avenge me.*

'Let her go!'

That was Victor's voice, the good-for-nothing idiot that her sister claimed to love. Sticking up for her against the monster. She ought to be thankful, but the thought of that idiot's voice being the last thing she heard left a sour taste in her mouth. Or was that blood? The dim light that had begun to filter in from above as Victor and the monster broke them a way out was starting to fade. The monster was so strong, but if she were able to manoeuvre she might be able to slip his grip and get away. She had spent the long, arduous climb gradually loosening the ropes securing her wrists, but her impatience had got the better of her. She had wanted to fight the monster right now, but she should have waited. It was too late—

'Kurou! Let go of her!'

She gasped in a desperate breath of freezing air as the monster's fingers relaxed. In an instant he was gone, shimmying up the shaft like a dirty, putrid spider, and the rope around her waist jerked hard, almost causing her feet to slip. She stuck out her hands even as she felt an uncontrollable dizziness coming over her, jamming her palms into the sides of the shaft to hold herself steady.

'Patricia, let go!' Victor shouted. 'We'll pull you up!'

She waited a few seconds before she replied. They had brought her this far, and if they had wanted her dead Kurou's fingers would have done their work.

She gave the rope a tug as if to confirm her agreement, then slowly relaxed her feet, letting the rope take her weight. For a second she just hung there, waiting for the rope to go slack and her descent back into darkness to begin, then the rope jerked, and she slowly began to rise up towards the light.

Kurou was standing a few feet away, peering around the corner of a building, as Victor hauled her the last few feet up to the opening and helped her through. His pasty, dull face was red with exertion, and his eyes filled with a childlike hope that she might offer some thanks. Instead she told him to fuck himself and then set about wiping the clods of soot off her ruined coat, a task she quickly gave up as a waste of time.

Victor glanced back over his shoulder at Kurou. The monster was muttering under his breath in a language she couldn't understand, and she thought about making a break for it, before realising that her rope was still attached to his ankle. Perhaps she could find a moment to strangle him with it, wrap it around his scrawny neck and choke the life out of him as he had almost done to her. She wondered where Victor's loyalties lay, whether it was with his lover's sister or the monster he had found in the depths of the abandoned dormitory building. Knowing Victor, his lack of spine would go with whichever option offered him the most safety, and he clearly had some kind of symbiotic relationship with this Kurou. Bottom feeders tended to stick together.

'Are you all right?' Victor asked. 'I'm sorry he tied you up.'

Habit required her to berate him, but she bit her tongue. She tried to reason with herself that he had saved her life twice now, but it was too easy to remember that she had come here because of what he had done to her brother. And what had he wanted to save her for? She had never offered him a kind word in anger. She had seen the way he looked at her when he thought she wouldn't notice. It was the same way other men did. No doubt he had seen an opportunity. She could imagine his soft, unattractive body grunting as he forced himself upon her. Only God knew what her idiot sister saw in him.

Kurou turned away from the corner and came marching back. He gave her a sour look, then clapped Victor on the shoulder.

'We'll soon have company, sire. Won't that be nice? A company of policemen are fast approaching.'

Their soot-covered clothes and faces stood out against the stark grey-white of the piled snow. Tracking them would be a breeze. All she had to do was alert the police to their presence—

Kurou crossed the space between them faster than she could have thought possible. She managed to get out a half-cry before his hand cracked against the side of the face, knocking her sprawling. She climbed to her hands and knees, splitting out a tooth amid a trail of blood.

'I'll kill you—'

He struck her again, on the side of the temple, his hand hard and lumpy like a jumble of bones in an old leather bag. She started to cry out, but a hand closed over her mouth, holding it shut. At Kurou's shoulder, Victor stood looking down, a helpless, terrified expression on his face, and in that moment she despised him almost as much as the monster himself.

'I'll see both of you dead,' she mumbled beneath his fingers.

'Silence might be rather appropriate in our current predicament, young lady,' Kurou said, his voice a birdlike squawk that mirrored his hideous face. 'It wouldn't be too difficult to draw a crimson line beneath your pretty little face and watch your poisonous blood create a mural of fading life on the snow around your feet.' He glanced up at Victor. 'Bring the rope, sire.'

It terrified her to see the way Kurou snatched the offered rope and sliced through a length with one long fingernail as though it was damp and rotten. She was a toy, his plaything. He could kill her at any time.

He jammed it into her mouth and tied it around the back of her head without any attempt at kindness. It bit into the sides of her mouth, and the only sound she could make was a throaty growl. She thought about making a run for it, but Kurou tied another part of rope back around her wrists and then looped the end around his waist so that he could lead her like a dog on a leash. Victor, she noted, was allowed to walk free.

'We need cover, sire,' Kurou said. 'Is there somewhere we can go? Haste might be a good idea.'

Victor turned in a slow circle, one finger on his chin. 'We can try my place,' he said. 'It's a risk, but its close. It might be that if anyone was looking for me they've already been and gone. Otherwise there's the old café, but it's a lot further and there's no heating. We'll freeze to death in a few hours.'

The sun was at its zenith. They had a couple more hours before the true cold set in, and the darkness began to descend.

'It might be worth a try, sire,' Kurou said. 'Let's hurry.'

He moved out from their cover, dragging Patricia behind him. At first she tried to resist, but the effort was too great to maintain, so she let herself be led. Victor voiced what she had been thinking when he said, 'What happened to the police you saw?'

Kurou grinned. 'I saw none, sire. I was just testing our young mistress's reactions.' He sighed. 'Predictable, as one … predicted.'

Victor led them back through the streets around St Peter's Place, away from the collapsed remains of the dormitory building, into a lower-middle-class district which was still poor enough to make Patricia turn up her nose. They were near to where her brother had died, and she knew that Esel liked to come down here for his entertainment, beating up and mugging low wage workers as they headed wearily for their beds, more for his own amusement than for any material gain. It wasn't her thing to come down here; she preferred the area around the station, where true wealth tended to be found.

After a few minutes of walking they reached a small street and Victor bade them stop. He pointed a few doors down to a nondescript terraced house, the kind of place that the government used to allocate to its lower class party loyalists, nothing to be proud of but a home nonetheless. It was a fraction of the size of her own family's home, and it was clear why Isabella always invited Victor over. Love or not, her sister wouldn't be seen dead in such a scraggly little hovel.

'That's it,' Victor said. 'I can't see anyone—'

'I can,' Kurou interjected. 'Street opposite. Two doors down, second floor. The curtain moved a fraction, sire. I'd suggest that going back to your little abode might not be the best idea.'

Victor turned to stare at him. 'How can you see that? I can barely see that house, let alone anything happening in the upstairs window.'

Kurou tapped the side of his beak, a hideous gesture that made Patricia's stomach crawl. 'Not just a pretty face, sire. One eye might have expired, but the other still works rather well.'

'Are you sure you saw someone?'

'As plain as the overlarge nose on my face, sire. By the inclination of our little snooper's eyes, I'd say it was at least nearly almost certain that he is waiting for your sweet return.'

Victor shrugged. 'We can't go to the café, it's too far. 'I have another place, a small workshop I rent, but it's not very comfortable. I've never planned to stay there more than a few hours at a time, so there's nothing we can sleep on.'

'Is it far?'

'A couple of streets.'

Kurou nodded. 'It might give us time to consider our next move, sire. A workshop, you say?'

Victor gave a goofball smile that Patricia ached to punch off his face. 'Just where I do a little tinkering.'

The clouds were closing in, latent with the threat of yet more snow. Kurou seemed to welcome it, as the gloom gave them more cover, but all Patricia could think about was getting free, killing these two fools and then catching the last train out of here with her father and sister. By her estimation it was set to leave tomorrow.

There was still time, and she had learned her lesson about patience. Next time she would be more careful.

After a few minutes walking through the snow, Victor led them down a dark, claustrophobic alleyway and came to a halt outside a corrugated iron sliding door which was secured by a heavy padlock crusted with ice. Victor squatted down and started digging away in the snow. Patricia was beginning to wonder what he was doing when he turned and held up a fat key.

It took him a few long minutes to pick away the ice around the lock to get the door open. Kurou pushed her inside, into a dark room which felt colder than the air outside, so cold in fact that she found herself gasping for air as her hands trembled. Kurou slapped her across the face, dropping her to her knees, but she wouldn't give him the satisfaction of hearing her cry out. She glared up at his ugly face, holding his gaze, as Victor shut the door and locked it.

'Wait a moment,' he said, then flicked a switch, casting a welcome orange glow over the room's contents. There was an old stove heater in the middle of the room, and he quickly set to getting it working as Patricia cast her condescending gaze over a number of workbenches and metal shelving units, some holding half-finished contraptions, the like of which she sometimes saw around her father's mining operations. Over near the window was a cleaning robot missing a head; behind the door was a strange thing that was even more spindly than Kurou which she knew was designed for scaling pylons to make repairs during high winds. Victor must have pilfered it from a dump somewhere, as it was missing a leg from the knee down.

Patricia quickly dismissed the room as an amateur inventor's junk closet and squatted down close to the stove to get some warmth on her hands, but Kurou was staring at the broken-down robots as if he'd fallen asleep and woken up in heaven.

'What is this place?' He reached out and ran a hand down the side of a robot's dented, rusty face as if caressing a beautiful lady.

Victor sat down on an upturned metal bucket and sighed. 'Oh, nothing really. It was just part of my dream.'

Kurou steepled his elongated fingers into a shape that resembled a fish skeleton. 'Oh, do tell.'

'I always wanted to be an inventor,' Victor said. 'Not just a handyman with a knack for electronics. I wanted to create something grand and elaborate, something that would cause awe and inspiration, and that would get me out of this town. I had this idea to create a kind of travelling circus, but instead of having men and women being the performers, I would have robots.' He gave a wistful smile and spread his hands. 'It was to be called the Circus of Machines.'

Patricia scoffed, but at a glare from Kurou she stifled it. 'And this is what you've built so far?' Kurou asked. 'A solid collection, I'll say, sire, albeit one a little basic.'

Victor was shaking his head. 'Oh, no. This is nothing.' The eagerness in his eyes betrayed a need to tell someone his secret.

'What is it, sire?'

'There's a place in the hills a few miles north of here. I discovered it last summer. I can't carry anything big, but it's where I found my tools. I know it's stealing, but it's just left there, abandoned—'

Patricia glared at him. Esel had always considered him a thief, and now she had proof. She wanted to tell him what she thought about him, but the rope was too tight in her mouth to form any sound. All she could do was scowl at him and hope he could read her thoughts.

'What did you find, sire?'

'Some kind of depository.'

'Of what?'

Victor looked so excited Patricia thought he might burst.

'Of machines,' he said.

20

___

THE END OF EVERYTHING

LIFTING his head from the armchair and wiping the weariness out of his eyes, Robert Mortin took a moment to register the knocking as coming from the house's rear door, rather than the front. As a muffled voice called his name, he remembered the phone call the night before and climbed up from the chair, shouting that he was coming. He didn't bother to adjust his appearance—two days now since he had changed his clothes, washed or shaved—after all, he was a grieving father.

The police had found his son's body the night before, partially buried in snow not far from St Peter's Place. Esel had been shot with some sort of explosive bullet that had penetrated his chest before wreaking havoc among his internal organs. The cold had preserved the body remarkably well, and until Mortin had looked on the wound he could almost have believed his son was sleeping.

That was one that needed to be avenged. He hoped there wouldn't be another.

He opened the door to reveal two grizzled men standing there in thick woollen jackets, their faces chapped and raw. Sergei Papanov and Yevgeny Franko. Ordinarily Robert would have turned his nose up at the sight of their sour, weather-beaten faces, the ghost of years of petty crime flickering in their eyes, but they were men who would do anything for coin. Papanov held out a bag.

'We did as you asked, Mortin,' he said. 'The good news, if you look at it that way, is that we didn't find her body.'

Robert looked up. 'Could she be alive?'

'I doubt it, but we found no bodies at all. Above the third floor the rubble was too thick, but we got down into the basements through an old ventilation shaft. There were the signs that some poor bastard was squatting down there, but no sign of your daughter. It's possible she got out somehow that we haven't figured yet.'

'Or she could have been crushed in the rubble.'

The man opened the bag and pulled out a square of silk. An elaborate floral pattern was soiled by dust and oil. At the sight of it Robert sagged, reaching out for the doorframe to support himself.

'My daughter....'

'Did this belong to her?'

'Her handkerchief. She took it everywhere.'

'It was in the lowest basement apartment. It was the only thing that wasn't ... putrid. She had been in there, either before or after the drone strike.'

Robert nodded. He went back into the kitchen and pulled a fat envelope from a drawer. Their work had cost him dear, but if it proved Patricia might still be alive, it was worth it.

'I want you to continue your search for another day. I have money.'

Franko stepped forward, putting a hand on Robert's doorframe. 'We need no more of your money, Mortin,' he said. 'We want passage on the train. The last one. We know you've got places on it, and we're pretty sure you can find a couple of spares if need be.'

Mortin hesitated. 'You'll have it when I have absolute proof of whether she is living or dead. Bring me that and it's yours.'

'Don't try to cheat us, Mortin,' Papanov said, his voice low.

They were both big men, heavily muscled, and with the kind of ugly faces that on another day Robert might have tried to bloody up, but he held his temper and his tongue. While both men now worked in the twilight world beneath the eyes of the law, Sergei had once worked in the mining industry as a specialist in mine rescue. Few other men in Brevik could have got inside the collapsed dormitory building, and no others would have done it without authorization from City Hall. Mortin had needed to call in a favour.

'Absolute proof,' he said again.

'We'll get it,' Franko said, stepping back from the door. Robert closed it and returned to the living room.

Upstairs, Isabella was still sleeping. He had slipped a couple of pills into a glass of wine to get her out of his way for a while. Her endless laments of sorrow were grating and of no help to anyone.

Where was that useless boyfriend of hers when anyone needed him?

Mortin paused, one hand resting on the drink cabinet where he kept the kind of whisky that could help him through a crisis like this.

Where was Victor indeed?

LENA FOUND it impossible to relax as the car bumped along the bombed out remains of the old highway. It had taken an hour to get through the many military roadblocks, but once they left the last soldiers behind a strange feeling of loneliness had set in. She was taking her turn driving, while Boris, one of her aides, slept in the back, and Stepan, the other, scanned the darkening countryside with a pair of binoculars from the passenger seat. Their inherent professionalism made the men poor company, and hours at a time would pass without a word uttered among them. As the vastness of the Siberian countryside stirred a sense of agoraphobia in her, she wished for just a little banality, anything to break the tension.

The highway was eerily deserted. From a few miles out of the city they began to pass the occasional abandoned car, some with their tyres blown out, others gutted by fire. The highway itself had been hit by drone strikes near the city, but further away it was more intact.

At last, Stepan stirred in the passenger seat beside her, dropping the binoculars and turning around.

'Lights,' he said.

'A house?'

Yeltzin scoffed. 'Not with electricity. Not out here.'

'Then what? A patrol?'

He gave a brief shake of his head. 'Not likely.'

'Then what? One of those robots?'

'It's not moving. Stop the car and let's go take a look.'

The idea was crazy, but the journey was driving her that way too. Getting out of the confines of the car for a few minutes might make her feel better. She pulled in to the curb and climbed out, leaving the engine running to conserve the car's heat.

It was bitterly cold outside, the temperature dipping into the minus double digits. After full night fell it would drop even further, to minus twenty or more, so cold that switching off the car might mean they never got it started again. They were sticking to the same routine they had on the way out, driving all night and sleeping in shifts, then stopping for a few hours late morning to rest the car.

The scent of something dangerous excited her, she had to admit. Back in her secret service days nothing had compared with the thrill of the chase; both the fugitives she hunted and the men she desired.

She drew her gun, a GSh-18 semi-automatic. Stepan gave her a thin smile and pulled his own weapon, an American-made Glock. In his eyes she recognised the same hunger for action.

'Let's go,' she whispered, after Stepan had woken Boris and ordered him to guard the vehicle. Lena took the lead, climbing up over a drift of snow and moving slowly through an ice-packed field towards the cluster of houses where Stepan had seen the light.

As they approached what appeared to be a small cooperative farming operation, with five outlying houses with barns, sheds and silos scattered among them, Stepan took the lead while Lena covered him, the pair moving in a zigzag to provide cover for each other until they reached the nearest building.

Stepan knelt down while Lena caught up. 'Round there,' he said. 'The barn at four o'clock, second from the right. I saw it again.'

'Inside?'

He nodded. 'It could be dangerous.'

Lena smiled. Danger was the only thing she truly loved. It made her want to fight; it made her want to fuck. It made her want to give up everything for one last rush of adrenaline.

'Let's check it out,' she said.

This time Lena took the lead, wanting to be the first to see inside the shed. Stepan hung back, covering her until she had reached the wall. When she had found a secure position, she waved him forward and he joined her just a few feet from the doorway.

They could hear sounds now, the hiss and click of machinery coming from inside.

'On three,' Lena said. Stepan raised an eyebrow, perhaps querying her order to charge, but he didn't object. He held her gaze as he gave a slight nod.

'On three,' he repeated.

'For Russia,' Lena said. 'For our great nation. For its people, and its ideals.' She stood up, the gun held at her shoulder. 'One, two … three.'

She burst through the door, dropping immediately down to the right, the gun trained in front of her on the cluster of figures in the middle of the room. Stepan followed her in, dropping away to the left, executing a neat roll and coming up behind a pile of boxes.

A few heads had turned towards her, and Lena didn't hesitate, pulling the trigger on the nearest, closing her eyes on the horror as the bullet found a mark.

'Run, Stepan,' she cried. 'Run for your life!'

She broke through the doorway and bolted for the cover of the building they had first approached. The sound of running feet came from behind her, then a mechanical whine followed by a gasp and a heavy thump as something fell, and she knew Stepan wouldn't make it back. Firing her gun back over her shoulder, she reached the corner of the building and ducked around it, making straight for the field and her vehicle beyond. She heard the sounds of pursuit but didn't look back, didn't dare or the fear might freeze her where she stood.

She had kept in shape, but by the time she got within a few metres of the car her strength was almost at an end. 'Start driving!' she screamed at Boris, and for once was thankful for his professionalism. He had jumped into the front and the car was moving forward in a slow crawl as Lena hit the road in a flat out sprint.

Behind her she felt fingers clawing at air as they tried to reach her, but she felt in her heart that she would not be claimed today, that while her own death might await her soon, it would hold off for a short while yet. It was waiting at her shoulder, but it would have to wait a little longer.

She screamed as she caught hold of the door Boris had flung open and pulled herself inside as the engine roared and the car jerked forward.

'What the fuck are they?' Boris was screaming at her, his voice hoarse and cracked. '*What the fuck are they?*'

Lena pulled the door shut and turned to look back. Three shadowy figures were receding into the gloom, the chase abandoned. She couldn't make out their features, but she remembered the cold touch of their fingers on her neck. It was a sensation that would give her nightmares for weeks.

'Where's Stepan?' Boris asked, glancing back as the car bumped along, slowly gaining speed as it left the last traces of civilization behind.

'He didn't make it,' she said. 'I'm sorry.'

'What were those things, Lena?'

She shook her head. Only time would let her make sense of them herself. She gave a slow shake of the head, and let out a long sigh.

'They were the end of everything,' she said. 'The end of us, of Russia, of the world.'

21

THE TIGHTENING NOOSE

PATRICIA AND KUROU WERE SLEEPING, the girl leaning back against a filing cabinet with a dirty blanket draped over her, and Kurou curled up like a stray cat in a space between two junked machines. Patricia was still tied, but despite Kurou's insistence that she suffer, Victor had replaced the rope in her mouth with a strip of softer towel. He had got no thanks for his efforts, but it had eased his conscience a little.

The gas heater gave them a circle of warmth about ten feet wide, beyond which the cold gradually began to set in. They had moved a few cabinets to try to hold the heat in better, but there was little they could do. In truth, Victor had never stayed overnight in the workshop outside of the summer months, and during the winter he worked with the heater stood at his feet. The place was too big to keep adequately warm and while Kurou preferred the cold, Victor was genuinely afraid for himself and Patricia. He had dozed off a couple of times, but he was too worried that the gas would run out and he'd wake up in a room with two corpses.

Or not wake up at all.

At first light they would head for the hills, but under cover of darkness it was too dangerous to attempt the journey, particularly with Patricia refusing to cooperate. The more time he spent with Kurou, the less Victor feared him, regarding him more like a dangerous pet that needed to be controlled. Kurou was still fearsome, but he responded to authoritative commands like a naughty child, and while there were moments when Victor still worried for his life, he had begun to experiment with the tones of his voice to see which ones had the most influence. Victor had got his way with removing Patricia's rope, and also that she have her hands tied around the front instead of the back, but when he had suggested that they set her free, the monster inside Kurou had bubbled back to the surface and Victor had backed down.

It was a strange feeling, being hunted. If Patricia had found Esel's body then others would have by now, and if Kurou was right that someone was watching his apartment then he was a wanted man.

The euphoria he had felt about the prospect of going up to the secret place was dying down. Kurou's genius with machines kept making him forget the rest, that the man was a killer and that they had a hostage in tow. Perhaps there was still part of a child in him, willing to overlook so much bad in order to get a little closer to his dreams. The right thing to do would be to free Patricia and either escape with her, or set her free to alert the authorities to Kurou's presence before he hurt anyone else.

Something wouldn't let him, though. He tried to tell himself it was his own cowardice, but that was a lie. It was Kurou himself. The man was special. Behind the monstrous visage was a person of precocious ability. Victor had lived his whole life in this nowhere town with nothing but his dreams and hopes. Kurou was a living embodiment of possibility. Victor had opened the curtains on to a burning bright sun that was so beautiful he couldn't bring himself to look away, even if at some deeper level it was slowly eating him up.

The heater stuttered. Victor sat up. He stared at it for a few seconds as if willing it to keep on chugging, but the oil gauge was teetering on empty. He would have to find more oil from somewhere, or at least some blankets. There was nothing in the workshop. There was oil at his house, but going back there was too great a risk.

Before he could talk himself out of it, he pulled on his boots and headed for the door. His idea was a stupid one, akin to putting his head into a lion's mouth, but he could think of nothing else. He had been at Isabella's house enough times to know where Mortin hung the key to the outhouse in which his burner oil was kept. It wasn't too far; he could make the trip in twenty minutes if he ran.

He pulled the door open and slipped out into the cold, gasping for breath against the freezing air as he slid the door shut behind him. It was a ridiculous idea—not to mention criminal—but he had talked himself into it. There was no letting go now.

Pulling his hood tightly down over his face, he turned and dashed off into the night.

THERE WERE lights on in Isabella's kitchen as Victor came to a lung-churning stop on the alleyway outside the back of the Mortin house. The locked outhouse stood at the end of an icy path leading down a set of steps from the back door and across what in summertime was a pretty little garden. The key was in a wooden nesting box hanging from the wall beside the door. Why Mortin kept it there, Victor didn't know, but it had always been there and he hoped that Mortin hadn't decided on a whim to change its location.

Half of the path was illuminated by the light from the back kitchen window. Victor wondered if it was wise having lights on after the recent drone strikes, but figured if anyone was in the know about what was going on, it was Robert Mortin. The man had his fingers in more pockets than most people had trousers, a network of connections that had got him far in the mining industry and kept him out of trouble with the government. Isabella rarely talked about her mother, but Victor guessed the same ruthlessness that had made Mortin rich had also made him a widower.

He crept up the path, trying to scuff his feet so that the footprints he had no choice but to leave might be more easily covered over in the event of a fresh fall of snow. He reached the back door and crouched as a shadow fell across the curtains in the window above him, holding his breath even though no sound could be heard through the thick double layer of glass.

Aware that the door might open at any moment, Victor reached up and slipped the key out of its box, putting it in his pocket. When he glanced back up at the window, the shadow had gone, so he crept back down the path and let himself into the shed where Mortin kept his kerosene tanks.

Several were too heavy to lift, but Victor managed to find a five litre plastic canister in a corner and a pump with which to fill it out of one of the larger tanks. He was just stepping out of the shed when he looked up and saw Isabella standing in an upstairs window.

For a few seconds he was dumbstruck, loitering there at the end of the path like a latter day oil commercial version of Romeo, the canister of kerosene a postmodern bouquet of flowers. Isabella went to the window and appeared to place a hand on her heart, as if dreaming of some lost lover, then she swept the curtains shut in a single frantic motion. For a moment Victor thought she had seen him, and he wondered whether he ought to take the chance that Mortin was out and knock on the door. The urge to speak to her was overwhelming, even if it was to incur her wrath at his absence.

And then he turned to leave and realised she had been staring at the two men now blocking his path.

They were both far bigger than him, their wide shoulders and thick chests only exemplified by the thick coats they wore. Hired muscle or underworld henchmen, Victor didn't feel the need to guess, but either way they could crush the life out of him with a single clap of their hands.

If he took them on, he would be squashed like a rotten fruit. If he tried to run they would catch him in seconds.

'Hey,' he said, hearing his own voice detached from his mind as if he had stepped out of his body in anticipation of an unavoidable beating. 'Give the key back to Mortin, would you, if you're going in? It's cold out and I need to get going.'

A hand he couldn't believe was his own flicked the key through the air towards them. The nearest of the two stuck out a hand and caught it, stared at it like an alien object, then put it into his pocket.

'Sure,' he said.

'Tell him I'll bring the tank back in the morning, and say thanks again.'

'Will do.'

Before his courage gave way, Victor hefted the plastic canister, huffing as if it were three times as heavy as it really was, and walked past them without a word into the alley behind the house. He gave an exaggerated sigh, then made a point of trudging loudly through the snow until he had reached an adjoining alleyway. Then, as quick as he could, he pulled the canister into his arms to balance its weight, and took off at the best run he could manage through the snow.

If they followed him he didn't hear it, but his ears were filled with the crunch of his own boots on the icy layer below the freshest snow. He didn't dare look back until he turned into the alley on which his workshop was located, but there was no sign of pursuit. Whatever happened though, sooner or later it would get back to Robert Mortin that a young man had been seen in his back yard late at night, stealing kerosene from his shed.

KUROU WAS STILL SLEEPING, curled tightly in a ball like a giant, hairless mouse when Victor returned. Patricia, however was awake, her eyes wide open, her body shaking with cold. Victor pulled off his coat and laid it over her, then got to work restarting the stove heater. Within a couple of minutes, a slow heat was spreading outwards, and Patricia's teeth had stopped chattering.

Victor knelt down beside her and pulled off her gag. He took one of her hands in his and rubbed her cold fingers against his warm palms.

'I'm sorry,' he said, quietly, fearful that Kurou might wake and overhear. 'I was as quick as I could. You know I would let you go if I could, don't you?'

'I don't know what my sister ever saw in you,' she said. 'You're nothing, a worthless nothing.'

Victor shrugged. 'Like I said, I'm sorry.'

It was quite obvious that Patricia wasn't about to forgive him, so he went over to check on Kurou, but the professor appeared to be soundly asleep.

How long did they have before they were found? Victor had always been secretive about his workshop, with no written record that he was renting it, paying in cash every month to a man so shady that Victor didn't even know his first name. There was nothing in his house to lead anyone here, and nothing here to link it to him. From time to time though, people had seen him come and go, and sooner or later the police would interview one of those people. Victor's skills with computers and electronics had made him well known in Brevik.

He felt like a noose had looped itself around his neck and was slowly closing. There was no way to know what would happen next, but Victor felt sure it was something bad.

Almost as a reflex action, he turned and looked back towards Kurou.

The strange professor had his one good eye open and was watching him. As Victor met his gaze, Kurou widened his mouth into a sinister little smile.

22

THE CLOSING OF TRAPS

IT HAD BEEN unusual for Pavel to hear Lena crying on the other end of the secure line. *Death is coming. It's unstoppable. Get on the last train and get out. Everyone who stays will die.*

Driving as fast as she could, she was a week away, she told him, maybe more, depending on the state of the roads. Some were destroyed, others intact, but of those many were now deep with uncleared snow. She couldn't guess at the speed of the approaching enemy; its advance slow and laborious as it ate up everything in its path, but relentless nonetheless. It was like a rising tide, slowly engulfing their country, and nothing short of the moon might drive it back.

Pavel picked up the phone, dialling a secure line. He asked the voice who answered for the code, listening as always for the length of hesitation before the list of numbers was reeled off.

'Is it ready? We leave for the mainline tomorrow.'

'The rails have been checked as far as Novilorsk. We're trying to assemble enough fuel to ensure we can reach the coast, but it's a journey our trains aren't used to making.'

'It has to be ready.'

'If we can get as far as Irkutsk perhaps we can find a connecting train—'

'No. This is it,' Pavel said. 'This is our last train. There will be no others. Irkutsk will prove no better than staying here.'

'As you wish, sir. I will ensure that the locomotive is as ready as possible. We depart at midday tomorrow as planned.'

Pavel hung up. For a long time after silence had returned to his office, he sat holding the phone receiver in his hand, trying to convince himself he had made the right decision.

For a moment she had dreamed that she had seen him, standing at the end of the garden path, waiting for her. Then the shadow had shifted and become two of her father's goons, come to deliver information or receive orders. Nothing ever changed in her family; her father used bullying and power to get what he wanted, an attitude that Patricia and Esel excelled at. Isabella, though, remembered her kind mother, the sweet eyes and the soft, soothing voice, telling her that a man should be honest and strong, and a woman should be brave and elegant.

Her mother was five years underground, taking her beauty and honesty with her beneath the accumulated years of her husband's merciless goading. Isabella had compartmentalised her parents, and while she had never forgiven her father for his role in her mother's decline into sickness and eventual death, she still loved him for what he was in a world her mother no longer inhabited.

Isabella felt a tiny pang of resentment towards her brother and sister. As twins, they had naturally attracted the majority of her father's attention despite causing the majority of the family's problems. Forced by circumstances to act like a surrogate mother, Isabella was both worried about their safety while enjoying a little more of her father's attention. Wrestling with the guilt of her thoughts had made it difficult to keep calm amidst the storm of having to prepare for leaving, and a double helping of guilt had been layered on when she realised that for a time she had forgotten all about Victor.

Simple ideals were the engine that drove her; the thought of marriage and children and peace, a nice house, a husband coming home at six o'clock and still having the energy to praise the way her hair looked or the dress she was wearing, and to offer her a smile of thanks over the meal she had prepared. Simple dreams for a simple woman, many would say, but Isabella didn't care.

Victor, for all his faults, had been perfect. Hardworking and talented—despite what her father or siblings had often said—he treated her well and she loved him, even if she had never really shown it. He needed to understand that she didn't mean it when she berated at him or told him to get lost, she was just insecure, just testing him. And now he had disappeared.

The horrifying possibility that he might be dead was one she wouldn't allow to muddle her thoughts. If she let it in, she would start to rely on it, make herself believe that the reason he hadn't come to see her was because he was lying beneath a pile of rubble somewhere.

The front door opened downstairs and her father came

stomping in, slamming the door behind him. Isabella had prepared him a light dinner that was probably now cold, and she had been planning to retire soon for the night. Packing for the train had preoccupied her as usual; trying to squeeze everything she might need into a single tiny case was providing her with a headache she didn't need. Still, if her father was tired, now might be a good time to ask him about letting Victor come.

After all, if her brother and sister were missing, surely their spaces would be free—

She cuffed herself around the side of the head. *Isabella, watch your thoughts. That's heinous, thinking like that.*

She headed downstairs to talk to her father, pausing at the living room door when she heard his voice. She cracked the door and peered in. Robert stood by the window, looking out at the street, a telephone receiver pressed to his ear.

'Has he come back? Are you sure? I'm not paying you to sleep.'

He slammed the phone down and uttered a curse that made Isabella blush. She started to open the door, but her father began dialling another number, this time sitting down on an armchair that faced the window and crossing one leg over the other.

'Yes? It's me. I need to talk to you about someone. Victor Mishin.'

Isabella put a hand over her mouth to stifle a cry and crept back out of sight, keeping the door open just enough to overhear.

'I think he might have had something to do with the death of my son and the disappearance of my daughter.'

Isabella clamped her hand tight over her mouth as tears sprang to her eyes. Her brother was dead and Patricia had disappeared? And her father thought Victor was responsible?

'You want evidence? I have it. I have witnesses placing him at the scene of my son's murder and the last place my daughter was seen alive. You get out there and you find that bastard, otherwise I'll take matters into my own hands. And if I find him first he won't make it to trial.'

Isabella could take no more. She turned and stumbled for the stairs, wanting to get to her bedroom and be alone with her sorrow, but she tripped on a bag her father had left in the hall and came down hard, crying out as her knee struck the stone of the bottom step.

'Isabella?'

Robert was standing over her. As Isabella cried out again he reached out and pulled her up, taking her into his arms.

'My daughter, my beautiful daughter,' he said, smoothing her hair back from her face. 'Did you hear that? I'm sorry I didn't tell you, but I didn't know how. That bastard has tricked you. Behind that mild mannered exterior is a cruel and evil man.'

'Father, not Victor!'

Robert half carried her into the living room and helped her down on to the couch. He sat down beside her and put an arm around her shoulders.

'I know this must be hard for you,' he said, 'but Victor Mishin has seduced you with his charms. Clearly he has a vendetta against our family. Perhaps he wants my money? Don't worry, Isabella, I won't let him hurt you. I'll have him strung up outside City Hall before our train leaves, I promise you.'

Isabella said nothing. She listened to the thud of her father's heart beside her ear, the thundering beat that sounded a little like the wheels of a train.

ALEK POLITOV PRESSED his face against the window, cupping his hands to view the darkness outside. He didn't need to use binoculars anymore, the battle raging on the distant hills was played out in an endless series of muzzle flashes and explosions as his brave soldiers tried to hold off an unstoppable enemy. In different circumstances, such an avante garde and decadent fireworks display might have been beautiful.

The room behind him was empty. He had bid his guards leave at the first sign of trouble, and despite the reluctance in their words he had heard the relief in their tone. They had left him food and water, and blankets to ward off the biting cold now that the electricity in the building had been switched off by his departing command crew. Not that he planned to use anything; it was delaying the inevitable.

Better to be halfway dead when the killing machines came.

He hobbled back to his chair and slumped back down again, closing his eyes, pushing his fingers up to his temples and rubbing the old skin there almost ritualistically.

I know you can hear me. You can stop this. Please.

The void seemed endless, his thoughts drifting off into space.

No.

Politov's eyes jerked open. The voice had come like a sudden flare out of the dark. 'So, you hear me after all,' he said. 'I always knew that you did.'

23

TREASURE AND KNOWLEDGE

VICTOR ROUSED Patricia an hour before first light. Kurou was already up, sitting in a chilly corner tinkering with a broken radio receiver that Victor had given up as junk. Whenever Victor looked across at him working, he felt both awed and nauseous. Kurou's fingers were literally a blur, moving so quickly over the component parts, twisting and shaping, reconnecting and discarding, soldering and fusing, that Victor couldn't follow. It was like watching a time-lapse video of a construction process happening right in front of him.

'Will you be quiet if I undo your gag?' Victor asked Patricia, but the girl shook her head. 'I'm sorry then, but I have to leave it on. I hope he'll agree to let you go once we're out of the town, but I don't know. He's … unpredictable.'

The girl muttered some curse that Victor couldn't understand. He figured it was probably just as well that he didn't.

'We have to go,' he said to Kurou, who looked up at him with his head cocked to the side, looking for all the world like a bird that had been disturbed in the middle of a meal. 'The town won't be quiet for long and we have a fair distance to travel.'

The professor picked up the contraption he was working on and put it in a canvas bag which he slung over his shoulder. 'Lead the way, sire,' he said.

VICTOR WENT FIRST, letting Kurou take charge of leading Patricia. At first the girl made a nuisance of herself, then Kurou whispered something to her that seemed to flick a switch in her personality.

Instead of dragging her feet or even trying to sit down, she began to cooperate, walking calmly along between them, her head bowed, not making a sound. Victor didn't want to ask what Kurou had said and the professor didn't offer, but he could get the general gist. He imagined it had something to do with their lack of food and Kurou's obvious taste for human flesh.

Brevik was eerily silent. Victor took them on the same roundabout route he had taken a few days ago, out towards the old café and then up a thin ring-road that arced around the outside of the town before joining up with the mining access road to the north. Victor was alarmed to see the heavy drifts of snow in places; it looked like no one had used these roads for a couple of days. The recent snowfall had been slight, but when the wind got up it caused drifts of fine ice to build up anywhere there was shelter, and in some areas half of the road had drifted three feet deep. It was hard going, and soon they were all exhausted.

Victor called a rest just after the v-shaped tree came into sight. 'We're about halfway there,' he said, but from now on it gets difficult. We have to go off the road.'

'And here,' Kurou said, 'we will let our little bird fly free.'

Patricia looked up at him, frowning. Victor was also surprised. After all, he had assumed Kurou would keep the girl until she was of no further use.

'Untie her, sire, but keep out of range. I get the feeling she bites.'

Patricia struggled as Victor untied her hands and pulled the gag out of her mouth. 'I'll gut you!' she screamed, taking a swing at him, but Kurou's fingers closed over her wrist, turning her away.

'It would be wise not to look this gift horse in its rather beautiful mouth, young princess,' he said. 'One is apt to change one's mind at short notice. Run along now, it's time to catch your train.'

At the mention of the train Victor felt a pang of regret, knowing that he would surely have no chance now of leaving with Isabella. Whether he would see her again he didn't know … but something told him their paths were beginning to diverge, and that from here on he had to make some tough choices. In all likelihood, once Patricia told her sister what a villain he was, he would have no chance to be with her anyway.

'One day I'll see you again and I'll kill you,' Patricia spat, as Kurou dropped her in the snow. She sat there for a few seconds, staring up at him with a petulant defiance in her eyes, then she pushed herself away and broke into a run back down the snowy mining road. Victor watched until she had turned a corner out of sight, then he turned back to Kurou.

'Was that wise? She'll have half the town looking for us.'

Kurou gave him a grotesque smile. 'Where's your trust, sire?

Have I disappointed you yet? One suggests you don't have the foresight that others have. Hold your assumptions a while, won't you?'

'We should go. The faster we leave, the more time the wind has to cover our tracks before Patricia returns with a lynch mob.'

Kurou nodded and gave a short bow. 'After you, sire.'

Victor led them in through the trees to the concealed road that led up to the valley to the secret place. It was hard going, the snow waist deep in places, and with the slow progress Victor was soon freezing cold, even as a pale sun rose above them to cast glittering light over the white landscape.

Half an hour later, they reached the viewing platform. Victor stopped and pointed down into the valley.

'Do you see anything down there? That's where we're going.'

Kurou smiled. 'Into that concealed cave entrance, no doubt.'

'You can see that? I know it's there because I've been down there, but from here....'

Kurou turned to him. 'When God refused me a human face, sire, he compensated me well. I guess you hear nothing but the wind and the rustling of the tree branches, don't you?'

'What else is there?'

Kurou lifted a misshapen eyebrow. 'Too much for you to need to know, sire, while there is still a distance for us to travel.'

'Is there anything else down there? I mean, people or vehicles? The other day I saw a blinking light.'

Kurou shook his head. 'Nothing, sire. But, I'm an old man now. Could be that my sight isn't what it used to be.'

'It's still better than mine.'

Kurou made a snorting sound that could have been a laugh. Victor decided it was time to end the conversation and get moving again. They still had at least another hour of hiking down into the valley.

MIDMORNING HAD COME by the time they reached the valley floor. The snow lay in thicker drifts here, but there was less wind so its depth was more even and it had settled better, allowing for quicker travel. By the time they reached the overhanging rock that concealed the entrance to the secret place, Victor was exhausted. Even Kurou seemed to be panting as he walked alongside.

In front of the jutting rock was a clearing which was usually thick with shrubs in summer, but was now a snow-covered basin. It was probably where vehicles had once parked, and whoever had planted the trees to conceal the access road had felt it unnecessary to hide the parking area too. Victor was pleased to see it still stood empty, and showed no signs that anyone had ever been here. The light he had seen still bothered him though, although there was no sign of it now. If someone had switched it on, they had since switched it off again.

Victor led Kurou under the jutting overhang into a cave space beneath where the snow blown in by the wind was only a few centimetres deep. Out of the sun it was bitterly cold, but the wind could no longer reach them, and surrounded by rock walls clear of snow, Victor felt mentally warmer, even if his body was still shuddering like an old train.

'We've arrived, have we, sire?' Kurou said. 'Best open the door for me, hadn't you?'

The back wall of the cave was abnormally vertical for something supposedly created over millions of years by the elements. The straight up, strangely coloured wall had aroused Victor's interest, made him go over and put out a hand to touch it.

And he had discovered it was a huge, heavy tarpaulin, covered with cement and rock chippings, hung from thick metal bars high above them, covering a huge set of metal doors behind.

It had taken Victor several days to find a way of opening them. He had searched everywhere for some secret opening mechanism or a keypad requiring a password, then in frustration he had jammed a knife into the gap between the doors and they had moved a fraction of an inch, enough to expose a secret that was so obvious he was kicking himself to not notice.

They were set on runners, and with a shove only hard enough to break the runner wheels through years of accumulated dirt, they slid easily back into orifices cut into the rock walls.

'They're a bit stiff,' Victor said. 'On my count, push.'

Ice caught up in the runners made them hard to move, but pushing together Victor and Kurou were able to move one of the doors far enough for them to slip inside. Kurou didn't wait, shimmying through the gap and leaving Victor standing alone outside. Giving Kurou a moment to discover the wonders of the secret place on his own, Victor went back out to the front of the cave and peered down the incline towards the rise they had descended. He couldn't shake a sense of unease, that something was going to go wrong, and as he looked up he thought he saw a shadow move out of sight behind one of the trees. It was so far away that it could have been a trick played on him by his tired eyes, but he didn't want to stay outside any longer, just in case someone out there in the woods had seen them.

As he turned back towards the door, he spotted the source of the light.

Set into the rock above his head, a bulb covered by a plastic cover about the size of a shoe was trying to flash through a crust of ice and snow that had built up over it, probably blown on to it by the wind. It was still working, something that unnerved Victor immensely. There was no sign that anyone had been here, but that didn't mean anything; there could be other entrances.

Victor slipped back inside the entrance and gasped.

The power was on.

A tall, sterile room with several doors leading off was illuminated by strip lighting. Victor had always used a torch when he came here.

A door to the left was open, a trail of dirty footprints on grey tiles marking Kurou's passage. Victor hurried after him, worried that Kurou might have run into danger.

The lights were on everywhere. Victor jogged down corridors far higher than his head, past numerous doors that led to empty offices and workshops stripped of their equipment. Last summer, he had explored this place a few rooms at a time, thinking for a while that it was abandoned and emptied out. It was a vast underground base, the corridors and chambers stretching for miles into the side of the hill, in places looking like the inside of some office building or hospital, in others hewn straight out of the rock.

And it was completely deserted.

But it wasn't empty.

On his third day of exploring, he had got up the nerve to descend into the depths, where he had come to a sealed door opened only with a keypad password. Walking almost bowlegged beneath the weight of his curiosity, Victor had wired up a battery to briefly power the door's electrics and used a computer tablet with a password breaking program to get the door open. He had then secured it with a series of large rocks he had carried down from outside.

What he had found inside had both terrified and thrilled him.

He found Kurou standing at the bottom of the steps, just inside the door which was still propped open. Kurou was statue-still, his hands clasped in front of him, his head craning forward.

'Kurou?'

The other man didn't move. Victor took a few steps forward until he could see Kurou's face.

He was crying.

With the lights on the cavern was more impressive than he had ever seen by torchlight, fifty feet high and several hundred long and wide, a space hewn out of bare rock. Overhead fans now hummed, and the icy, subterranean air that Victor remembered even during the summer months had been replaced by something like warmth as ancient air conditioners cranked back into action.

'What is this place, sire?' Kurou moaned. 'Have I died? Have I died, sire?'

Victor had felt a similar sense of euphoria as he walked along the aisles of the great cavern, swinging his torch across its contents.

'It's a storage facility,' he said. 'I'm guessing it is owned by the government. Why they decided to seal it away and disguise the approach road is anyone's guess.'

In front of them, illuminated by bright strip lighting in the walls and roof, and large panels set into the floor, robots and machines and other kinds of military equipment stood lined up in rows, hundreds upon hundreds of them. To their left were huge caterpillar tread machines that looked like futuristic tanks, while to their right were hundreds of metal body suits hung on great rails several deep. The aisle directly in front of them was lined by metal cases and wooden crates, which Victor had discovered on his previous visits contained tools and parts, many of which were beyond description.

He had camped out here for several days at a time last summer, spending his time wandering around, trying to make sense of the place. The vast majority of the equipment was too heavy to move, so he had contented himself with picking through the boxes of old tools and computer equipment, poaching as much as he could carry to take back to his workshop. He had felt like a thief, but from the rust around the edges of many of the machines he could tell no one had come here in decades.

'The greatest toyshop in the world,' Kurou suddenly screamed, his arms high over his head like a mad professor. Before Victor could respond, he had dashed off down the wider central aisle, screaming at the top of his voice.

Victor didn't know what to make of it. The spindly body receded towards the rear of the cavern, then Kurou was gone, vanishing into one of the side aisles. His footsteps echoed off the countless rows of war machines like the notes of a piano built from old car parts.

It was some minutes before Kurou returned, huffing and puffing from an aisle to the left, his coat fallen off his shoulders to hang around his waist like some gypsy shaman.

'Sire, we must get to work.'

'Doing what? We came here to hide.'

Even as he said it, he wasn't sure he believed it. He had wanted Kurou to see this place, just as he had wanted to meet the strange man who had been fixing up his battered old machines. He couldn't get over the childlike view that he was in the presence of some kind of Santa Claus of machines, and that what he could learn from Kurou might change his life forever.

'There are workshops, yes? Computer mainframe rooms? Testing chambers?'

Victor nodded. 'The upper floors are all research laboratories. Some of them are filled with machines I couldn't guess at the use of. Others are filled with scientific equipment. I always got the impression that this place had been left ready for use in the case of a future war. One rather like the one we have going on right now. At least so it seems.'

'Joy and jubilee,' Kurou said. 'More candy than a crow could ever want.'

'I don't think we should touch anything. I only ever took a few tools and a couple of old computer parts. There are whole rooms just full of junk.'

'You are too meek, sire,' Kurou said. 'This is a goldmine shining so bright I fear for my poor remaining eye.'

He rushed off again before Victor could respond, disappearing into the aisles. Victor sat down on the ground beside Kurou's bag to wait, unsure what to do next. Bringing them here had been the extent of his plan. It was the only safe place he knew of, and he had to hope that the city council didn't know about it either. With the last train set to leave this afternoon, he was beginning to think they were in the clear. Even if Patricia had followed them long enough to discover the entrance to the secret place, she wouldn't have time to get back to town and bring help before the train left. If she wanted to escape, she had to go soon.

It was quite possible that by tomorrow the town would be near-deserted, inhabited only by wraiths and those too poor to buy their way on to the train. If this place had remained hidden for so long, there was a chance the approaching enemy might roll right over the top of them without ever knowing they were here.

On the floor beside him lay the bag Kurou had brought. Victor reached out and picked it up.

Something inside was giving off a faint clicking noise.

He reached inside and pulled out the old radio from his workshop. He had never been able to get it to work, but now an LED was flashing red. The tuning control had been ripped out and replaced with a click button that Kurou had taped down. Victor had no idea what Kurou had done, but it had been tuned to a station broadcasting in a computer language Victor didn't recognise. He was about to press the button to see what happened, but he thought better of it and put it back down just as Kurou reappeared.

'Your radio is making clicking noises,' Victor said.

Kurou sat down on the floor beside him. 'Very interesting indeed, yes,' he said.

'What is?'

'This.' He pointed at the radio.

'What's that sound?'

'Binary, sire. Computer language. These are commands being relayed from a mainframe to the drones it controls.'

'What radio frequency is that?'

'Digital, sire. A secure line.'

'How can that radio—'

'I made a few adjustments, added a couple of components from some you had lying around. I calibrated the coordinates to where I suspected the mainframe computer was based, and intercepted all digital signals within a certain area. Easy peasy, sire.'

'And you can understand what its saying?'

Kurou leaned theatrically towards the radio and cupped a bony hand behind his ear.

'If I pay attention, sire. Fluency isn't my strong point, but I can get the general gist.'

Victor gave a disbelieving shake of the head. Understanding binary by ear? That was quite a skill.

'And what's it telling the drones to do right at the moment?'

Kurou smirked. 'It's telling them to bomb a railway line about five miles east of here.'

24

LIES AND BLACK STAINS

ROBERT WOKE from a fitful sleep to find himself slumped on the sofa with the manila envelope of photographs scattered on the floor around him, an empty bottle of vodka lying on its side in the middle.

It was already midmorning, a cold sun breaking through a gap in the curtains. He got up just as the door opened and Isabella appeared, carrying a tray of food and coffee.

Her eyes were bloodshot, her face sore.

'I thought we should have a good breakfast on our last day here,' she said, giving him a weak smile.

Her resolution reminded him of how much he did love her, even if she was a weaker prototype of his second beloved daughter.

'I know this has been hard for you, Isabella—'

'Hard?' She looked about to say something else but bit her tongue. 'It is what it is, Father.'

'That doesn't mean I'm happy about the situation. Victor Mishin might not have been my choice for you, but before this terrible business...' He shrugged. 'I guess there were worse possible suitors.'

'The train leaves at twelve, Father. I packed some things for you.'

Her organisation was impressive. In the midst of trying to find his other children, he had done nothing for himself. In truth, he couldn't see himself leaving until he knew what had happened to Patricia. There might be no more trains, but he had all-terrain vehicles up at the mine. He could use one of those—

A knock came on the back door. Isabella turned white, and looked about to drop the tray, so Robert took it from her and put it down on the table in the corner.

'Stay here,' he said, heading for the kitchen.

It was Papanov and Franko. Their eyes were bloodshot, as if they'd not slept. One of them kept coughing as if he'd contracted influenza overnight.

'Do you have proof?'

'We found a busted up chimney around the back of the Lenin Building,' the first said. 'Looks like someone escaped from that basement apartment after all.'

'Patricia? Then where is she?'

We found tracks, looked like three people,' Papanov said. 'Difficult to tell with tracks in the snow. Looked like boots, couldn't be sure of the size.'

'Do you have anything solid for me or not?'

Franko sneered. 'Did your daughter have a favourite colour, sir?'

'Blue.'

Franko reached into his pocket and pulled out a square of blue cloth, holding it up. There was a black stain in the middle. 'Looks like a handprint of soot smeared a bit by the snow to me,' he said. 'Wouldn't you say it looks like a message? Perhaps a cry for help?'

Robert snatched the cloth out of the man's hand and stared at it, turning it over, running his fingers over it. The so-called handprint was more of a smudge, barely discernible as anything. It was true, though, that Patricia's favourite colour was blue. As a small child he had taken her ice fishing, and she had spent hours just gazing down at the surface. He remembered her asking him, rather sinisterly, 'Is my heart that colour, Daddy? Because I wish it was.' He had assured her that her heart was red like the comic book hearts in the books she had liked to read, but by her early teens he was not so sure.

If it really was a sign from Patricia that she lived, like the handkerchief found in the basement apartment that was definitely hers, then she was still out there somewhere. Papanov and Franko had done what he asked, proving that she was still alive, even if the cost to Robert had been high.

'The train leaves at two,' he said, holding the first man's gaze. 'The station doors will open at one. When you arrive ask for me.'

A smile spread from one man to the other. 'Thank you, sir,' Papanov said. 'We'll spend the time beforehand looking for your daughter, just as a service to you. I can't promise we'll find her, though.'

'Knowing that she lives is a grace you have given me,' Robert said. 'Thank you.'

'We'll see you at one,' the first man answered. He tipped his hood to Robert, then they headed back down the path.

As Robert closed the door and turned around, he gasped at the sight of Isabella standing just a few feet behind him.

'Was that wise, Father? If they find out you lied to them—'

'Those men are common thugs,' Robert said. 'I paid them well. I owe them nothing more, and the train is full. They can die here with the rest of the worthless.'

'But what about Patricia?'

'I will stay behind and wait for her.'

'No, Father! What about me?'

He put his hands on her arms. 'Isabella, you are a grown woman now. You can look after yourself. If your sister has been kidnapped, I have to stay behind to look for her. I wouldn't abandon you, and I can't abandon her.'

'You *are* abandoning me!'

'I'm sending you to safety!'

Isabella thumped her small fists against his chest, then turned and fled upstairs, sobbing into her hands. Robert sighed and headed for the living room. He was just opening the door when a light on the stove heater began to flash, signalling that it was out of fuel.

He thought about heading out on to the streets to look for Patricia, but Isabella would probably come downstairs soon to collect a few mementoes from the shelves, and it was minus fifteen outside, even at ten a.m. In all likelihood, he had no hope of finding Patricia before the train left, so it wouldn't hurt to fill the heater up before he headed out.

But when he went to take the key from the little bird box outside the back door, he found it missing.

Frowning, he headed down the back path, wondering if he had left it in the door to the shed. The footprints of the two goons were still fresh on the path, and Robert scowled, thinking again about how much money he had paid, and what he had promised them, all for a little empty hope.

The door to the shed hung ajar. Feeling his anger begin to rise, Robert went inside and looked around.

A five-litre plastic container was missing.

Footsteps on the ground led back outside. It looked like one set, but he couldn't be sure, as they seemed to mingle with the two lines that led up to his back door. Perhaps one of them had stood guard while the other stole the gas. From the look of the footsteps, they had probably done it last night before they came to see him.

Manipulation was something Robert understood, because he had employed it on many occasions. Straight out theft though, that was low.

He hurried out of the back gate, looking up and down the alley for Papanov and Franko, angry enough to ring out a thumping drumbeat on their faces, but it was empty. For a moment he just stood there, weighing up his options, whether to attempt to find them or to give up and go back inside.

He was just turning away when something yellow lying in the snow a few feet up the alley caught his eye.

It was a square of cloth with a black stain in the middle. When he bent down to pick it up, he found two more: one green, one red.

The bastards had tricked him. They had taken a chance on Patricia's favorite colour being a common one and it had paid off. Now they thought they had bought themselves a ride out of town on a lie.

There was no proof then, that Patricia was alive. It was all a set up to exploit him, and he had fallen for it.

They would die for this.

He headed back inside, slamming the door behind him. The clock on the mantel read ten forty.

They had nothing else to wait around for.

'Isabella, get your bags,' he shouted up the stairs. 'We're leaving for the station.'

She came running out to the landing. 'You've changed your mind? You're coming with me?'

He hesitated just a moment before he gave a reluctant nod. In all likelihood, Patricia was dead. If he stayed behind, he would join her. There were vehicles up at the mine that might get him a few miles, but the train was their only real chance.

'Hurry up, now,' he said. 'We don't have much time.'

25

———

THE LAST TRAIN OUT OF HELL

PATRICIA FOUND herself using more energy to kick at trees than for walking. The icy blue sheet of the sky provided the best visibility in days, but all it did was show her how much further she had to go.

It had been a surprise that they had freed her. She had expected at some point to die at the evil one's hands, the same way her brother had, but she would have drawn as much blood as she could. Her hatred for Victor paled in comparison to the way she despised Kurou. If there was one thing she could do in her life it would be to see him die.

The words he had whispered into her ear would remain with her always.

I saw the light fade from your brother's eyes, and I laughed at him. One day I will watch the light fade from yours too, princess.

Her brother's murderer could not be allowed to live.

As soon as she was out of sight, she had doubled back and crept after them, following as they made their way up the rise through the forest, then watching them from a viewing point as they continued down into the valley. She had hoped for a chance to ambush them, but the trees were so far apart she couldn't get close enough.

Still, she had seen where they went: into a cave down in the valley. She had waited for fifteen minutes or so and seen Victor briefly appear again, only to head back inside. So, they were planning to hide out up here. She guessed that Victor had arranged for some food and heating materials, otherwise it was suicide, but it was obvious they would be staying long enough for her to get help.

Her memory of the days before her capture was hazy. There was a train leaving town sometime—was that today or tomorrow?

She thought it was tomorrow. She had time to find her father, get a group of men together to catch—and if she had her way, kill—Victor and Kurou, and still make the train out of here.

Her brother's eyes would haunt her, but it was the best she could do.

It was close to noon when she finally made it to the outskirts of town. Her thighs were aching from hiking through the knee-deep snow, and her lungs were burning as if she had run a marathon. The town looked deserted. A few cars were parked along the roadside, but she saw no sign of any people. Brevik was rarely busy, but by now there should be some sign of life, a door slamming, the muffled voice of a woman berating her husband, a gang of children playing in the street.

At first she thought she'd mistaken the day and that the train had already left, but as she got further into the town she heard a low humming sound, like the roar of a distant football match.

She had mistaken the day, but that was not all.

Heart pounding, she broke into the best run her tired legs could manage, heading for the train station that dissected the town nearly in two, running in an east-west arc a couple of streets south of City Hall.

Finally, she began to see signs of people, family groups standing outside their houses, husbands comforting crying wives, men berating each other, groups of children playing in the snow oblivious to what was going on.

The old Soviet-era station was up ahead. Rounding a corner, she came upon a great mass of people, several hundred, crowding around the entrance. People were screaming abuse at others that were out of sight, demanding entrance, demanding access to the train.

'What's happening?' she asked an old man near the back.

'The bastards have sold out our lives,' he screamed at her, not turning around. 'They're leaving us to die.'

'Who are?'

'The lucky ones,' he shouted back. 'I worked fifty years in those fucking mines with barely a day off and this is my recompense—to be left behind to die.'

She didn't have much time. Her father would get her on to the train, but she had to somehow get past the mob and into the station. She started to skirt around the back of the crowd, heading for the left corner of the building, hoping to find some other way inside.

'Look! There's Patricia Mortin!'

Patricia turned before she could check herself. A middle-aged man near the back of the crowd was pointing at her, pushing at someone else's shoulder, trying to get his companion's attention. She recognised the first man as a money launderer she had met in the bars in the backstreets opposite the station. For a suitable fee she had warmed his bed a couple of times before finding better opportunities elsewhere, but clearly the cost of her body was a fraction of the value of her life.

'Grab her!'

Several other men had taken notice of the money launderer's words. After a few seconds of confusion, a group broke out of the crowd and began to give chase.

Patricia stared in dismay. Perhaps they thought to use her to bribe their way on to the train, or maybe they thought she was in possession of some golden train ticket that they could steal, but Patricia had had enough of being someone's prisoner. She turned and bolted for the nearest side street.

The backstreets around the station had been her haunt since she was old enough to understand how easy it was to manipulate and exploit the kind of men who frequented the bars. She knew every nook and cranny, every blind alley, every fire escape that offered a shortcut on to an adjacent street. Within a couple of minutes she had lost her pursuers, but as she slowed again to a walk she knew that she had missed her chance.

The train was about to leave, taking her father and sister away with it.

She was alone.

'WERE you going to tell me? Goddamn it, were you?'

Kurou just cocked his head. 'Tell you what, sire?'

'About the drone strike on the train!'

'What matter is it to you, sire?'

'All those people will die!'

Kurou shrugged. 'So?'

'What do you mean, *so?*'

Kurou put a hand on Victor's shoulder and leaned close. Victor tried to stare into the man's single working eye rather than let his gaze drift over Kurou's misshapen face.

'You know as well as I that there's no one on that train worth saving.'

'My girlfriend will be on it!'

Kurou shrugged again. 'Replaceable.' With a smirk he added, 'She'll need to be, because those drones don't tend to miss.'

'We have to stop the train!'

Kurou started laughing. 'In my younger days I shared your invincibility, sire. I thought I was unstoppable, that there was nothing I couldn't control.' He spread his hands. 'And look what happened to me.'

'There must be something we can do.'

Kurou shook his head. 'Sometimes the only thing we can do is watch.'

Victor jumped up. He looked around him at the rows of ancient machines, all silent and cold. There had to be another exit to this place, somewhere the machines could leave. They couldn't have been constructed down here. If one of them worked....

He ran over to the nearest vehicle, a huge people carrier with wheels as high as his waist. He climbed up on to a foot step and yanked at the door to the cab.

Nothing happened except a shudder of pain ran through his shoulders. It was either locked or rusted solid.

He jumped back down, rubbing at his shoulder. Kurou had sat down on the floor and was watching him like a school kid at a pantomime, hands propping up his tilted face. When Victor glared at him Kurou just shrugged.

This was no use. If these machines could be used for anything it might take days to get them operational. There was no telling how long they had sat here in this freezing subterranean chamber.

Victor did a couple of calculations in his head. After it left the town, the train line angled north for a while before it cut back towards the southeast and the Trans-Siberian mainline two hundred miles distant. For a mile or so it ran alongside the northern highway. The nearest of the mining operations was a short distance north of here. There was bound to be an access road running alongside the train line somewhere. If Victor could steal a vehicle big enough to block the train line—

'I have to go.'

Kurou raised an eyebrow. 'Where?'

'I have to help them. I don't expect you to care, but I can't just stand by and do nothing.'

Kurou shrugged again. 'Godspeed, sire. I'll see if I can't poach us a few forest creatures for a little barbeque upon your safe return.'

Victor had no patience for Kurou's eccentricities. He shot the professor a sour look then raced for the stairs, taking them three at a time.

Outside, the beaming midday sun seemed to be mocking him. It would take him at least an hour to retrace his steps, by which time it would likely be all over. He'd be picking through the burnt out remains, looking for pieces of Isabella.

Then he noticed a gully a short way north of the cave entrance. It angled up the hillside, then fed into what looked like a series of switchbacks that headed up the hill and disappeared into the trees on the crest.

Perhaps it was a hiking trail. The hill faced away from the wind on that side, so the snow cover was lighter. It was probably still a couple of feet, but it would save him time.

Taking a deep breath, Victor started running as quickly as he could for the foot of the gully.

———

HE WAS RIGHT. Less than twenty minutes later he reached the top of the rise, squatted down in exhaustion, and turned to look back at the valley below. From here the overhanging rock was invisible, blending in with the valley floor. Although buried in snow, the trail he had climbed up had felt manmade under his feet, crude steps hewn out of the hillside.

A few minutes later he waded out of the trees on to the road. He was close to the end of his strength, but finding the snow cover much lighter underfoot spurred him on, and he broke into a staggering jog as he headed for the nearest of the mining fields. Massive billboards began to appear beside the road, advertising the copper and zinc mines in the area. To the naked eye Siberia might have appeared to be a wild, snow-covered wilderness, but beneath the ground were riches beyond compare.

When he reached the mining operation he headed straight for the nearest line of loading trucks, but found that the transmission lines had been cut on all of them, as if the departing mining crews had wanted to leave them unusable by the invading armies.

Time was running out. Becoming desperate, he circled around the back of several squat, temporary offices, looking for personal vehicles.

Several old four-wheel-drive cars were parked up against the edge of an old slag heap. Victor ran over and tugged on doors, trying to find one that was open. He was near the end of the line before his frustration got the better of him and he used a rock to smash the window of an old Ford pick-up truck.

Most of the newer cars were thief-proof, designed to lock down their systems if an improper starting method was employed. Victor didn't have the skills to hotwire one, so the old pickup, with its cracked windscreen and rusty wheel rims, was his only hope.

He had just climbed in and got the engine started when some sixth sense caused him to look up.

Far above him, three black specks were moving across the clear blue sky.

Pavel had organized a small militia, but as the crowd locked outside the train station bayed for the head councillor's blood, he wished he'd hired a few more.

Most of those authorised with passes had already arrived and boarded: three hundred members of the city's elite and those others rich enough to fill Pavel's palms with enough favour to buy their way on. The word had been passed around to arrive at a certain place and time, and Pavel's hired guns had ensured that the station was open long enough for them to enter. Now, with the doors closed and barricaded, he was waiting on a last few engine checks before they could depart.

Gunshots had already sounded from the east. Hired mercenaries were protecting the line from potential saboteurs. He had promised them a ride; they would find out too late about a politician's promises.

Even up front in the arbitrary first class carriage, the seats were full and the aisles were packed. Pavel had to push and shove just to make it up to the driver's cab. Outside on the platform, a fight had broken out among a group of people struggling to get on.

The door to the carriage opened suddenly and a thin-faced, overdressed girl climbed on, followed by a thickset man in his early fifties with short cropped hair and a chiselled chin. The cold grey of his eyes marked him as a Siberian man born and bred, hard and uncompromising like the landscape which had brought him kicking and screaming into the world. For a transferred Moscovite like Pavel, he felt the automatic need to take a step back and give this man space.

Unfortunately, there was nowhere to go.

Robert Mortin took one look at him and unleashed a punch that Pavel didn't even see coming. As he slumped to his knees, his vision blurring, his skull reverberating from the blow, he waited for Mortin to speak, but no words came. They didn't need to. He had felt the town's satisfaction in Mortin's fist.

As the mining foreman and his daughter pushed past him to look for seats, Pavel climbed to his feet and knocked hard on the door to the cab.

'It's time,' he shouted, his jaw throbbing, possibly broken.

It was going to be a long journey, he thought. In more ways than one.

THE SEATS her father had reserved were at the back of the first class carriage. Three people were sitting in their berths, but after her father had knocked the town mayor to his knees, they got up and moved without a word.

'Take the window seat,' her father said, guiding her with his hand on her shoulder. 'I have to talk to some people. If anyone tries to take your seat, shoot them.'

Her eyes widened as he pushed a small pistol into her hand. It was barely long enough to extend beyond her palm, the kind of weapon that while deadly over a few feet was useless at any kind of range.

She didn't like the idea of killing someone, but as her father headed off down the aisle, the other passengers nearby made a point of keeping their distance, their eyes down, not looking at her.

Hopefully her father would be back soon.

She tried to look out of the window to take her eyes off things, but the platform was a melee of pushing, shoving people, some with tickets, others who had managed to sneak in and were trying to bribe their way on. Men with assault rifles walked up and down the platform, but many looked uncertain, untrained, as if the position of guarding the train had been thrust on them at short notice. Everything seemed on the verge of a meltdown, a rope twisted so far it was set to fray and break.

If only Victor was here, she thought. He had always been such a calming influence on her.

As she thought about his kind eyes and the way he had always treated her with care and respect, tears sprang to her eyes. She had never been nice to him, always expecting him to compromise his nature to put up with her tantrums and moods.

She promised herself that if she ever saw him again, she would tell him how much she loved him.

Outside, the men walking past on the platform appeared to be sliding, caught on a freeze frame that was shifting out of view, and she realised the train had begun to move. Where was her father? She had promised to stay in her seat, even though her gut instinct was telling her to get up and go and find him.

Instead, she pressed her face to the window and watched the town and everything she had ever known slowly slipping away.

IN AN EMPTY ROOM not far from the main entrance, Kurou found something that made his heart thunder with excitement. A bank of machines, coin operated, all offering pre-packaged culinary delights the like of which he hadn't tasted in half a decade. Chicken fried rice, spaghetti with meatballs, pork curry, beef goulash ... the list was endless.

For a while he forgot all about young Victor with his hotheaded dreams of heroism as he headed down into the bowels of the research facility, looking for a way to turn the water back on and transform the packets of dried nothingness into actual real food.

With the machines finally operational, he busted open the coin banks and scrapped the rust off the few coins he found left behind. The mechanisms were gummed up and lethargic with age, but after a few false starts he got one of the machines to work.

An **LED** countdown timer informed him that he had three minutes to wait for his meal.

When the **READY** light flashed, accompanied by an ancient musical jingle that was slurred and out of tune, Kurou did a little dance of joy.

For his first meal he had gone with a simple beef stew and mashed potatoes. The smell when he opened the little plastic box was enough to tell him that the decades of disuse had left even dried food a lot to be desired, but for a man used to dining on the dried meat of murdered drug addicts, it was gourmet indeed.

Delighted at the way the stodge masquerading as beef and mash warmed his hollow stomach, he ordered a second portion.

As he sat down at a plastic trestle table to eat, he wondered how young Victor was getting on in his attempt to save the world.

26

DISASTER IN THE SNOW

SHE WAS TRAPPED HERE. As Patricia stood on the street and watched the last train carriage passing through the level-crossing three hundred metres distant, she felt a great pair of hands pressing down on her shoulders. An immense feeling of failure fought to push her to her knees, but she resisted, grabbing hold of a nearby lamp post for support as her legs sagged beneath her.

Never before had she felt so hopeless, so saturated with despair. The train was gone, and she was trapped here with the dregs of Brevik's humanity, the leftovers, the unwanted, the rejected.

It wasn't in her nature to give up. Life had never been easy, but she had always squeezed the best out of it, but now she had to face her greatest challenge.

Her house was just a couple of streets away. When she arrived, she found the front door locked, as if her father had just gone on a short vacation. Breaking in through a window at the front would likely be a calling card for every potential vandal in the area, so she took the subtler option and broke in round the back, smashing the kitchen window and climbing inside.

The house was nearly as cold as the street, and the oil in the living room had run out. The stove's lid was open as if her father had planned to refill the kerosene, but had never got to it.

Patricia switched on the television, but the banality of the rerun dramas and documentaries made a dozen years ago was too much for her to handle. There was a computer on a desk in the corner, so she opened it, but the screen had been smashed with a hammer. With a frustrated sigh she pushed it aside.

On a table by the window she found a scattering of photographs. She picked one up, and nearly screamed as she saw a grainy image of Kurou's fireplace, a pile of dirty blankets on the ground in front of it.

People had searched for her, and managed to trail her to Kurou's apartment. What did her father think had happened to her since then? Did he think she was dead?

In a fit of anger, she ripped the cluster of photographs into pieces, tossing them away across the floor. In a cupboard against one wall she found a bottle of her father's vodka, and took a couple of long swigs before flinging it across the room.

The sound of it breaking against the wall was so loud it frightened her, and she staggered a few steps backwards, still feeling the burn of the vodka in her throat, and bumped into a corner cupboard, knocking the door open.

Something rattled inside, followed by a metallic thud. Frowning, Patricia turned around and peered inside.

Her eyes widened at the sight of something she had never seen before.

On numerous occasions she had sneaked into her father's drinks cabinet. Sometimes for the thrill of it, other times because in her early days of trolling the bars by the station she had needed a little courage to do what she did for the fistfuls of cash she craved. Other times she had picked though the cupboards in the bedroom looking for old Soviet loot passed down from her grandparents that her father had collecting dust. Old watches and war medals, antique computer equipment and fine, still-boxed pairs of boots; all of it had collected good prices in the back rooms of bars, where people passing through Brevik gathered to see what treasures they could accumulate before hopping on the next train out of town.

The living room cupboards, however, which contained various knickknacks of family life, china plates and framed photographs, rows of books and movie discs and some old Communist statuettes complete with their engraved slogans and rallying cries, had never interested her. If there was no gain, Patricia could spare no time for anything.

In the corner cupboard, a stack of her father's old books had collapsed, revealing something hidden behind.

A rifle.

Patricia shoved the rest of the books aside and pulled it out. There were a couple of boxes of ammunition back there too, with some other musty objects that looked to be used for cleaning or dismantling it. There was also a strap that fitted into two clasps on the gun's side.

Patricia knew little about guns. The thought of using it unnerved her until she closed her eyes and saw Kurou's ugly face, heard that sarcastic laugh.

And she thought of her brother, lying dead in the snow, and she knew what she had to do.

THE VEHICLE SEEMED ONLY capable of driving in second gear. Every time Victor tried to change up, it wheezed and spluttered as if preparing to die on him, the wheels would spin in the icy ruts in the road and his breath would catch in his throat until the gears caught again and the car leapt forward.

Half a kilometre south of the mining operation Victor found the train tracks. They were glistening in the sun, cleared of the overnight ice by the thundering of dozens of wheels. The train had already left, perhaps just minutes before. Up in the sky, the circling dots were almost invisible to the naked eye, but they were up there nonetheless, biding their time, waiting for their orders and calculations to align.

He found the small road that followed the train line, used for maintenance access during the warmer months, but it was covered with a thick blanket of snow that reached Victor's waist. For a car it was impassable.

Heading back the way he had come, he returned to the mining operation and then carried on north towards the highway that the mining trucks used to transport their ore to larger cities in the west and east.

Potholes and seemingly random drifts of snow made the journey hazardous even at just a few miles per hour. Soon Victor's arms were aching from jerking the tired vehicle from side to side, and as he found himself rounding yet another heap of snow, with the remains of a wrecked vehicle protruding out from underneath, he wondered whether he ought to turn back.

And then he crested a rise and far below him he saw the train, chugging slowly along between hills of white peppered with snow-veiled trees.

The hillside dropped away towards the distant train line, but the highway arced back around to the south, heading away. Victor stared in dismay at the road ahead, blocked with rubble, overturned cars and more snow than he ever wanted to see again. The hillside angling down towards the train line was open and clear of trees, perhaps a vegetable field in summer. The cold had packed and hardened the older snow, and the wind had stripped the freshest layer away. From here it looked as smooth as a ski run. Victor stared at it, wondering whether he had enough luck left to take a chance.

Then something whizzed over the top of the car and Victor

caught a glimpse of a grey smear just before it slammed into the side of the slowly moving train.

ROBERT HAD RETURNED to sit beside Isabella as the train moved out of the station, finally leaving the sound of gunshots and the rioting crowds behind. She kept her hands on her lap and her eyes politely on the snowy landscape outside, trying to focus on the small things —the trees, a protruding fence post, a rundown shed in the corner of a field—anything rather than close her eyes and go searching for Victor's face.

It didn't matter what her father claimed. Victor wasn't a killer and he wasn't a kidnapper. Whether it was in his nature or not wasn't in question; he was simply too meek, too shy, too much of a pushover. And Isabella realised, as she watched their life together receding behind her, that all the things she had outwardly hated were the very things that made her love him. He was a fool and a dreamer, but he had belonged to her, and she had left him behind to die.

A wave of nausea began to accelerate up her throat, and Isabella jerked to her feet.

'Bathroom,' she gasped in response to her father's astonished stare.

'You can't,' he said, motioning towards the crowds filling every available space, but Isabella wasn't to be denied. If her final act of rebellion before accepting the role of submissive refugee was to push and shove her way to a place where she could vomit in peace and privacy, then so be it.

It took some effort, but she finally made it to the end of the carriage and the small cubicle lodged into the space where the carriages joined. Someone had taken up residence in there, using the toilet as a spare seat, but Isabella remembered her old way with charm, and a few kind words got the man to move.

She went inside, closed the door, and then the world quite literally turned upside down.

EACH OF THE six carriages took a direct hit, the missiles striking and exploding in a rapid line from left to right like a firework chain reaction. Victor's scream was lost over the roar as the train became an elongated fireball. Shoving the reluctant vehicle into gear, Victor swung the car on to the top of the downward slope and floored the accelerator.

Accumulating snow and ice quickly clogged the wheels, and the car ground to a halt a few hundred metres short of the smoking inferno that had once been a train. Victor kicked the door open and climbed out, struggling across the snow towards the burning carriages.

His initial terror that everyone had been killed was quickly relieved by the sight of a few dazed passengers stumbling around in the snow. The first three carriages had derailed and rolled over, the impact with the snow helping to stem the spread of the flames. The rear three had remained on the tracks, and as a result the fire was raging strongest there, giving off a heat that made them hard to approach.

As he staggered through the snow he tried to find the strength to scream Isabella's name. He stumped towards the front of the train where the damage was lightest, with a vague plan to start there and work his way back. Even in the face of this tragedy he wouldn't let the mathematical part of his mind lose control. If he let his heart mislead him he might have no chance of finding Isabella at all.

He was within ten metres of the first carriage when a hand reached up out of the snow and grabbed hold of his ankle.

Victor cried out and tried to stumble sideways, but the grip was strong and he succeeded only in crashing down into the snow. As he twisted around he found himself staring into the bloody, charred remains of Robert Mortin's face.

'You bastard,' Mortin wheezed, blood splattering on the snow around him. 'This was your fault, wasn't it?'

27

A GAME OF CAT AND CROW

PATRICIA FOUND that pulling the trigger and ending someone's life was remarkably easy when you no longer had any care for your own.

As the young man sprinted across the icy street towards the car that had been left idling with its doors flung open, Patricia lifted the gun, aimed at the young man's chest, and fired.

He jerked and spun in midair, his arms flailing and his legs kicking out. Patricia screamed soundlessly, the roar from the gun so loud that everything else around her cut out, replaced by a ringing hiss that wrapped itself around her head like a rubber shawl.

She didn't hear the thump as the young man's body struck the ground, his limbs still twitching.

She rubbed her aching shoulder as she dashed for the car. She wondered if this was what dislocation felt like, a dull thud of misplaced blood that throbbed so hard she though her skin would burst. She wanted to rub it more, but she had the gun in one hand and needed the other to pull the car door shut.

It was as freezing inside the car as it was out. The sub-zero temperatures had done their work wherever they could, icing up the windscreen, the side windows, and the door mechanisms. Patricia threw the rifle down on the passenger seat and hauled at the door with both hands, wincing at the pain in her shoulder, getting the door closed and the lock down just as the sound of running feet appeared further up the street.

Others would see an idling car as the same gift she had. Locks and a rifle wouldn't protect her from a mob, and with Brevik raging at its abandonment one would form quickly. Patricia put the car in gear and lurched forward blindly, scraping at the windscreen with one hand in an effort to see out.

As the shouts and cries became louder, she increased the car's speed, seeing the road ahead from memory alone, keeping the car as central as she could, trying to recall where other vehicles had been parked.

The street had been empty as far as—

The car jerked as it collided with something on its left side. Patricia heard the crunch of metal and then the passenger side window burst open, pierced by the protruding face of a street sign, showering her with safety glass. She screamed in frustration. She had no hope of ever clearing the windscreen so she lifted the rifle, pointed its barrel at the glass, and then squeezed her eyes shut as she pulled the trigger.

The windscreen exploded. Patricia wiped glass shards out of her hair, feeling blood trickling down her face. Freezing air billowed around her, but at least she could see again. The street ahead was clear of cars, but several people had appeared in doorways to watch her bumbling escape attempt.

She stamped the accelerator just as someone leapt in front of the car. The bumper connected with a heavy jacket with a muffled thud, then the wheels were bumping up and over the fallen body. Patricia hadn't seen it closely enough to know if it was a man or a woman, but as she felt the front wheels land she urged the car faster. The back wheels hit the body so hard that the rear bumper thumped down on the snow.

Don't feel. Don't think. Just drive.

Shock would be setting in amongst the townsfolk. Shock that they had been abandoned by everyone they had ever looked up to, and shock that they were now left to fend for themselves amidst a growing sense of anarchy. The sounds of violence and vandalism came from the side streets she passed, and the billowing smoke of several fires was already rising up over the houses. When night came the cold would drive people back inside and dampen their anger, but for the next few hours of daylight people would riot and rage.

There was only so far she could get in the car on the snow-clogged roads. It took her as far as the point where Kurou and Victor had released her, but from there she had to continue on foot. To disguise her passage, she turned the car around, then released the handbrake and jumped out, letting the vehicle trundle back down the road until it veered too close to a snowbank and overturned.

She hadn't thought to bring any supplies. She had the clothes on her back and her father's rifle. It would have to be enough.

Climbing up into the trees, she followed the line of the valley as Victor and Kurou had done, eventually happening across a few footprints not filled in by the wind. By the time she had made it to the lookout point overlooking the overhanging rock where she had seen them disappear, the sun was starting to dip, and she had perhaps an hour of daylight to make it before she risked getting lost in the snow.

Unlike Kurou and Victor had done, Patricia took a more direct route down through the trees, in places slipping and rolling in the deep snow. She even dropped her gun a couple of times, feeling a momentary horror on each occasion that it would discharge and give her away, but she made it to the valley floor quicker than she would have done by following their tracks. Here, where the wind was less intrusive, she was able to see their passage easily. Their tracks headed up through fluffy thigh deep snow to disappear under the huge, overhanging rock.

They had to be holed up in a cave. With no way to keep warm other than building a fire with frozen driftwood, eventually they would have to come out and head back to the town. Patricia checked the gun and found she had three bullets left. It was enough.

Arcing around to the right, she tried to find a good viewpoint to see beneath the overhanging rock. A fire ought to be visible, but in the darkness beneath the lip of the rock there was nothing.

She could only wait for so long before she would also freeze to death. The temperature was already several degrees below zero, and would plummet as soon as the sun dipped below the edge of the valley. It was already low in the sky, shining wanly through the snow-covered tree branches.

If you won't come out, I'll come in.

She had felt Kurou's strength up close, but he had no weapons. If she kept him in sight she could kill him. He would be the trickiest of the two, but Victor would be like executing a lame deer, almost too easy. Checking the gun was cocked and ready, Patricia crept towards the overhanging rock, peering into the darkness, waiting for her eyes to adjust.

The rock was looming high above her when she realised there was no one there.

Instead of the people she had expected, there was just a pair of large metal doors.

AT TIMES, as the huge overhead lights revealed the contents of one giant cavern after another, Kurou found it difficult not to spur his patchwork body into pirouettes of glee. Decades before, he had hidden great hordes of his own treasure in vaults around the world, and while the advancement of his own work made this dusty museum collection look positively antique, it was a meal for a starving man, the oasis for a weary traveller dying of thirst.

Part weapons storage and part research facility, several vast chambers contained lines of old military vehicles parked so closely it was impossible to squeeze between them. Others were vast ammunition stores, while some stone rooms were turned metallic by guns of all description stacked high. It was enough to arm a small country, albeit with archaic weapons that wouldn't stand much chance against a modern army. Whatever invisible enemy Victor feared would barely scoff at such a thorn of resistance, but pitting one war arsenal against another was not a path Kurou had any intention of pursuing.

The machines of the larger caverns were of little interest. The true treasure lay in the smaller caverns further below ground.

Laboratories and research stations, testing rooms filled with dusty robots and banks of computer equipment, they pierced Kurou's long disused mind like a drug. As he wiped the dust off an old leather chair, wheeled it over to a laptop that creaked when he lifted the screen and pushed an optimistic finger against the start button, he felt the years shedding off him like a snake's discarded skin. As the screen flickered into life, a beautiful butterfly of intelligence began to stretch its wings, years after taking refuge in the dark.

Once, the whole world had been his canvas, until the fear of enemies more powerful than himself had made him blow out the light.

Now it was growing bright once more.

Of course the computers were encrypted with protection software, security too powerful for most hacking programs to break through. But within a couple of minutes Kurou was in, his hooked, twisted fingers buzzing over the keyboard as he executed a series of complex operating system shortcuts and bypasses that he had years before committed to memory. Once he had access, fearing other levels of tripwire security, he hacked into the mainframe and reconfigured the network and all associated security systems to answer to one person and one person only.

Its new master.

With the computer systems under his command, Kurou then got to work discovering just what extent of riches innocent little Victor had found beneath the Siberian snow, and how he might use it to his own advantage.

The world will see the strokes of my brush again, I swear it.

Patricia sat beside the doors for a long time, trying to decide what to do. She had found one set of footprints heading away, and from the clumsy way they moved through the snow, she guessed they belonged to Victor. The temptation to hunt and execute him was nearly overwhelming, but he was the easy one. He could wait.

Whatever else lay beyond the doors, Kurou was in there. She stood up and swung the rifle back over her shoulder, wincing at the lingering soreness.

There had to be a way to open the doors. If there was, she would find it.

Within minutes of accessing the internet for the first time in half a decade, Kurou realised that the rot that had begun to set in years ago was now near absolute. Rather than fight it, people had instead begun to work the corruption to their own advantage, flooding the internet with so much fallacy and misinformation that the very nature of trust had been turned on its head. He found an article series denouncing the internet and declaring it dead, then another denying the claims of the first. It seemed that over time the infiltration had oozed forth from the computer screen into all forms of communication, to the extent that television broadcasts were routinely faked and that only commands given face to face could be trusted.

Years and years of unchecked corruption had made the whole fabric of organised society unstable, to the extent that no one could be quite sure what was true and what was not beyond the borders of their own vision. Wars were fought blind, governments were falsely elected and then pushed from power without the players themselves ever having known.

It was, in short, a right fucking mess.

It would take some time to wade through the debris of what had begun as mankind's greatest invention.

Luckily, time was something he had in abundance.

Pulling his chair closer so he was hunched over the screen, his keen eyes flicking over the lines and columns of data, he got to work, fingers clacking on the keyboard like a piano player for the dead.

Victor, that pea-brained fool. Terrified that the doors would seal him outside, he had left a small square of rock jammed into the sliding mechanism. As soon as Patricia spotted it the way in revealed itself, and five minutes later she was standing at the end of a long corridor with the cold trapped outside. Somewhere from inside the walls came the soft hum of heating units, and Patricia felt a maddening urge to just sit down by the wall and enjoy the warmth.

She pinched her fingers in between the gun barrel and the wall, causing a sharp pain that forced her to focus. Kurou was in here somewhere, waiting to die.

Kurou had never panned for gold, but he understood the concept. Digging through the shredded remains of the internet in search of something useful and meaningful was rather similar, hours on end of trawling through shit in the hope of unearthing one little nugget of fortune.

Unlike the hopeful shifter squatting in the middle of the river, he realised quickly that nothing of any use would come from anywhere that had once been trusted. All of the major websites he might have once browsed for information were a hacked, ruined mess. It was a thrill of sorts to tap into the defining fabric of each site and watch the battle between the hackers and the defenders play itself out in fluid lines of code, but trying to walk through the middle of the war and pick up some vegetables was a pointless, thankless task. After witnessing the same raging battle on the websites of several major governments and news agencies, he retreated to his old haunts in the corners of the internet where he had once planted his own seeds of misinformation, to the forums and the blogs and the nothing sites, the low-traffic, uneventful, simplistic pages that few hackers would ever feel the need to infiltrate.

Even there, though, he found corruption, the fingers of decay stretching far, but out in the furthest reaches of the internet, on the sites long ignored and mostly abandoned, he began to use his own skills to find a way in, to sort the misinformation from the truth, to spin his own web around the hackers that were controlling everything and very slowly piece together what the fuck was going on in the world.

It was impossible to keep the smile from his lips as he worked. The years of hiding were over and he had thrown open the doors to reveal the light.

He wondered if the world had been waiting for him.

For the return of the greatest hacker of them all.

It would be beautiful. It would be flawless. The world would be his canvas once more, to be seared and burned and painted with the blood of its subjects.

Kurou took a deep breath and muttered a little prayer. He could feel his wings spreading out around him, so long clipped. Soon, he would fly once more—

Something cold and circular and hard pressed into the back of his head, nestling itself into a little nook of scar tissue. It felt almost comfortable.

'You're dead, you ugly fucking freak,' came the sibilant hiss of a girl's voice that sounded vaguely, remotely, intrinsically … like that of his own long lost daughter.

28

REMAINS IN THE SNOW

THE INTERN DOUBLED over as the butt of the gun struck him in the stomach. Sergei Papanov lifted the gun to finish the man off, then thought better of it, some small inkling of mercy slipping into his thoughts as the heavy, scored teak was set to thunder down.

'Leave him,' Yevgeny Franko said. 'Not his fault, is it?'

Sergei waved at the two heavies waiting in the doorway. 'Make him talk,' he said. 'If he knows anything, get it out of him. I want to know about vehicles and guns. Food stores. Anything that might keep us alive.'

The two heavies dragged the intern away. Sergei turned towards the window, looking out at the snow-covered town below. A few groups still huddled in the streets, but most of the remaining townsfolk had returned to their homes. The cold had sucked the fight out of them.

'I won't just sit here and wait to die,' Sergei said, sensing Yevgeny coming to stand beside him. 'They abandoned us, but they also abandoned this town and everything in it. Fuck them. We'll find a way out.'

'Or we'll die when the enemy rolls through. We should surrender. There are laws, you know. The Geneva Convention—'

'Fuck the Geneva Convention. We fight or run or we die.'

Yevgeny was silent a moment, thinking. 'You don't think it could be all bullshit, do you? All this talk of war? What if there's no enemy? What if it's all made up? They say hackers can do anything—'

Sergei turned towards him. 'Then you stand by and do nothing. But I intend to be prepared. If those bastards want a fight I'll give them one.'

PAIN AND WHITENESS. This was what Isabella had heard death was like, and now she believed it. The pain came from her shoulder, where a large triangle of glass had slashed a V through her dress and the flesh beneath; the whiteness was the floor below where the door of the toilet cubicle had once been.

And then she reached down, and realised it was snow.

She could hear people screaming now. She had been sitting on the toilet, sobbing into her hands, when a massive explosion had sent the world revolving around her. A lump the size of one of her mother's antique vases now burned from her temple, probably the reason why she remembered nothing in the immediate aftermath of the explosion.

'Father?' she called softly, wondering if the enemy army had found the train and were now massing around it. She looked down at the shard of glass on the ground and wondered if pulling it across her throat might not save her from days of rape and torture at the hands of the heathen enemy soldiers.

The thought of killing herself was terrifying. If only Victor was here—

'Isabella!'

His voice came out of the haze of her misery like a swooping silver bird, and for a moment she was certain she had actually died in the catastrophe which had befallen the train. She had to be dead, she had to be dreaming.

'Isabella! Where are you? Are you alive?'

'Victor!'

'Hold on!'

The sound of breaking wood came from outside, then the head of an axe appeared in the toilet door.

'Stand back!'

The axe landed a couple more times, then a boot came smashing through the splintered wood. Isabella screamed as splinters showered her, then the remains of the door flew open and Victor held out a hand.

'Thank God you're alive,' he said. 'Come on. We have to get away from the train in case the drones come back.'

She didn't want to ask what he was talking about, but she let him lead her out of the wreckage, climbing over the remains of the carriage and its mangled wheels, past heaps of burning wood that stank of cooking meat.

'It might be best if you close your eyes,' Victor said.

She tried, but her curiosity got the better of her. All around them were the remains of the train, some of the carriages ripped in half, others standing on end, most engulfed in flame. Dead and dying people lay everywhere.

'I had to get you away from the train,' Victor said. 'There's a siding shed about half a mile back up the line. The survivors are heading there. There's nothing to eat or drink because the supply wagon took a direct hit, so those who can walk will head back to Brevik and bring help for those who are too injured to move.'

'My father…?'

Victor nodded. 'He's alive. He's in a bad way, but he'll live. He'll be happy to see you.'

Isabella wanted to thank him, but as she opened her mouth to speak, a sudden dizziness came over her. In an instant her vision had gone blurry, and only a little gasp came out as her knees wobbled and she collapsed to the ground.

VICTOR'S RELIEF at finding Isabella alive was quickly replaced by frustration as she fainted in his arms. She didn't weigh much but he was at the end of his strength, so carrying her through the knee-deep snow was an arduous chore. At the end of it her father waited, something that didn't exactly spur him on, so as she started to come around he lowered her back down and tapped her cheek lightly until her eyes opened.

'Are you all right?'

'Victor, what happened to us?'

'A drone strike. The whole train was hit. It must have been targeted by the enemy.'

Isabella started to cry. 'What happens to us now? We can't go back to the town or we'll all be killed.'

Victor nodded. 'I know somewhere we can go, but it's a long walk.'

'What about my father? I need to see him!'

A plan began to manifest itself in Victor's mind. The siding shed was still some way distant. Mortin had wanted to look for his daughter, but with a leg broken in at least two places as well as a broken arm and dislocated shoulder, he'd had no choice but to let two other survivors strap him to the charred remains of a partition door and drag him away across the snow. After surviving a volley of expletive-laden abuse, Victor had promised to search the wreckage for Isabella and bring her—dead or alive—to the siding shed.

Now, that didn't seem like such a good idea. There was too much danger back in the town, both from the people left behind and the approaching enemy. The only safety for either of them was in the secret place.

'How well can you walk?' Victor asked.

'My feet are like frozen lumps of ice and I'm sure one of my ankles was nearly severed by a piece of glass.'

'Hmm. But otherwise okay?'

'I'll never be okay again!'

Over the course of their relationship Victor had learned to understand Isabella pretty well. The louder and more argumentative she became, the better she was feeling. Right now she could probably manage a Himalayan trek.

'It's this way,' he said, pointing up the slope. 'It's quicker if we go this way.'

'Where are we going? Are we going to find my father?'

'Yes, of course.' Victor said, hoping that by the time she figured out that he'd lied to her it would be too late to turn back.

ROBERT MORTIN SHUDDERED at the screams coming from the corner, where a man with terrible burns was in the midst of dying. He'd heard several other survivors mention how it would have been more humane to leave the guy to die in the snow, but a couple of do-gooders had dragged him up here to the siding shed to inflict his misery on the rest of them.

As if they didn't all feel in their death throes already.

Victor had yet to appear, which meant Isabella was probably dead. The fool wasn't likely to show up empty handed, so Mortin feared the worst. The weight of losing his son and both daughters in the space of a couple of days was like a hammer thudding Mortin repeatedly over the head, but rather than any thoughts to end his own painful life and join them, all he could think about was revenge. Someone somewhere had to die for this, painfully and slowly. Killing himself was definitely an option, but not until he had wreaked his vengeance on as many people as possible.

'We have to go back to Brevik,' a voice said from nearby. Mortin looked up to see Mayor Andrev, his arm in a sling and a vicious gash down the side of his face, standing over him. 'We have no choice.'

Andrev was right, but that didn't make it any more reassuring. They would all die if they stayed here, whereas if they went back to the town only some of them would die.

'You know that we'll be at the mercy of whoever assumed control in our absence? And that there's no other way to get back to the town before nightfall other than follow the train tracks back in?'

'I understand all of that.'

Mortin sighed. 'So when do we leave?'

'Immediately.'

YEVGENY COULD BARELY KEEP the smile off his face. 'You'll never guess what just came slinking back in,' he said.

Sergei turned away from the window and the few twinkling lights of the twilit town. 'What are you talking about?'

'The train. It got destroyed. A trail of survivors just came limping back in along the train line.'

'Where are they now?'

'They've headed straight for St Peter's Place. I think they're heading for the town hospital.'

'Have them intercepted and rounded up. I want them all in the city cells. We'll decide what to do with them tomorrow morning.'

Yevgeny didn't move. 'You sound like him, you know.'

'Who?'

'Mayor Andrev.'

'So?'

Yevgeny took a few more steps into the room. 'I was just wondering who put you in charge.'

Sergei lifted the gun he had been concealing in his sleeve, pointed it at Yevgeny and pulled the trigger without hesitation. The blast seemed to fill the room, reverberating off the walls. Sergei walked over to Yevgeny's twitching body and put two more shots into his former comrade, one in the chest and one between the eyes.

'I did,' he said.

29

BARGAINS AND BRIBES

'No!' Kurou screamed. 'Don't kill me, sweet princess! Don't kill me or your father will die!'

Her finger had tightened on the rifle's trigger, but now it paused.

'What are you talking about?'

'Your father! He's going to die!'

A bony elbow slammed in to Kurou's face and he found himself lying on the floor with the girl straddling him, the rifle barrel pressed against his throat.

'Tell me what you meant!'

Kurou hoped his black eyes made it difficult to see that he was looking around, searching for a way of escape.

'I guess you're not too caught up on the latest news—'

'*What* news?'

'That little escape train belonging to your dear townsfolk just got rather annihilated by a series of drone bombs.'

'Liar!'

'Um, perhaps a glance out of the door might reveal a distant column of smoke?'

Uncertainty appeared in the girl's eyes. Aware he was quickly regaining control of the situation, Kurou made a point of tensing his arms and legs to give the impression of nervousness. It was important that the girl still thought she had the ascendancy.

'You said my father might die. If that train was bombed—'

'But your father survived! And right now he's being held prisoner back in your pretty little town. They're going to kill him, a little execution, yes.'

The look in her eyes showed she was convinced. It was a pretty good estimation, Kurou thought, based on the likely sequence of events. Of course he could be completely wrong, but right now all he needed was a little time to figure out how to get the gun barrel away from his throat.

Hurting young Patricia's feelings was the least of his worries.

'If you release me we can figure out a way to save your father!'

She appeared to be considering it, her brow furrowed in concentration. Ah, the female mind. So much easier to manipulate with emotion than a man's—

She flashed him a wide grin, then the gun swung round and the hardwood butt end crashed into his forehead, sending him spiralling down into unconsciousness.

WITH ALL THE pain he had felt over his long life, it was remarkable that there was still something that could hurt enough to surprise him, but when he opened his eyes Kurou was immediately bombarded with two completely separate hangovers, one behind his eyes and the other on the crown of his head. The isolation of such pain in two distinct locations was something that he would love to investigate … on the corpse of the girl standing above him.

He tried to sit up, but he was tied up good, his arms pressed so tight to his sides they might as well have been nailed there.

The girl was a quick learner, he had to admit. His daughter, his dear sweet Nozomi, had once been the same.

'We can talk about this,' he muttered, surprised at the absence of a gag. It was understandable now he reasoned it—calling for help was unlikely to do someone as ugly as he any good. Being killed privately was quite possibly preferable to a public lynching.

'Shut up,' she said.

'There's no need to be hasty now, is there? A penny for your thoughts and all that?'

She turned and threw a spanner at his head. Luckily his one remaining eye hadn't deteriorated with the rest of him and ducking out of the way was relatively straightforward.

'I can understand how you might be upset—'

'Shut up!'

As she reached for another tool of some metallic description lying nearby, Kurou decided now might be a good time to do just that. He sucked his thin lips together and made a mumbling sound to indicate he was in agreement. She glared at him, but put the tool back down.

Patricia was fiddling with one of the computer screens he had activated, pressing random buttons with excessive ferocity. She had no clue what she was doing; he didn't need her frowns to tell him that. He had been in the process of setting up a communications scrambler that covered a thirty-mile radius, as well as a proxy firewall so it wasn't obvious to any hackers that the scrambler's origin was nearby, keeping him off the radar for any further drone strikes.

Such was the nature of warfare these days. He felt almost nostalgic for the days of swords and spears.

'Stupid thing.'

Kurou said nothing. He turned his head slightly so that Patricia would think he was staring off into space. His monochrome eyes had fooled many a potential victim, but he was watching every move she made, analysing every motion and shift of her hands and body, reading her like some might read a book, picking out information.

In years gone by, he could have picked a hiding rabbit out of a field of grass at five hundred metres, and although these days his vision was a fraction of what it used to be, he could still see the rise and fall of her pulse in her neck, see how her heart rate was rising as she became increasingly frustrated. He actually felt more concern for the computer terminal than for himself, because unlike a complex mainframe, he was relatively easy to fix.

'How does this fucking work…?'

He said nothing. Patricia tapped a couple of buttons and frowned. An image appeared on a screen of a dating site profile, a muscular man in his mid-twenties pouting at the camera. Kurou felt his cheeks redden as he read the profile's name: Mark Crowe.

Patricia turned to him with a look of disgust on her face. 'What the hell were you doing?'

Had it not been for the ropes binding him so tight, Kurou would have shrugged. 'Oh, I was just seeing if I'd had any views since last time I logged in … it's been several years, you know….'

'What *are* you?'

'They say I was born a man….'

'You're not anything. You're like a worm under my foot.'

Kurou was happy enough just to get her talking. Insults really didn't hurt in the same way that fire, electricity, and thrown metal tools did.

'I'm a worm who's rather useful with computers….'

Patricia glared at him a moment longer, then turned back to the computer. She peered around the back of the screen, then looked under the desk. With a sigh of frustration, she stood up.

'I guess if it doesn't move I have no choice but to move you,' she said.

'I don't bite!' Kurou pined.

Patricia, taking no chances, looped a metal hook into Kurou's bonds and dragged him across the floor to the computer terminal. Then she hauled him upright and pushed him into the chair.

'That's much better,' Kurou said. 'I was getting terrible double vision lying down there.'

'I want you to open the back gate,' she said. 'I know there is one, because I found it on a map.'

'Most observant of you. Um, I'll need the use of my hands.'

Patricia shook her head. 'Tell me which buttons to press.'

The girl wasn't to be bested—at least not yet. The entrance that Victor had found was only secondary to a larger set far more well hidden in the forest, but opening them via the computer was a long, arduous process that drove Kurou near out of his mind. Command by command he instructed Patricia how to open up the mainframe and then access the computer program that controlled the base's systems.

'Okay, there you have it,' Kurou said, as the command tab for REAR ENTRANCE flashed up as OPEN. 'Best not leave it like that too long, lest a draft gets in. I'm rather susceptible to a little grippe these days, especially with the long winters that we have.'

'Get up,' Patricia said.

Kurou did as she indicated, walking ahead of her towards the door, the rifle barrel pressed into his back.

'Pray tell me where we're going?' Kurou said. 'I do love a family outing.'

'We're going back to Brevik. I'm going to offer them a murderer and kidnapper in exchange for my father's life.'

'Oh, how delightful. Did you pack some sandwiches?'

He was sure the girl gave a little chuckle, but the net result was a harder prod with the gun barrel.

'Goddamn it if I'm not going to cut out your tongue before I hand you over,' the girl said. 'I hope you're enjoying it because it's not staying in that mouth of yours for too much longer.'

'Hold him still.'

The two men lifted Robert Mortin upright. The big man winced as his splinted leg was straightened, sweat breaking out on his brow despite the cold. With one arm in a makeshift sling and his face bloody and blackened from minor cuts and burns, he looked beat up enough already, but Sergei owed him one.

'You lied to me,' he said, slamming a fist into Mortin's face. 'You dirty Mongolian. You lied and you left me to die.'

Mortin barely flinched. His cold eyes continued to stare into Sergei's, who was struggling to contain his composure. Mortin was like granite. Sergei was sure he had broken a knuckle, but he couldn't let Mortin see his weakness. When it came time for the mayor to take his turn, Sergei would use a weapon.

Mortin's big head swung towards the nearest guards. 'How much is this idiot paying you?' he asked. 'I'm guessing not much. I'll double it.'

'Silence! Take him out to the gallows,' Sergei shouted. After a short pause during which a few uncertain glances were passed around, the guards turned Mortin back towards the door and headed out.

Pavel Andrev now stood alone in his former office, his hands bound behind him. The head councillor looked untouched by the train disaster that had left some two hundred townsfolk dead.

'You made a mistake abandoning us,' Sergei said. 'I run this town now.'

Pavel smiled. 'You're nothing but a petty thief,' he said. 'The people won't follow you.'

'Rather me than the man they trusted to protect them who left them behind.'

Pavel looked sheepish. 'You'd have done the same in my situation.'

Sergei gave him a light slap across the cheek—with his good hand. 'Oh, quite possibly. But I wouldn't have got caught.'

***

IF SURROUNDED by idiots is how I have to die, then so be it.

The huge floodlights, beaming down from the roof of City Hall on to the square where crude gallows made of metal scaffolding poles had been set up, were like a dinner invitation for more drone strikes. The suddenness of Sergei Papanov's ascension to power was disturbing, but Robert had seen enough doubt in the guards' eyes to know the gangster had a tenuous grip at best. Whether they would overthrow him before the gallows did their work on the captured exiles was another matter.

Robert wasn't the only one being made an example of under Sergei's new regime. A couple of dozen other prominent figures had also been handpicked to be strung up from the wire nooses hanging in the air fifteen feet above him. The rest of the survivors had been rounded up and either detained or allowed limited medical treatment. All had been promised that punishment was imminent, that their possessions were no longer their own, and that death would likely be a mercy.

It wasn't quite the homecoming Robert had hoped for.

'It's time,' boomed a voice above him, fading in and out of the microphone. Sergei clearly wasn't used to public addresses. 'Let's get these traitors in the ground.' He paused for dramatic effect, but the response from the sparse crowd was muted. 'Guards, you know what to do!'

A few of the mayor's less reliable guards who had been left behind and a handful of small-time crooks and unsavoury civilians now dressed up in guard clothing began to move the captives up the metal steps towards the gallows platform.

'The mayor will begin the proceedings,' Sergei boomed.

Pavel started to protest, but hatred for him was greater than for anyone else. He struggled as a guard looped a noose made from electricity cable over his head, then gave a muted scream as two more guards hoisted him up into the air.

Robert winced as a trickle of blood dribbled down on to the platform, the crude noose cutting into Pavel's neck. For a few seconds the mayor's feet kicked, then his body slumped forward.

'Next!'

There seemed to be no set order, although Robert expected he might be saved for a final coup de grace. Around him the scaffolding shuddered as a second man—one of Pavel's council aides—was strung up beside his old boss. Rather than bay for blood like Medieval crowds of old, the assembled people looked more disgusted than anything else, but no one made a move to challenge the new order. Near the outermost fringes of where the floodlights could reach, several small groups were slinking away. It was possible Robert would die in front of a deserted square.

The sound of an engine made him look up. The crowd parted, many people running in fear, as a large military transport vehicle burst into the square and skidded to a halt in front of City Hall.

A hatch opened in the roof and a young woman climbed out, a gun clutched to her chest. Robert's breath caught.

Patricia.

'Who's in charge here?' his daughter shouted. 'Show yourself, you sorry dog.'

A flame of pride ignited in Robert's heart. If the boy and the stupid one were dead, it no longer mattered because Patricia was alive.

A torch swung up towards the balcony where Sergei had appeared. He'd found some of Pavel's old ceremonial robes from somewhere, although even at this distance it was obvious he had arranged them wrong and looked more like court jester than a mayor incumbent.

'I am,' he shouted down, his voice still amplified by the microphone held in one hand.

Patricia scoffed. 'You? Are you serious?'

'Guards, arrest her. I'll let her warm my bed tonight, although it'll be for far less coin than she's used to.'

Robert strained at his bonds, sending shudders of intense pain through his legs and arms. If intent could kill he'd be a mass murderer.

'Wait!' Patricia shouted. 'I brought you something.'

She turned and pointed her gun inside the hatch, barking orders at someone inside. A spotlight swung across to train on her as a monster unlike anything Robert had ever seen climbed up into the light.

Gasps came from the nearest members of the crowd and some people tried to shrink away.

'I found you a demon,' Patricia said, poking the man in the back until he stood up on the front of the vehicle. He was dressed in rags, trussed up like a swine ready for the spit. There was something wrong with his face, but the shadows caused by the shaking floodlight made it difficult to tell.

'This is the man responsible for the murders in the Lenin District,' she said. 'He's a monster who eats human flesh. I offer him in exchange for my father's release.'

A ripple of excitement spread out among the people left in the square. Many of those who had come were close to the murders: the town's unemployed, downtrodden underbelly. If Sergei knew what was good for him he would take the exchange.

'I appreciate your offer, young lady,' Sergei boomed, after a pause for consideration, 'But I will not be bowed by the weight of bribes. Unlike my predecessor, I am a man of honour and integrity. You will hang like the common whore you are with your father and this murderer on either side of you. Seize them!'

As guards rushed for the military transport, Patricia opened fire. Two floodlights immediately burst, showering the crowd with glass and plunging the square into near darkness. Chaos ensued as people rushed back and forth, away from the gunfire, away from the rushing guards, away from the falling glass. Patricia and her prisoner were lost in the melee as more shots rang out, one taking a chunk of masonry out of the balcony ledge just inches below where Sergei stood.

From the platform on the makeshift gallows, Robert had the best view of anyone. A riot had kicked off between the guards and the crowd, but within a few minutes the guards—fighting for their lives rather than their assumed new leader—had brought it back under control.

Patricia, held by three guards, was dragged up on to the platform. At the sight of Robert, she started to cry, sinking to her knees in defeat. He screamed at her to get up, but she just shook her head.

'Those idiots!' she screamed. 'They let him get away!'

Robert frowned. It took a moment for him to realise that she was referring to the prisoner she had brought with her, the rather unusual looking man who was apparently a multiple murderer.

30

POLITICS AND MACHINATIONS

As HIS TROOPS routed the city, the man who had gone under many guises and aliases throughout his long and eventful life looked up at the tall hotel on the other side of the square. An old Soviet monolith, forty storeys of bland functionality, it had remained untouched on his command while the rest of the city burned.

He felt uncharacteristically nervous as he took his first steps through the snow, churned up by hundreds of running feet. The building's doorway loomed close, a black cavern like a giant's mouth.

The elevator was still working. That was a surprise considering the power was off in most of the city. He took it up to the top floor, not needing to guess where his old friend might be; their thoughts were linked like two cups on a piece of string.

The door to the penthouse suite was closed, but not locked. He opened it and went inside, gasping a little in surprise at the wall to ceiling window that gave a panoramic view of the west side of the city. It was an effect he would have to remember if he one day had need to design an apartment of his own.

He closed his eyes, shutting down his thoughts, listening for his old friend's breathing. It was there, near the window, but weak, the breathing of a dying man.

'Alek, are you there?'

The old man was slumped in an armchair, wrapped in blankets. His weak breath turned to frost as it left his lips, and only when the newcomer put a hand on the old man's arm did he open his eyes.

'You're still alive.'

The old man's eyes flicked across the younger man's face. 'I waited for you. You took longer than I expected.'

A smile. 'I was enjoying the scenery.'

'It's been a long time, Massi. Despite everything you've done, I always hoped I would see you again.'

'Is now about the time you tell me I was the child you never had?'

The old man sighed and shook his head. 'No. I would never have wanted a child like you.'

For some reason, the old man's words cut deep. 'You wronged me, Alek. From the moment you laid eyes on me you wronged me. Everything that I've done stands at your door.'

'I don't dispute that. But it's never too late to stop. While you live you can end this.'

'It can't be stopped until I have what belongs to me returned. I will raze every tree, burn every field, kill every man, woman, and child until I have back what was taken from me.'

The old man sighed again. 'Then you are already dead. Your heart wasn't always black, Massi.'

'Goddamn it, stop calling me that.'

'Whatever monster you became, you were always that little boy with the curious eyes and the kind smile.'

'That boy died the day he was stolen from his mother.'

The old man shifted his head in the blankets, finally allowing their eyes to meet. 'Then I look on no one. Goodbye, Massi.'

The old man gave one last long, gradual sigh, then his eyes closed, and his head slumped forward on to the mound of blankets covering his chest.

The man he had called Massi stared for a moment, his mouth wrinkled in disgust. 'No! Alek, you do not die unless I command it!' *Do you hear me?*

But for the first time in more years than he could remember, there was no voice to reply to his thoughts.

———

THE SUDDEN CONFUSION had been unexpected, but welcomed like a former lover come back to warm his cold, empty bed. Sharpened bones hidden in folds of skin where the fingertips would be on a normal man had made short work of the bonds, but they had never been much concern. The girl's rifle had been more so, but most deadly had been the look in the girl's eyes. The ease with which she might end his life had made patience essential.

And now it had been rewarded.

No one cared what a skinny, ugly man was doing while bullets were flying and glass was showering the crowd. Within seconds he had rolled off the top of the armoured vehicle and away into the crowd. Within a minute he had found the shelter of an unguarded doorway, and within five he was safely out of harm's way.

He surveyed his new abode with something like excitement. While getting back to his playground of new toys was his highest priority, he had landed on his feet with his choice of hiding place.

If there was anywhere he could turn to his advantage, it was the office of the town mayor.

IT TOOK some considerable time to secure the girl, but eventually she was captured and brought to the cells on the lower floor of City Hall. Sergei scowled as he followed his newly appointed head jailor down the freezing corridor towards the cells at the end.

In the gunfight and proceeding chaos, the gallows had been damaged, the frame collapsing under the weight of the two dead men. With the crowd all but dispersed it had made sense to hold the other prisoners until a second execution ceremony could be arranged in the morning. Impressing the remaining populace to get them on side was imperative.

What then, though? That idiot Yevgeny was dead, so was the mayor. Everyone else capable of opposing him was in the cells. Yet still his power was tenuous, on the verge of collapse. He had stood up in front of the people and assumed control, yet even his hired guns were barely loyal. His promises of rewards from the coffers he had yet to locate would only hold them so long. He had allowed them to take their pick of the townsfolk's women for their bed partners, something which had temporarily appeased them, only to incite the rage of the wronged families in its place. The freezing temperatures had sent people back to their homes, but they would be rapping on the door of city hall come daybreak.

He was starting to think that power wasn't worth the effort.

'Here, um, sir,' the head jailor said, pointing towards a closed cell door. 'That's where we put her.'

'Open it.'

Inside, Patricia, looking slightly worse for wear, was sitting on a concrete bench wrapped in several blankets. The air temperature was suitably freezing, and the girl's teeth chattered as she glared at him.

'You have one chance to avoid death at first light,' he told her. 'You will come to my bedroom now, and you will do whatever I ask.'

The girl snapped her teeth together sharply. 'Not that it's not small enough already,' she said.

'You little brat. I should have you shot.'

She smiled. 'You won't be long behind me. Your supposed rule will be over before you know it. Once the people realise you're just a small-time crook.'

Sergei shrugged. 'Everyone has to start somewhere.'

The girl stared at him. There was something in her eyes he found unnerving. He was just taking a step forward to knock that look off her face when she flashed a smile.

'He got away, didn't he? Good luck out there. Make sure you lock the door on the way out. There's no way I want him getting in.'

Sergei scowled at her. He tried to think of a suitable retort, but failed. He barked at the head jailor to lock her up again, then headed back up towards his offices, where at least it was warm.

He had to admit he had barely thought about the supposed murderer she had captured and brought to trade for her father, but now that things had settled down again he got to thinking about the room he had found in the basement of the bombed dormitory building, and the strips of meat he had seen on the floor that belonged to no animal he had ever seen.

So what if the man was out there again? He'd been loose before, so what had changed?

Sergei scowled again.

Only everything.

As he headed for the upper floors, he resolved to put an extra guard on the entrance, just to make sure.

ISABELLA COULD BARELY STAND by the time they made it to the underground base. She was so exhausted that Victor didn't even need to explain where they were. The lights were still on and the heating systems were still pumping hot, musty air from ceiling vents, but of the professor there was no sign.

Isabella was ready to fall asleep on her feet, so Victor guided her to an old office and laid her down on a cracked leather sofa. She was asleep before he had reached the door. He didn't want to leave her, but he needed to know what was going on.

Searching through the offices, labs, and hangars, he found evidence that Kurou had been here, but no idea where he had gone. Then, in a small control room adjacent to the largest of the hangars, he found a smashed computer screen and signs of a scuffle.

One of the computer terminals was still online, so Victor sat down and searched through the files, looking for access to the security cameras he had seen hanging in the corners of some of the rooms.

When he finally accessed the digital feeds and wound them back a few hours, he stared at the screen in shock.

31

THE COUNCIL OF WAR

SERGEI PAPANOV WAS HAVING a wonderful dream. He was sitting out in the sunshine, holding a vodka cocktail in one hand while a woman knelt in front of him. All around him, people were cheering and waving flags.

He felt rather disappointed when the sensation of something nudging him broke off his dream at the stem and pulled his eyelids open. The ache of a vodka hangover immediately hit him, and as he looked up into the face of the tall, beautiful Russian woman standing over him, he wondered if he had merely ascended to a higher level of dreaming.

Then the woman lifted a SS-issue pistol and held it up between his eyes.

'I wanted to meet you before I killed you, you bastard,' she said. 'Your fun is over. This is for Pavel.'

Sergei heard rather than felt the bullet as it entered his head and then exited again nearly immediately, condemning him forever to a level of dreaming from which there would be no escape.

PATRICIA OPENED her eyes to the sound of a heavy key scraping in the lock. She opened her eyes to see Sergei's head jailor, flanked by two soldiers. She pulled the blankets up around her, the chill forgotten as the fear of immediate execution clouded everything, then she noticed the resigned smile on the head jailor's face as he stepped inside and motioned to her to follow the soldiers.

'A changing of the guard,' he said as she passed him. 'Leave the blankets, please. I'm sure I'll need them.'

ROBERT MORTIN WAS RESTING in a hospital bed when Patricia walked in. The guards had taken her straight to the hospital after freeing her. Her father was a mess of slings and plaster casts, but he was alive.

'Patricia … I thought….'

'I'd slap you if you weren't already broken,' she said, giving him the best hug she could in the circumstances.

'I waited as long as I could. I thought you were dead like your brother. I hunted for you—'

'You can save your excuses for later. What happened last night?'

He smiled. 'Lena Patrova returned. Mayor Andrev sent her out on a reconnaissance mission some weeks ago. She's always been the darling of the people and she didn't desert them like Pavel Andrev did. She walked right into City Hall without so much as needing to lift her gun. Sergei Papanov didn't stand a chance.'

'Daddy, that man who captured me—'

'Will be hunted down like a dog and killed. If either of my arms were working properly I'd rip him in half myself. Why I let that bastard Victor Mishin hang around your sister so long, I can't fathom. I know she was never the brightest spark, but even so….'

Patricia opened her mouth to say something else, then closed it again. There was too much to get out, too much to explain, that she couldn't manage it all at once. For now, she was just happy to see her father alive, even though the bitterness at being left behind was still ripe on her tongue.

'What happens now?' she asked.

'Councillor Patrova has called an emergency meeting for tonight. I am required to attend.'

'How…?'

'I've assigned you as my official aide, so you'll be coming too. You'll need to push my wheelchair, but that's it.'

Patricia gave him a sweet smile. 'Anything for you, Daddy.'

Anything that will get me closer to knowing what's going on.

KUROU FOUND what he needed in a small room at the end of a corridor on the fourth floor of City Hall. It was an old computer terminal, perhaps once used by a secretary or accountant. The system was slow and cumbersome, but once he had cracked into the council's wi-fi connection and realigned the system to use a power-saving bandwidth, he found it was adequate to his needs.

He quickly tapped into the City Hall computer systems and

from there hunted down the online marker he had set up on the mainframe computer at the underground base, just in case such a situation as this occurred. Within a few minutes he had regained complete control of the base's systems, and had taps on all incoming and outgoing phone lines and signals in a five hundred-metre radius. He was ready and prepared to create havoc if necessary, but for now it was probably a good idea to sit tight and watch, find out what was going on. He knew what he knew, of course, but what did they know?

As he browsed through the base's video cameras, surprised to find Victor up there with some new woman, he felt it was no wonder no one trusted the internet any longer. It was like a thousand million balls of string all intertwined, with blind men tugging on the loose ends of each one.

But just in case Victor managed to find a little intimate time with the girl, Kurou ordered a nearby vending machine to dispense a long out-of-date packet of cigarettes. He had heard that a post-coitus smoke had once been the done thing.

PATRICIA KNEW RATHER MORE of the assembled people than she would have liked. Most of the former council members were absent due to death, so Lena Patrova had compiled a round table of the city's best leftovers, a handful of businessmen who had made it on to the train, and a handful of crooks who had not. From where she stood at her father's shoulder on one side of the room, it was obvious that before anything useful could be achieved the bitterness that had been fermenting since the moment the train departed would need an opportunity to air itself.

'You fucking traitors!' shouted one man, a well-to-do restaurant owner from just outside the train station. 'You fucking left us to die! Every one of you should be strung up. That idiot had the right idea.'

'Mayor Andrev did what he thought was best,' Lena interjected. 'Yes, it was an abuse of power, and yes it was wrong. But what's done is done. When you hear what I have to say I think you'll agree that we have no choice but to work together. It's vital for the survival of us all.'

'Fuck you, you damn whore,' the man shouted. 'Who the hell are you to come in here dictating terms? How can we believe anything you say? You were Andrev's right hand, and for all we know you were in his pants as well.'

Lena glared at him. 'Had you said that on the street a bullet would be nestled between your eyes right now,' she said. 'But in the interests of public safety, I'll let it pass.'

Patricia couldn't help but grin. This was the kind of woman she admired, not idiots like her dumb sister.

'We were thinking of ourselves, I'll admit,' Robert said, making to stand up, then wincing in pain and sitting back in his wheelchair. 'But wouldn't you have done the same? What we face is total annihilation.'

Lena stared at him for a long time. 'You don't know the half of it,' she said.

She let the arguments go on for a few more minutes, giving people a chance to air their grievances. Patricia was impressed; by the time they were all done the hate was smouldering rather than enflamed. The woman clearly knew how to deal with angry men.

Finally, Lena raised a hand. 'I think it's time I told you what is coming for us,' she said. 'If you'll all look up at the screen, I managed to get a few photographs.'

Patricia turned as Lena switched on a projector, immediately displaying a view of a ruined city. Fires burned in the foreground, while what might have been bodies lay amongst the rubble of a collapsed building.

'This was ten days ago,' she said. 'We got lost, trying to escape the oncoming army, and for a while we ended up behind them.'

The images flicked over a few ghastly wartime scenes, then paused on one of what looked like a fallen humanoid shaped robot.

'They're machines,' she said. 'They're controlled by an unknown source. All I know is that they're eating their way across Russia like a wave of mechanical locusts.' She paused, and wiped something out of the side of her eye. 'Quite literally.'

A few more images flicked past. There were ruined buildings, dead people, then a close up of a corpse that brought gasps from the assembled group.

'What the hell happened to it?' the restaurant owner asked.

Lena sighed. 'One thing I could establish about these machines, is that they're self-maintaining. They don't have a base, they don't get serviced, they don't sleep or stop. When my contact explained their food source, I didn't believe him. Then I caught one refuelling.' She gave a little cough as her voice began to crack.

'They run on bio-fuel,' she said.

'Plant matter?' someone asked.

Lena gave a slow shake of her head. 'No. They run on the bodies of their victims. Their fuel is human flesh.'

Shocked gasps gave way to outrage. 'So, you bastards left us to this?' one man screamed, standing up to throw a cup at Patricia's father. It bounced off the metal frame of the wheelchair, spilling vodka on to the carpet. 'We have to leave!' another man shouted. 'We have to leave right away! We'll walk if we have to!'

Lena tapped the table until the commotion stilled. 'On our side is that they're moving slowly. They move on foot, covering only a few miles per day. I saw no sign of any heavy artillery, only a few drone aircraft which appear to serve the dual purpose of surveying the area and taking out any potential benefits to the defenders. We are being defended, by the way. Those were dead Russian soldiers. The army is broken and in disarray, but it fought like only our people can.'

A general mood of pessimistic solemnity fell over everyone. The fight was gone, the ire that some had shown now doused.

'What do we do?' the restaurant owner moaned. 'What *can* we do?'

'As I see it,' Lena said, 'we have two choices. You saw what happened when a large scale evacuation was attempted. That drone strike on the train wasn't a lucky shot. They were watching.' She tapped a finger into her palm. 'There's a chance that small groups might get away, but most of the roads are now blocked, and there are no ways to refuel for hundreds of miles. It's a huge risk.'

'What's the other choice?' the restaurant owner said.

Lena's face hardened. 'We fight. We stand up like warriors and we fight to defend our town until the last man is dead.'

There were one or two small cheers, but the general reaction was muted. Patricia saw her father's face harden and knew that he was resigned to die here. There would be no more attempts to escape.

'How?' someone asked.

'I don't know,' Lena said. 'We'll pool our resources, find what's available in the town, use whatever we can.'

Patricia raised a hand.

'Yes?'

She felt like all the eyes in the room were on her as she muttered, 'North. There's a base north of town. A military base.'

Lena's eyes widened. 'What are you talking about?'

'I was kidnapped and taken there. I escaped, but I can show you where it is. It was full of military vehicles—'

Lena gave a slow nod. 'So they were right,' she said.

'We're saved!' the restaurant owner shouted, jumping up out of his chair.

'Wait!' Patricia raised a hand. 'They were ancient, in bad condition. I don't know how to get them to work—'

The words cut off in her mouth as for a moment an image appeared to flicker on the screen, overlaying Lena's photograph to show the outline of an animal, a bird.

No, not just any bird.

A crow.

It was gone in an instant, and Patricia blinked, aware that every pair of eyes in the room was staring at her. Perhaps it had all been part of her imagination, but imagination or not, the threat to the town was real. They had no choice but to fight, and hope for some kind of a miracle.

'I can take you there,' she said again, and Lena gave another slow nod, as if she too knew that there was no other choice.

32

ISABELLA FINDS A THRONE

THE THOUGHT of starting work on another canvas was making Kurou's skin tingle with anticipation. It was all so perfectly arranged that he felt divine intervention had set him up like this. He had his materials, his paints, his technology. He had everything he needed to make this the greatest work of his long career.

'The big one,' he muttered. 'The one that puts all the others to shame.'

So, the townsfolk wanted to fight. Without him, of course, they were just a little square of ice ready to be melted by the morning sun. But the machinery was just sitting there, waiting to be harnessed like a seam of newly discovered gold.

All it needed was the right man to do it.

He logged back into the computer and ran through the inventory of the underground base. More than half of the arsenal was made up of standard but out-of-date military vehicles and weaponry: tanks, armoured cars, guns and mortars. He might as well send the townsfolk out with rocks.

Level Three, the lowest level of the complex that contained storage hangars, that was where things got interesting. The research and development bay, the experimental robotics technology.

It was all so primitive by his standards, pale in comparison to his birdmen and his spiders, and his fondly remembered masterpieces, the bears. Yet with a little tweaking....

The day was not lost. He had a little time. A week or two at least before the enemy came storming through.

And the enemy, what of them? There was something familiar about it all, about the face he had found hidden deep in the darkest recesses of the internet that was allegedly behind it all.

They had almost met before, and as a result Kurou had spent the last five years in hiding, keeping his continued existence a secret. This other, this creature—for it was surely no man—was not just his equal, but perhaps something more.

Perhaps his eventual slayer.

'A little jousting, a little jousting I do enjoy,' Kurou muttered. 'Why not a little dance together, Grey Man? A penny for your thoughts, grand sire?'

THERE WAS nothing Victor could do about Kurou for the time being. He had to make sure Isabella was safe, and only then could he figure out how to help the professor. The girl had a number of minor cuts and bruises, but luckily nothing serious. In a lower level medical bay Victor found some medicines and bandages that were vacuum sealed and still in perfect condition. With Isabella a little drowsy from some painkillers he had found for her, he set about patching her up.

'Victor,' she moaned, as he cleaned a shallow cut on her wrist, 'what do we do now? Can we just stay in this place until this crazy war is over?'

He shrugged. 'I don't think so. I'm sure they'll find us eventually.'

'Oh Victor!' she wailed. 'Don't say that!'

Victor shrugged. 'I think its best to be pragmatic about all this. That way we might be better able to figure out a solution.'

'Where are we?'

Victor shrugged again. 'Somewhere that probably shouldn't exist. From what I've seen it's obviously military, but it's also old. And if even the town council doesn't know about it, then it might not belong to the army at all. It might belong to someone else entirely.'

Isabella stayed quiet for a while, barring the occasional yelp of pain. There was something in her eyes that Victor found unsettling, worrying even. For all the time he had known her, she had been a bastion of innocence in the middle of a dark, dark room, purity in a place where purity had long ago been consigned to memory. He knew what her father and sister thought about her, that she was naïve, ignorant, even dumb; but they were the fools as far as Victor was concerned. They were walking down one street with their eyes on another. Isabella had it right; everybody else had it wrong.

But now something had changed. She had seen so much death and destruction that even her thick drapes of denial had been forced open.

'I'll just go and get us some water,' he said, unable to look at her eyes any longer. 'I'll be back in a moment.'

There was a sink in the medical bay but the water supply was dry, the pipe probably long ago rusted solid. Luckily, a little way down the corridor was a washroom with a tap which after a few minutes of coughing up brown, putrid liquid, had begun to run clear. The base, despite its obvious age, had been built to last.

As he filled up a plastic beaker under the tap, he wondered if it wasn't indeed possible that they could stay here undetected from the oncoming invasion. The base had been hidden so long, of course, but there had to be a way to conceal the entrances. On the video footage, Patricia had exited via a long tunnel that opened out into the woods further down the valley, a second entrance even more secret than the first. There could be others, but Victor didn't see why they couldn't be sealed. The base had an air-circulation system, water supplies, food machines—and even a cigarette vendor, judging by the packet he had found randomly dispensed on the floor outside the old mess hall—so there was no reason why they wouldn't be able to wait the war out, even if it took years.

The skeptic in him however, wasn't convinced. The oncoming army was relentless, and who wasn't to say that they were coming here for the very reason of reclaiming this base? Victor and Isabella might find themselves an unwilling welcome party.

He was still mulling over the best course of action when he walked back into the medical bay and found Isabella gone.

***

'OUR BIGGEST ISSUE WILL BE FUEL,' Lena was saying from the front seat as the old jeep jerked and skidded through the drifted snow on the road heading up into the hills north of the town. 'Whatever we find in this base, the fuel supply will likely be unusable. Refined oil and petroleum have a shelf-life like everything else. If it's spoiled, anything that requires fuel will be useless.'

'Then what the hell will we fight them with, snowballs?' Robert said beside her. Despite having one leg in plaster, one arm in a sling, and another shoulder heavily bandaged, Mortin had insisted on coming. Patricia's father was nothing if not tough.

'Guns will still work, provided we clean and oil them,' Lena said. 'Though what use they'll be, I don't know. I'm praying there'll be some kind of oil-refinery on site, or at least some alternative form of energy.'

'Nuclear? A couple of nukes would certainly help slow down the invasion.'

Lena gave Mortin a cold look. 'I think we've learned our lesson about nukes already,' she said. 'It's possible that some of these machines will have atomic power supplies, though. That's what I'm hoping for. And that they haven't decayed or leaked, of course.' She gave Mortin a sideways look. 'But then in all likelihood we're going to die anyway.'

Patricia sighed. On either side of her sat Lena's trusted guards, staring out of their respective windows at the bland snowy landscape, seemingly obvious to the conversation going on in the front. For her part, Patricia was just hoping she would find someone worth taking her frustrations out on. Victor or preferably Kurou, although one was likely hiding in the town and the other probably dead. Maybe she would have to settle for smashing up some of these machines Lena was counting on.

Up ahead, the road angled down into a hollow, then turned sharply uphill. Where the road turned back on itself a pair of tracks led out of the woods.

'There,' Patricia said. 'That's it.'

In the gun battle, the armoured truck she had brought down from the secret base had been damaged, its tyres blown out by stray bullets. The jeep had no chance of making it up to the tunnel entrance, so Patricia told Lena to pull over.

'It's only a couple of hundred metres, but it's hard going,' she said. 'Father, perhaps you should stay here?'

Mortin glared at her. 'You know me better than that, girl,' he said.

Patricia nodded and held up a pair of fold-out metal crutches. She just hoped his stubbornness wouldn't hold the rest of them back.

'ISABELLA!' Victor shouted, jogging through the corridors, his panic slowly rising. She had just vanished into the air. Many of the floors were coated with a fine layer of dust, but he couldn't find even a trace of her footprints. It was as if she had floated away.

'Where are you?'

His own voice came bouncing back. She couldn't have gone far, yet he had looked down all of the adjacent corridors, and there was no sign of her. Instead, he headed for the control room on the lower floor, sure he would be able to find her on the security cameras.

As he descended the stairs to the lower level, he passed hangar after hangar of ancient machines. Caked in a dry grey dust, everything looked so empty and desolate, a graveyard of technology. It was a soulless, dead place, one which he had dreamed of inhabiting until he had brought Isabella here.

Now all he wanted to do was get away.

'Isabella!' he screamed again, and this time a faint sound came back to him.

'Victor? Over here!'

He turned to see her at the far end of the nearest hangar, standing among rows of tall humanoid machines, her foot on the bottom rung of a stepladder pointed towards the nearest one.

'What are you doing? Stay away from there!' he shouted, but Isabella, being Isabella, just shrugged.

'Look!' she shouted. 'They have places you can climb inside. I think they're meant to be driven by people like we drive cars.'

For a few seconds she just stood there at the foot of the ladder, in front of the tall machine, and Victor felt something popping in his chest, like a link to his heart going boom. He tried to scream at her to get the hell away, but his words came out as a dry, constricted croak.

'Look, I told you,' she said, reaching up and moving out of sight beneath another one of the machines.

'No!'

Victor sprinted as fast as he could, but as he reached the machine Isabella was just struggling into a tight concave alcove in the robot's chest cavity, sliding her arms into control ports and ducking her head into a semi-circular chamber with a visor that fell down over her eyes.

'Get out of there!'

'Just a minute, Victor—oh, I ... I can't!'

Something whirred and something else clicked. A series of lights came on along the machine's flank and then a metal plate slid out of one side of its chest, arced around in front of Isabella's wriggling body, and attached itself to a locking mechanism on the far side, sealing her in. Below it, her feet still kicked out, but a moment later braces jutted out of the machine's lower torso and encircled her ankles, pulling her tight.

'Hang on,' Victor shouted. 'I'll get you out!'

'I'm stuck!'

Victor climbed up the ladder and reached out for the shield covering the front of the machine, but when his fingers touched it a bolt of electricity surged through his body. One moment he was reaching for Isabella, the next he was lying on his back, looking up at the rock roof of the hangar far above.

'Victor? Victor, are you all right?'

His muscles felt like cast iron as he inched his head around to face her. 'I'm fine,' he muttered out of a mouth that was reluctant to work. 'What did you do to me?'

'Nothing, I swear it!'

'It … it shocked me.'

'I didn't touch anything! I can't! It feels like my hands are trapped. I can't move anything. Victor, please help me!'

Victor tried to get up, but it was like climbing out of thick mud. He stared at his hands, compelling them to move, only to see them inch slowly back towards his body like he was reeling in a fish from a tar-filled pond.

Perhaps if he rolled on to his front he might have a better chance, he thought. He craned his neck to the left, trying to use the momentum to turn himself over, but all he felt was a growing neck ache. Sensation was starting to return to his legs, so he kicked out with his feet and was finally able to turn himself over, flopping on to his front to stare back up the hangar towards the door he had entered through.

Two people were standing there. Victor tried to gasp, but all that would come from his throat was a crushed wheeze.

He didn't recognise the taller of the two, an elegant but coldly attractive woman wearing a heavy fur jacket open at the waist where a gun holster was poking out. The other was shorter, younger, and apparently unarmed, but he considered her far more dangerous.

His wannabe angel of death: Patricia Mortin.

33

VICTOR IMPRISONED

THE GREY MAN closed his eyes, reaching out to his soldiers. They were spread out now, stretched wide across the Siberian plateau to maximize their effectiveness, but the cold was starting to wear. He'd lost three only yesterday, brought down not by enemy gunfire but by the relentless freezing air working on their control systems.

It didn't take long to go to work. Once the controls shut out, the heating systems switched down and their riders quickly died. He had teams heading out to retrieve those he could, but sometimes the riders were too integrated, and the system died with them.

His head was thumping with pain like he hadn't felt in decades. The skin on his arms was beginning to lighten again, after years of staying the same tint of grey-white. He knew his control was beginning to waver, that before long he would begin to lose his soldiers one by one and they would either regain autonomous control or perish in the harsh conditions. He was learning so much about himself at the same time as exacting a long overdue vengeance, but the time was coming when he would have to go underground again.

Still, there was time left yet. Time for a little more devastation before he turned his attention back towards his primary objective: recovering what had been stolen from him.

With his fingers pressed into the wooden window ledge until they left imprints and cracks in the paint, he reaffirmed his single command to his soldiers, the one solitary objective that had made controlling so many so easy:

Destroy.

ONE OF THE guards landed a token punch in Victor's stomach as the other opened the door. Together they tossed him into the storage room and pulled the door shut.

'Stand guard,' Lena told one, then dispatched the other to fetch Robert from where he was resting upstairs. Turning to Patricia, she said, 'Now let's go see what we can do about your sister.'

Patricia hurried to keep pace with Lena's long strides as the councillor walked back up through the hangar towards the machine where Isabella was trapped. The tall woman had been quiet ever since they had discovered the machines, barely even noticing Isabella's screams and struggles.

It appeared that Victor had managed to pull Isabella from the train wreckage and bring her here, but while Patricia was happy because she would be able to tell her father and cheer him up, she was far more excited about the rooms of machines they had discovered.

An entire war host was here just waiting for them. If only they could use the machines to their advantage, they might not have to give themselves up as lost.

Isabella was still screaming when they returned to her. The machine hadn't moved, but Isabella's face was pale and her eyes were darting around as if following motes of dust floating in the air.

'How do we get her out?' Patricia asked. 'My father will be heartbroken if she's hurt.' When Lena gave her a sideways glance, Patricia added, 'So will I.'

'There must be a mechanism on this thing. Perhaps he knows where it is?'

Patricia scowled. Victor, whom they had found lying on the floor in near paralysis, claimed Isabella had climbed into the machine of her own accord. Patricia didn't believe him for a second and had wanted to execute him on the spot. Lena had insisted they spare him, but his time was coming. Patricia had no intention of letting him leave the storage room alive.

'Isabella, can you find a catch or an unlocking mechanism?' Lena shouted, but Isabella just began to cry, shaking her head back and forth.

The problem was the folded brace around the front of the machine. Isabella had warned them not to touch it, but if they could break it open somehow they might be able to free her.

Back near the entrance to the hangar Patricia had seen a workshop. 'Wait here,' she said to Lena, leaving the older woman to stare up at the machine with a thoughtful look on her face.

A lot of the tools were too heavy to carry, but in a cupboard Patricia found an old circular metal saw which still worked when she tested the power. Grabbing a couple of armfuls of cable, she ran back downstairs to the machine.

Lena was still staring up at it with her eyes furrowed now. Isabella had gone quiet. A low noise was coming from the machine.

Patricia found a plug and had switched on the saw before Lena looked up. 'This will get her out,' Patricia said, hefting the saw and arching it towards the central body guard, even as Lena screamed, 'No!'

The saw struck the metal casing, bounced off and narrowly missed severing Patricia's arm. As it fell to the floor and began cutting into the concrete, Isabella's screams filled the air.

Lena jerked the cable from the socket and the saw's noise cut out, leaving just Isabella's high-pitched wail. The skin on her face was stretched unnaturally tight, her mouth open so far she resembled something from a horror movie.

'Isabella, I'm sorry! What's the matter?'

'It hurts!' the girl screamed. 'You're hurting me!'

'I didn't touch her,' Patricia said. 'What's she talking about?'

Lena was shaking her head slowly. 'We need to think about this. It's connecting to her in some way, perhaps running an electrical current through her. If you don't want to hurt your sister, we need to be more careful.'

'Hey! What's going on? Isabella? Isabella!'

At the far end of the hangar Robert Mortin had appeared, hobbling forward on his crutches. At the sight of his older daughter a wide beaming smile broke out on his face. Patricia felt a pang of jealousy, remembering how it had been Isabella who had made it on to the train and not her. She wished she still had the saw in her hands.

'What's happened to her? Get her down,' Mortin said, hobbling up to them, then leaning back on his crutches, breathing hard.

'She's trapped,' Lena said. 'This thing, this machine … it's like the ones I saw, but older, more basic. Those were far smaller and more compact. This is big and cumbersome, but it's something. We can use it to fight.'

Mortin glared at her. 'All I want right now is my daughter out of that thing.'

'We don't know how.'

'Well who does?'

Patricia glanced at Lena. Without a word they started walking back towards the storage room where Victor was trapped, Robert Mortin hobbling after them.

Victor looked up as the door opened and a looming figure blocked out the sudden burst of light. Sticks poked out from its sides and his dark-adjusted eyes initially thought it was a robot. Then the glowering face of Robert Mortin loomed over him.

'What did you do to my daughter?'

Victor was tempted to respond with the truth, that he had dragged her from a train wreck and brought her to safety, but Mortin didn't look in the mood for sarcasm, and in any case, Victor had only just begun to recover from the electric shock. More than a few words felt unnecessary.

'I don't know,' he said. 'She ran off.'

'I'll kill you, you worthless turd—'

Victor winced as a heavy wooden crutch rose into the air over his head. He wanted to lift his hands to protect himself, but they were still tingling and he knew it would make no difference.

'No!' Councillor Patrova had stepped in front of Mortin, her gun raised. 'I'll handle this,' she said.

'She ran off,' Victor muttered again, waiting for her to turn the gun on him.

'I need you to help me, Victor,' Lena said. 'How do we get the girl out of that machine?'

Victor shook his head, waiting for his still-tingling lips to get into position to form the words. 'That machine is called a War Horse, Prototype Level One. I saw it listed on a computer inventory.'

'Level One? My contact told me the ones coming towards us are level six. How can we get Isabella out of it?'

'I don't know.'

'You bastard!' Mortin shouted, pushing Lena aside. 'I never should have let you near my daughter!'

As he brought the stick up to strike, Victor screamed, 'But I know who does!'

Mortin paused. 'Who?'

Victor opened his mouth to speak, but it was Patricia who answered.

'His name is Kurou,' she said with a long sigh.

34

KUROU PLAYS WAR GAMES

KUROU FOUND the mayor's office much to his liking. With Lena Patrova gone off looking for Easter eggs up in the northern hills, he slipped in through a side door the guards waiting outside knew nothing of and calmly locked the main doors from the inside. Then, brewing himself a pot of expensive coffee that was most likely not available to the starving masses, he sat down at her desk to make some use out of her far more impressive computer.

Connecting to a satellite orbiting high above the Siberian Plateau, he used an online scanning system to locate any of the Grey Man's drones in the area. There were two, a couple of hundred miles to the north, casually picking off civilian factories with laser guided missiles. One had just run out of ammunition, but the other still had a couple of payloads left.

Hello, Grey Man. Any chance you remember me?

Hacking into the drones' communication systems and taking control of them was easier than unlocking a computer game. He reconfigured the command codes, blocking out any attempt by flight navigators on the ground to assume manual control, then set the drones back on a path that would take them home. The loaded drone would unload its two remaining missiles into its command centre, then both would make a last lovers' dive, kamikaze style. Whatever atomic power source was keeping them up in the air would make a bit of a mess upon impact.

Kurou sat back and rubbed his hands with glee. Then he set about hunting for more drones.

PATRICIA FELT RATHER resentful that Lena had allowed Victor a hot drink from the vending machine in the upstairs lobby, but as he sat holding it in two hands, she listened as Victor outlined his plan.

'I know he's dangerous. He's a murderer. But he's also a genius. We need him on our side.'

Her father, reluctant to move, had stayed down in the hangar with Isabella, but Patricia refused to let Victor out of her sight.

'How do we find him?'

'From what I know of Kurou, he'll be watching. Some way or another, he'll know where we are, and if we get out in the open long enough he'll come to us. But, if he thinks we're a threat, he'll stay hidden.'

'Search every house in the town and drag him out,' Patricia blurted.

Victor shook his head. 'No. You don't understand him. I barely do, but what I've learned is this: you can't force him to do anything. You have to let him think he's in control, that he's doing it by free will.'

Lena, who had taken her gun from its holster and left it lying on the table in front of her as if worried Victor might make a dart for freedom, said, 'How?'

'He's very childlike in a way,' Victor said. 'You have to let him think he's going to the circus, that it'll be fun for him. That he's playing games.' He smiled. 'And I have an idea….'

LENA'S COFFEE had kept Kurou awake longer than usual, but finally he retired to an ante-chamber in part of the Head Councillor's suite —after first setting up an alarm triggered by facial recognition using the camera outside the building's main doors—and took a few hours rest.

He was feeling groggy when he woke, and the wound in his side was weeping a little again. Outside the window night had fallen and a light snow was building up on the window ledge. The room, centrally air-conditioned, was a pleasant temperature, so before getting back to work, Kurou spent a few minutes poking through the recently departed mayor's cupboards and refreshing his attire, finally settling on a pinstripe suit—to wear beneath a fur coat if necessary —and a top hat that appeared to have come right out of a British period drama. He finished off his new look with a pair of white leather gloves and a fat Cuban cigar.

Feeling too dapper for words, he ambled back to the desk and sat down, one leg crossed over the other, then set about reviewing what had happened since the afternoon.

'How delightful,' he mused, noting that the two hijacked drones had found their mark, destroying a non-descript office building far away in St. Petersburg. The satellite map had no other drones in the immediate area, so Kurou went searching a little further west, picking up a small group of them moving in this direction. With a few musical taps of his white-gloved fingers, he hijacked them, breaking into a code that had been modified and strengthened since he had retired to bed, then for good measure adding in a calling card, an image of a crow that would appear on the screen of anyone trying to take control from the ground.

Then he sent them home.

Most likely the other command centre would learn from the mistakes of the first, and evacuate the building at the first sign of trouble, so therefore Kurou reconfigured the destination coordinates of the drones so that they would attack all of the major buildings within a five hundred metre radius of the exact source location.

Just to mess with their heads.

With that in place, Kurou spent a few minutes browsing wildlife websites and watching some aerial footage of Roman Bald Eagles on a video sharing website, before figuring he ought to check on how his absent friends were getting on.

Scanning the security cameras that scattered the town in the hope of seeing Lena Patrova's convoy returning, he was somewhat surprised to see a lone figure standing in the middle of St. Peter's Place, snow falling all around him as he held a bundle in his hands.

Kurou ordered the camera to zoom in.

'Victor…?'

His old friend was holding something the size of a baby. Kurou squinted at the screen, wishing the resolution was better, then, as if hoping to be seen, Victor turned around and was caught in the glow of an overhead street light.

In his arms was a tiny, broken robot.

'A gift for … me?' Kurou cawed gently, under his breath.

THE TEMPERATURE HAD to be twenty below zero, and Victor was so cold he could barely keep hold of the thing in his hands, despite the heavy fur coat and thick woollen hat he wore. He had been walking the streets for the last hour, and was at the end of his strength. Ten more minutes, and if Kurou didn't appear he would head back to Robert's house, where Lena and Patricia were waiting.

He had found the robot in amongst Kurou's things at the bottom of the chimney shaft. Guards had lowered him down with a couple of torches attached, but descending into the bowels of that great ruined building had brought back hideous memories, and it had taken all his willpower to resist crying out in horror every time he brushed against the walls.

Down in the basement apartment, the poverty of Kurou's existence returned in the flickering lights like some acid trip horror movie. The rooms stank of sickness and death, litter lay strewn across the floor amidst a clutter of machine and computer parts, strips of clothing, pieces of old, near-decayed meat. Victor had wanted with every fibre of his being to be out of the place, but he needed Kurou to see his sincerity. He needed a token that would make the professor believe.

In a corner of the main room, buried among a heap of wires and computer components, he found it.

A child's robot, handmade from pieces of junk. One leg was loose, one arm missing, but when Victor pressed a switch on the back the twin LED eyes briefly flashed before going dark.

He found a clean strip of cloth, carefully wrapped the robot, and tucked it into a pocket in his coat.

The fresh, winter air that wrapped around him when he emerged from the shaft had never been more welcome.

Despite the cold, the man standing across the plaza seemed unaffected. Victor knew immediately that it was Kurou, because the figure was skeletally thin, a black silhouette against a grey background, a tiny glowing light announcing his presence like a miniature signal fire.

Kurou was wearing a black suit and a top hat. On his feet, heavy snow boots were farcically out of place. The glow came from a cigar poking from the side of his mouth beneath the looming, crow-like beak. As Victor approached he removed the hat and gave a flourishing bow.

'Well met, squire. I see the years have been kind. Did you bring my coxcomb?'

Victor didn't even bother to ask what Kurou was talking about. Instead, he just held out the robot so that Kurou could see it in the glow of a nearby street light. Fat flakes of snow landed on its casing, one in its eye.

'I recovered it for you. It's a gift.'

Kurou stared at it for a long time, and Victor sensed the shedding of his performance piece. The real Kurou looked up at him.

'It's a replica,' he said. 'Of the first robot I ever built. *He* broke it when he came to see me. He broke it.'

'Who?'

'Rutherford Forbes. The Englishman. The man who bought me from my mother.'

Victor sniffed. A rapidly freezing tear popped from his eye. 'Do you miss her?'

Kurou looked up, only one beady eye visible. 'That old whore sold me down the Yangtze River for a washerwoman's dime. No, I don't miss her. But there are days when I miss *him*.'

'Forbes?'

'I never had a father otherwise. He gave me everything, except this.' Kurou lifted the little robot out of Victor's hands, put it into the top hat and replaced the hat on his head.

'I need your help,' Victor said. 'The whole town needs your help. You can come out of the dark, Professor. You're not the villain anymore. We need a hero.'

Something in Kurou's eyes changed. The sensitivity was gone again, hidden away back in its shell. The showman, the circus master, had returned.

'I am but a poor artist,' Kurou said, spreading his hands wide. 'I have no colours to paint with except those I find around me, and the surrounding world is so sickly grey, isn't it? You ask a great deal, young sire. If you ask, I will answer, but do not ask lightly. A request once received can never be withdrawn.'

For a moment Victor considered getting down on his knees, but he was so tired he doubted he could stand again. Instead, he put a hand over his heart. 'I have lived my whole life in Brevik,' he said. 'My parents were from this town, and their parents. The girl I love is from this town. It's nothing but a Communist throwback with too much snow and not enough love. Most trains don't even stop here because no one gets on or off. The people, for the most part, are assholes. But despite all that, I don't want to see it destroyed.' He took a deep breath. 'In that base there are rooms of old military vehicles and robots. Half of them look broken, the rest don't look capable of fighting their way out of a paper bag. Yet they're there. They're all we've got. With someone at the controls who knows what he's doing, perhaps we can put up a decent fight and not just lie down and roll over against the enemy that's coming for us. If I could do it myself, I would, but I can't. I don't have the skills. But you do. We need you, Professor. Everyone in this town needs you.'

Kurou took a long tug on his cigar and puffed a wide ring of smoke up into the night. It floated among the falling snow like a cancerous halo. Kurou gave a small cough, and when he spoke his voice was low and gravelly like the crunch of caterpillar treads on an icy street.

'I will build your war machines,' he said.

PART III

THE BATTLE FOR BREVIK

35

KUROU LEADS A WAR COUNCIL

As the door opened and Victor entered, brushing snow off his coat as he was followed in by Kurou, dressed bizarrely like a 18th Century British politician, Patricia made sure Lena Patrova stood between her and the new arrivals. Her father had stayed up at the base with Isabella, who was becoming less and less coherent, rambling on about strange dream sequences and feelings of being transformed into a machine. Victor promised that Kurou might be able to help her, but she would rather see him dead, and if her sister had to be sacrificed, then so be it.

Victor and Lena exchanged a curt nod. Kurou stuck a tongue out at Patricia then removed his top hat—the robot inside rattling around—and gave Lena a short curtsy.

'Charmed,' he said. 'I don't believe we've met, although I've enjoyed the pleasure of your offices these last few hours. Not a fan of the décor—a leftover from your unfortunate predecessor, was it not?'

From the look on Lena's face it was clear she found Kurou difficult to look at. She didn't offer him a hand but instead pointed to a chair on the far side of the room. Victor sat down beside him. Patricia stayed where she was while Lena took her father's favourite armchair.

'We need your help,' Lena said.

Kurou nodded. 'Dear Master Victor here has already informed me of the direness of your situation. Such a travesty. Human against human … when will it ever end?'

'So you'll help us?'

'My young friend brought me a gift. What kind of monster would I be to ignore such kindness?'

Patricia wrinkled her nose. Her fingers clenched around an imaginary gun and she pumped the trigger once, twice, three times. She bit her lip to keep her mouth shut.

'If we don't fight, the enemy will overrun us within weeks.'

Kurou raised an eyebrow. 'They're nine days west of us. I've already offered their overlord a few minor distractions, but they'll be coming on regardless.'

Lena leaned forward. 'You know about them?'

Kurou shrugged. 'I have ways of wading through the mess that used to be the internet that most people don't. More often than not it's a case of what it doesn't say that's most important.'

'Professor,' Victor said, 'who are we fighting against? Who's behind this?'

Kurou started to laugh. Patricia gripped the armrest of her chair as a shiver went down her spine. She remembered his face close to hers, his spindly fingers touching her. She would gladly die in a hail of machine gun fire to see him die first.

'Our greatest enemy is our own misinformation,' Kurou said. 'Teams of hackers have broken down the communication systems all across Europe. They're *your* teams of hackers, working for the Russian government, but they've been infiltrated. They have no idea that what they've been primed to do is turn your own army in on itself.'

'Are you saying that we're fighting a civil war?' Lena asked. 'What are you talking about? That's not possible.'

The whole of Eastern Europe and Russia has been ravaged by a war where no one knows who's on who's side. To one such as myself, with no great love for humanity, it's rather hilarious.'

Patricia started to stand, but Lena put a hand out to stop her. 'Sit,' she barked, as if reprimanding a schoolchild. As she lowered herself back into the chair, Patricia shot an angry glare at the back of the councillor's head.

'Those things I saw,' Lena said. 'They weren't part of any Russian army.'

Kurou grinned again. Sitting at his shoulder, Victor looked increasingly nervous, as if all he wanted to do was go home and watch television. Picking the first one of the pair to die would be difficult, Patricia thought.

'Let me see if I can describe what you saw,' Kurou said. 'Four legged robots seemingly with humans carried in the undercarriages, like a joey in a kangaroo's pouch? Between seven and nine feet high? Feeding off the remains of the dead like pigs snacking at a trough?' He leaned forward. 'Bristling with weaponry like a porcupine's spines?'

Lena glared at him. 'One might consider that you've seen one before.'

Kurou matched her stare. 'Only on paper,' he said. 'Signed by yours truly.'

'What are you talking about?'

'Up in that little grotto under the hill you have a couple of hundred older models. The company I worked for—and might I say built—was once provided with a series of inefficient prototypes and contracted to improve them.'

'You built those things?'

Kurou spread his hands. Patricia stared at his white gloves, wishing she could cut them off. He looked like the devil's own conjuror.

'Do I look like a common labourer, my dear? I most certainly did not build those things. I merely took a bad design and made it good.'

Until this point, Victor had sat quietly beside Kurou, saying nothing. Now he looked up. 'If you designed them then you know how to stop them.'

Kurou turned to stare at Victor as if noticing him for the first time. 'Do I look like the kind of man who would make fallibilities in my creations, sire? Do I? Is it really that likely that I would build something so easy to stop? The request was for an upgrade on a machine designed to kill as many people as possible that was cumbersome, flawed, and fuel inefficient. I honoured the contract to the letter, crossing the Ts, dotting the Is.' He spread his hands again. 'As any good contractor would.'

Patricia shook her head. 'You disgust me. Do you care anything for human life?'

Kurou shook his head. 'No, not at all. I wish for every single one of you to perish.'

'Then how do we know you're going to help us?'

Kurou grinned. He leaned forward, his beady eyes piercing. 'You don't.'

Lena put up a hand. 'Look, this isn't getting us very far. Is there any way to fight those things, to beat them?'

Kurou lifted two fingers to his temple and made a popping sound. 'The best way to kill a soldier is a bullet in the head,' he said. 'How many bullets do you have?'

'Can you jam their communication systems?' Victor said. 'If you can figure out what we're fighting you must be able to do that.'

The spark of total confidence vanished from Kurou's face as his eyes dropped, and Patricia knew that for all his bluster, there were things he didn't understand, couldn't figure out.

'It might be possible,' Kurou said. 'I'll need time. Probably more than you have. In the interim, raising a small army might not go amiss. Something to greet the Grey Man when he arrives.'

'The what?'

Kurou looked up at Lena, suddenly flustered as if caught with his hand in the cookie jar. 'It's nothing,' he said. 'Just a little blanket term to describe our enemy. Comes from the colour of their armour plating, don't you know?'

Lena gave a slow nod, but Patricia watched him a while longer. He scratched at an ear, crossed and then uncrossed his legs, fidgeted in his seat.

He knew something, a secret he was keeping to himself.

I'll cut it out of you if I have to, you bastard. We have unfinished business yet.

Kurou put the top hat back on to his head and stood up. 'If you don't mind, dear princess sisters, it might be wise of me to go back up to our little treasure trove and begin making plans. I'll need my assistant here, of course.'

Patricia stood up. 'I'll come too. I'm not letting you out of my sight.'

Kurou turned on her. 'On the contrary, my dear. I'm afraid this bird likes to fly in select company. Assuming you still wish to receive my assistance?'

Lena put a hand on Patricia's arm. 'Let them go,' she said. 'We have no choice.' Turning to Kurou, she said, 'I have council business in the town to attend to. We will meet you up at the base tomorrow morning to begin preparations.'

'That sounds like a delightful arrangement,' Kurou said. 'Myself and my good assistant will endeavour to stay out of Mr. Mortin's way until a suitable human blockade is made available.'

Patricia stared at him. 'How did you know my father was up at the base?'

Kurou grinned. 'The same way that I know that without my help in nine days you'll all be dead. By using my eye and ears, and my intuition. It's never too late to begin your tuition, sweet princess.'

As retorts rattled in Patricia's brain like old bolts, Lena hissed at her to keep quiet. Kurou gave a final bow and then headed out into the night, Victor at his heels.

As soon as the door was closed, Patricia turned on Lena. 'Are you crazy? He's a *mass murderer*. And you've enlisted him to help us? Are you out of your fucking mind?'

Lena sighed. 'On the contrary,' she said, doing a poor mockery of the professor's mannerisms, 'a mass murderer is the very thing we need right now.'

AS THEY HURRIED through the snow towards the jeep that would take them back up to the base, Victor turned to Kurou.

'Who is he?' he said. 'Who's the Grey Man? I heard you say that name, and I know you didn't mean to.'

'Should an assistant question his master so?'

'Just tell me. Do you know or not?'

Kurou's face was a shadow in the gloom. 'I don't like to speak with confidence on things I don't truly understand,' he said. 'I trust you've gathered that, sire?'

'I got that impression, yes.'

'This Grey Man—as he appears to call himself—who is commanding these War Horses, is something of an enigma. When you first encountered me, did you not feel something of the same, sire?'

'I still think you're an enigma.'

Kurou smiled. 'Your honesty is fascinating. While it is perceived as true, I am but a simple artist with the whole world as my canvas. I get the impression that this Grey Man might be something of the same.' He paused, touching his huge overhanging nose with one white glove. 'And it is my estimation that there might not be room for the both of us. That, particularly, is my cause for concern.'

36

KUROU RAISES AN ARMY

EVEN AT TIMES LIKE THESE, when half of everyone you knew was dead, the comfort of a sofa and the companionable chatter of the television remained a welcome constant. Dimitri had seen the drama a dozen times before, but in those oft repeated scenes he was able to forget the nightmares going on outside. He had been unable to get a ticket for the last train—thankfully so, after what had transpired—but had decided to stay out of all the rioting that had sparked off around City Hall. He had heard the gunshots and the roars of the crowd from the safety of his own living room, having fitted extra deadbolts over his window shutters and on his front and back doors.

Still, avoidance didn't mean there wasn't a threat. Dimitri just saw no reason to partake in anything that was proportionately likely to get him killed.

The picture on the screen flickered, and Dimitri instinctively glanced up at the ceiling, as if something was messing with his signal. It had happened before the last drone strikes, shutting down as if severed, and also before what he later found out was the hit on the departed train. He stood up, gathered up his bottle of vodka and the biscuits he was eating, and turned to head for the basement, where he had a bed set up all ready. His only gun was down there too, propped up against the wall at the bottom of the concrete steps.

On the screen, the picture flickered again, but didn't cut out. The drama disappeared, replaced by a dark room with a silhouette of a thin man standing in the centre.

'Greetings, dear citizens,' came a reedy, sinister voice. Dimitri paused in the doorway to watch. He had an overwhelming urge to leave the room, but there was something in the way the man's white-gloved hands were moving that he found strangely compelling.

'My name is General Crow. You may not recognise me, but that's because I've been hard at work repairing all the damage your town council has done. The situation has, unfortunately, degenerated into one where I am forced to ask for your help. As you may or may not be aware, an invasion force is quickly approaching the city. Without a little resistance, we will all die. We do, however, have some hope. A military weapons cache lies just to the north of the town, and it might prove strong enough to repel the invaders. However, with no one to operate the machinery it stays lifeless and dead, and useless. Therefore, I ask for your help, dear people. I ask for you to volunteer to help us repel this terrible enemy. I ask that you gather in City Hall Plaza at midday tomorrow. There you will receive further instruction. Good night.'

The TV appeared to be rocking up and down, then Dimitri realised it was because he was nodding. It made perfect sense. He had to help. Would he need his gun though? He supposed not. He would definitely need a coat, however.

Of course he had to help. He was a patriot, wasn't he? And his town was in dire need. It would be an honour to die in the line of duty.

Still nodding, he stared at the clock, willing the seconds to tick around to midday. There was a long way to go, but what were a few more hours?

Wow, he thought, as his eyes glazed over, the clock face becoming a blur of black and whites, there had been something special about that man's hands.

THEY HAD nothing at all among them except the old television and the broken wooden chair it stood upon. The six men, all former mining workers, had lost everything in the pit closures, and their lives had spiralled downwards into whatever numbing pastime they could find. Now, all high, hollow-stomached and empty hearted, they watched with something like wonder as the television screen flickered and morphed into the image of a tall spindly man wearing a black suit, a top hat, and white gloves.

They listened as he promised them everything. As one they nodded, and as one they began to cheer.

THE SHEER NUMBER of people assembled outside City Hall came as a surprise to Lena. For the previous two days she had spent her time knocking on individual doors, doing miniature pep rallies in front of disillusioned townsfolk who either loathed her or had no idea who she was or why they should care. Kurou had insisted on doing the intercepted television broadcast, but she had told him he was wasting his time, that if she couldn't persuade them in person they couldn't be persuaded at all.

Yet here they were, some four hundred of them, a few enthusiastic, gung-ho volunteers at the front whooping and cheering with every stirring word of her rallying call, but most standing motionless in orderly rows, barely even blinking. She had hated this place on sight, she recalled now, on that dreary, supposedly spring day so many years ago now that the best days of her life should have still been ahead of her. Instead, the mood of this grim, outlandish place with its glum-faced residents had vacuumed the youth out of her, and here they now stood, come to mock her resilience one last time.

'…and we have no choice but to stand up against this invader, or perish in our homes like cowards.' She suppressed a sigh, hoping her speech, shamelessly plagiarized from dozens of old war movies, might have some effect. Now, for the coup de grace. 'So … are you with me? Do we stand together and fight, or do we die alone in our homes?'

For a second there was only the lonely cheering of the handful of volunteers at the front. Lena braced herself for a slow handclap, or even a roar of laughter. Then, so suddenly it made her flinch, four hundred right fists thrust up into the air, accompanied by a roar of approval.

'*Fight!*'

I would hate to have gone to school in this shithole, she thought.

'Together we can win this!' she screamed into the microphone, unsure whether she believed it or not, but feeling the need to say something. She was de facto mayor, after all.

THE GREY MAN didn't need to look at the report printing itself out on the fax machine on his newly commandeered desk. He had felt the people die. In his mind he had heard their screaming as the building burned and collapsed. He had been sleeping at the time, and sometimes it was difficult to differentiate such disasters from simple nightmares. This time, their pain had been almost tangible, breaking him from sleep with a jolt.

That the drones had been taken over wasn't the worst thing of all, it was that it had happened without his knowing. Someone had cracked their systems and turned them back on their programmers. As a result, he had ordered all remaining drones to be grounded. It had happened once, and then it had happened again. Until he understood the threat, he had no answer, and he risked losing control of his entire fleet.

Someone was out there, standing up to him, breaking through the communications mist that his teams of hackers had created, revealing the truth and then finding a way to fight back.

He had been so, so, thorough this time.

Who are you?

The prints were still coming, falling from the table to the floor and scattering at his feet. Soon, the fax would run out of paper. Lines and lines of figures and statistics and garbled computer-based reports detailing the damage, so much unnecessary detail—

He nudged one sheet aside with his foot, then reached down to pick it up. It was an image, a black silhouette of a bird that took up the whole page. There was some detail at the bottom that mentioned how it appeared on screens when attempts were made to regain control of the drones.

The Grey Man frowned. He remembered an assignment he had given to Halo some five years before in Barcelona. A madman had turned La Sagrada Familia into a lake of fire and Halo had been lucky to escape with his life. The madman had disappeared. The madman's name had been....

Kurou.

I remember you. Is that you out there? You're taunting me, aren't you?

Five years ago, the trail had gone cold. A man named Park had died because he wouldn't accept failure, but even though he had moved on to other things, the Grey Man had never forgotten the genius that had brought ruin to the greatest of European cities, and civil war to Spain.

The Grey Man pulled a few more sheets from the floor, more interested now in the data he couldn't extract from his mind's own wanderings.

The two pairs of hijacked drones had been flying nearly a thousand miles apart, but between them was an endless expanse of almost nothing, pinpricked by a few mining settlements and two larger towns. One was in the process of being razed by his War Horses, but the other....

He closed his eyes and concentrated, sending out his mind's feelers in that direction. As always, the greater the distance and the more people to be encountered the weaker his strength became— the crowded nature of cities were so overwhelming as to leave his powers almost ineffectual, but out here in Siberia he had much greater strength—but there was a large gathering of minds, like an army marching in file.

Could these people be planning a resistance? And could they be harbouring the one who had destroyed two of his command centres?

The Grey Man closed his eyes.

If you're out there, I'll find you.

37

THE TALE OF A HORSE AND ITS RIDER

A KNOCKING WAS COMING from two doors at once, and Kurou wished he'd chosen an office with only one entrance, or better still, none at all. Who would lose patience first became a moot point as simultaneously one door sprang open to reveal Lena Patrova, while the other rattled in its bearings, the sound just audible over the shouting of Robert Mortin.

'I'll deal with him,' Lena said. 'Once you give me an update.'

Kurou pulled a map up on the largest of his computer screens. 'Here in the centre,' he said, 'that little blue dot is our delightful Brevik. Five miles north we have the mining operations, creating a useful barrier for where we sit right now in this base, three miles due northwest of town. Protecting us to the west are these pine-forested hills, but you know all this already, don't you?'

'It's easy to see why they chose this place to hide all this junk,' Lena said. 'It must have come as a surprise that the town grew so big.'

'A lot of greedy fingers can squeeze into a pot of gold,' Kurou said. 'Or in this case, a dry bowl full of cheap aggregate.'

'So our best line of defence is this forest. Particularly if we can hold the ridgeline.'

'As long as possible would be good,' Kurou said. 'We have six hundred War Horses, but we can only spare three hundred men. They're coming at us with a force of roughly two thousand.'

'Jesus.'

'And they're much newer models. Faster, more agile, better weaponry.'

'Do we have any chance at all?'

Kurou grinned. 'Not so much. A thrill, isn't it? The art of war? A battle of wits and skill, like one gigantic game of chess.'

Lena glared at him. 'I can see why people tend to dislike you.'

'I do not crave friendship. Respect, however, is rather more valuable.'

Lena pointed at the map. 'If we don't have the numbers to fight them in open battle, we need to trap them.'

'A woman after mine own heart,' Kurou said. 'A spider to my crow.'

'You charm me,' she said with a flat smile.

'Our weak points are to the south and east,' Kurou continued. 'The railway valley is a particularly smooth line of attack. Our only chance is to sacrifice the town. The Lenin District to the south is crowded with narrow streets and tight alleyways. If we can draw them inside, make them believe we have a larger force, that we're fighting a tactical retreat towards City Hall, maybe, just maybe … we have a chance.'

Kurou clicked on the map and it zoomed in, showing a wider view of the town. He pointed at a street winding up towards St Peter's Place.

'The route of the old highway,' he said. 'They will have no aerial support. I will make sure of that. Therefore, we put our strongest forces in the hills to the west and around the mining operation to the north. We make them go around, draw them into the town from the south, make them advance along the route of the old highway. Most of the buildings there are abandoned. We load them with explosives and weaponry. When they come—', he snapped his hands together, the white gloves making a *whump* sound like something bursting into flame, '—we pop them like bugs on a hot plate.'

'Will it work?'

Kurou shook his head. 'It might. It might not. The longer we can stall them, the better. If I can find a way to jam their communications systems, then perhaps we can shut them down.'

'Why can't you?'

'Give me time, give me time,' Kurou said, flapping his hands in the air. 'Their systems are not as they should be. The way they're being controlled, it's not….'

'Not what?'

'Natural.'

Thuds came from the other door again. Something heavy struck the handle from the far side and the metal hinges screeched.

'He's back again,' Lena said. She went to the door and pulled it open.

Robert stood there, crutch poised for another strike. 'No thanks to you but we got her out,' he said.

Kurou stood up. 'That pretty girl? Are you sure?'

'I got a team of engineers together and we busted her out. You bastard, two men are dead now.'

'And I'm to blame exactly why?'

Robert lifted his crutch. 'I'll cut off your ugly head, you freak,' he snarled, taking a couple of shaking steps forward using his other crutch for support.

Lena got in his way and lifted a hand. Robert shook his crutch one more time, then put it back under his arm.

'You really should have left her in there,' Kurou said. 'I told you I was working on it, and when a crow makes a promise … did she survive?'

'She's resting.'

'Oh, how lovely. Tell me when—or if—she wakes up.'

'What do you mean, "if"?'

Kurou picked up his top hat from the desk beside the computer terminal and put it on his head. 'I think I should accompany you to the princess's bedchamber.' He smirked. 'Or would you rather I went alone?'

A GUARD STOOD outside the private room on the corridor outside the medical lab. As they approached he muttered something about Victor trying to visit but being shooed away, then he was holding the door open for them to go inside.

Robert glared at Kurou like a hawk at a lame mouse from the other side of the bed where Isabella lay, tucked in beneath a musty quilt duvet with faded floral patterns. Among the train survivors had been a couple of doctors, and they had hooked Isabella up to a heart monitor which beeped gently in the background. An oxygen mask was fitted over her face, and her slow breathing came in long, ragged draws.

Kurou raised an eyebrow at the sight of her. So pale she might as well have been dead, some of her hair had even fallen out. Her cheeks were sunken as if she hadn't eaten in weeks, and a nasty red welt stained the left side of her neck.

'A regular sleeping beauty, isn't she?' Kurou muttered. 'I guess there's always the recycling. I could recommend a couple of good websites. We might even be able to hack up her price a little bit—'

'Kurou, shut up,' Lena said. 'Mortin, has she spoken or opened her eyes?'

'Not once. She was coherent until we broke her out of the machine, but apart from a few minor injuries there appears nothing wrong. The doctors have examined her and can't find anything physically wrong, but as you can see, she's wasting away.'

Kurou sighed. 'As useless as the dumb bear you resemble. There's a reason I told you to leave her in the machine until I had a way of freeing your precious baby figured out. Now look at her. If I were you I'd keep a watch on her and hope for a miracle.'

'What are you talking about?'

Before anyone could stop him, Kurou gave Isabella a pat on the head. 'Doth thine anger burn like thy father's crown?'

'You babbling fool.'

Kurou grinned. 'You can keep my coxcomb. Now, I have work to do, sire. Good day to you.'

He hurried out before anyone could stop him, but Lena caught up with him in the corridor. 'What's happened to her?' she said. 'We have another three hundred of those things that we need to fight for us. Is this going to happen to everyone who rides one?'

Kurou stopped so quickly that Lena had to sidestep into the wall to avoid hitting him. 'Yes,' he said, his single eye fixing her with a piercing glare. 'The riders of the War Horses, they don't just assume physical control, but mental too. They make a connection with the machine. They're symbionts. You can't just separate them. That buffoon and his clown army might as well have taken off one of her pretty little legs.'

Lena's gun was out of its holster and poking into Kurou's face before he had seen her draw it. *Must be getting slow,* he thought, trying to ease his great curved nose to the side so the gun didn't scratch it.

'We're relying on those machines for our survival,' she said. 'Are we going to have the same situation with each of them?'

'If we remove the riders by force then yes.'

'Is there any other way?'

Kurou shrugged. Lena lowered the gun but didn't put it away. 'One of the design flaws that I was asked to fix was the difficulty in disassociating a War Horse with its rider. When they were damaged during military exercises the riders inevitably died after being cut out. Some of them held on for a few weeks, but it happened one hundred percent of the time.'

Lena stared at Kurou until he looked away. 'You knew about this, didn't you?'

Kurou lifted an eyebrow. 'I care nothing for these people I send to war,' he said. 'I care only about the victory.'

'How can your heart be so cold?'

Kurou grinned. 'Now, now, sweet Lena of the green pastures of grand Russia. If I compare thee to a summer's day wouldst thou not compare me to every government in history? Since when have the lives of a few mattered to the survival of the many? You call me cold, but I am just a product of the humanity from whence I came, as are you, my dear. Would it not be time for a little redefining of the term "humanity"?'

Lena said nothing. 'Are you trying to find a way to save them?'

'Among other duties, yes. Their deaths, while of no direct consequence to myself, are a hindrance in our efforts to win the day.'

For a long time, Lena said nothing, she just stared down at the dusty tiles of the corridor floor. 'So, the girl might die, and the others we use for those machines might die also.'

'Yes. Are you okay with that?'

Lena took a deep breath. 'Do what you must, Professor.'

'With Godspeed, sweet princess.'

As the footsteps echoed away down the corridor, a side door opened. Victor waited until he was sure they had gone, then he lifted a hand and wiped away a sheen of sweat from his forehead.

His heart was thundering. He had overheard every word, but most of it had passed in a blur, overshadowed by the knowledge that Isabella would almost certainly die.

Only days before he had dragged her out of a burning train. Now she needed saving again.

Without a clue of what he was going to do, he headed off back to the control room and the hangars beyond, hoping to come up with some sort of plan before the love of his life wasted away before his eyes.

38

SECRETS AND REVELATIONS

Without fear of the drones spotting them from the air, the valley with its steep, forested sides was ideal for weapons practice. Kurou had selected ten men to enter the suits, while the rest of the chosen stood around in groups, watching as the ten lined up and discharged their weaponry into the forest.

'Feel free to take notes,' Kurou shouted through a megaphone as the boom from the first round of arsenal discharge died away into a dull ringing. 'You'll need these to take out anything bigger than a truck, but remember to aim a little in front of the target as they'll be much faster than you. Got that, amigos?'

He doubted that the glum ranks and file of the volunteers got anything. He was already starting to regret his little hypnotism trick, as revising their hypnosis to follow orders was more trouble than it was worth, requiring man-to-man attention. All of the genuine volunteers had been assigned to more demanding tasks, such as laying mines or trip-explosives, setting up surveillance cameras or moving heavy artillery into position. Those in front of him assigned as riders for the War Horses were mere cannon fodder, and while Lena might have agonized over their inevitable sacrifice, Kurou's only concern was that they would put up too little of a fight.

There was not enough fuel or ammunition for proper weapons training. Unlike the War Horses that were coming en masse from all sides—which ran on bio-fuel taken cannibalistically from their fallen enemies, a quirk which Kurou himself had introduced in the new designs—these old ones ran on regular gasoline. On Kurou's command, Victor had led a team back into the city tasked with siphoning off the petroleum left in domestic cars and running lines into the town's few refuelling stations to drain them. Their defence was only likely to last a couple of days anyway, but in the event that they managed to hold out longer they would be beaten by their own lack of fuel.

At least the fusing had gone well. The men already saddled up—as Kurou wryly referred to it—had become more autonomous than their peers, with the machine's controls influencing them. With all of them controlled remotely by computer, the only downside would be their lack of human-influenced reactions in the heat of battle.

Lena came up behind him. 'How are they?'

'Heavy and cumbersome, slow and easy to hit, but raw food is a hearty meal to a starving man, is it not?

Lena sighed and nodded. 'Is there still no way we could evacuate?'

'I would share no concerns were you all cut down running west while I sneaked away east through the battle lines themselves,' Kurou said. 'In terms of survival though … you have no chance. Not enough transportation vehicles or fuel, and the roads have now been left unploughed for several weeks. Where, of course, they've not been bombed.' He turned and patted her on the shoulder, making her flinch. 'Good luck.'

'How much time do we have?'

'To the west about four days. To the north, east, and south, perhaps five, giving them a little more time to circle around. We will assume battle formations the day after tomorrow.'

Lena nodded and made excuses to leave. Kurou watched the gun testing for a few more minutes, then headed inside, leaving the machines in the charge of one of the volunteers.

Down in the room he had taken for his control centre, he logged back into the communications satellite he was using to track the progress of the incoming War Horses. As expected, they were beginning to converge from the north and south, moving in a pincer-motion towards the town.

'You know we're here, don't you?' Kurou muttered. 'You're coming for the party.'

It should have been a relatively simple procedure to hack into the communications systems for the Grey Man's War Horses and take control of them, even taking into consideration the level of autonomy that each rider had. Sure, it would mean searching through reams of code and hours of programming, but it should have been possible. Yet, nothing was working so far.

It was as though there was some other form of communication that Kurou couldn't breach.

The technology was far in advance of what he had to work with, but compared with some of his own creations it was primitive. Yet still … nothing would give. He was at the end of his patience, and starting to believe the way the Grey Man was controlling his War Horses was something darker, unexplainable.

Something that would render his efforts worthless.

He picked up a computer monitor and hurled it across the room in frustration, then headed back outside. High above, a cold sun was leaning towards the end of another day. Most of the War Horses had been moved back inside, but Kurou waded out through the snow and up a path to a clearing where one of the War Horses lay face down in the snow. Three volunteers, one former radiologist and two who had been pharmaceutical assistants, stood around watching it, taking measurements with a variety of electronic equipment that Kurou had painstakingly—and at times angrily—taught them to use. They flinched at his approach, but despite their guarded looks they stood to attention.

'Success?'

The nearest man nodded. 'Eighteen hours and the rider still lives. The machine is creating an artificial heat source to protect them both.'

'And the upper surface temperature?'

'Base levels. The additional heat generation is only on the rider cavity, so that if the machine is lying face down the heat source is undetectable from above.'

Kurou clapped his hands together. 'Perfect. Then we begin deployment tomorrow. Good work, gentlemen.'

He left them standing around the face-down machine and went back to the base, hoping they had made no mistakes. The ability of the War Horses to protect their riders in times of extreme cold was essential to their success. The cumbersome machines were an easy target out in the open, so he needed to employ the old trick of surprise to give them the best chance of success.

Victor was in the control room when Kurou returned, looking at something on the computer.

'Success, my young apprentice?' Kurou asked.

Victor's nod was a little too enthusiastic. We filled three tankers,' he said. 'One of the fueling stations had been keeping a secret stock to sell at inflated prices later in the war.'

Kurou grinned. 'A businessman after my own heart.' He pulled off his top hat, gave the robot who had been riding in it continuously for the last three days a little shake, and put it down on the desktop.

'I have another task for you,' he said.

'Yes?'

'I need three size seven screwdrivers from hangar bay four. There are some in the little workroom by the entrance.'

Victor stood up, giving a quick glance back at his computer screen. 'Um, sure.'

'Hurry along now, sire. On the double.'

With a nod, Victor plodded out, closing the door with a soft click that was almost nervous. Kurou sat stock still for a few seconds, his acute hearing picking up Victor's footsteps as they receded down the corridor towards the stairs at the end. Satisfied that the young inventor was out of the way, Kurou went over to the workstation Victor had been using and quickly restored the browsing history that Victor had been so quick to delete.

Kurou frowned, cocking his head. A computer model of a War Horse from the hangars below appeared on the screen. A central area was flashing red, and Kurou zoomed in to take a closer look.

The highlighted area belonged to the life support systems.

So, it seemed young Victor was lovesick, still clinging to the hope that his girlfriend could be saved.

Kurou almost wished it could be true, but not quite. He had far more pressing matters than a young man's grief, like how to get one over on the Grey Man.

———

Patricia slipped the fist-sized incendiary device into a pocket of her thick winter jacket. She looked around to see if anyone was watching, but none of the other volunteers on trap-laying detail were paying her any attention. She nodded to herself, then squatted down and pulled another of the timed bombs out of the box and fitted it into a crevasse in the collapsed wall of the old bank, covering it over with a thin layer of gravel.

She had four others already secreted away in a tree stump not far from the entrance to the base. While her choice of hiding place made her feel a little like a psychopathic squirrel, she didn't dare keep them near her sleeping quarters, or get caught with them on her. Kurou had eyes everywhere, and where he didn't have eyes, he had cameras. Her father might be able to call him off publically, but Robert was still restricted to crutches, and there was only so far his influence could reach.

Each device had an individual code, which was keyed into a triggering controller about the size of a pocket calculator. From there, various detonation options were available.

She had also stolen a controller.

When the time came, part of her didn't want Kurou to die instantly. She wanted him to watch her as she put a boot on his neck and ended his sorry excuse for a life.

39

KUROU MEETS THE LOST PRINCESS

VICTOR HAD to wait until midnight to be sure that Robert Mortin would be sleeping. He had come armed with some fake orders in case he was denied admittance, but the guard outside Isabella's door was also snoring quietly in a plastic chair, his head lolling against the wall.

Inside, Mortin was sleeping on an adjacent bed, his face turned to the wall. Victor tiptoed across the room, wincing at every creak and groan of the floor as he went. Robert Mortin was fearsome even on crutches, but Victor just wanted a few quiet minutes with Isabella. Maybe she couldn't hear him, but he needed to say the words anyway.

On a low table beside her a single dim lamp lit the room. Victor crossed to the side of Isabella's bed opposite Mortin, ready to duck out of sight if the man woke. Isabella was lying on her back, her pale, gaunt face looking up at the ceiling. Wires connected her to a ventilation machine, and a tube in her arm led to a fluid drip. The room stank of formaldehyde, even though someone had put a bunch of dusty, plastic flowers in a vase on a corner table and sprayed it with dryly pungent air freshener.

Victor reached up and took her hand, wincing at the chill of her skin. 'Can you hear me, Isabella? It's Victor.'

She made no response. Victor stared at her face, hoping only for the flicker of eyelids to indicate she could hear, but nothing came.

'I wanted you to know that I haven't given up. I'm trying to find a way to heal you, but I'm not quite there yet. I just need more time. Stay strong for me.'

No response.

'Some people might have given up on you, but I haven't. I'm

nearly there. I've nearly got it figured out. I just need a little more time, then we can get out of this place forever.' He paused. 'I love you, Isabella Mortin. Please don't die.'

Over on the adjacent bed, Robert snorted and rolled over, for a moment his head lifting off the pillow, one hand reaching up to wipe his nose, then he relaxed and began to snore again. Victor sat motionless in the gloom, listening to the beat of his thundering heart.

Sensing Robert would soon wake, Victor gave Isabella's hand a last squeeze. The flesh beneath the cold skin felt hard, almost metallic.

'Wait for me,' he said. 'I'll come again soon.'

As he crept out of the room, past Isabella's snoring father and the guard sleeping in the chair outside, Victor prayed that he could keep his word.

As Kurou moved through the deserted streets, the cane he had found to go with his gloves and top hat swishing through the fresh snow, he tried to ignore the blistering air temperature, chilling even for him as it dropped to the region of minus thirty centigrade. He had considered discarding his costume or replacing it with a thick Russian jacket, but it helped him stay in character, and right now his character was the only thing that might get him answers.

While his own army's preparations for war were going better than he had could have hoped, considering the age of the resources available and the limited fuel sources, not to mention the technical infallibility of his workforce, he had failed to make further progress in his attempts to stop the Grey Man's approaching horde.

With the right resources, Kurou felt capable of controlling anything. His were skills learned through myriad hours of intricate practice, his knowledge of electronics, computer systems and genetic manipulation technology advancing until they were without peer, but this was something different.

Controlling the drones had been like stealing a kid's toy and taking over the controller. Once you knew where the controller was, it was a case of plucking it out of whatever hand—real or digital—was holding it.

But taking control of the War Horses—the very same machines that he had helped to design—was different.

He could feel their systems. He could tap into their memory banks and read through their data, count the kills, the remaining fuel, even view the emotive charts which displayed the current status of the human-machine link, but he couldn't take control of them in the way that he, Kurou, had designed them so that he should be able to.

Something else was blocking them, a form of technology of which he had no knowledge, and the implications of that were terrifying.

He couldn't beat an enemy he couldn't see.

The Lenin District was deserted and almost pitch dark, the electricity having been diverted to add power to the underground base. A handful of emergency street lights were too dim to even cast him a shadow, an irony that did not go unnoticed. Even in the gloom his keen eye picked out the tracks of his volunteers, and he was careful to keep away from the streets he had allocated for booby traps and other little welcome parties for the Grey Man's troops.

He had to take a scenic route through several dark, deserted streets to get to his old haunts in the far south of the Lenin District, where most houses were abandoned shells, haunted only by the ghosts of former mining workers and the wraiths that kept them alive.

With a memory better than any photograph, it was easy to find the house where he had spoken to the girl. It was likely she was dead or gone; while he hadn't seen her among the volunteers, the last time he had seen her, in the days before Victor had found him, she had been a hair's breadth from a welcome death.

The house was as he remembered it, putrid smelling, freezing, veiled with the aura of the dead or nearly so. The downstairs rooms were empty, but he quickly found the place where he had left the remains of his last human meal, the floorboards creaking underfoot. In a back room he found a small television, its screen dirty, its power chord frayed. Several wooden stools surrounded it, the remains of some kind of animal—most likely a household pet—shared among several plastic bowls in front of them. Some of these men were now saddled into War Horses and preparing to ride into battle; he remembered the same foul stench on their unwashed bodies.

The stone staircase was cold underfoot, in places sticky from the residue of a carpet long ago taken away. On the second floor landing, three doors stood open to reveal empty rooms littered with trash and drug paraphernalia.

One door at the end was closed.

Kurou opened it silently and peered into the darkened room. The girl lay on the bed, beneath a pile of filthy blankets that smelled like rotting cattle hide. A fire in one corner flickered weakly beneath the charred remains of a stool similar to those encircling the television.

Her eyes were closed, her breathing shallow. Kurou tapped his cane lightly on the floor until she opened her eyes and squinted up at him.

'Do you remember me?' he said. 'I have come back for you.'

The girl gave a weak smile. 'The worst thing in the world. Self-styled. Like a character from a comic book. You know nothing, Mr. Caricature.'

Feeling a surge of anger, Kurou knelt down and gripped the girl's chin in his fingers, squeezing her mouth open. He gave her tongue a kiss before she could shrink away.

'Tell me what I ought to know.'

'He's coming.'

'The Grey Man?'

'Yes.'

'How do you know?'

She gave a weak smile. 'I hear him. He doesn't know I can hear, but I can. I remember him.'

'Who is he? What is he?'

The girl started to laugh. 'He's the end of all things. Isn't that who you wanted to be? He's looking for you, you know. He doesn't appreciate being made a fool of. Not by a man, not … by a Crow.'

'Tell me how he controls them. How does he speak to you?'

The girl smiled again. 'He is with me all the time. In here.' She lifted a hand and pointed to the side of her head. 'Sometimes I hear him talking, other times it's only his thoughts.'

'Talk to me in the same way. Do it now.'

'No.'

'Why not?'

'I don't want to see inside of you. I'll go to hell soon enough as it is.'

Kurou slapped the girl across the face. 'Who are you?'

'Don't you mean, what am I? Isn't that it? One of the rejected, I guess you'd say.'

Kurou stared into her eyes, and as the firelight flickered there he saw she was older than her face suggested, older than he was, older than he might ever be.

'What's your name?' Kurou asked.

The girl chuckled. 'I don't remember what it was, but it was pretty. I remember that.'

'You knew him, you were close to him.'

'Once. We come from the same place. The same level of darkness.'

Kurou slipped one hand under the mass of blankets. The girl didn't react as his fingers traced lines across her cold skin.

'Why can't I hear him?'

'Because he only speaks to humans.'

Kurou smiled. Whether she was humouring him or not, he didn't know, but he took it as a compliment. He pushed the blankets back further and lifted himself up into the bed, pulling the covers back over them both.

'Call him,' he said. 'If he can hear you, call him. I want him to hear your sighs, your moans, your cries. Call him, lost princess.'

The girl closed her eyes. She sighed and lowered her head back on to the pillows.

'Call him,' Kurou said, beginning to move back and forth. 'Tell him Kurou looks forward to meeting him. Tell him to come with all might and prepare for darkness, even in the depths of light. Tell him I'll be waiting.'

The girl had begun to groan. Kurou scowled as he pushed himself forwards, enjoying a pleasure he hadn't felt in years. Then, as the wind rattled the shutters of the bedroom window, he lifted his cane and lowered it across the girl's throat. She made no motion to stop him, but her eyes jerked open, staring straight ahead.

'Tell him Kurou waits in the passages beneath ground,' he said. 'Tell him to come to me if ever he wishes to avenge his lost princess.'

He leaned forward on the cane as he rose inside her. For the briefest of moments her arms reached up to grip his shoulders, then her mouth widened, a low moan escaping her lips. Kurou gasped, pushed down on the cane one more time, then relaxed, pulled himself free of her embrace and climbed out of the blankets, lowering them back down over her empty, dead eyes.

'Goodnight, flown angel,' he said, breathing hard. 'I'll tell your old friend you wished him well.'

40

ISABELLA'S SITUATION WORSENS

THE GREY MAN opened his eyes and sat up with a start. A tear trickled down his face and he wiped it away with a flourish of his big hand. Had he been dreaming?

Lost princess.

The words reverberated inside his skull. Who was she? Where was she?

He closed his eyes, reaching out. There was nothing, the link was dead. All he had was the residue of her thoughts.

The passages beneath ground. Kurou waits. Prepare for darkness.

He climbed up from the chair and looked around, feeling suddenly disorientated. The girl … she had spoken to him. All these years she had listened in silence, waiting for him, but now she had spoken.

'You know me. You know what I am….'

He reached out again, but the link was truly gone, as if it had never been.

'No—'

She had spoken to him under duress, he saw that now. This Kurou, he had found her, made her open a link to him, made her issue a challenge.

And then … he had killed her.

The might of his army was waning. Soon he would have to go to ground or begin a new form of offensive against the many who had wronged him. But for now … there was enough.

'I will scorch you from the world,' he muttered, his voice as deep as a rumble of thunder. 'I will wipe you away.'

He closed his eyes, reaching this time to his soldiers, those still answering his commands.

Faster, he bade them. *As fast as the howling wind.*

'WHAT ARE YOU DOING?'

Kurou turned to see Lena standing behind him. She pointed at the trucks. 'Can we spare the fuel for these?'

'None of this equipment works,' he said. 'It is useless, so we will make it useful. A magic trick.'

'How?'

'For barricades and obstacles, among which our own soldiers will hide.'

'Will it work?'

'We will engage our enemy on our terms,' Kurou said. 'There are no guarantees. We only need to slow them.'

'Have you discovered a way to block their communications systems yet?'

Kurou started to shake his head, then thought better of it. Lena was ready to assume control as soon as he was of no further use, he could tell from the look in her eyes. If she knew he had failed, then he could find himself back behind bars, or even worse—his dead eyes might watch the battle from the top of a flag pole outside City Hall.

'It has proved my greatest challenge,' he said. 'Yet one that will be conquered.'

'Good. We're counting on you. We won't be able to hold them for long. They'll overrun us in hours. I've seen what these things can do.'

You're talking to the man who designed them, you arrogant whore. Out loud, he said, 'I'm sure it was a horror like no other.'

Kurou turned back to watch the volunteers loading the junked machinery on to the trucks with forklifts and a digger they had brought down from the mining fields. He gave a small shake of the head. Far too many of the machines in the hangars had proven worthless, the years of stagnancy fraying their wires and rusting up their joints. More than half of the War Horses had to be abandoned, and it was unlikely that many of the rest would last long before breaking down.

Heaped in the roadways they might still have a use. Among the broken robots Kurou would hide others, ready to ambush the Grey Man's invaders. The battle—while far from won—wasn't quite over yet.

An angry shout came from behind him and he turned, groaning at the sight of Robert Mortin hobbling among the workers towards them.

'Here comes Nuncle,' Kurou muttered with a sideways grin, wondering if there was some way he could slip away, but it was too late, Mortin had seen him.

'You!'

'To what delight do we owe this pleasure, grand king?' Kurou said. 'Hast thou split thy kingdom amongst thy undeserving daughters?'

With a growl Mortin swung a crutch at Kurou's head. The speed caught Kurou off guard, and while he avoided a direct blow he caught a stinging glance on the shoulder. He clenched a fist, feeling his knife-like nails cutting into his palm.

'You ignorant bastard,' Mortin spat. 'When this is done I'll use your skin for a doormat. My daughter is getting worse. I need you to see to her immediately or I swear I'll cut your throat.'

Kurou sighed. He threw a glance at Lena, who was taking an unnatural interest in the loading of a broken War Horse into the back of the nearest truck.

'I've told you, I'm doing everything I can to find a way to fix her.'

'She's not one of your damn machines!'

'If she were, she would be significantly easier to fix, sire.'

Mortin swung the crutch again, but this time Kurou was ready for it. He stepped back out of range as Mortin stumbled, his good knee landing in the snow. Lena ran to help him up, then glared at Kurou as if it had been his fault Mortin was a blathering idiot, rather than a combination of inbreeding and growing up in the shithole to end all shitholes.

'If it will ease your troubled mind, sire, I will waste a few of my precious superhero moments to visit her,' Kurou said. 'Just remember that I am a scientist, not a doctor, and that removing her from the machine was a mistake made by your dear misguided self.'

Mortin turned to Lena. 'How can you stand him? I'd cut his throat after five minutes of listening to this crap.'

She shrugged. 'You learn to filter him out after a while,' she said, offering Kurou a smile that was almost friendly.

With witty retorts flying off his misshapen tongue like sparks of electricity, Kurou let Robert lead them back up to the tunnel entrance where he had commandeered a jeep for his own private use. Within a few minutes they were standing around Isabella's bed while a couple of doctors from the town hospital stood in the corner, looking sheepish and helpless.

Kurou had seen corpses in better condition. Isabella's face was gaunt and colourless, the veins on her neck poking up, the hair that fanned out around her left in clumps on the pillows. The sound of shallow breathing came from the ventilator hooked up beside her, and the soft bleep of the heart rate monitor was like a ticking clock.

'She's worsening,' Robert said, reaching down to pat one of her hands. Kurou stared at the way it took a few moments for her skin to even out again, the elasticity almost gone.

'Double her food doses,' Kurou said. 'She's wasting away.'

'I can see that, you fool. How can you make her better?'

'I'm working on it.'

Mortin's face was like a sky heavy with the threat of rain. 'You said that yesterday. You've done nothing that I've seen. I'm giving you one more day. If she dies, you die.'

Kurou sighed. The fool would not be put off. When the inevitable happened it would be best to keep out of the old man's way, lest a swinging crutch take a chunk out of the back of his head.

While he would not admit it to Mortin, he'd done nothing at all to investigate Isabella's condition. Her life meant nothing to him and he had far bigger concerns to focus on, namely ensuring that he came out on top in the forthcoming class of armies. Soon enough there would be all the emergencies that the doctors could deal with, and the girl would be forgotten in the rush of mutilated bodies and severed limbs. He didn't like to admit it, but unless he could find a way to stop the Grey Man's army, they would be annihilated. He had designed the War Horses to be fast, efficient, and savage. They would do him proud, and he hoped he could get far enough away that he could appreciate their handiwork without risk to himself. Surely they wouldn't turn on their own creator?

'Kurou, you bastard, are you listening to me?'

'Of course, Nuncle,' he said, giving Mortin a wide grin. 'It's just that I have a war to prepare for. Now, if you don't mind....'

'Heal her, Kurou,' Mortin said, his voice menacing.

'Yes, yes, I'll do one's best,' he said, retreating from the room with Lena following behind.

'Will she die?' Lena asked, when they were alone.

'Certainly,' Kurou said. 'Twenty-four hours at most.'

Lena gave a slow nod. 'Then there's nothing we can do.'

Kurou sighed. 'Within a few hours, we'll have a lot more death on our hands than just that one girl,' he said. 'Are you ready for a little bloodletting, princess?'

PATRICIA LEANED BACK against the side of the truck, her cheeks burning. Robert hadn't even noticed her standing just a short distance away. Had he forgotten her so soon? That useless bitch

Isabella had got herself into trouble and all her father could think about was her.

She shook her head, punching the side of the truck. Since when had his attention meant so much to her? She didn't need it; she never had before. Yet she couldn't shed the feeling of resentment towards Isabella that had been brewing ever since the old dimwit had been taken on the train while she had been left to rot in Kurou's dungeon. It didn't matter what her father said, that he had sent people to find her, if he loved her he would have stayed behind and let Isabella go alone. What kind of parent would trust that their child was dead without seeing the body? He didn't love her, he couldn't have. He had loved Esel, and he loved Isabella, but Patricia?

She punched the side of the truck again. What did it matter? She didn't need him. She didn't need anyone.

With anger filling her heart she stalked off, wanting to be alone for a while. A knife bounced around inside her jacket and she wondered if it wouldn't be better to head out into the forest and pull it across her wrists. It wasn't like anyone would care.

Then she turned a corner and ran right into Victor.

'I'm sorry,' he muttered, his eyelids fluttering like a village idiot caught stealing ice cream, a can of oil shaking in his hands. Was he really scared of her or was it just the cold?

With more warning she might have buried the knife into his chest, but it would require her to unbutton her jacket and the pause would give him time to get out of range. Instead, wanting to see him hurt, she said, 'She's dying, do you know that? That stupid girlfriend of yours, she's dying. Happy are you? It's all your fault.'

His eyes looked wounded and for a moment she thought he would cry. She wanted him to, she realised. She wanted him to feel some of the resentment and turmoil that she felt.

'I wish I could help her,' he said, then before she could reply he had hurried past. He dropped the oil can down in the snow and broke into a clumsy run.

Patricia watched him until he went out of sight behind a distant truck. It made her a little sick to think it, but she wanted Isabella to die, just to see his misery.

Around her, the snow had begun to fall harder. The oil can Victor had dropped was already almost obscured, the snowflakes piling up on top like a little white skullcap.

41

VICTOR HEADS INTO BATTLE

HIS NAME HAD ONCE BEEN Wilheim, a carpenter from Moscow who had signed up for a military experiment because the fee was more than he could earn in a year, and he had a daughter who dreamed of going to university somewhere far away, Paris or London or Rome. He didn't tell his wife, because the interviewers at his initial contact interview said he would only be gone a few days.

Easily covered as a work trip out of the city.

He never returned. War had broken out, and he had found himself fitted into a four-legged killing machine that made his bones ache with the speed it covered the ground and his heart hurt with the terrible deeds it carried out in the name of its faceless master.

Over time, he had stopped being Wilheim, and had become WH4-73, and the ache of the killing had ceased to be bothersome. His body no longer hurt because the metal skeleton of the machine had become his body, its warmth had become his warmth, and its orders had become his pleasure to carry out. Together as one they marched across the land, pillaging the enemy, dealing out the justice that was necessary and deserved.

The human part of him had lost count of the towns ransacked and destroyed, but the machine part had logged each one in its database, and his kill count gave him shivers of pride. He was among the most successful killers in his division, and felt sure that if such a thing as promotion existed, he would be deserving.

But all great things had to come to an end, and now his fuel reserves were running low. He had feasted in the last town, but the next campaign would be his last. Even if he feasted well again, his reserves were too low to get him much further.

He was within fifty miles of what would be his last town. WH4-

73 would ride one final time, and he would spill the blood of his enemies in his master's honour.

Fifty miles. The order had come in to make the greatest of haste, so he urged himself forward through the snowy landscape, the blizzard so thick he was forced to use his sensors to detect upcoming obstacles. The going was slow, and it would get slower, but fifty miles was fifty miles. Even at a gentle walk he would be there by nightfall.

And then the excitement would begin.

THERE HAD TO BE A WAY. Kurou stared at the computer screen, his fingernails drumming on the desktop.

He could see from his satellite radar links that his liaison with the girl had got the Grey Man's attention. The tiny flashing dots that indicated the oncoming War Horses had begun to move more swiftly, while those from further away—which had initially been uninvolved—had turned towards the town. The Grey Man was coming with one purpose only—to destroy the town and everyone in it.

Good.

The first War Horses would arrive within hours. Whether they would gather en masse before attacking or come in small groups remained to be seen. It depended on how well the Grey Man understood their capabilities and whether he thought the town could launch a decent defence. It was Kurou's belief that they would come like a swarm of locusts from all sides at once, meaning the battle would be over in hours unless he could find a way to halt them.

The only way he could comprehend that the girl and the Grey Man had shared a telepathic link was to assume it was a level of science that he—and most of humanity—was yet to break down into its component parts. It was something that existed out there and that one day a human being would break it. However, while he would like to be that person, there wasn't time. He had to work with what he had.

The human side of the War Horses was untouchable. If their orders were to move forward, pillage and destroy, he could do nothing about it. All he could do was try to manipulate the machine side, the part which he had designed.

He punched the table, letting out a whoop of delight.

'Mind's eye going like the others,' he muttered, shaking his head, his fingers racing with that familiar, comforting speed over the keyboard.

Victor woke up slumped against the workbench, his body shaking with cold. He shoved himself roughly to his feet, angry that he had fallen asleep at so crucial a moment. The scattered tools lay around him in a circle, some pushed into the bag he had brought, others lying loose. The tiny electric component saw he had been trying to fix when he decided to close his eyes for just a second lay beside his left hand. He picked it up and stared at it, trying to remember whether before he passed out he had fixed it or not.

He pressed a little button on the side and the blade began to whir, so at least something was going right. Water was dripping from a cracked pipe across the ceiling, beating out a rhythm like a ticking clock. Victor didn't dare look at the time, in case it was already too late. Instead, he gathered up the tools and quickly put them into his bag.

All night he had sat up, trying to figure out a way to save Isabella. He had finally stumbled upon something that might work in the early hours of the morning, and headed down here to collect what he would need from the bowels of the military base, out of sight of Kurou's war effort.

He tried to appear as innocuous as possible as he made his way up the stairs to Hanger Three, where Isabella's machine still stood. He passed a couple of people heading down, but no one paid him much attention. Kurou, with his obviously distinctive looks, was regarded both as a demi-god and a demon, but Victor, despite being his designated assistant, was the kind of person that eyes saw past. Right now, as he headed into the hangar to find the machine, he was thankful that he wasn't attracting any notice.

There were few people around. Victor walked through the entrance and into the hangar proper, then stopped, staring in disbelief, a feeling of lightheadedness coming over him.

Isabella's machine was gone.

He ran forward a few steps, sure he must have come to the wrong hangar by mistake, but the whole section was empty, the entire line of War Horses gone. Now that he looked around, he saw the hangar was in the process of being cleaned out, just a couple of troop vehicles left in one corner.

Back by the stairs, he interrupted the first man he saw, who was pulling a cart full of old computer monitors towards the row of broken elevators.

'Where's everything gone?' Victor said, struggling to keep the hysteria out of his voice.

The man gave him a square look, frowning. 'Where you been, sleeping? It's all hands on deck, don't you know. Everything that's not working has been taken into the town.'

'Why?'

'They're building roadblocks down there or something. Don't ask me, I just lug stuff where I'm told.'

Victor thanked the man, who just gave him a rude shrug and headed off, pushing his cart of computer monitors in front of him. Victor ran for the stairs, taking them two at a time until his heavy bag of tools began to sap his energy.

In the control room on the first floor, there was no sign of Kurou. Victor jumped on to the nearest computer terminal and pulled up the list of War Horses, hunting for the serial number of Isabella's. It was in a folder marked INACTIVE, but when he opened the file he was able to get a tracking signal that opened a link to a local satellite map.

He let out a slow groan. There it was, flashing on the screen on the southern edge of town. Victor expanded the map to pinpoint its location.

The Lenin District, right on the edge of St Peter's Place.

Victor rubbed his eyes and let out a long, frustrated sigh. The damaged robot had been moved right to where Kurou expected to meet the oncoming army, on the very front line of the battle.

Isabella was perhaps hours from death, and the robot was in the worst place possible. With no other choice, Victor climbed to his feet and headed for the door, the bag of tools slung over his shoulder.

42

A LOST TREASURE IN THE SNOW

LENA HAD no intention of hiding away like many leaders might. The headquarters of the town's only major banking corporation stood on the northern edge of St Peter's Place, and from the ninth floor there was a view of most of the surrounding streets, particularly the wider thoroughfare cutting up through the town from the southern highway. The snow was still falling heavily, limiting her visibility to a few hundred metres, but it was enough to make out the lines of barricades Kurou had ordered to be built across the roads. Set back every fifty metres or so, they ranged in height from a few metres to ten or more. Built entirely of junked machines from the military base and cars taken from the streets, they were snow-covered, jagged mountains of metal blocking the way into the town. This was where Kurou had planned their biggest stand, with thinner lines of defence along the ridge to the west and the valley to the east. The mining operations to the north had been rigged with hundreds of mines and other booby traps, but with the largest concentration of War Horses set to come at the city from the south, it was the defence of the Lenin District that held the greatest importance.

Lena shivered. She had barely slept in days; those few hours she had grabbed filled with nightmares. The blood on the lips of the machine creatures snapping at her heels was not something she would ever forget, but she had a feeling she'd be seeing a lot more of it before the day was out.

Through the snow the smudgy shape of a midday sun was beginning to appear. Lena didn't know if she wanted the snow to stop or not.

A red light appeared in the snow to the south, just beyond the town limits. A short distance away it was joined by another one, then another. Lena put a hand over her chest as her heart began to pound. They were coming, oh God, they were coming.

She had to reach out for the window ledge as more lights blinked on. Her legs felt unsteady beneath her, and the gun in her other hand so useless.

This was the charge of a cavalry that such primitive weaponry could not down.

The barricades stood still and silent. Not a thing moved anywhere below her except for the lights moving through the snow, coming closer.

You're not exactly trying to hide, are you? You feel no threat from us.

Then something started to crackle above her, and she looked up, frowning. The sound wasn't in the room but coming from outside, from higher up the building.

'What the hell?'

The sound of flutes joined piccolos and oboes. A broad grin broke out on her face as she recognised the piece, Wagner's *Ride of the Valkyries*, booming out across the Lenin District from a hundred speakers she'd had no idea Kurou had even ordered to be set up. As the first of the War Horses came into view, the red lights glowing from their LED eyes, bombs began to go off. Kurou's own War Horses rose up out of the metallic scrap heaps like warriors rising from the dead, their weapons blazing, tearing into the attackers with a ferocity that was breathtaking. As clouds of smoke obscured the streets, the cacophonic symphony blared so loud it almost masked the explosions as the War Horses on both sides tore each other apart.

As the enemy came on, breaking through the defensive lines with clinical speed and power, only to find another line of defenders rising up in front of them, she could only shake her head in awe. As the battle unfolded in the snow to the backdrop of booming classical music, Lena could almost imagine herself as a child at one of Moscow's huge state theatres, watching the unfolding of some dramatic ballet.

Tears streamed down her face, and she began to laugh as her gun fell uselessly to the floor at her feet.

———

WH4-73 HAD NEVER FELT such excitement. As he rushed into battle, opening out his hand-to-hand weaponry to engage the machine rising out of the rubble in front of him, a bigger, more cumbersome version of himself, all he could feel was the bloodlust.

It was like a fire in his belly making him burn brighter and hotter and brighter and hotter—

He ripped into the enemy machine with all his might, his iron claws splitting apart the machine's underside, tearing a hole in the casing where its rider was enclosed, ripping right through the inert man's torso, drenching the snow around them with human blood. In its death throes the machine collapsed forward on to him, but WH4-73 reached into its body cavity and ripped right up through, tearing the metal apart, throwing the two pieces of the robot aside as he stepped through the piles of junk in search of his next conquest. He wanted to pillage and destroy, he wanted to ravage and kill and maim, he wanted to crush and tear and annihilate....

To his left another machine was moving, smaller, more agile, one of his own, a brother, yet this brother was moving too slowly, too lethargically to be up for the fight, one leg dragging along the ground, some of its hydraulics broken. WH4-73 turned towards it, feeling a sudden surge of hate that was as welcome as it was unfamiliar. This robot was letting them down and it needed to be destroyed; he had never felt anything more certain. With a roar, he turned towards it, locking on with his missile systems.

The other War Horse knew nothing as WH4-73 unleashed the full power of his missile armoury. Four twin surface-to-surface warheads turned the War Horse and its rider into a heap of scrap metal.

You bastard, WH4-73 thought. *You let us down. You weren't fighting hard enough. You're no better than the enemy. You're all one and the same, you cowards.*

LENA STARED. She leaned closer to the window, wiping away a sheen of condensation to see better. What was going on?

She could swear that one of the enemy War Horses had just fired on another. Even as the lines of Kurou's troops were retreating under heavy losses, the enemy was in disarray, the War Horses turning on each other, some even fighting hand to hand. One on the corner of St Peter's Place suddenly turned on another, throwing it back against the wall of a nearby building as a timed bomb went off nearby, blowing it apart.

Still more were coming, the red lights blinking on back in the snow and advancing into the town, but there was as much a battle between the enemy robots as there was between them and the defenders.

'Kurou, whatever you've done, you're a genius,' she whispered, just as the entire wall in front of her exploded in a deafening roar of cracking mortar and shattering glass.

KUROU SAT at his main computer terminal in the control room, watching the battle unfold through a series of cameras his volunteers had set up around the town. He groaned as one suddenly blinked out and kicked the desk in frustration. Through the rising smoke and the snow that still fell, it was difficult to make out much of what was happening, but aided by the statistical chart displayed on an adjacent screen, he could follow the way the battle was going.

His forces had been decimated, overrun along the ridgeline to the west, shattered in the valley to the east. To the north, the booby-trapped mining area had claimed its share of the spoils, but he was down to just four operational War Horses, all of which would likely fall within the hour.

In the old Lenin District, his forces had put up a far greater fight, dancing with the Grey Man's soldiers in a vast, apocalyptic war dance while some of his favourite music roared in the background. Even there though, the lines had been broken through and his forces would be reduced to spare parts by the day's end.

From an outsider's point of view, it might appear that his army had not just lost, but been routed. That might have been the case had the enemy not also been fighting itself.

Adjusting the emotive settings on the Grey Man's War Horses had been a huge but calculated risk. Turning up the anger to maximum might have caused them to fight harder, overrunning his forces even quicker, but his estimation had proved correct, that the overload would cloud their judgment, causing confusion, causing them to see all other machines as the enemy. While his troops had fought bravely but ultimately in vain, the Grey Man's army had fought a magnificent battle amongst itself.

Satisfied that there was nothing further to be done, Kurou began to switch off his computer systems, transferring the necessary data to a small handheld tablet, in preparation for the final battle, one which was fast approaching, and one which he would have to fight alone.

He was reaching for the button to disable the video screens when he caught sight of a tiny figure running through the snow in St Peter's Place while bombs exploded, buildings collapsed, and War Horses died around him. Impressed by the individual's bravery, Kurou zoomed in to take a closer look.

'Young Victor? What on earth are you doing?'

THE TRACKING DEVICE in Victor's hand was flashing quicker, even though he could no longer hear the sound of the accompanying bleeps over the roar of the battle around him. He had configured the handheld tracker to the radio frequency given off by the damaged robot, and he knew he was getting close from the way the flashing light was now almost a solid dot of red. All around him the world was turning to hell, huge robots blowing each other apart, their stray missiles bringing the façades of buildings crashing down into the street.

Something rose up huge and dangerous to his left, and Victor dived for the cover of an overturned car as a second robot crashed into the first, huge mechanical forearms ripping at the other machine's torso. As the first machine rolled on to its back, Victor got a glimpse of human legs flailing, then it was behind him as he ducked into a tunnel made of piled machinery, briefly given a respite from the battle above.

Then the world was shifting, something landing heavily on the metal over his head. He dived for safety once again as the space in which he had been standing disappeared beneath a cascade of twisted steel. He screamed, but his voice was silent, lost in the grinding, squealing cacophony of war.

Brushing dust and snow out of his eyes, he realised the tracker light was now fully solid. He looked up, and there was the machine right above him, jammed into a space between an upturned truck and another damaged War Horse. He could see the way its torso had been crudely cut open to get Isabella out.

Climbing up into the body cavity as the ground shook around him, Victor pulled a torch out of his bag and got to work. Blood dripped from a couple of shallow cuts in his face and froze solid in the creases of his coat. All around him the air was thick with the smell of cobalt and burning flesh. Victor flapped a hand in front of his face as often as he could spare one, but what he had to do would have been tricky enough in the quiet of an empty laboratory. His hands trembled and he tried to hold his tools steady as he slowly cut his way up into the machine to retrieve the single component that might save Isabella.

His arms were aching and his back was sore from sitting so awkwardly when he finally pulled away a panel to reveal a small object that resembled what he had seen on the computer screen. It was a tiny square box with a protruding rectangle on one side like a port dock to fit into a computer.

Somewhere nearby an explosion sent an avalanche of masonry crashing to the ground. Victor coughed as his lungs filled with concrete dust. Covering his mouth with the sleeve of his jacket, he put the component carefully into his bag and climbed down from the underside of the machine.

With the exception of the occasional stray missile crashing into the higher floors of the tall buildings around St Peter's Place, the battle seemed to have moved on towards the town centre. Victor peered out from behind the corner of a fallen robot at the expanse of bloody, junk-cluttered snow that separated him from an alleyway offering more shelter. He counted down from five then darted out across the street, running low with the bag clutched against his stomach.

He almost made it. The battle had churned up the snow that had been accumulating in the streets ever since the abandonment of the town, and Victor's foot caught on something metallic hidden beneath its surface. He fell face down, then scrambled up to his knees and turned around, just as something detached itself from the nearest junk pile and lurched across the road towards him.

It was a man, or had once been. Naked, so gaunt he was almost skeletal, his chest crisscrossed with wires, the only real sign of life was in the bloodshot eyes and bared teeth. Victor tried to stand as the man came rushing for him, but his foot was still trapped and he fell backwards in the snow. The man was on him in a moment, jaws snapping. Only the bag trapped between them kept the man's teeth off his face, but with his foot still trapped there was only so long Victor could hold him off.

One clawed hand got a grip on his jacket. Victor, with that arm trapped beneath his bag, tried to roll to the side, only for the man to follow him, and suddenly there was nothing between them. Victor closed his eyes, unable to avoid the inevitable, then a blast of sudden heat passed in front of his face and the weight that had been on top of him wasn't there anymore.

Victor opened his eyes to see the gaunt human lying dead in the snow beside him, a gaping wound in his chest that wasn't bleeding at all. A short distance away stood his old surveillance robot, its caterpillar tracks now repaired. A light flashed on its body, seemingly in greeting.

'I know that was you, Professor,' Victor said to the machine. 'I don't know how you found me, but thanks.'

If the machine's light flashed an acknowledgement Victor didn't see it. He was already up and running back toward the military base with his bag and its precious contents tucked under his arm.

43

A DUEL OF KINGS

No one could ever tell Kurou he didn't dress appropriately for each occasion. Looking dapper in his suit and top hat, with the cane clacking on the corridor tiles, he strolled through the deserted corridors of the military base, impatiently awaiting the arrival of his expected visitor. The battle, he considered, had been both won and lost, with the armies on either side nearly decimated. The Grey Man's conquest of Siberia had fallen on its own sword, and would likely wind down over the next few weeks as hackers cleared the mess that was the internet and saw things for how they really were, a ragtag group of damaged robots near the end of their strength. The Grey Man's remaining forces would be routed, and a form of peace would once again reign over the land.

All that remained was the final act, the duel between champions, to see who went home with the spoils, and who bled out on the ground.

Five years he had hidden from this confrontation, but now he felt confident he would win the day. He appeared to be immune to that which he most feared, that the Grey Man could enter his thoughts, and without that advantage, a man was just a man.

His cane clacked on the tiles, tapping out the melody of a centuries old classical piece. He had just begun to hum, when slow footsteps from the far end of the corridor began to disrupt his musical accompaniment.

A long shadow fell across the tiles, and then a tall, broad-shouldered man in a long trench coat stepped into view, his arms folded across his chest.

'Well met, Cousin,' Kurou whispered, the sound of his voice echoing along the corridor. 'We meet at last.'

The Grey Man stopped. Like a statue he stood, blocking the far end of the corridor, his hands falling to his sides like a gunslinger ready to draw.

'Your application for a place at my side has been noted,' he said, his voice a deep, chocolatey hum, almost seductive. 'Yet, alas, I must decline.'

His hands swung up, and Kurou found himself tumbling back along the corridor as if caught by a sudden vicious wind. He scrabbled at the floor to try to slow himself, managing with one hand to hold on to his top hat and cane.

'I guess you don't like to get too close,' Kurou said, climbing back to his feet, refusing to dwell on what kind of power the Grey Man was able to wield. 'Well, neither do I.'

He lifted the cane and pressed a button on the top, activating a clever little modification he had made the night before. A line of nails flashed through the air, their points razor sharp, but mere metres from their target they dipped and slammed into the ground at the Grey Man's feet.

Kurou stared. The Grey Man smiled, lifting another hand.

This time Kurou ducked sideways into a connecting corridor as a vibration in the air wafted past him, pulling his top hat from his head. The computer tablet fell from his pocket and spun away across the floor. He darted after it, gathering up his hat at the same time with a hooking motion of his foot, feeling the little robot inside bouncing around. Then he was on his feet, scrambling away down the corridor as behind him came the sound of heavy footfalls giving chase.

A set of metal stairs at the end led down to a lower floor, turning back on itself at a middle landing.

Kurou leapt down the first flight, using the wall of the landing to stop his momentum. Something in his right forearm cracked, but there would be time to worry about his injuries later. Behind him, the Grey Man's presence filled the corridor.

Squatting down as he spun around, Kurou pulled the computer tablet from his pocket as the wall above him exploded, showering him in small pieces of masonry. He pressed a button on the touchpad, and a line of timed explosives activated along the corridor ceiling. As smoke wrapped up around a cacophony of sound, somewhere back in the chaos the Grey Man cried out in pain.

'Strike one,' Kurou muttered, pushing himself up out of the rubble and hurrying down the second half of the stairs to the floor below. A short way along the corridor he ducked through a side door into an empty storage room and slid down against the wall behind it, pulling out his computer tablet. In a few seconds he had a visual from the cameras in the corridors outside as the Grey Man appeared out of the smoke at the bottom of the stairs.

The looming figure took a few steps forward then stopped, peering up at the camera. Kurou raised a misshapen eyebrow, surprised. The camera was hidden in the ventilation shaft above the corridor ceiling, invisible unless you knew it was there. The Grey Man stared up at it, giving Kurou a good look at his adversary. The man looked even bigger than in the grainy images Kurou had found buried on the internet, his shoulders broader, more imposing. His eyes were a deeper crimson, but his skin was more white than grey, as if time itself was bleaching him. Through the lens of the camera Kurou felt they were sharing a moment that bordered on respect.

Then the Grey Man smiled. The image shimmered and then exploded.

'Not playing games, are you, sire?' Kurou whispered, so quietly even a hawk would be unable to hear. Somewhere outside the door came the sound of heavy footfalls moving away, and Kurou let out a long slow breath.

THE TUNNEL into the base inclined upwards at an angle that quickly stole the remaining strength from Victor's legs. He had left most of his tools behind in the snow, with the exception of a heavy wrench he carried for protection and those he would need when he got the machine component back to Isabella. In truth, he didn't know for sure if his plan would work, but when everyone around him seemed to be dying, it felt appropriate to try to give life rather than take it away.

He soon slowed to a walk up the gently inclining concrete road, his feet leaving prints in the old dust between the lines of tyre tracks. The base was nearly empty now, everything of use sent to help defend the town.

Up ahead, the entrance to the base came into view at the end of the tunnel, a wide set of steel doors some five metres high that had opened the first time on operation after Patricia had kidnapped Kurou and then got stuck, remaining open ever since. They led into the hangar on the third floor, the one containing most of the War Horses as well as several old tanks and transport vehicles, although most were gone now.

Feeling a little nervous about so much open space, Victor kept close to the wall as he headed for the stairs that led up to the medical bay on Level Two. Empty, the hangar was uncomfortably large, some two hundred metres across, a great circular cave carved out of solid rock. Only as he got to know the complex better had Victor realised that the hangars were built at staggered intervals to limit the threat of collapse. The complex was quite literally a giant staircase heading down into the bowels of the earth.

Victor was nearly at the foot of the stairs that would lead him to Isabella when a tall, pale man stepped out of an entrance a quarter of the way around the side of the hangar from where he stood.

Victor instinctively threw himself back into an alcove as the man strode a few metres out into the centre of the huge cave and looked around. A sudden cold wind seemed to rustle in the air. Too terrified even to think, Victor stared at a crack in the dusty rock floor and dared not move.

Where are you?

The words came so loud and clear in Victor's mind it was as if they had been spoken right into his ear. The initial terror was so great that he just shut his thoughts down and listened, aware that in some manner that he couldn't fathom they were coming from the man standing in the middle of the hangar, who only needed to turn a little to the right and look up to see Victor cowering against the wall.

Come out and play, Kurou.

Was this the Grey Man that Kurou had talked about? Victor could understand the description. While the man's clothing was all black, his face and hair were a shade of off-white that made Victor feel like he was looking at a picture cut out of an old newspaper. The man glowed with power and strength, but in his newspaper cut-out face was a darkness that Victor could barely imagine. This was the man, he recalled, who had brought a wave of annihilation crashing across Siberia, and while he lived he was a threat to them all.

Isabella.

Victor couldn't keep the thought out of his head any longer. He knew he had made a mistake as the Grey Man tensed and started to turn. Victor wasn't even properly concealed, the slight bend in the rock barely deep enough for a man half his size to hide.

With no choice other than to stand and die, Victor made a dash for the stairs, his bag bouncing against his waist as he ran. He didn't look up, but something wrapped itself around his legs, pulling him sideways. He glanced down, *saw nothing there*, then crashed to the hard floor, rolling on to his back. The Grey Man was ahead of him, looming like a colossus, his hands raised above his head, face twisted with anger. Victor scrabbled for the bag, trying to get the wrench, then his hand jerked back, striking the floor hard enough to crack his knuckles. As he slid closer, he wondered if he would just split apart, circumnavigate the Grey Man in two wide semi-circles, then come crashing bloody and bruised back together again on the other side.

Then a fat silver ball struck the Grey Man in the chest, opening out like a butterfly from a cocoon to spread silvery tendrils around his torso. Victor felt the force dragging him along the ground vanish as the Grey Man struggled against the wires that had engulfed him, roaring with both pain and anger as he tried to free himself from the net that was constricting tighter with each movement.

'You may leave us now, young sire,' came a familiar voice from behind him, and Victor turned to see Kurou standing back by the corridor entrance, in one hand a gun with an overlarge barrel like an old fashioned blunderbuss, his cane in the other. He still wore his top hat, although it had been partially crushed and now tilted to one side. 'I have a little private business with our visitor.'

Victor didn't wait to be asked twice. He climbed up and staggered to the stairs. As he reached them he turned and looked back, lifting a hand to Kurou, wondering as he did so whether it was a wave of goodbye, or a wave of thanks. Kurou cocked his head for a moment, and his one eye appeared to wink. Then he turned away, walking slowly towards his enemy. Victor watched him for a second, then hurried up the stairs. By the time he reached the first landing the professor was out of sight.

THE GREY MAN tried to roll to his feet, but the wires had wrapped themselves around his chest and arms, and any attempt to move caused them to bite into first his clothes and then his skin. Already he was sticky with blood across one shoulder and the underside of one arm. What kind of weapon was this? He was caught like a deer in a barbed wire net.

Kurou stopped a short distance away, the weapon tucked under one arm and a cane under the other. 'Impressed, sire? I discovered this antique down in a basement. A few modifications made it my own. Delightful, wouldn't you say? It's been so long since I've felt such a level of mastery over anything; it was a feeling I had almost forgotten.'

The Grey Man waited. He had been hasty too many times in the past, and it had cost him dearly. Despite the hate smouldering inside him for this insolent fool, Kurou held the upper hand. He had to wait for an opening.

Kurou took off his hat and reached inside, pulling out a tiny robot. He turned it over in misshapen hands disguised by white gloves.

'That young man you just tried to harm gave this to me,' he said.

'It is an exact replica of the first robot I ever built, too many years ago to remember. It is … special to me.'

He squatted down and set it on the floor in front of the Grey Man. 'And now, I think my work here is done, sire. If my duties are no longer required, I think I will retire for the night.'

'I could make great use of your skills,' The Grey Man said slowly. 'I control most of Russia. Soon I will head west, to make my presence known in Europe. I have great power that you do not understand and many people stand in awe in my shadow. A man like you could create great things if given the freedom and the resources to do so. I can give you all of those things.'

Kurou sighed. 'I was given them before,' he said wistfully. 'I held the world in my hands, just as perhaps you think you do now. I lost everything; my wealth, my power, my looks … even the one I considered my daughter.' He smiled. 'That hurt more than most. Losing one I considered dear, watching her walk away.' He shrugged. 'Well, she tried to kill me first, but let's not complicate things, shall we? Tell me, sire, have you ever lost anyone dear? Have you ever lost anyone close to you?'

Was this fool mocking him? The Grey Man felt a renewed surge of anger. Holding himself as still as possible, he made hands with his mind, reaching out for whatever he could take hold of, finding only the wires encircling himself and the tiny robot sitting in front of him. Kurou's mind was like an impenetrable wall.

'A lady friend, perhaps?' Kurou gave a hideous lopsided grin. 'After I was done with her I told her I would say goodbye.'

The Grey Man roared, trying to leap up, but it only served to pull the wires tighter, cutting into his flesh. He collapsed on the floor as agony surged through him, hearing behind him the slow *beep beep beep* of something counting down. He pushed out at the ground with his mind and managed to roll himself over, only to see the little robot standing in front of him, its eyes flashing in turn, one by one.

The flashing lights were gradually repeating faster and faster.

He barely noticed that Kurou was nowhere to be seen, seemingly having vanished into the air. With nothing else he could do, the Grey Man reached out with his power and smote the tiny machine back across the hangar towards the stairway and the distant exit, praying that he could get it through the door before the explosive went off.

The more distant something became, though, the weaker his hold over it, and the tiny explosive came to a bouncing stop in the shadow of the stairwell. Too late, the Grey Man realised what he had inadvertently done.

The little robot exploded, bringing the stairwell above it crashing down to cover the cave entrance, sealing the only way into or out of the hangar.

He had sealed his own tomb.

Kurou's laughter seemed to come from everywhere, and a moment later he realised that it did, from speakers fitted high up in the walls. The Grey Man tried to sit up, looking around, searching for some other way out or something he could use to first free himself from the wires encircling him, then unblock the entrance so he could escape before he ran out of oxygen.

Then, almost as if the curtain was coming down on the final act of mankind's greatest stage performance, the lights went out, plunging the cavern into total and complete darkness.

44

HELLOS AND GOODBYES

VICTOR HAD JUST REACHED the medical bay corridor when he felt
the explosion on the level below. A blast of warm air made him
blink, then everything went quiet. Whatever had happened, only
one thing was certain: he didn't have much time left to save Isabella
and get them both to safety.

He took the wrench from his bag and crept along the corridor,
staying close to the wall as he approached the turn before the door
to Isabella's room. He peered around it, his eyes going wide at a
sight of disarray. The walls of the corridor were seared with burn
marks and scarred from some kind of explosion. The door had
buckled and in front of it lay the twisted remains of a chair.

The guard's body lay in a heap several metres further along the
corridor, thrown there by the explosion, his clothes ripped and
chard. Feeling nauseous, Victor looked down, and saw the imprints
of a small pair of shoes leading through the dust of the explosion
and up to the door.

A sudden fear for Isabella overwhelmed everything, but even
then he hesitated. What if she was already dead and her killer was
waiting for him?

He put a hand on the damaged door and eased it open a few
inches. From inside came the beeping of Isabella's life support,
accompanied by the rustle of the ventilator. He breathed a sigh of
relief and pushed the door a little wider.

When it was halfway open it stopped, blocked by something on
the floor behind it. Victor eased into the gap, looked down, and saw
the end of one of Robert Mortin's crutches pushed against the edge
of the door. He tried to kick it out of the way, but it was held in
place by the weight of Robert Mortin's body on top of it.

Robert was lying on his back, spread-eagled on the floor, one crutch at his side and the one blocking the door stuck beneath him. He had been shot in the face, but his head had lolled to the side, shadows hiding the worst of the damage.

The room was in semi-darkness, the only light coming from the monitors and a small table lamp. Victor felt the need to close the door, as if it would block out all the world's troubles. He pushed it as far closed as he could. Only then did he realise that Isabella wasn't the only person in the room.

The girl was sitting on a chair in the corner, a gun on her lap. She didn't move as he came in, but he heard her give a quiet sigh.

'Hello, Victor. You took your time.'

'Patricia.'

Victor's heart was thundering. He had considered a thousand eventualities on his way up here, but Isabella's little sister hadn't crossed his mind. Over the last few days the girl had been nearly invisible, helping with the war effort and staying out of sight.

'What happens now?' she said, patting the gun against her knees. 'I wondered if you'd come. I thought you might. Not much else left for you, is there?'

It felt like he should say something heroic, or meaningful, or even diplomatic, but all he could muster was a quiet, 'No.'

'I'd like to blame you for everything that's happened, for the war, and the train crash and my father's death, and a thousand other things. I'd like to say that everything is your fault, but it's not, is it? You didn't start the war, and you had no real involvement in ending it. Nothing much was your fault really.' She cocked the gun. In the gloom Victor couldn't even tell what kind of gun it was. 'No, the only thing I can really blame you for is the death of my brother.'

'I didn't—'

She raised a hand, rolling her eyes as if he was a complaining child. 'I know, I know. Don't waste your breath. I know you didn't kill him, that it was Kurou's machine. Whatever. Who cares now? You're not listening to me, Victor. I *could* blame you, but that wouldn't be right. It wasn't your fault, just like what happened to Isabella wasn't your fault. Nothing was your fault.'

She lifted the gun and fired it into the ceiling, causing a cascade of dust and concrete. In the tiny room the sound was incredibly loud. Victor shrank back, clutching the bag to him like a comfort blanket.

'You see, Victor, I can't blame you for anything. You're such a spineless pathetic weed that you've drifted through your whole life doing nothing of any importance or note, making no impression.' She leaned forward into the light, and the pure, uncontained rage on her face made him flinch. 'You're such a worthless, nothing of a human being that I want to blow your fucking face right off your skull.'

The ferocity of her hatred was stunning. It took Victor a few seconds of uselessly working his jaw up and down before he could muster forth a reply.

'I ... I ... I can save Isabella.'

'*Save* her? You think that condemning her to a life with you is saving her? The only way to save her is with this gun.'

Patricia stood up and pointed the gun at Isabella's face.

'No, don't hurt her!'

She turned towards him. 'Are you going to stop me? Go on, Victor. I'll make it easy for you.'

To his astonishment she turned the gun over in her hand and held it out to him.

'Go on, take it. Kill me, and save your beloved girlfriend. Take it!'

Victor stared at the gun, then looked back up at Patricia. Isabella lay between them, a sacrificed Juliet on her mechanical altar.

'Why did you kill your father?'

'Take the gun, Victor.'

'Why?'

Her bottom lip trembled. 'He wasn't my father. He left me to die. He took Isabella, but he left me behind.'

Victor shook his head. 'There was no choice. He thought you were already dead. He was just trying to save himself and Isabella.'

'He could have waited!' she screamed, almost as loud as the gunshot had been. Victor took a step backwards as she turned the gun and held it first up towards his chest, then down at her father lying on the floor.

'He did wait,' Victor said, voice trembling. 'Isabella told me, he did wait. Those men he sent looking for you, they told him they found your body, but they lied. They tricked him. He left because he thought you were dead.'

While he wasn't entirely sure he was right, having pieced together the words from Isabella's incoherent mumblings during their climb back up to the base after the destruction of the train, he felt certain Patricia wouldn't know either.

All he needed to do was keep the gun from pointing at Isabella or himself. If he could just calm Patricia down, he might even be able to enlist her help.

The girl was still staring at him. 'I don't believe you,' she said.

'I can't prove it so you'll have to.'

'I don't believe you!'

Victor jumped aside as Patricia lifted the gun and fired. The bullet hit the door behind where he had been standing. Patricia started to come around the bed towards him, but Victor grabbed Robert's loose crutch and swung it at her feet. It caught between them and tripped her. The gun went off again, this time the bullet hitting the floor just in front of his face. Then Patricia hit the ground, grunting as she landed heavily on her shoulder. Victor grabbed her wrist, turning the gun away as she tried to aim it back towards him.

The girl was wild, but Victor was far stronger. He twisted her around in front of him, holding the gun arm against the floor. She struggled for a few seconds, but he held on to her tightly until she went still.

'Look, your sister is going to die if we don't help her soon,' Victor said. 'I can do it. I have what I need in my bag. You can help me.'

'You really want me to help you?'

'Yes.'

Patricia sighed. Victor thought he heard a sniff, and wondered if she was crying. 'I'll help you if you help me,' she said.

'Sure. What do you want me to do?'

'Take the gun. I can't trust myself.'

Her request was a little strange, but she had gone limp in his arms. He eased his hand along her arm until his fingers closed over the cold metal of the gun. He pushed her fingers aside and eased his over the handle, pulling it out of her grasp. She didn't move as he slid the gun back towards his pocket.

'Victor?' her voice was meek, like a child's.

'What?'

'Remember my face.'

Before he could respond, she grabbed his arm, catching him off guard. She twisted the gun up towards her, pushed his fingers over the trigger, and pulled them tight.

The blast was deafening. Victor cried out and rolled away from Patricia as the girl's body slumped against the floor. He wiped her blood off his face, tears filling his eyes. He stared at her, a thousand unsaid reassurances racing through his mind. The gun had spun away across the floor and he wanted to take it up, point it at his own face and silence all the bitter voices telling him how much he had failed, how many people had died because of him.

Then, as the ringing in his ears began to ease, he heard the low rise and fall of breathing.

Isabella.

She was the one chance he had left to redeem himself. He climbed to his feet with the lethargy of a dying man reaching a mountaintop, and pulled his bag of tools up on to the bed.

He couldn't be sure this would even work. As he stared at

Isabella's gaunt, ashen face, he wondered if it wouldn't be better to just switch off her life support and be done with it.

No, a voice whispered at the back of his mind, and he wondered who it could belong to. Surely not Kurou, the Grey Man, or even his long dead mother. Perhaps, he thought, wistfully, it belonged to himself.

Save her, it whispered again.

So he tried.

EPILOGUE

LIGHT, DARKNESS, UNCERTAINTY

IT WAS A FINE, frosty morning on the first day after the end of the world. Kurou strolled through the remains of the town, his cane tapping on the hardened snow underfoot, and the occasional piece of metal or rock debris lying close by. The greatest beauty in such an unforgiving climate, he thought, unable to forget the scars that covered his body, was that it didn't allow fires to burn for long. A few wisps of smoke drifted up into the air from the fallen machines and the bombed-out buildings, but a layer of snow and ice had already formed as the Siberian wastes staked its claim on the remains.

Never one to dwell too much on the past, Kurou turned his mind back to his future plans. With the war as good as over and the Grey Man dealt with at last, it seemed a corridor of uncertainty had opened up in the direction of Northern Europe, so it might be best to head that way for a while. The joy his latest masterpiece had given him would only last so long. In time he would feel the urge to create something new.

He didn't know how far south it was to reach the Trans-Siberian Express, a train that according to reports on the internet was still operating. It had to be several hundred miles, but he was a resourceful fellow, he thought, as he gave his cane a twirl. There would be something somewhere that would take him.

———

THE LAST OF Victor's strength was almost gone as he stepped out into the light. All around him the valley shone crisp and clear beneath an aquamarine sky. The snow was pristine and untouched all around, but there, poking up through the snow by his feet was the shoot of something green, something that would soon grow into a beautiful shrub or flower. A long overdue spring was on its way.

He hoisted Isabella in his arms and took a few steps forward, the sun warming his face. He looked down and saw her eyelids flutter. Her lips moved slightly, then she groaned and settled back into sleep.

The bulge just below her neck was barely perceptible under the thick jacket he had dressed her in, but the robot component had fitted well, clearly pleased in its artificial way to be reunited with its human companion. Managing it would take time, as would her recovery, but Victor felt quietly confident. The last few weeks would never fade from his memory, but there was no point looking back, only forward.

Looking down the valley at the hint of a path that would take him back to Brevik and whatever lay behind, Victor took the first step into an uncertain but welcome future.

***

HE HAD BEEN SLEEPING, but when he opened his eyes nothing had changed. The wires still bit into his body, the air still felt thick and dry.

Moving his body would do nothing to help him, so he stayed still, conserving his strength. Instead, he closed his eyes again, and let his mind drift, reaching out.

Old friend, he called. *Can you hear me? I have need of you.*

******

ACKNOWLEDGMENTS

Thanks to all those who have helped and guided me with this and other books, including Su Halfwerk, Elizabeth Mackey, Lee Burton, Emily Hetherington, Jenny Twist, John Daulton, Matt Koeler, and Fiona Ninnes. A special thanks goes out to my friends at the Retreat for your continued inspiration.

Until next time…

C.W.